PENGUIN BOOKS

COLONY

Rob Grant was born in Salford. Despite being hopelessly and incurably tone-deaf, he spent ten years at Chetham's School of Music. He maintained his place in the soprano section of the cathedral choir long after his voice broke by silently mimicking the lip movements of the person in the opposite row. Even though insanely liberal lecturers provided the exam questions months before the exams, he managed to fail his second year at university without ever sobering up. He has been fired from every job he ever had, including selling ice-cream and shoes, moving drums around in a chemical factory and an eighteen-month stint putting paper into one end of a computer printer and taking it out of the other. He spent what he can remember of the eighties churning out radio scripts for every living comedian before moving into television. He co-created *Red Dwarf* for BBC television in 1983, and in 1988 BBC television actually got round to making it. He recently created and wrote the pre-medieval comedy *Dark Ages* for ITV, and the alien-invasion comedy *The Strangerers* for Sky.

Colony is his first novel since the international bestseller *Backwards*.

He has the chiselled body of an Olympic athlete, makes love like a Greek god and has the vivid imagination of an incurable congenital liar.

Colony

ROB GRANT

PENGUIN BOOKS

PENGUIN BOOKS

Published by the Penguin Group
Penguin Books Ltd, 80 Strand, London WC2R 0RL, England
Penguin Putnam Inc., 375 Hudson Street, New York, New York 10014, USA
Penguin Books Australia Ltd, 250 Camberwell Road, Camberwell, Victoria 3124, Australia
Penguin Books Canada Ltd, 10 Alcorn Avenue, Toronto, Ontario, Canada M4V 3B2
Penguin Books India (P) Ltd, 11 Community Centre, Panchsheel Park, New Delhi – 110 017, India
Penguin Books (NZ) Ltd, Cnr Rosedale and Airborne Roads, Albany, Auckland, New Zealand
Penguin Books (South Africa) (Pty) Ltd, 24 Sturdee Avenue, Rosebank 2196, South Africa

Penguin Books Ltd, Registered Offices: 80 Strand, London WC2R 0RL, England

www.penguin.com

First published by Viking 2000
Published in Penguin Books 2001
15

Set in Monotype Dante
Printed in England by Clays Ltd, St Ives plc

To my Lily and my Rose

PART ONE
Lucky Town

'Who would true valour see,
Let him come hither.
One, here, will constant be,
Come wind, come weather'

(John Bunyan: *The Pilgrim's Progress*)

I

Eddie O'Hare considers himself to be the unluckiest man in the entire cosmos. And, bluntly, he's got a damned fine point.

He's standing at the smoked glass window that takes up an entire wall of a top floor room in a hastily built hotel, staring down at the fickle crowds thronging the neon splattered street below. His stomach is gurgling like a freshly skewered rat dying slowly in a stinking sewer. Tomorrow, the streets will be empty. The town will die. There'll be no reason for it any more. And unless his luck changes, unless the universe stops throwing snake eyes with Eddie's dice, Eddie's going to die along with it.

In his sweating fist, he's clutching his one last hope. A single gaming chip. A fifty. He's trying hard to think of the number he should place it on. That's all he has to do: pick the right number. A thirty-six to one shot.

If he can just do this one thing right: one right thing right, then all he has to do is pick another right number. That can be done. That's do-able.

And then, the last and final thing he has to do is let all those winnings ride on just one more right number.

He has to pick three right numbers. That's all. If he can just do that. Beat those odds.

But the thought stops as abruptly as a marathon runner with a stitch just a few seconds after the starting gun, jerks around in agony on the side of the track, and expires.

Maybe a hardcore gambler could convince himself he could ride that tide. But Eddie's not even a softcore gambler. In the pornographic scale gamblers seem to measure each other by, Eddie's not even the swimwear edition of *Sports Illustrated*. He's an accountant. He can work out the odds. He can't help himself.

Forty-six thousand, six hundred and fifty-six to one . . .

That's what it will take to turn this sweaty gaming chip into the two and a quarter million he owes to people who would break all of his ribs one at a time with a toffee hammer for a handful of change.

Face it, Eddie: it's not going to happen.

Who's he trying to kid with this positivity nonsense? Good things like that hardly ever happen to truly lucky people. And Eddie? Eddie isn't even partially lucky. The only time Fate gives Eddie anything good is so Luck has something juicy to whisk away from under his nose just as he's reaching out to grab it.

He opens his mouth to sigh, and his tongue actually makes a Velcro ripping sound as it tears clear of the roof of his arid mouth. He tastes his own blood. He imagines he'll be tasting a lot more of it before the morning. Plenty of that particular delicacy coming his way. A few pints he'll quaff. Well, on the bright side, it should help to ease the passage of his smashed teeth down his stomped gullet, and take away the taste of leather toecap.

He's startled by a long creaking noise that sounds like a deck shrinking in equatorial heat on a doldrums-bound ship. It's his stomach.

He looks down at the doomed street again. He starts to count people who are laughing. He gives up when it starts to become clear that absolutely everyone is laughing. Every single member of the crowd below is giggling, chuckling or guffawing with that unbridled delight normally only enjoyed by children, the freshly in love, and undeserving movie award winners.

It seems everyone, everywhere is relishing life and having fun, except for Eddie O'Hare, who will never smile again.

Because he owes two and a quarter million to . . .

To . . .

His reflection looks back at him from the blue smoked glass. A sad ghost full of pity for a soon to be sad ghost. The spectre shakes its head in sympathetic disbelief. The cruel twist is: it's not Eddie's fault that he's living this nightmare. He didn't actually do anything wrong. He didn't actually steal from the people he can't bring himself to name in his thoughts.

The money was stolen by a computer. Not a hacker. Not a living-flesh human trickster using superior technical skills to break through firewalls within firewalls, hack through uncrackable chains of encrypted passwords, and bypass the most sophisticated alarm system in security history. It was stolen from Eddie's computer *by* Eddie's computer.

Eddie doesn't have any idea where the money went. One nano-second it was there, the next it wasn't. No sign the system had been accessed from the outside. The computer just up and disappeared the money. And for reasons currently unfathomable to Eddie, it left behind an electronic trail that led to him.

He's been framed for a non-existent crime by a mass of wires and hot electrical circuits.

Now, you try explaining that to the . . . to those kind of people.

No. Eddie was left with just two alternatives: somehow replace the money before it was missed, or spend the rest of eternity as a small portion of the foundations of some unfinished hotel no one would ever check into, with ice picks lodged in his decomposing testicles.

He liquidified as much of his assets as possible in the time – what a meagre haul that had seemed, set against his ludicrous debt – and headed for what he considered to be the fairest casino in town.

It had taken him seventeen years of virtuous thrift and parsimonious self-denial to amass his pitiful savings. It took considerably less than seventeen minutes to lose it all.

So now, here is Eddie O'Hare, in a free hotel suite the casino reserves for its biggest high-rollers, for the people who lose the most money the quickest, clutching a fifty chip some big-time winner has tossed him in pity. And that chip is the last thing between Eddie and a very brutal . . .

Eddie sees the big hole appear in the door before he hears the sound of the gunshot. The huge smoked window he's gazing through cracks across the middle and the top half seems to sigh, then collapses without protest down towards the thrill below.

The door has already been kicked down and two men are standing in the doorway, silhouettes against the corridor's glow. Tight-fitting grey suits, ties as thin as stiletto blades, trousers slightly too short, exposing fluorescent pink socks above black suede loafers.

The uniform.

How did they find out so fast? How did they find *him* so fast? Eddie doesn't really have time to think, as the men start to cross the room briskly and businesslike in his direction. Just doing a job. Dum de dum.

Eddie briefly contemplates hurling himself after the window. Then he realizes that would be fairly silly, since that's probably what the men are going to do to him, if he's lucky.

The first man reaches him. Eddie sees his features. He has startlingly red hair. He's not smiling, but he's not looking angry, either. For some reason, Eddie finds this reassuring.

Wrongly.

The man grabs him firmly but not violently under his arms as the second man arrives, his gun freshly holstered. He's bald, this other one. Shiny bald. He grabs Eddie behind the knees, and swings him up. Hammocked between the two men, Eddie feels strangely guilty that he didn't put up some kind of a fight. Some sort of struggle at least. A verbal protest, even.

They swing him back, ready to pitch him through the window. Eddie's aware of the aftershave of the man holding his arms. He thinks it's quite nice. In other circumstances, he might have asked for the brand name.

One of the men speaks. The redhead.

'Mr Bevadino would really like to know where his money is.'

Eddie looks out of the window at what has suddenly become a beautiful night sky. The moon really does look blue, just like in the song. He thinks about the long fall he's about to undertake.

He's not looking forward to it.

It's not the prospect of the crushing, mangling impact that fills him with dread – he believes that he'll be dead before he's splattered over the pavement like so much regurgitated Saturday night kebab. No, what he's really dreading is having his life flash before him. It was bad enough going through it once. Such a nothing of a life. Such a safe, riskless, funless excuse for a life.

'Last chance, pilgrim. It's a busy night.'

A thought strikes Eddie, and he voices it. 'Who's Mr Bevadino?'

The two men make eye contact over Eddie's horizontal body.

'Ahmed Bevadino? Ring any bells?'

Even though he knows the name means nothing to him, Eddie genuinely tries to remember. He makes a real effort. That's Eddie for you. He doesn't want these men angry with him. He shakes his head. 'I . . . sorry. No. Don't think I recall a Mr Bevadino.'

'You don't?'

'Sorry.' And then, feeling this isn't enough, Eddie adds: 'I know a Mr Beverley.' What is he thinking of ? Is he hoping they'll shrug, say 'That'll do', and launch him out of the window anyway? Bevadino? Beverley? That's close enough? Get a grip, Eddie.

The bald man with the holstered gun lowers Eddie's legs. 'You'd better not be wasting my time.'

Or what? Eddie thinks. But he doesn't say it.

Baldy walks to the door, which is prone. He looks down, then looks over at his colleague. 'This is 888.'

The man with an arm lock on Eddie says: 'You sure? It looked like 886.'

'Yeah. There's a little nick out of the last 8.'

'A little nick?'

'Yeah. Tiny chip in the number. Makes it look like a 6.'

Redhead releases Eddie and steps back to what Eddie thinks is probably perfect karate kick distance. Eddie hopes he never gets to find out. 'What's your name, pilgrim?'

Baldy takes some folded sheets of paper out of his back pocket.

'My name?' Eddie's mind is galloping now. Should he give them his real name? What if these men also work for the people Eddie's angered, as well as Mr Bevadino? What if his name's down on their list, only later on? Maybe next, even. They could be working their way along the corridor. They said it was a busy night, didn't they? On the other hand, what if Eddie's not on the list, gives them a false name, and it turns out to be the name of someone who *is* on the list? Perhaps even the name of the wretched unfortunate they thought they were about to defenestrate. For Eddie, that's not far fetched, it's a real possibility. Eddie believes he really might be *that* unlucky.

'Edward.' Eddie hopes that might be enough. It isn't.

Red reaches into Eddie's pocket and tugs out a pathetically slim wallet, with an unnecessary 'Excuse me.' He flips through the maxed-out credit cards and finds some ID. 'Edward O'Hare?'

Eddie nods.

'Like in the airport?'

Eddie nods. He's about to launch into his well-polished story about O'Hare airport, but decides, just in time, that this isn't a terrific platform. Out of the corner of his eye, he tries not to notice Baldy thumbing through his lists for Eddie's name. Lots of sheets of paper. Lots of limbs to twist, digits to break and bodies to hurl. The pavements are going to get plenty messy tonight.

'You're not Harrison Dopple?' Red's comparing Eddie with the photograph on the ID. It's probably a very old picture. The only photo identification in Eddie's wallet is his sexual activity clearance card. It expired about a decade ago.

Eddie tries as hard as he can not to look anything like anything any Harrison Dopple might possibly look like. Hard to pull off, given he's never even heard of the guy. Still, he tries. He straightens his stance, in case Dopple is short, and tilts his head to one side, trying to offer an un-Dopplelike profile. 'Not me.'

Red hands him back his wallet. 'What can I say? You're not our next appointment. This is uncustomarily unprofessional.'

'Don't mention it.'

'I'd hate you to think we go around throwing people out of windows willy-nilly.'

Willy-nilly? Eddie snorts playfully, trying to suggest the very thought is preposterous.

Baldy is standing impatiently in the corridor now. Keen to make up for lost time. Keen to keep the next 'appointment'. Red looks over, nods, and crosses towards him. Eddie realizes that, for some reason, he's waiting until the men have gone to breathe properly.

'Like I said: it's a busy night.' Red pauses in Eddie's shattered doorway. 'And if I were you, pilgrim, I'd renew that sex clearance card.'

Eddie smiles and nods. 'I'll do that.'

Red winks. 'You never know when you might get lucky.'

2

It's a strange night in a strange town. A town with just one night to live.

In the record books, it's Afortunado City. To the people who use it, it's simply Lucky Town.

Its one, long street is a chaos of humanity. Thousands of people who will have no need of money tomorrow, eager to spend what they've got, and the rest of the population just as eager to relieve them of it. There are just a few short hours for the dealers to deal, the grifters to grift and the hookers to hook. Prices are inflating by the second.

Stepping out of the hotel on the very perimeter of town, Charles Perry Gordon experiences a bolt of heat in his stomach. The closest he's ever come to a sense of completeness. Fulfilment. He *imagined* this town. It sprang out of his mind's eye. He conjured it up, reclining in his big leather chair, at his desk in his office in Rio.

And here it is.

He had nothing to do with the architecture, or the technical nuts and bolts side of constructing Afortunado. He merely *predicted* it. It was a place that, to Gordon's mind, simply had to exist. The Project is the biggest operation ever undertaken by the human race, with a budget to match. It employs tens of thousands of people and pays them extravagantly well. Naturally, they need somewhere to dispose of their income and blow off steam. And Afortunado was born to give them somewhere to do just that. A pleasure city, carved out of the unforgiving desert of snow. An 'O-ice-is' it's been called. And though Gordon's seen it many times in his head, this is his first brush with the wonderful reality of it.

Standing at the top of the steps, he looks right into the human tumult thronging the main street like a vast, slow-motion particle explosion. He listens to the complex yet primitive music of human voices clamouring for attention.

To his left, he squints at the shimmering heat haze of the hotwall, the thermal barrier that separates the town from the lethal wilderness of the Antarctic peaks that surround it. Across the street, a group of youths in Bermuda shorts, fledgling goatees and brightly coloured shirts are tossing empty beer cans through the barrier, just to watch them flare and vanish. Curious to see them, in their casual summery gang uniforms, just metres away from a hostile desert of snow. Without the hotwall, their life expectancy would be measured in minutes.

Sometime tomorrow, when the last of the temporary town's inhabitants have straggled on to the last of the transports, the wall will be powered down. Within a week, Afortunado City will be buried under tons of compacted ice and snow, reclaimed by the wasteland from which it was carved. Gordon predicted that, too.

'Hey, pilgrim! Need a lift?'

Gordon looks down the steps, where an ancient oriental man is looking up at him hopefully. There is a lighted sign on his headband, flashing the promise: *Taxi*. 'A lift?'

There are no passenger vehicles in Afortunado. No need, Gordon predicted. The entire strip is less than a kilometre long. No journey longer than fifteen minutes on foot.

The taximan turns around and hikes a thumb over his shoulder. He's offering Gordon a piggyback. The old guy is eighty if he's a day. His tattooed limbs look like flimsy bulrushes loosely wrapped in a pirate's treasure map. A good gust of wind would snap him at the knees. Gordon shakes his head. 'I'll walk, thanks.'

Without dropping his smile, the taximan makes a strange but clearly sexually insulting gesture, barks a bizarre exclamation, clearly an expletive, and jogs off towards the next hotel, disappearing into the blast of people.

Gordon sighs. People disgust Gordon, on the whole. Especially people who are inferior to him. Which is, in fact, most people. He strolls down the steps after the taximan.

Technically, he should go straight to the Project, but he can't resist at least one short inspection of the town that sprang from his mind. Who would blame him? Besides, he still has some money left over from the trip, for emergencies that never happened. Might as well spend it. Tomorrow, it will be so much waste paper for him.

He's pictured this scene a thousand times, but in his imagination he didn't hear the sounds: the cacophony of uncomplementary music duelling painfully out of neighbouring bars, restaurants and casinos – the techno throb invading the Dixieland, which in turn is polluted by the string quartet, which yields to the rock anthem; the indistinguishable jabber of hawkers, beggars and pleasure seekers, melding into a pulsating discord of voices. And he never imagined the smells: the hot rasp of frying oils, animal fats, spices and aromatics from all the world's cultures streaming out of the gutter cooks' food wagons; the colognes and perfumes assaulting the nostrils, but failing to mask the all too human fragrances of sweat, vomit and excrement. Disgusting, yet strangely thrilling.

Gordon strolls on. A woman leans out of a darkened doorway and offers him a hand job. He looks down at her proffered palm which sports a genetically grafted vagina. He smiles and thanks her, politely turning her down.

Even in the midst of all the mêlée, Gordon feels perfectly safe. There are no police in Afortunado. The rule of law is preserved by an extremely efficient consortium of organized-crime groups. Gordon had foreseen this would be the best system, and the franchise had been put out to tender to the top contenders. An alliance of Las Vegas mafiosi, Russian mafyia, and Hong Kong triads had secured the job, portions of which were sub-contracted to smaller groups. It all works terribly well. Violent crime is non-existent, except for the odd over-enthusiastic debt collection incident. The streets are safe.

Just as this thought flits through Gordon's mind, a savage blow to his kidneys drops him heavily to the ground. He looks up to see his assailant: it's the old taximan hurtling along at an unlikely pace, with a fat business-suited man on his back. It could have been an accident that the passenger's briefcase poleaxed Gordon, but he doubts it. As a curse forms on his lips there is a dull explosion overhead.

Gordon looks up. A large sheet of blue smoked glass is tumbling from the top floor of the Hotel Felicity. The crowd below it does its best to scatter, but the bodies are packed pretty tightly on Easy Street tonight, and a few are too close to the impact as the window shatters on the pavement, sending dozens of large, potentially lethal projectiles towards the terrified stragglers.

If the taximan hadn't knocked him down, Gordon would have been among them.

Lucky man.

He picks himself up and looks around. There are ten, maybe a dozen injured. Some quite seriously. The town's one hospital is a small, flimsy affair: no traffic, no violent crime, why would any other provision be necessary? A small emergency room, a burns unit and a cardiac ward, that's all. Anything more chronic would have to be shipped out.

Gordon dusts himself down and steps over a screaming woman. The screeching is annoying him. He wants to get away from it.

He sees the sign for the Felicity Casino, and decides he might as well spend his money in there.

He kicks away the injured hand that's clawing at him and skips down the steps.

3

Eddie is looking out of the wall-to-ceiling void that used to be his window. He's staring down at the street he almost became a part of. Another man might be thinking what a lucky escape he's just had. Another man might take a glorious lungful of sweetly processed air and bless the entire concept of existence, might take a moment to wonder at the bizarrely sturdy fragility of life.

Not Eddie.

Eddie's frozen in the glaring truck headlights of fear. Eddie's thinking he's just had a little taster of his immediate future. An *amuse-gueule* to whet his appetite for the bone-grinding bloody terror of the slasher movie fate inexorably awaiting him. In his right hand, he's turning the sweaty betting chip over and over.

This is wrong.

Eddie has to *do* something. He has to *try* something, or the awful terrors of his imaginings will most certainly come to pass. But this is precisely Eddie's problem. Eddie's a do-nothing guy. He unconsciously subscribes to the theory that the best way to tackle a terrible twist of events is the old, dismal, double-pronged non-attack: first and foremost, do nothing, absolutely nothing at all, because doing something, *any*thing, might very well make the terrible thing worse, and second, the even more pathetic strategy: hope against all the laws of logic and reason that the terrible thing will go away and never happen. It doesn't matter to Eddie that this approach almost never works. It doesn't matter to him that this lifelong passion for uneventfulness has left him with a dry, unenviable past; a life not worth remembering even in the drastically truncated flashback form supposedly induced by a lethal plunge from a high building.

The most peculiar aspect of this non-living approach to life is that Eddie thinks himself 'sensible'. And if you could poll any of Eddie's acquaintances, they would concur that Eddie is indeed a sensible guy. Sensible is the word that comes to mind.

So here's old Eddie, sensibly waiting to have the life smashed out of him, when there's another muffled explosion and another shattering of glass, and he sees another window lazily tumbling down the side of the Hotel Felicity's hasty façade. For a terrible moment Eddie's terror finds a new, higher gear. He thinks it's the . . . men, coming back for him. Then he realizes he has no more window left to shatter. The . . . fellows are paying a visit next door.

Eddie listens with a peculiarly interested detachment. It's as if the scene that had just been rehearsed in his life is now being replayed in room 886, only properly, for real. Eddie was just a stand-in. Now his part is being played by the real star, the real Harrison Dopple, and Eddie's curious to hear how he might have performed his role better.

There are angry shouts, Dopple's voice, presumably, and loud, dangerous threats, again Dopple's. There are crude expletives and loud violent curses, counterpointed by quiet, dangerous mumbles. There is smashing furniture and scuffling – major scuffling – and the strangely flat, unmovielike sound of fists impacting on flesh and bone. There is, in short, a big kerfuffle.

Eddie shakes his head. He wishes he could have done that. He wishes he could have kerfuffled more. Or a little, at least. That's what a real man does. Eddie didn't kerfuffle at all, not a bit of it. He minded his manners. Harrison's not minding his manners. He's not trying to ingratiate himself with a couple of cold-blooded murdering bastards intent on his demise. He's fighting for his life. Eddie imagines, rather romantically, that the unseen Mr Dopple must live one heck of a life, to make it worth all the kerfuffling. A thrilling life, full of promise, excitement and gusto. A big, exhilarating roller coaster of a life. A life to kerfuffle for.

Eddie is actually beginning to feel envious of the man who is being murdered next door.

And worse, much worse than that, Eddie will very soon come

to wish he really had been Harrison Dopple. He'll come to consider being splattered all over the pavement as preferable to his own fate.

There is a dreadful silence next door, now.

It's broken by the start of a count.

'One . . .'

Suddenly, Dopple's voice changes tenor and volume, and now he's speaking very fast, very low. Pleas, not threats.

But the grim count continues.

'Two . . .'

And all the while, Dopple is gibbering his soft entreaties.

And from the cadence of the count, Eddie realizes that it's never going to reach four. But they're just threatening Harrison, surely. Surely Eddie can't be about to see a human being murdered before his eyes. Surely they're not going to count out . . .

'Three.'

The entreaties stop, and there's a double grunt. Eddie correctly estimates it to be precisely the double grunt generated by the effort it takes two men to launch a third man to his death out of a top-floor hotel window void.

Eddie looks away, but too late. Too late to avoid registering the look on Harrison Dopple's suddenly silent face as gravity grabs him at the top of his upward arc, and he starts his inexorably fatal acceleration downwards. That look will be burned into Eddie's brain for ever. What's more, Eddie is brutally aware that his mind will file it, as it always files his most horrific recollections, in exactly the same image library it stores all his erotic memories, so it can crop up randomly as he approaches the peak of his solo passion and deflate him instantly, and without hope of resuscitation.

And it's the understated bathos of Harrison's expression that Eddie finds so peculiarly ghastly.

The soon-to-be-late Mr Dopple doesn't look afraid. He doesn't look angry. He's not flapping his arms and legs wildly, as Eddie probably would, in a risibly desperate last-minute half attempt to acquire, somehow, the gift of flight.

No. None of that.

The soon-to-be-late Mr Dopple is smiling.

It will take Eddie a while to interpret that smile correctly. In fact, Harrison Dopple is smiling in disbelief. His primary reaction in the face of inevitable death isn't fear, or even anger: it's surprise.

He can't believe that death is a thing which is actually, definitely, going to happen to him. To *him*.

Incredibly, he's danced his last dance (badly and drunkenly, a long time ago), eaten his last meal (mercifully, a deliciously unhealthy and highly anti-social microwaved burrito), enjoyed his last orgasm (thankfully, only minutes ago, courtesy of the round-the-clock hotel porn channel). And now he is actually smiling his very last smile. And even though he's known, all his life, that all human beings always die, he's managed to nurture and protect the nonsensical, irrational conviction that, somehow, the death thing would never happen to Harrison Dopple.

In the meantime, some good, at least, has come of Harrison's shocking demise: Eddie is no longer wallowing in self-pity. He is wallowing in pity for Harrison Dopple. He turns and moves away from the window. He doesn't want to hear the impact, much less see it. The momentum carries him towards the flattened door of his suite.

He pauses briefly in the doorframe. He'd rather not bump into redhead and baldy as they leave the apartment next door. But they'll be checking their grisly roster, fairly soon. They'll be crossing off Harrison Dopple, room 886, Hotel Felicity, and looking for the next appointment in their busy, busy schedule.

And that next appointment could conceivably be Eddie O'Hare, room 888, Hotel Felicity.

Eddie would rather not risk that possibility.

He carries on down the corridor, turning his face away from the flattened door of 886 as he passes. Pointlessly, as it turns out. A full-length mirror spans the corridor opposite the suites, and Eddie unwittingly makes nerve-grinding eye contact with the killers' reflections. Inexplicably, the one who used to have red hair is now bald, and the formerly bald one is sporting a convincing blond mane.

Eddie tries to smile in a way that demonstrates he still feels a kind of recent-acquaintance-type affinity with them, without actually appearing either to condone or condemn their . . . career decision.

It's not much of a smile. More of a tortured grimace, really. Still, the newly bald ex-redhead acknowledges it with a brief distracted nod, before returning his attention to his grim list, with the formerly bald blond.

Lips still locked in the lacklustre leer, Eddie manages, rather neatly, to accelerate down the corridor without actually appearing to go any faster.

4

Eddie reaches the lifts, and even though the casino's in the basement, and he's nine storeys above it, and time is in desperately, desperately short supply, he elects to take the stairs. Not as a means of escape: if Eddie's next on the list, using the stairs won't foil any pursuit. No. It's this: Eddie doesn't think he can maintain his wretched limp and fake smile for the duration of the lift journey, should the . . . should the . . . men elect to join him, and he doesn't want to try.

There is no relief in the stairwell from the invariable perfect temperature, which Eddie is beginning to find a kind of torture, but there is a strange smell, which triggers off some sensory memory in Eddie's brain.

It's a wet, somehow metallic smell. So intently is Eddie trying to place it, the sound of the stairwell door opening a couple of flights above him registers only peripherally, and the urgent clacking of hurried footsteps is almost on him before he realizes the hitmen are following him down the stairs.

What to do, Eddie? The killers still might not be after you. And if you run, you'll certainly look suspicious. They'll certainly scrutinize their list of business appointments most thoroughly if they catch you fleeing, and there's a good chance you'll be on it.

On the other hand, if they *are* after you, an accelerated downwards trajectory just might get you into the casino with a sufficient lead to hide among the milling crowd. This is an important decision, Eddie, and, without wishing to rush you, it's a decision you have to make in less than a second.

Less than astonishingly, Eddie opts to do nothing. He opts to keep a clear head, a steady, unhurried pace and brazen it out. What cool, he congratulates himself. What élan. What poise. Unfortunately, Eddie's legs immediately chicken out of the cool, élan, poise option and start leaping down the stairs five at a time.

As he stumbles blindly down, his hand reaching out for the rail and occasionally grabbing it, but more frequently stubbing his fingernails painfully against the wall, Eddie tries to assess how far his possible pursuers are above him.

Did they hear him take off ? Did they accelerate after him? Are the terrible trademark pink socks closer or further away?

And as Eddie's attention is above and behind him, he fails to notice the fire exit door he's heading towards lurch open.

He fails to notice it so completely, it crunches into his lunging face and thumps him backwards, so his coccyx cracks into the rim of a concrete step, exploding Eddie's reality into a white-hot eruption of electrified suffering.

This, Eddie is dismally aware, is not one of those run of the mill collision injuries that will eventually disappear and leave no legacy. This one will result in an intermittently crippling shooting pain that will periodically plague him for the rest of his natural life.

And arguably, to those who embrace certain religious beliefs, well beyond.

The one good thing about the pain: it makes Eddie forget, at least for a tiny while, all of his other considerable problems. As the agony haze subsides, and Eddie's able to focus out of it and take in his surroundings, he sees a strange face peeking round the fire exit door.

'You OK, pilgrim?' The man has druggy wild eyes with pinprick pupils that dart around randomly in a crystalline-induced sham panic. He is wearing what looks like a filthy green bandanna around his head, and a similarly green, similarly filthy smock, with curiously shiny brown stains all over it. He is the source of the smell Eddie couldn't place.

Eddie recognizes the smell, now, and consequently the stains.

Blood.

'You in need, pilgrim? Can I offer you some enhancements?'

Eddie shakes his head. 'No.' And, because he's Eddie, he adds: 'No, thank you. I'm fine.'

The man is a backstreet grafter. He is offering surgical augmentation. It's illegal, of course, but very popular. Very fashionable. He wipes a rubber glove over his forehead, leaving a cloyed bloody smear across his eyebrow line. 'You certain, pilgrim? You couldn't think of a use for another penis? Your life wouldn't be dramatically improved by some eyes in the back of your head?'

The grafter widened his eyes with such pathetic hopefulness, that a big piece of Eddie wanted to accommodate him. Here we are. Eddie, with the last few grains of sand tumbling through the hourglass of his life, with a contract out on him and a couple of hitmen on their way downstairs in his direction, is willing to consider a lengthy pause in his schedule to undergo unnecessary, dangerous and undesirable surgery, from a patently incompetent sleep-deprived speed junky, just because he doesn't want to see this stranger disappointed. Is Eddie a nice guy, or is Eddie an idiot?

He drags himself painfully to as erect a stance as he can manage. He shakes his head again and tries to smile. 'Thanks, but this is really not a good time.'

'I've got a whole lot of end-of-line stock.' The grafter smiles and slowly yawns open the fire exit door to reveal, crowded on the metal spiral stairs, a terrible tableau that will lodge in Eddie's permanent memory, nestling, as usual, in the worst possible location, among his top-of-the-line masturbatory fantasy images: a miserable group of wretches who are waiting to sell their body parts. Eddie looks away, but not quickly enough. He can't avoid seeing the sodden bandages on recently truncated limbs, the bloody off-white eye patches, the stomachs criss-crossed over major internal organs with hasty, inept stitching, the makeshift wheelchairs and carts, the jerry-built crutches, the pinned-back sleeves and knotted spare trouser legs, and, worst of all, the eager glints in the eyes of those who still have eyes.

The grafter licks his amphetamine-dry lips ineffectively. 'Last chance, pilgrim. Closing down tonight.' His leer widens unpleasantly. 'Everything must goooo.' And just as Eddie thinks his sense of revulsion has peaked, there is a sudden rustling at the grafter's crotch, and the hand of a grafted third arm bursts through the flies and beckons him towards the door.

Eddie steps back involuntarily, just as two sets of footsteps hit the top of the stairs behind him.

With a painful wrench of his head, Eddie spots them. The pair of them now sport that kind of Superman black hair that's almost hair. Eddie marvels at not only the quality, but the astonishing variety of their hairpieces. The hitmen look angry. Eddie instantly regrets having run off the way he did. This is not a pair of gentlemen he would wish to aggravate needlessly.

On both their faces, simultaneously, the angry look is wiped away by a sinister spreading smile.

They unharness their guns and head down the stairs in their matter-of-fact, businesslike, resolute way. No rush, but no hanging about, either.

Professional.

As they reach him, Eddie tries not to cower, but fails. They carry on past him. They fling open the fire escape door, Mr Red/Bald/Black calls out: 'Jimmy Duffle?' and they plunge into the human butcher's yard inside. Eddie should go now, but he doesn't. He listens.

Sure enough, there is a kerfuffle. Eddie wonders if he's the only appointment who never kerfuffled. Scuffing on steel steps. A lot of yelling. The almost clinical, flat, slapping sounds of fists striking face, then the door bursts open again, and the hitmen emerge carrying their battered appointment, in his stained white smock all ready for surgery, between them.

The bruised man is yelling. 'Please, I'll get the money. I'm selling it. Look: it's worth a fortune, I swear. Just let me show . . .' He struggles a hand loose and frees his penis from the slit in his smock. It is an undeniably impressive beast, if blatantly riddled with unpleasant disease. 'Check that baby out. It'll make a mint. Trust me. Hey!' He sees Eddie. 'Hey, pilgrim: you could use a monster pecker, could you not?' He whips his member around like a rubber hose in a Chilean interrogation room. 'Look at it! It's a beauty. Work it up to performance level, you could go punting with it! Come on! You'll never get a better bargain.'

The killers stand their appointment at the top of the stairs. Bald/Blond/Black puts his gun to the man's temple. The other one – Eddie, believe it or not, has come to think of him as the 'nice' hitman – raises his eyebrows in Eddie's direction, and, over the doomed man's gibbering pleading, offers the advice: 'I were you, Eddie, I'd take the elevator.'

'Can do.' Eddie smiles and nods. The smile is to mask his intense disappointment that he is recognized, and his name is remembered. He turns and walks painfully back up the stairs towards the previous floor, trying to shut the door behind him before the gunshot, and more than that: before the terrible wet slap of warm brains against wall, but failing, failing.

5

The Project.

Say 'the Project' and nobody asks you 'What project?'

In its time it has been variously known as the Generation Project, the Pilgrim Project, Project Colony, and, in a short-lived blast of unwarranted glory grabbing, best forgotten: the Gwent Project.

But now, it's grown so big, so important, so famous, no adjective is required.

Now, it's simply the Project.

And with good reason. It has a large ambition, the Project. It aims to save the human race from extinction.

Vast resources have been lavished on it. Every nation of the world has contributed. All but the smallest and most paranoid have allocated even the monies normally set aside for national defence. There isn't a whole lot of planet left to defend. And the little that remains won't be around much longer.

The Apocalypse is indeed at hand. It's no longer the exclusive property of doomsayers and cranks. It's happening. The end of the world. Not with the prophesied sudden holocaust of an Armageddon, or the feared swift might of a meteoric conflagration: it's happening by degrees.

The Apocalypse is coming in slow motion.

Global warming has shrunk the Earth. The melting ice caps have raised the oceans, swallowing up vast tracts of land in the low-lying regions. There are few left alive who remember a country called Holland. Fewer still who could point out on a map the area of water now covering what used to be Belgium, and none who'd want to. The United Kingdom is reduced to a series of islands and atolls, though with characteristic defiance, it refuses to change its name.

Everybody finally agrees global warming is a serious problem, now they're up to their necks in water.

And as the land masses shrink, as resources drown under the swelling waters, the world population has exploded. There are more people alive now than ever lived in the whole of human history. Billions upon billions trying to scrape a life from the receding land and its dwindling supplies. More born every day. And every day, just a little less land, just a little less food.

The only hope for the human race is to expand. To spread. There are small colonies establishing themselves on the more agreeable planets in the local system, but life there is harsh, and unlikely to get much softer in the predictable future.

Humankind has to raise its sights a little. It has to reach for the stars.

And that's what the Project is for.

It would give a false impression to say that a gigantic spaceship is under construction. It's much, much more than a spaceship: it's a city. A mobile metropolis, built for space travel. It has parks, apartment blocks, factories and schools. It has a sports stadium. It has its own transway system, and twenty-seven channels of its own entertainment broadcast network. It's designed to accommodate a complete community.

In a heavy-handed attempt at PR positivity, the ship has been named: the *Willflower*.

And it is *large*. Far, far too large to be launched from the Earth's surface. The energy required for take-off would split the planet in two. So it's being put together in orbit above the point of least spin: the South Pole.

It's tethered to the drowning Earth by the tallest structure in human history: the Hoist. The Hoist – or, more romantically, the Stairway To Heaven – is a giant elevator that ferries supplies and personnel to and from the ship.

In theory, at least, the crew represents the cream of humanity: individuals at the top of their professions, at the peak of their abilities. It is supposedly an honour to be numbered among the

Selected. But then, it was supposedly an honour to be a kamikaze pilot.

The Selected are not prepared to dedicate merely their lives to the Project, they are prepared to dedicate the lives of their unborn children. And their unborn children's unborn children.

The *Willflower* is a generation ship. Even travelling at the fantastic speeds it hopes to achieve, it will take several lifetimes to reach its destination. Quite how many lifetimes is much underplayed in the news media.

Because the Project is just about the only good news the human race has to relish.

Its objective is the nearest Earth-like planet. Or, to be more precise, the nearest planet that most closely resembles the Earth before humans started dickering with it.

It's impossible to say which planet this will be – the distances involved make such precision impossible – but it's a long way away. A long, long way away. The crew of the *Willflower*, the Pilgrim Parents – more PR spinnery – will ready the planet for the mass exodus of the human race from its original home. By that time, it is confidently predicted, space travel will have evolved sufficiently to render the journey achievable in years, rather than decades.

At least, that's the official version.

The reality is considerably less palatable.

Even in the best-case projections, and ignoring the effects of time dilation, which the best-case projections all do, the voyage will take centuries.

But who would care to broadcast that news? And who would want to hear it?

Because the Project really is that important.

It's the last and only hope for the long-term survival of the human species.

6

The lift is not a good place for Eddie.

The strip lights are too bright, and the mirrors on the three walls reflect an infinite number of Eddie O'Hares, each one looking with thinly disguised disgust at each of the others. These are the mirrors to be avoided at all costs. These mirrors show you in the worst way possible.

They show you as other people see you.

The furious noise of the casino swills into the elevator car long before it reaches the basement and spills Eddie out into the greedy chaos.

There are bright lights, flickering, blinking, flashing. There are sequins. There is glitter. There is a wall of noise, human, mechanical and electronic. But most of all, there are people.

Eddie blinks. This is only his second visit to a casino. The first was just a few hours ago, and it lasted less than fifteen minutes. The place hadn't seemed quite so alienating then. Eddie had his money, then. A lot of money, for Eddie. True, he didn't manage to keep it for long, but it had given him a sense of comfort, a feeling that he had a *right* to be there, alongside other casino types. Now he has almost nothing to lose, he feels like an interloper.

He turns the fifty chip over in his hand, his last, sweaty link to any kind of future, and tries to work out where to be.

Everyone else in the place seems to know where they should be, and they're all standing there, or sitting there, or heading there with confidence and conviction. He hears a yelp of delight, and a slot machine to his right chunkles out its prize generously. Almost instantly, to his left, a loud, vicious expletive erupts and an expensively tuxedoed gambler snatches a ludicrously bejewelled watch from his wrist and crushes it under his well-heeled heel.

Eddie's father was a gambler. Yet even though he's seen the disease that close up, he still doesn't understand it. You lose and, in frustration, you stamp an expensive watch to death. Where's the sense in that? He believes that gamblers, fundamentally, are looking to lose. He can deal with that. It's not sensible, but it makes sense. What baffles him is this: what do gamblers think of money? Do they hold it in such high esteem that nothing else in life really matters? Or do they hold it in such low contempt that money, and consequently everything else in life, is utterly meaningless?

Either way, there's no time for piddling little details like taking care of your family. Of your son.

He's remembering, now. Going back to Christmas time, his eighth, he thinks. There was this toy he'd been coveting. Hardly a toy, really: an electrically powered junior hover car. An exact working replica of a Ferrari Velocemente, quarter size. And hardly coveting it, either. Even then, he was aware it was absurdly expensive. He'd seen it in one of the few remaining department stores that still actually had things out on display. It had seemed so impossibly beautiful. So unattainable.

The last day of term, he came home to find an enormous present, gift-wrapped, under the Christmas tree. The package was precisely the size and shape of a quarter-scale Ferrari Velocemente junior hover. It felt like a Ferrari Velocemente junior hover, too. To young Eddie, it even seemed to smell like a Ferrari Velocemente junior hover. He remembers folding open the gift card attached, struggling to keep his hands from trembling long enough to actually read it. It was addressed simply: 'To Eddie, from Santa'.

Naturally he pestered his father about the contents of the parcel, and naturally, his father denied all knowledge and teased him mercilessly, offering ludicrous alternative suggestions: a dead sheep-dog, a goldfish in an oversized bowl, a pair of bloated kippers. Eddie was too young, then, to work out that the old man had won some big-time gamble, and was on the high, extravagant end of his mood-swing scale. He thought all dads yo-yoed between drunken misery and outrageous, flamboyant generosity.

Eddie resisted the urge to peek, though the temptation was achingly strong. He made do with caressing the parcel when no one was watching. With creeping downstairs in the wee hours to feel its sleek curves and smell its rich leather promise.

When Christmas morning finally had the good manners to arrive, around seventeen million years later, Eddie crept downstairs one final time. But the parcel had shrunk in size. Dramatically. Where once it had dominated the room, Eddie now had to scrabble under the tree to find it. Same gift card. Same paper, though substantially less of it. And there was a model car inside it, but it was a 125th-scale model.

And it wasn't a hover.

It wasn't even a Ferrari.

Eddie didn't work it out for a long time, but his mother did. That was the last Christmas Eddie's father spent in the family home.

But this is inappropriate. Eddie shouldn't be indulging himself in these maudlin memories. Not now. He's still no closer to deciding where to chance his chip, and time's a-ticking.

It has to be a roulette table.

The accountant in Eddie knows roulette offers the longest odds that most fairly represent the laws of probability, assuming the table is straight. Which is a rather huge assumption tonight, of all nights.

A roulette table, certainly. But which one?

He scours the unwelcoming room for a feeling, a sense of destiny, a sign of some kind. And, being Eddie, he feels no disappointment when nothing comes to him. And then a magical thing happens in Eddie's totally unmagical life. He sees something. Something unmistakably portentous.

In the far corner, one of the tables has a flashing arrow pointing to it. And a message in lights reads: *Eddie to Win*. He strains. He must have misread it.

But no, it's flashing away there, for everyone to see. *Eddie to Win*.

And not even a loser like Eddie can resist a lure like that. He pushes his way over to the table, watching the sign all the while. And when he gets there, it feels *right*.

He looks up at the sign again. But now it's reading: *Ready to Win?* Can he really have misread it?

It doesn't matter. For once in this long and staccatically violent night, Eddie truly feels he's in the right place at the right time.

He fights the accountant's urge to play the short odds, the best probabilities: the red or black two-to-one shot, or the odd or even. That's too sensible for the occasion. The occasion requires him to multiply his stake by forty-six thousand, six hundred and fifty-six.

But that's not the way to think of it. Thinking like that will just freeze you up and get you all sweaty, Eddie. What you have to do, *all* you have to do, is pick the right number three times.

Now, that doesn't sound too hard, does it? It doesn't have to be three *different* numbers, even. And with just three correct guesses, he'll have the two and a quarter million he owes, with a little under eighty-three grand left over. Piece of cake, my friend. Slice of gateau.

Eddie stares at the green baize, waiting for a number to jump out for him.

Dozens of people are at the table, clunking chips all over the place. Some of them are playing the sensible low odds, some of them are making complicated wagers, combining numbers in bizarre cluster combinations that bewilder Eddie, but most are looking for the quick riches of the single number.

And what is the number for Eddie? His birthday? No. No one could call that a lucky-number day. His age? His hat size? The length of his penis in inches? What? What? What?

Then Eddie sees something. He sees the reason why whatever it was that directed him to this particular table directed him to this particular table.

A man with the same build, the same colouring; a man who looks so like Eddie that even Eddie has to look twice.

Of course, Eddie thinks this man is better looking than him, but

Eddie would. In fact, the biggest difference between the two of them is that this man, the non-Eddie, is calm. His hand isn't sticky and sweaty. He doesn't seem to care whether he wins or loses. And he's putting a large pile of unstinking, sweat-free chips on a single number.

There must be a grand's worth of chips, there. With a scientist's disdain for superstition, he's putting it all on thirteen. And in a flash of certainty that goes far beyond confidence, that's where Eddie puts his stenchy, sticky lifeline of a chip.

Thirteen.

Unlucky.

Just like Eddie.

And as soon as it's down, Eddie wants to take it off. But the croupier's called, and the ball is spinning.

What was he thinking of? He should have watched a few plays first, at least. He should have tried to divine some kind of pattern, a bias, even. Some kind of kink, some deviation in the wheel. A hint of a sequence. He should have done something a whole lot more sensible. And now it's too late. He's not only cursed himself, he's cursed his unwitting partner in luck, the innocent Eddie lookalike.

And now the silver ball's slowing down. Its orbit is decaying. It's tinkling, now, against the compartments of the whirling wheel; bouncing back to the outer rim and clattering again into the wheel, and it seems to Eddie that the tiny ball is disproportionately loud for its size, that its incessant clack-clackety-clack is drowning out the massed clamour of the entire casino, this one, teensy, tiny ball thundering with metallic explosions around the roulette wheel. And there's an inexplicable thudding, tha-*dump*, tha-*dump*, tha-*dump*, which turns out to be the blood pulsing through Eddie's temple. And the ball has stopped, but the wheel's still spinning, so you can't quite see what number the ball is resting in, and it looks like . . . it looks like . . . No.

No.

No.

No!

Eddie's life is over.

He's a dead man. Just tag his toe and toll his bell.

Eddie will have to race upstairs and start auctioning his limbs and organs to try and raise the shuttle fare out of here. If he's lucky, he'll be left with a leg, so he can at least hop to the shuttle port.

Because with the fickle cruelty that dogs Eddie O'Hare's every move in life, the ball has landed in compartment thirteen.

Wait.

Is that *thirteen*?

Thir*teen*?

That's Eddie's number!

Eddie's number is thirteen. He's won.

Eddie involuntarily jumps and punches the air. He looks around, to share his wide-eyed joy, the sensational sensation of a one thousand eight hundred, count 'em, one eight oh oh big ones, instant profit with his fellow punters, but all eyes are on Eddie's *doppelgänger*, who has clocked up closer to thirty-six thousand. He's shaking his head, smiling wryly. As if he truly didn't care about winning.

The croupier stretches out to push the winnings towards the thirty-six thousandaire, but he holds up his hand and nods down at the table.

He's going to let it ride.

Thirty-six thousand on the spin of a ball.

And now the croupier is about to shunt Eddie's meagre haul towards him. But Eddie holds up his hand.

Can he really be doing this?

He nods down at the number thirteen.

Is this really sensible Eddie?

Is he really going to let it ride?

But that's so not sensible!

One thousand eight hundred big ones.

Let it riiiiiiiiiiiide!

The little silver ball, Eddie's shiny friend, grinds around the outside of the wheel.

And he wants his money back.

He immediately wants to rescind the bet. What part of him made this insane decision, and by what authority? Where was this discussion held? Where was this meeting of the mind taken, to which Eddie's consciousness was not invited? Who voted? Not Eddie's sanity, that's for sure. He could at least have taken back his *stake*. He didn't have to leave it all on there, risking everything.

But it's all too late now. No amount of sensibleness can take back what he's done. The orbiting ball seems distant, this time. Like he's watching it through the wrong end of a telescope. His skin, the skin on his face, seems to be buzzing.

The wheel's slowing down, now, and the little silver ball makes one last hop, one last clack, and bobbles in the thirteen slot. Bobbling . . . bobbling . . .

And it stays there.

Around Eddie, people are shouting silently.

Eddie thinks they're probably making a noise others could hear, but Eddie's on a different level, now. He looks up at his likeness, who may or may not be on the same level. Certainly they share a private moment together, a look, before Eddie's awareness slips back down to reality and the noise thunders back into his world.

Eddie now has nearly sixty-five thousand. Small change compared to the Eddiesque fellow on whose luck Eddie is piggybacking. Just a tickle under one point three million is due in that direction.

Eddie is getting ready to gather his chips. Take a break, drink a cola, gather his thoughts, but the croupier reaches over to shove Eddie's lookalike's winnings over, and Eddie's lookalike holds up his hand again and nods towards the thirteen square once more. The croupier looks troubled. This is a big bet, now. Way over the floor limit. She shoots a glance towards a serious-looking individual Eddie hadn't seen arrive. The serious man in his serious suit pauses a second, and nods his permission. A tiny little nothing of a nod, given the amount that's riding on this spin.

One million, three hundred and sixty thousand.

There are lots of people round the table, now. Eddie is finding it hard to breathe. Almost as an afterthought, the croupier reaches to push out Eddie's comparatively small pile, and cocks her head, quizzically. As if it's a foregone conclusion that Eddie will let his sixty-four thousand, eight hundred winnings ride on.

Eddie's lost, here. This is way out of his sphere. We left the land of Sensible long ago, and we're deeply into the uncharted waters of the Cape of Loonyness, now. There be sharks, here, Eddie. There be dragons.

Oh boy.

Could this happen? Could a thing *this* good happen in a life as unlucky as Eddie's? He looks around the crowd of eager faces. They all want him to bet. To win. They want a happy ending. They want to see someone beat the system.

And if he wins, if he *does* win, he wins so much. He gets his life back. His insides stay inside him. His brains don't become sloppy, random graffiti on a stairwell wall.

And if he loses . . .

But that's not even worth contemplating. This is what we call 'a streak' here. For the first time ever, Eddie's on a winning streak. It may not, technically speaking, be his *own* winning streak, but he's hitching a ride anyway.

He's going to do it.

He's raising his hand and turning his head towards the Eddie lookalike, to exchange a smile of mutuality, of defiance, of confidence, when he stops. The Eddie lookalike isn't looking at him. He isn't looking at the croupier, or the table, or the wheel. He's looking at his watch, then over towards the exit. What is this? Millions, literally tens of millions at stake on this spin, and the man is *bored*?

And it suddenly dawns on Eddie what's going on, here. This man doesn't *care* about winning or losing the odd million or two. And not because he's rich – he's *beyond* rich. He's with the Project. He's a bona-fide *pilgrim*, and tomorrow morning, and for the rest of his life, he'll be living in a world where money doesn't matter.

He'll be leaving the planet Earth, with all its concerns, all its pleasures and its pains and all its currencies behind.

Eddie can't risk his life on that basis: gambling an insane gamble in tandem with a man who doesn't give a flying hootenanny about winning or losing. And Eddie changes the motion of his hand, beckoning for his winnings. The croupier shrugs – what does she care? – and sweeps Eddie's chips over to him.

The crowd all look away from Eddie. He's embarrassed them with his cowardice. But that's all right with Eddie. That's fine with him. He scoops up his chips clumsily, cradling them between his arms and his chin. He knows the croupier's shooting him a contemptuous sneer for not slinging over a few chips to tip her. But Eddie doesn't care about that, either. Like she deliberately let him win, or something? More important to Eddie, he has to get away from the table. Quickly. Before the clattering silver ball settles.

He must never find out where that ball winds up on this spin. Because, either way, he doesn't think his heart could take the strain.

He turns from the table. Some chips tumble out of his clumsy grasp. He wants to leave them there, at least until this spin is spun, but he can't. He can't afford to lose any of it. He has to let every chip multiply if he's going to save his life.

And as he's scooping up the stragglers, he hears the ball stop clattering. And there's a silence. Is this a real silence, or is it one of Eddie's perceived silences?

It's real, all right. It's broken by the croupier's voice. Though Eddie has never noticed before – it's been drowned out by cheering or by the tha-*dump*, tha-*dump* thudding of Eddie's blood circulating past his ears – she always calls out the winning number and the colour of its square.

'Thirteen, black.'

And under the tumult that follows, Eddie tries not to do two sums, but, naturally, he fails.

He has turned his back on over two and a quarter million, and the man who wanted to lose has just netted an eight-figure fortune in the region of forty-six million, six hundred and fifty-six thousand. Tax free.

Eddie needs a drink. A big drink. But first, the anal accountant in him wants to tidy up his chips. He staggers over to the cash window and tips his winnings into the dip on the counter. The cashier asks him if he wants cash, but Eddie shakes his head and orders the largest chips they have.

When he reflects on this, Eddie will come to believe he made the two biggest mistakes of his life in as many minutes.

He collects six ten-thousand chips, four one-thousands and some change, and turns to head for the bar. In the short space of time it's taken Eddie to change his chips, a very long and unruly queue has formed behind him. Foolishly, Eddie doesn't think about why this might be, and heads for the bar.

The bar is strangely deserted and it takes quite a while for Eddie to order his cola successfully.

So what's the plan now? He needs one more number. One more successful bet. That's all. He sips at his soft drink, trying not to think of the bet he just didn't make. There is a furore behind him, but Eddie's wrapped up in his own little furore. He has to make that one last bet. He needs a number. He looks for a sign, but sees nothing. The bartender presents the bill. Absently, Eddie says to put it on his room. The bartender asks for his room number. Eddie says eight, eight, eight and slides over his key. And still Eddie's looking for a sign. The barkeep repeats the number. Eight, eight, eight. And Eddie wishes this guy wouldn't keep interrupting his thought train while he's looking for a sign, for some indication where he might put his money. On top of which, the over-loud tannoid is making some earsplitting announcement so a man can hardly think straight. 'That's right.' Eddie raises his voice, as close to bad-tempered as Eddie's ever been. 'Eight, eight, eight. That's what I said. That's what it says on the key fob. That would be eight, followed by another eight, followed by a third and final . . .'

And Eddie's off his barstool and standing at the nearest roulette table, which is surprisingly devoid of custom. Eddie puts his chips down on the number eight.

The croupier ignores him. He's talking to a waitress.

Eddie coughs. 'Excuse me? Is this table closed?'

The croupier turns and looks at Eddie's bet. 'Are you serious?'

'Deadly serious. Sixty-four thousand, eight hundred serious.' Eddie sips his cola. He's secretly delighted to have impressed a hardnose like this croupier, who looks like he's seen a lot of serious gambling action. Eddie's definitely a hardcore gambler, now. For this one final spin, Eddie's triple X-rated.

The croupier offers a facial shrug to the waitress, who giggles flirtatiously, and with an exaggerated flourish, he lifts the silver ball out of its housing in the middle of the wheel.

'Any more bets?' He calls with comic theatricality, which is to say unfunnily in the grossest way.

The waitress, astonishingly, leaps on to the table and sits with a thump that knocks Eddie's neat tower of chips over. 'Yeah,' she grins, 'I bet my ass on red.'

Eddie tries not to be thrown by this inexplicable levity. He stacks his chips neatly again, and tries to ignore it.

The croupier says: 'Sorry, lady, but your giant *ass* appears to be placed on the red *and* the black.'

She giggles again. 'Whoopsy.' She shifts her buttocks, so only one cheek is on the table. 'Better?'

'I'm afraid not, lady. It's still on the red and the black. It's also on the odd, the even and about half a dozen other numbers . . .'

The croupier ducks to avoid the waitress's flung stiletto-heeled shoe. He calls: 'No more bets.'

He spins the wheel.

Eddie sips the cola. He'll complain about the staff later. When he's a millionaire.

The croupier flings in the ball, with another pantomime flourish.

This time, Eddie has no nerves. There is no feeling of suspense. No doubts. No fears. Just a certainty, a cool, unshakeable conviction that the ball will bobble into compartment number eight. Just that.

And it does.

Sweet as a teat.

'Eight, black.'

Eddie smiles a smile that qualifies as 007 wry. Superiority. Satisfaction. Aplomb. Two million, three hundred and thirty-three thousand, give or take. He's a double and a third millionaire. He's safe. He's free. He's going to live.

But the croupier doesn't acknowledge the win. He doesn't seem even to notice Eddie. No, instead the croupier flings his croup in the air and yells: 'The lady loses her ass to the house!' and starts advancing on the waitress with mock menace. She yelps, clambers on to her hands and knees and starts backing across the roulette table, growling. Eddie can clearly see her fine skimpy satin underpants which admirably just barely accommodate her far from giant ass. Under any other circumstances, the view would be enough to silence Eddie, to distract him completely, at least for a few moments. He certainly could use a few good images for his erotic memory library, to counterbalance some of the erection nobblers he's acquired tonight. But Eddie has won a considerable amount of money here, and this behaviour is a very long way from appropriate to the situation. This is wrong.

Eddie says 'Excuse me' through his smile, but the croupier keeps advancing, crowing, 'That ass belongs to me, young lady. I must collect that ass.' And the waitress keeps backing off on all fours, growling and snarling, her beautiful satin-thonged *derrière* wiggling in Eddie's face.

Eddie thumps the table, hard. This does get the staff's attention. 'I don't want to break anything up here, but there is the small matter of my bet.'

The croupier looks round at the table. 'Your bet?'

'Number eight.'

'You won?'

'Sixty-four thousand, eight hundred globals. All on numero eight, my friend.'

The croupier registers the tower of chips, raises his eyebrows and nods. 'That's right. You won your bet.' There is a long and unseemly pause. A smile struggles not to cross the croupier's lips. He sniggers, then barely manages to cough out a falsetto: 'Congratulations!' before collapsing into a bizarre giggling fit. The waitress joins in.

Eddie looks around for some kind of help. What is going on here? Did he inadvertently wander into some part of the casino reserved for the mentally derelict? His fortune, his lifeline, his very future currently lies in the hands of a maniacally giggling lunatic. This is bad. This is very, very bad. What if they cart the guy off in a straitjacket? Who's going to believe Eddie actually placed his winning bet? This is too much, too cruel.

Eddie grabs the guy by the lapels. Not violently, that's certainly not in Eddie's nature, even under this level of provocation. He just wants the man's attention.

'Look, you can fool around all you want to, friend, you can cash in the waitress's backside at your leisure, but first, you have to pay me my winnings.' And in case that sounded too confrontational, Eddie adds: 'Is that OK with you?'

'Sure.' The croupier snickers and calms down. 'I'm sorry. Take it.'

'Take it?'

The croupier waves his hand expansively at the neat banks of chips by the wheel. 'Take it.'

'Take my winnings? Myself ? Help myself to two million, three hundred and thirty-two thousand, eight hundred globals?'

'Whatever you want! Take it all! Think big, my friend. Take all of it.'

Eddie's face doesn't know what to do with itself. His mouth doesn't know what word to form. It attempts a couple of vowels, but the larynx isn't co-operating. He looks from the chips to the croupier and back again. There is clearly something wrong here. Something very, very, very wrong. He looks back at the croupier and manages to verbalize a 'b' sound, which exhausts his current conversation bank.

The croupier gently removes Eddie's hands from his waistcoat lapels. 'Didn't you hear, pilgrim? The casino's closed down. Some lucky son of a bitch won almost fifty million. Broke the bank. All bets are off.'

Eddie's mouth attempts a few more vowels and a hard consonant or two, but his voicebox just won't join in.

'Hey, I'm sorry. I thought you knew. Everybody else seems to know.'

Eddie looks around. The casino certainly does have an after-the-party look about it. The staff have all loosened their ties and they're chatting in groups. The few punters still remaining are operating some tables for each other, making ludicrously large, meaningless bets.

'OK.' Eddie gathers his wits. 'OK. So I didn't win the bet?'

'Hey. Sorry. I thought . . . I mean, it was just fun. You were just having fun, right?'

'But my stake . . .' Eddie struggles to keep a whimper out of his voice. 'My stake, that's still good.' And even though the croupier's shaking his head sadly, Eddie carries on. 'I can still cash in my original stake, of course. That's real money, still, is it not?'

'There was an announcement.' The waitress is joining in now. 'Everyone must have heard the announcement.'

Eddie sucks in his lower lip.

'It was a very *loud* announcement,' the waitress adds, infected suddenly by Eddie's patent misery.

'Sooooo.' Eddie's lips have trouble moving on from the 'o' shape. 'Thooose chips are, what? Worthless?' Eddie tries to pitch the penultimate syllable high, to induce a note of *faux* levity, but his mouth is too dry and his voice cracks, and his lower lip begins to quiver before he can suck it in again.

The croupier and the waitress look away. This level of barely contained anguish is close to unwatchable.

'But they *have* to pay. Don't they? I mean, there is a legal contract, here. There is a binding agreement. A tacit bargain. In law. Is there not?'

The croupier shrugs.

'I mean, surely . . . surely they should pay off the rest of us, before they pay out the full fifty million. So what if Mr Break The Bank only gets forty million and change? So what if his sky yacht has one less propeller? What about us? What about the little people?'

The croupier sighs. 'You have to be realistic, pilgrim. Say you're a casino. What would worry you most? A lawsuit from a bunch of little people who've probably lost most of their money anyway, or a lawsuit from a multi-millionaire?'

Eddie nods. That does make sense. That makes good business sense. That's exactly the advice Eddie would probably have given if he'd been the accountant here.

Eddie simply stands for a while, waiting for his skin to stop buzzing, but that isn't going to happen any time soon. The croupier coughs quietly and tries to fasten up a button on his waistcoat that isn't really undone. Of all the things Eddie has to feel bad about, he begins to feel bad that he's ruining a moment of sexual excitement for these two young people. He nods, forces a truly dismal smile, and catches the word 'thanks' before it leaks inappropriately out of his mouth, managing instead to turn it into what he hopes might pass as a macho grunt of farewell, but sounds, in fact, closer to a piggy death squeal, and turns towards the exit.

He has no idea where he can go from here. No idea what he can even try to do. He's the walking dead. He's a zombie.

The next time he's aware of his surroundings, Eddie is at the casino door. The speakers are stuttering a very old recording, certainly pre-digital. Pre-stereo, even. The song is 'The Man Who Broke the Bank at Monte Carlo'. His eyes are smarting. He doesn't know why.

7

Now Eddie's on the street. He doesn't know how far from the casino. Some sound has snapped him out of his shocked state. He hears it again. That flat, unreverberating, non-movie sound of real human-on-human violence. He glances to his left. A man is on the floor, being kicked mercilessly by two other men. Eddie doesn't look up at their hair, but he does register the pink fluorescent socks swinging with businesslike regularity.

Eddie wonders how far down the alphabet the boys are now. Still on the 'D's, possibly. If Eddie is on their list, he's probably got an hour or even two before they work their way down to the 'O's. Though, of course, some systems classify Eddie's name under 'H', in which case he's probably got considerably less time.

He looks up at the sky, shimmering above the thermal dome. In Afortunado, it rains for seven minutes every seven hours, which the designers hoped would give a semblance of randomness. For the long-term inhabitants, the street vendors especially, it's become a sort of Chinese water torture. This doesn't look like a rain hour . . .

Eddie snaps to towards the end of a shower. He wonders how long he's been walking. He tries to get his bearings, and spots the Hotel Felicity on the next block. He's spent an hour, maybe two, going nowhere. This is crazy, Eddie. You can't just give up. You still have time. You need a plan. You need to make something happen.

But that's not how Eddie's life operates. Eddie doesn't make things happen. Things happen to Eddie. And now, just when he needs it most, something mercifully does happen to him.

There's a bar, a low-rent tavern over the road. There's a neon sign over the entrance. Bizarrely, the bar appears to be called the This is Where You're Meant to Be, Eddie Inn.

He blinks.

That is definitely what the sign says. He looks around. Nobody else is looking at the sign. Why would they?

Eddie crosses the road. He looks up at the neon sign again. Now it says The Loser's Blues Bar. But Eddie's past caring. He pushes open the door and steps in, anyway.

He's in a bar. A dark bar. This is the darkest bar Eddie's ever been in. The major light source is a handful of neon alcohol brand signs over by the serving area. The dismal illumination these provide is dissipated by thick plumes of disturbingly untobaccolike smoke.

Eddie has never walked into a drinking establishment where he felt comfortable or welcome. In Eddie's mind, the piano always stops when he enters a bar. All eyes flit in his direction, and the brains behind the eyes immediately start calculating precisely when to jump him, and just how badly damaged to leave his poor, pilfered body.

And for once, this really is such a place. This is a dive at the bottom of all dives. A dark, impenetrable place, where dark figures plan dark deeds and perform dark acts.

Eddie waits for his eyes to adjust to the gloom enough for him to find the damned door *out* of the place. He tries not to contemplate the strange noises around him: the whispers, the gruntings, the barking of mad laughter, the smashing of glass, and the inexplicable wet sounds.

It was a big mistake, coming in here. This is probably exactly the kind of place frequented by the people he's trying to avoid. They probably pop in here after a hard day's murdering to throw back a few cold ones.

He finally realizes his eyes are never going to adjust, and decides to try backing out through what he hopes is the way he came in.

His heel connects with something animal on the floor. He hears the rattle of a chain, a worrying hiss, and the thick muscle of his calf erupts with a stinging pain.

He jumps in a direction which he prays is away from the danger, and collides with a chair. His right hand reaches down involuntarily for balance, but grabs a handful of hair, and elicits a heart-squeezing curse.

Even though Eddie snaps his hand back with cobra speed, he feels a wet warmth spreading over it, which can only be the product of a swift encounter with a very sharp, very ready blade.

He puts the back of his hand to his mouth and sucks at the salty blood pumping copiously through his neatly sliced flesh. He waits for the pain to come, hoping it will be sufficiently excruciating to help him blank out the agony in the back of his leg, which is thrumming very unpromisingly.

What *was* that thing that stung him?

He's praying it was just a large, grizzled old bad-tempered cat with inexplicably sharp claws. But the truth is, it felt more like a snake.

Or, possibly, a scorpion.

From the size of the punctures, it was big snake, too.

Or an unbelievably large scorpion.

Could there truly be a big snake chained to the floor here? Or a giant scorpion in fetters? Or, best of all, one of those illegitimate genetic/surgical hybrid guard animal/insect/reptiles, banned on every continent and colony in the solar system, but nurtured openly and apparently adoringly by hairy tattooed men with shaven heads? This certainly is the kind of establishment where the management might find it amusing to keep such a lethal, nightmarishly ugly predator as a bar pet.

So here's the big question: is deadly poison currently coursing through Eddie O'Hare's veins?

And, if so, should he *really* be sucking his own blood?

Eddie's waiting for the first sign of paralysis to hit him. Waiting for the muscular spasms, for the uncontrollable juddering of his legs, for the frothy bile to start foaming out of his facial apertures. And it comes. His arm experiences an involuntary jerk. *This is it*, Eddie's thinking; *Here I go*.

And there's another jerk, and another, before Eddie realizes someone's tugging his arm with increasing urgency. A final tug impels him into a chair.

He's in a booth. Eddie wonders what kind of person would require the additional privacy of a booth in a place like this. In a place where the bar staff would require infra-red night scopes and sophisticated sonar equipment just to collect the empty glasses. He peers through the gloom, still sucking on his probably poisoned blood, and finally decides there is definitely someone else occupying the booth opposite him.

There is a voice from that general direction: soft, but not threatening. 'Recognize me?'

Eddie can't help a little snort escaping, and now he has the taste of his own blood in his nose. 'I'm sorry, friend, but it's pretty dark in here. I can barely recognize *me*.'

'Well, that's good,' the other voice smiles. 'Because I want you to stop being you.'

Eddie wonders how, with all it's been through tonight, his stomach still feels athletic enough to churn mildly, let alone perform a full-blown Fosbury flop.

He stops sucking his hand, which is now beginning to hurt more than his apparently venom-free leg wound. 'You want me to stop being me?' Eddie tries to indicate an air of intriguement, with a tinge of amusing engagedness, rather than petrifaction, with a *soupçon* of unwitting bowel movement.

'That's right.' The voice gets closer, bearing on its breeze the aroma of expensive cigar. 'From now on, I'd like you to start being me.'

8

And so the luckiest man in the cosmos finally gets to speak to the unluckiest man in the cosmos. At last, the irresistible force meets the movable object.

Eddie's feeling very sticky here in the darkness. His clothes are gooey from the drying rainwater and reluctant sweat. His face is gluey from cloying blood mingling with that same sweat and his own saliva, a rapidly dwindling resource. He doesn't want to think about what he'd look like with a bright light trained on him. Certainly, small children would scream at the sight. Caught unawares, he might even scream at himself.

But here, in this dark nook in the darkness, he can pass himself off as a reasonably regular individual. He leans back, trying, pointlessly, to pinpoint the incumbent of the seat opposite and meet his invisible gaze. 'You want me to start being you? You want us to swap identities?'

'No, no. Why would I want to be you? No. *I* want to be me, as well. I just want you to stop being you, and start being me.'

Eddie wonders if he can leap up and reach the door before this madman produces a chainsaw and starts on some kind of rampage. But there's the chained stinging-or-biting beast to worry about. And the slash-happy razor man. And who knows what else is lurking there in the dark between him and the exit?

And so Eddie tries politeness and reason. 'Listen, friend, I don't want you to think that I'm *against* your plan, in principle. And I don't want to put any flies in any ointments, here; but if I become you, who's going to be me?'

Eddie spots a red circle opposite. It glows, briefly illuminating the lower face of the man who wants Eddie to be him, then darts out of sight. There's something about that half face, that nose.

Eddie catches the scent of cigar again. It makes him wish he were a smoker. There is a long, sibilant exhalation, and the man speaks. 'There's very little time here, so forgive me if I'm wide of the mark. I saw you in the casino. You looked like a man who needed to win. Who needed to win very badly. When you walked in here, you didn't look like you had won. At least, not enough to get you out of whatever mess you were in.'

Eddie wonders how anyone could have read all that just from his expression in the brief moment his entry was illuminated by the lights outside. He concludes you probably don't need to see him. He probably reeks of it. Eau de loser. Effective at fifty paces.

The cigar voice croons on. 'Tell me now if I'm wrong, but I think we're both running on a very tight schedule, and I think we can help each other out.'

Suddenly the memory of the half face in the cigar glow clicks with Eddie. 'It's you. You're him! You're the man who won –'

Eddie's shin bursts into pain. The man hisses: 'Keep it down. I'm trying to keep a low profile on that subject. What d'you think I'm lurking in this dive for?'

'Well, I don't know.' Eddie's shin feels like it's doubling in size. 'I don't know what you're doing in a place like this. You should be having some fun, somewhere. I mean, some serious fun.' And this is so. In this man's place, even Eddie would be having fun, with all the good-time girls he could lay his tongue on. Of all persuasions in all the colours of the rainbow. Who in his right mind would celebrate the acquisition of a tax-free fifty-million fortune in a darkened, joyless pit where the clientele sit in the gloom with one hand on a drink and the other on a spring-loaded cut throat razor?

'I shouldn't be here at all, friend. I should be at the Project.'

Of course. Eddie had spotted the man as a pilgrim. 'I see.' Eddie rolls it over in his mind. 'You're expected there. But now . . .'

'Circumstances alter cases. I'm a very rich man, now. I stand to make around five million a year in interest alone.'

'That's right,' Eddie's calculator brain steps in. 'You're raking in around ten globals every minute, day or night, sleeping or waking.

And that's assuming a basic non-compound interest rate of only ten per cent, which is well short of –'

'The point is: I'd like to *enjoy* this money. I don't want to join the Project any more.'

'And who could blame you?'

'They could. And they will.'

Point made. Point taken. Pilgrims were the modern equivalent of kamikaze pilots. Their families were richly provided for. Their debts were all written off. In return, they signed an iron-clad contract. The mission demanded a full complement. Desertion would be ferociously and, if the rumours were true, terminally discouraged.

This was actually starting to sound good to Eddie. This sounded like a fine deal in the making. Eddie O'Hare would avoid the lethal retribution awaiting him by ceasing to exist. And in exchange, he would become a member of an elite group of Earth's finest: the best of the best, on a lifelong voyage to the stars. For the rest of his life, his every need would be provided for.

And this is the pretty pass to which Eddie has come. The prospect of ceasing to exist is not only the best thing that's been put on his table tonight; it's the best thing that's ever happened to him.

But Eddie, being Eddie, has to perform a little dental inspection on this gift horse. He has to check the bridgework.

'All right. Say I agree. Let's say I become you. How would I pull that off ? Who are you, anyway?'

'I am . . . you are Charles Perry Gordon.' Eddie is aware of a document file being pushed across the table. 'Everything you need to know is in here. You're a community planner.'

'I'm a what?'

'Relax. It's a walk in the park. If anybody asks you a question, all you need is an opinion. It doesn't even have to be a good opinion. It's a Social Science. It'll take years before anyone realizes you don't know what you're talking about. It's – how would the Americans distort the language? – a totally no-risk scenario for you.'

'"Charles", you said? "Charles" . . .' Eddie runs the name over his tongue, while he tries, pointlessly, given the ambient light, to sift through the paperwork. "Chaaaaarles". Is that what people call you? Please don't say they call you "Chuck".'

'Nobody out there's met me. I worked out of Rio de Janeiro; never been on site. To the people on the Project, I'm a photograph on a CV. I'm a bunch of papers, articles and emails. They'll call you what you want them to call you.'

'And you're sure they'll believe I'm you?'

'Why wouldn't they? We're of similar build, similar colouring. You'll have my ID. They won't even think about it. They'll have a million other things to worry about up to the launch.'

'How about "Cee Pee"? I think that has a certain ring.'

In the darkness, the real Mr Gordon is beginning to have his doubts about this man's ability to pass himself off as a human, let alone as one of the Selected. But the Devil's driving here. Needs must. Needs must. '"Cee Pee" sounds charming. The question is: how can I be sure you'll keep to the bargain?'

And with difficulty, because saying it out loud, admitting it, explaining it to another person makes it seem even more terrifyingly hopeless, Eddie tells him. He tells him about his situation.

And the real Mr Gordon doesn't express sympathy, doesn't remark on Eddie's luck. He simply relaxes in the darkness and holds out his hand across the table. 'So we have a deal?'

Eddie senses rather than sees the proffered hand and, without thinking it through, offers his own.

The exuberant handshake bursts Eddie's sticky scab, and his wound starts to bleed again with all its original enthusiasm.

Eddie might see this as a sign. Blood to be spilled. If he were a religious man, he might even make a connection with stigmata, and sacrificial lambs. But he isn't, and he doesn't.

Poor Eddie.

9

Eddie is looking at Afortunado from a different perspective, now. From many different perspectives.

He's a new man. Literally.

He's cleaned up. He has fresh clothes. He has luggage! He has a new identity, new papers, a new career. He has a *future*. He even has a little money. Enough to hire him this spindly, ancient, yet astonishingly sturdy oriental taximan to ferry him and his cases to the Project shuttle station.

He's looking down on the crowds swarming Easy Street as the taximan hurtles through, yelling strange curses and barging aside the drunk, the drugged and the just plain dopey, and he feels above it all. Superior. Even though the frenzy is mounting, is yet to peak, the town is tumbling inexorably towards its grave. Come the morning, it will be dead.

He's bobbling towards the thermal wall at the edge of town, now, and to the gate of the shuttle station just by it. Armed guards in uniform woman the entrance. Eddie wonders why. Most of the pilgrims will be at the Project already. Just a few stragglers left to show up. And Eddie.

Suddenly, he's nervous again. Armed guards. To keep out curious tourists, chancers and . . .

. . . and impostors.

Armed.

The taximan stops abruptly and drops Eddie's cases. But he doesn't set Eddie down. He barks up at Eddie. Some kind of demand, or order.

Eddie says: 'This is it. This'll do nicely,' and tries to dismount, but the taximan grips his legs, both of which are injured anyway, and barks the incomprehensible demand again.

Through gritted teeth, Eddie tries to explain that he's happy with the destination, and he'd really like to get down now, while what's left of his blood is still circulating around what's left of his legs. He tries variations on this theme in a few languages, concluding with an appalling attempt at pidgin English, including the humiliating phrase: 'Leggee hurtee', before he realizes the taximan won't release him until he's paid his fare.

This is wrong. The fare's already been paid by the real C.P. Gordon, who was keen to ensure Eddie's safe arrival at the station. A very generous fare, too, not to say extravagant.

But the taximan knows when he can milk a profit, and he wants another fare.

Not a problem, as soon as Eddie can remember which pocket he put his wallet in. And, indeed, where any pockets might actually *be* in the unfamiliar official garments of Project personnel. He tries to ignore the pain in his legs and pats his jacket, grinning in the direction of the guards, who look on dispassionately.

Finally, he tracks down what feels like it might be a wallet in a pocket halfway down his right thigh. With difficulty – the trouser material is being pulled taut, he has minimal feedback from his increasingly numb leg, and the taximan is not disposed towards being in any way helpful – he drags out the wallet between his thumb and forefinger and flips it open.

His heart performs a small somersault when he sees the false name below his ID photograph, but he collects himself, extracts a hundred bill and hands it down to the taximan.

The taximan scrutinizes the note, without in any way relaxing his grip on Eddie's legs, and tucks it into some inscrutable fold in his curious, baggy trousers. Eddie leans forward to facilitate his dismount, but it's not going to happen just yet. The taximan holds up his hand again.

'Keep the change,' Eddie says, and adds foolishly: 'Keepee changee.' But the taximan's hand stays where it is. Eddie looks hard, but the hand is empty. He wants more? This was a five-minute trip. If Eddie had a stone, he could turn and hit the pick-up point from here, even with his pathetic, girly throwing technique. But the taximan wants more. He knows a sucker when he's got one on his back.

Eddie fishes out another note. He only has hundred bills. He tries to tell himself this money will be useless when he reaches the Project, but it's hard. Eddie's an accountant, and it's hard. 'You are, in fact, mugging me, you realize?' Eddie thrusts the bill into the waiting hand. 'In full view of armed law-enforcement personnel.' He glares over at the disinterested guardswomen. 'Do you truly expect to get away with this?'

But, of course, the taximan truly does get away with it. He gets away with the first two hundred, and with three hundred more. When he's finally convinced Eddie's wallet is truly empty, he sets Eddie down.

'Thanks a lot.' Eddie rubs his knees to try and coax a little blood through the bruised canals of his veins. 'Nice trip. As soon as I get my next million, we can go all the way round the block.'

The taximan leers a single-toothed grin, waves Eddie's wad in the air and says what could be either: 'Hard knife dagger' or 'Have a nice day' – either of which, in Eddie's book, constitutes an unnecessary taunt – and hares off at Olympian speed back towards town.

Eddie's dilemma now is when to start walking the few short steps towards the security gate. Does he move straight away, and risk looking like a man rising from a wheelchair at Lourdes? Or does he wait ten minutes or so, by which time he might be just capable of mimicking the walk of a brain-eating zombie?

The decision is made for him. To his right, he hears a yell, a pleading yell, and a scuffle. The guards barely flick their eyes in the direction of the altercation. But Eddie knows what it is.

It's a kerfuffle.

Two men, wearing neat pork-pie hats, are swinging a third man between them.

The third man is struggling, and the other two are sporting bright pink socks.

The pink-socked duo are trying to work up sufficient momentum to hurl their appointment over the laser safety cut-outs and into the lethal thermal wall.

Eddie starts to move towards the station entrance, hoping to get there and get through before the horror is played out. But his oxygen-starved legs can hardly hold him up, let alone carry him along with any kind of speed, and he's still several tottering steps away from the guards before the scream and the flash occur.

Eddie doesn't look back, but the image conjures itself up in his brain anyway, thank you very much, and files itself where it simply isn't wanted.

Eddie staggers up to the security gate and flashes his ID, hoping this will be enough to get him through. It isn't. One of the guards holds her hand out, and Eddie's forced to pass it over.

He tries to look vaguely in the direction of the guards, without appearing to be either averting his gaze or staring them out. He's also trying not to look as if he's mentally undressing them, or conjuring up lurid sexual imaginings involving the electric cattle-prods dangling from their belts, but he's not sure how long he can keep it up.

What's the delay here? The guard seems to be comparing Eddie's face with the photo on the ID. This shouldn't be a major problem. After all, it's a photo of Eddie, taken only minutes ago. Eddie attempts to strike the facial pose on the photograph exactly. Unfortunately, it's a bizarre, unnatural kind of half smile, and Eddie can't maintain it for too long without feeling he looks like an axe murderer. His nerve fails and he looks down at an imaginary bug he hasn't heard wriggling on the ground.

This is taking too long. This should have been a quick check, possibly a double take, and a wave through.

Eddie toys with the idea of feigning indignation. After all, he's a Pilgrim. Pilgrims are notoriously arrogant. He thinks he might try: 'Is this going to take much longer? Only some of us have an interstellar spaceship to catch.' But he knows he won't. Not Eddie.

The guard looks up and says: 'Mr Gordon. Glad you could make it. They were just about to push the button on you.'

Eddie fakes a smile. What's that? Push the button? What could that mean?

The guard reaches out for Eddie's left hand before Eddie can react. 'If you don't mind, sir. We just need to check your DNA signature.'

'My . . . ?'

'It's just a formality.'

Before Eddie can protest, he feels a prickling sensation in his arm and hears the hiss of his blood being withdrawn.

The guard holds the vial up to the light. Enough to fill a fountain pen. Eddie's surprised he's got that much blood left in his system.

'Is this absolutely necessary?' Eddie's tone is depressingly short of arrogant.

'Just a formality,' the guard repeats, and inserts the vial into her desktop console.

Eddie's in a real bind now. Running, of course, is out of the question. He could try to waddle away, but what would be the point? The worst thing that could happen to him, here, is to get turned away. To be released to the less than tender mercies of the pink sock brigade. But the jig is surely up. Even if he were good at bluffing, which he is not, Eddie couldn't bluff his way through a DNA mismatch.

The computer emits a series of unpromising sounds. The guard turns from the screen and looks at Eddie. She is most definitely pissed off.

'Well, you could have saved us a little time, here, couldn't you?'

'In what way?' Better. Much closer to arrogant.

'In the way that you might have mentioned this is the first time you've reported to the Project. That your DNA wasn't on record.'

'Well,' Eddie smiles, 'it is now.'

The guard grunts, hands the wallet back, and nods tinily towards the embarkation point. Relief flushes through Eddie's extremely overtaxed nervous system, as he hauls his poor body towards the boarding gate. It is with some satisfaction that he overhears, as he is meant to overhear, the guard muttering, slightly too loud: 'Arrogant bastard.'

There are only a couple of other passengers on the shuttle, and neither of them pays much attention to Eddie. One of them is an extremely good-looking woman. She offers him a brief smile. Far too charming a smile to interest Eddie. She is definitely not his type.

Eddie's type, for the record, Eddie's kind of gal, is the type that Eddie will fail to attract. Usually some breed of male hater, who wouldn't be attracted to *any* man, let alone such a pitiful example of manhood as Eddie O'Hare. They're not even lesbians, as a rule, though Eddie's wasted a substantial amount of his unrequited allure, not to mention his insubstantial salary, on them. They're not even, necessarily, unattractive, though looks are not of major importance to Eddie's libido. They just have to be aloof and unattainable to get Eddie's juices flowing.

Why?

Who knows?

Perhaps he *wants* to fail with women. Perhaps there's some awful part of his DNA that knows it shouldn't try reproducing itself. Perhaps it's a natural selection thing – Eddie's so wishy-washy and nice, he needs to mate with pure horror to balance things out.

Whatever the reason, the results speak for themselves. On the extremely rare occasions he's managed to persuade or trick one of the objects of affection actually out on a date, the evening has never lasted through an entire movie, got past the first interval at a play, or gone as far as the pudding course in a restaurant.

She's busy working, this woman that Eddie wouldn't date because she might possibly still be hanging in there while he's arguing over the bill. The other occupant of the cabin, an earnest, honest-looking man in a dog collar, is also working.

Eddie should be working, too. He should be ploughing through C.P. Gordon's files. He should, for instance, in a perfect world know who he actually *is*. He should probably also know what he does. He should know who his colleagues are, who he reports to, who reports to him. It would be nice to have the odd autobiographical fact to hand, too. Like his mother's name. His nationality. His sexual orientation. All those little details that could trip him up. It might even be handy to find out what the consequences would be if he *does* get tripped up. Will they give him a sharp slap on the wrist and withdraw a few privileges, or will they stuff him into a garbage canister and shoot him out into space through the waste disposal?

But as the shuttle lifts off, Eddie can only look out through the window and wonder how to feel as Afortunado shrinks away, as he leaves his life behind. As he leaves the planet Earth behind.

And when the last light from the tallest tower is definitely no longer visible, and hasn't truly been visible for a good ten minutes, Eddie finally grabs hold of the file, spreads the papers over his seat table and sighs like a bouncy castle going down. Gordon has agreed to pay off his debt, and send a million to Eddie's mother's bank account. No loose ends. Everybody happy.

There is another sigh, almost simultaneous, and almost as contented, on the ground.

Gordon has watched Eddie board and take off. He watches the shuttle through the heat haze of the thermal dome until it can no longer be distinguished from the ice-capped peak of the mountain that is its destination. He smiles, very broadly. He has no intention, naturally, of paying off Eddie's debt, or sponsoring Eddie's mother, touching and cute as the dismal thought might be.

No.

He has good use for his money.

He can use it to sow the seeds of the perfect society he's dreamed of. And he'll see the results now, in his own lifetime, not just imagine them, generations hence.

In a little under four hours, the *Willflower* will have launched. In a little under four and a half hours, Gordon, looking suitably beaten up and bedraggled, will file a report to the effect that a man answering Eddie O'Hare's description jumped him, drugged him and stole his identity papers. O'Hare will be arrested and . . . dealt with. It will, of course, be too late for Gordon to join the mission.

No loose ends.

Everybody happy.

PART TWO

Generation I

'There's no discouragement
Shall make him once relent
His first, avowed intent
To Be A Pilgrim.'

(John Bunyan: *The Pilgrim's Progress*)

10

Eddie stays on the shuttle for as long as he can, desperately cramming up on Gordon's notes. Initial impressions are not good. Community Planning, it transpires, is one of those strange social sciences you have to study for decades before you can understand what it actually is, and even then can't define it. He finally acquiesces to leave the cabin just before the irate steward starts getting physical with the portion-control bags of macadamia nuts.

He bundles out of the craft, still trying to stuff the papers back in the file, so he almost collides with a very serious-looking group of individuals, standing at the entrance to a huge cylindrical tower. One of them, a silver-tinged black-bearded man of indeterminable age – he could be a very well-preserved sixty with distinguished colouring, or a gone-to-seed forty with inadequate access to hair dye – holds out his hand and says: 'Mr Gordon, I presume?' Which is deemed sufficiently close to a joke to exhort a mild snicker from two or three members of the party.

Eddie doesn't hesitate, doesn't look around for this Mr Gordon who's being talked to: he acts the part, he pulls it off. He immediately shoots out his bandaged hand in response, and prays for two things: he prays he doesn't have to return some kind of secret handshake, and he prays that this group isn't in any way representative of the average sense of humour level on board.

Only the first of those prayers is answered.

'Community Director Gwent,' the bearded man offers, clasping Eddie's injured hand with unsuppressed gusto, despite the bandage. Great. This bundle of fun looks like he's Eddie's superior. But it gets worse. The buffoon mocks a *commedia dell'arte* level 'Whoops!' and strikes his brow with the flat of his hand. 'I mean *Captain* Gwent!' This draws a major laugh from all the lackeys, and a deep, heartfelt guffaw from Gwent. Eddie snickers along and tries not to look bewildered. 'Don't worry,' the Captain slaps him far too heartily on his shoulders, 'I won't be holding it against you, Charles.'

Holding what against him? 'I hope not,' Eddie tries, and then attempts an amused: '*Cap*tain,' which all but brings the house down. This is the biggest laugh Eddie's ever got in collected company, and he's no idea what it is that's supposed to be so funny.

The Captain thumps Eddie between the shoulder blades with the same force a normal man might use to attempt the Heimlich manoeuvre on a choking gorilla, drapes a matey arm around his shoulders and steers him towards the cylinder's entrance. Eddie knows what this is: it's the famous Stairway to Heaven, officially designated as one of the seven wonders of the modern world. It looks less impressive from this angle than the computer simulations he's seen, but the cloud cover is very low, and only a small portion of the tower is visible.

Gwent makes some remark in what sounds like Latin, but could be classical Greek, or even, for all Eddie knows, Etruscan. Whatever the language, it is clearly understood by everyone else in the party, since it's greeted by a great woof of delighted laughter. Eddie tries a little chuckle, as if to imply he obviously gets the joke, but he doesn't think it's all that funny. This seems to meet with Gwent's approval. 'They told me you were *finally* on your way, Charles, so I made a special journey down to greet you.'

Eddie's meant to be flattered. He acknowledges as much with a slight inclination of his head. He wishes he'd corrected the Captain the first time his name had been used. He'd much prefer to be known as CP. He doesn't feel like a Charles at all. He doesn't really feel like a CP, come to that, but CP would be better than Charles. CP is more of an action guy, the kind of guy you'd like to hang out with in a bar, or have as a racquet ball partner. Charles is too goody-goody. He still calls himself what his mother calls him. Still, too late now. The moment's gone. Charles it is. Ah, well.

Eddie's been too fixed on this, perhaps trivial, thought train.

Understandable enough, though. This is a new beginning for him; a chance to shake off the useless clutter of his wasted past. This is important, in its way.

But now, the assembled group is staring at him, and the Captain has withdrawn his arm. Clearly, he's been asked a question, and he's failed to respond for a rude amount of time. He tries a stab at a humorous recovery. 'I'm sorry? Could you repeat that . . . *Cap*tain?'

This time, he meets only a blank silence. What's wrong? It's the same useless joke. Why isn't it funny any more?

A thin woman, attractive, even though her features are a little pinched and her dark hair is dragged back in a severe bun which fails to be unfeminine, steps in: 'Are you, perhaps, buying time, Mr Gordon? Or is it that a true and honest answer might damn you, *and* your profession?' She parts her lips, which are painted a Gothic dark purple, in a predatory smile.

Eddie's not going to get any help from these quarters. He's in strange company here, where daydreaming isn't part of the mental make-up. And further dithering is definitely out of the question. He elects to go bold. 'Absolutely not. I would say . . . on the whole . . . my response would be . . . positive.'

There is a small but deep silence. It's broken by the Captain's guffaw, and another ill-judged blow between Eddie's shoulder blades which Eddie feels sure has fractured several vertebrae. He is led onward, towards the great tower. The Captain leans closer to him, pointlessly, since his voice is only capable of one volume, which is just below the level of an elephant's death bellow. 'You'll have to forgive Section Leader Peck,' he trumpets. 'She's a hard, hard scientist. It's a religion with her. Anything less than pure mathematics belongs in the waste compactor just above psychology.' He spits 'psychology' in the austerely fetching Ms Peck's direction. A private 'joke'. Eddie's not sure how many more of these jokes he'll have to take. Unfortunately, his mind can work it out. At the rate of one per minute, which seems to be the average here, with eight hours a night off for blessed sleep, he can expect to face around another forty-one million, if his projected life expectancy pans out. He can only pray it doesn't.

'No, no,' the Captain broadcasts on. 'Most of us think Afortunado is an astonishing achievement. No *sane* scientist' another joke? 'could expect a hundred per cent successful implementation of such a sophisticated social model. Unless of course chaos theory has suddenly joined the social sciences!' Everyone snorts at this one, except Eddie and Ms Peck, at whom it's directed. Just a little tickler of a gag. Still, nauseating none the less.

They're inside the tower, now, and stepping into what must be the elevation tube itself. It's . . . well, it's large. You could have hidden the Pacific Fleet from the Japanese bombers in this space. The source of the Nile could be lurking in one of the corners, and you'd never find it. It's a big, big space. Eddie dreads what the acoustics might do for the Captain's voice.

He is not disillusioned.

'Your first trip, Mr Gordon,' the Captain rock concerts, 'and my last. Alpha and omega. Come.' As the double doors slide closed and the airlock whispers, the Captain strides over to the opposite wall. The rest of the party follow in various degrees of punctual respect. 'This is the view.'

Eddie looks out at the view, which is bewilderingly monochrome and featureless. He shoots a quick glance at the Captain, whose sanity already has a big question mark over it, then realizes they are still at underground level. The view, as yet, is merely of rocks of ice.

There is a grinding sound which is, for Eddie, far too reminiscent of a rust-ridden fairground ride, and the room lurches. The ice falls away, and the spectacular view is now the monochrome blue-black of a polar night sky. Eddie peers fruitlessly into the gloom, but gloom is all there is, all around them.

Then the window is filled with white again, as the hoist achieves cloud height. Eddie would like to utter some kind of awe-filled mumble to justify the Captain's pronouncement but, as yet, he hasn't been able to make out a single feature of the panorama.

'Any moment now.' The Captain holds up a finger and listens. Fans kick in. 'Yes. Fifteen thousand feet. Oxygen required.'

And upwards, through layer after layer of fluffy cloud. Eddie is beginning to feel embarrassed for the Captain. Some view. A small child could reproduce the spectacle by holding a glass tumbler to his eye and wiggling a wad of cotton wool over the end of it.

And then the cloud falls away.

A cannon goes off in Eddie's ear. Gwent. 'The edge of the troposphere. There is no weather above this point. No more weather for us, Charles. We have cursed our last rain shower, constructed our last snow person, squealed through our last sea squall. Humbling, no?'

Humbling? No. But now, suddenly, there *is* a view. The cloud blanket drops beneath them and curls away towards a lowering horizon, with an astonishingly clear, bright view of the stars and space beyond, unhindered by atmosphere. The clouds start to break up and curl into wisps and smoky strands over the ball of the strangely fragile Earth beneath them.

This is humbling. Even Eddie, who is, let's get real, not exactly unhumble anyway, is further humbled by this view. Imagine how humbled the arrogant bastards around him must feel.

So he isn't the only one who fails to see the Captain draw a gun.

He is, however, the first to leap back at the sound of the weapon cocking, and he cowers the lowest when the Captain yells, quietly on his scale, 'Now, stand back, one and all.'

And that's all the warning anyone gets as the barrel of the gun booms and jerks and the transparent wall through which they had all just been admiring the view smashes spectacularly, to be replaced by what Eddie can only think of as a 'big hole'.

And out of this 'big hole' charges the air that Eddie had planned to be breathing for the next few minutes of the trip.

Eddie's lungs are being dragged inside out. His eyes are bulging like a dodgem fare collector's jeans. His tongue feels like it's unravelling. He looks back towards the Captain, whose greasy silver black hair is whipping forwards all over his grinning face.

The Captain raises his voice over the roar of the escaping air. 'Charles,' he screeches. 'Would you like to talk us through this next bit?'

Eddie thinks, on the whole, that it's probably best it all ends here, messily, insanely and inexplicably, before they reach the ship. God alone knows what madness is waiting for him up there.

With a great effort, he lurches his neck around, in the vague hope that one of these butt-licking idiots might have some kind of contingency plan for the emergency strangulation of the senior officer in the event of blatantly demonstrable frontal lobe failure. But no. All eyes are on him. They're waiting for him to answer the Captain's question, as if they're in some kind of tutorial group in the cosy comfort of a lecturer's sitting room, rather than standing in a glass canister with a big hole in it, far above the Earth's atmosphere, within scant seconds of having all their heads explode like rotten fruit in a shooting gallery. He swings his head back to face the Captain.

'We-ell,' Eddie yells, 'I would have to highly recommend hurling you through the hole in the direction of the troposphere, Captain.'

The Captain raises his chin and begins to judder. Eddie worries that he's suffering a terminal and messy aneurysm. But no. He's laughing. This is great. Eddie could get the job of ship's jester without even practising.

The Captain guffaws: 'A sane response.' Right. Like he would know. 'But wrong. No. We simply wait and watch.'

Eddie forces his face towards the rupture. Bizarrely, it's beginning to shrink in size.

Perhaps his vision is being distorted by the tears in his eyes, partly caused by the savage rush of air, mostly by hysterical fear. He blinks. No, the hole is definitely getting smaller. And as the fissure diminishes to non-life-threatening dimensions, the sound of escaping oxygen decreases, and Eddie can hear the material in the wall knitting itself back together, and by the time the hole has dwindled to basketball size, he can actually see the discrete sections of the fabric melding with each other energetically.

In less than ninety seconds after the gunshot, the rupture has repaired itself, and no evidence of any damage remains.

Eddie is still curled over, like a Lowry hunchback, with one hand on the floor. The other occupants of the hoist are calmly smoothing back their hair and unruffling their clothes.

'Spectacular demonstration, eh, Charles?' The Captain drags an expensive comb through his steely locks, and briskly fluffs up his beard.

Eddie can manage no response beyond a passable impression of a freshly landed gagging halibut.

The Captain slips his comb into a top pocket. 'The material from which this beauty is constructed is organic.'

Eddie tries not to plan murder.

'SR²OM. It's organic, yet it's synthesized. A synthetic living fabric. Airtight, stronger than steel and self-repairing, which is the part you're probably grateful for.' The Captain nods a chuckly kind of nod, and Eddie's murder plans can no longer be resisted. 'The ship is constructed from the same material.'

There is a jolt, and everyone staggers as the upward motion ceases. Then a series of clicks and whirrs as machinery negotiates with machinery. The hoist has reached its destination. They are docking.

They are aboard the *Willflower*.

Eddie feels a small pang of disappointment. 'We don't get to see the ship? From the outside?'

Section Leader Peck looks at him with something approaching repugnance from the wrong direction. 'What for? It's a ship. It's a big ship. It's dark. It's a big dark ship.' Eddie suddenly feels like he's in nursery school again. 'There's nothing *to* see.'

'It's where I'll be spending the rest of my life. I'd have liked to see it, that's all.'

Peck shakes her head and turns away, like he's a battlefield casualty with a stupidly inoperable number of bullets in his brain, and she has more promising wounded to attend to. She's a brutal, intolerant, unromantic woman, and probably casually cruel to boot. Eddie is starting to feel incredibly horny.

The hoist is plunged into temporary darkness. Eddie tries to use its cover to shuffle over towards Section Leader Peck and stand very close to her. Not to touch her or fondle her or anything crude like that. Just to stand close. Perhaps even close enough to breathe in her perfume. But the darkness is too complete, and he can't be sure whose body he's pointing his nostrils at. He breathes in hopefully, anyway. He's at the wrong party. The person he's sniffing smells very strongly of carbolic soap.

Then a bright green light burrs across the floor and starts passing over them like a giant luminous hula hoop. As it reaches their faces, Eddie is astonished to find he is indeed standing close to Peck. For reasons probably best left unconsidered, his heart balloons at the thought that this woman scrubs herself with carbolic soap. In the passing green glow, she looks at him with a perfect combination of confusion and disgust, and by the time the light has hit the ceiling and expired, Eddie is in love.

In the small ensuing darkness he senses her moving away, but he doesn't try to follow. Instead, he directs a wonderful, short, erotic mind-movie of Officer Peck curled over in a small tin bath, scrubbing away at some stain, perhaps some imaginary sinful stain that can never be removed, with a bar of the stern-scented soap that will never lather, no matter how brutally she rubs. No pornographically graphic body parts, not so much as the suggestive swell of a breast. Just the relentless scrubbing of the wet bare flesh, and a rogue strand of hair dangling from the otherwise ruthless bob. The soundtrack: utter silence, punctuated only by a handful of resilient, breathy, slightly desperate grunts. It goes straight to number one in Eddie's mental movie chart.

He's still replaying it when the lights flicker back on. He blinks and looks around for the real, flesh-and-blood Peck. She's a long, long way from him. She must have been sprinting in the dark to have made it that far away in that space of time. Eddie's getting more aroused by the minute. He barely notices the hoist doors haul themselves apart.

It is, perhaps, a sad indictment of the male mind that Eddie should be thus distracted at what is undeniably a momentous event in his life. This is his first sight of the ship on which he will spend the rest of his existence, on which he will eventually die. But he has to drag his attention round and slap its face like a Gestapo interrogator before he can take it in.

He feels only a mild sense of disappointment.

It's a corridor on a spaceship.

It's larger than he expected but, apart from that, unremarkable. There are people using the corridor, who look quite a lot like the rest of the people in the hoist. He feels as if he's just arrived at a happily anticipated holiday destination, only to realize as soon as he steps off the plane he's going to hate it in about three days.

The Captain sweeps him into the corridor. 'Naturally, Charles, you'll be wanting to see how your models have been practicablized.'

Practicablized?

'Why don't you slope off to your quarters, shine up your bits and have a wander. We'll meet up for a bite of supper in, say, an hour or so? You'll have a million questions for me doubtless. I certainly have several millions for you.'

Eddie grins and tries to say 'Great!' and think 'Bugger' and manages not to get them the wrong way round. Millions of questions. Not just one or two. Way beyond the bluff zone. Eddie has some serious cramming to do if he wants to avoid being shot out into deep space in a garbage canister.

Gwent strides off, leaving Eddie lost and a little confused. Presumably, he's meant to know the way to his rooms. After all, he is supposed to be responsible for planning the layout here.

Thankfully, the Captain stops, wheels round and bellows back at him: 'Oh! Room's been re-allocated, Charles. Haven't been fiddling with your blueprints, but something came up. Somebody can show you up.' He looks around and spots Peck walking away as fast as she can without breaking into a trot. 'Jezebel!' She stops instantly, like a bolas has been hurled around her legs. 'You can do the honours.'

She hangs her head slightly and barks, 'Fine.' Without looking back, she says, 'This way, Gordon' – Savage. Not even *Mr* Gordon – and hurtles off.

Jezebel, eh? Cruel. Eddie likes that.

It takes him three twists of the corridor to catch her up, even though he's calling 'Whoa' and 'Slow down' most of the time. His legs have still not recovered from the taximan's tender attentions, not to mention the brutal kick on the shin and the possible insect sting or potential reptile bite. He's breathless and in quite a bit of pain by the time he intercepts Peck at the doors of an internal transway stop.

She's looking up at the transway's readout, trying to will it down faster.

Eddie's still summoning up the courage to attempt a conciliatory advance, an I-can't-help-feeling-we-got-off-on-the-wrong-foot kind of approach, but Peck kills it stone dead. 'I can't help feeling we got off on exactly the right foot, Gordon. You've made it perfectly clear what kind of man you are, and precisely how far you're prepared to go to ingratiate yourself with the community leader. You are slime, you are filth, you are insectoidal excrement, and I want as little to do with you as humanly possible. Now and for the rest of the mission.'

The rest of the mission? Isn't the mission supposed to last for the rest of their lives, and beyond?

Now, what is this all about? Eddie got lost halfway through her diatribe, there. He started out thinking she was ticking him off for standing too close to her in the hoist. Which would have been understandable. Although it was a small and relatively inoffensive thing to do, he feels guilty about it anyway – probably because of those insanely lurid erotic bath imaginings. But then she seemed to veer off on some bizarre tack about him sucking up to the Captain.

'Whoa, slow down.' Is Eddie going to spend the rest of his life repeating that phrase? 'If this is about what happened in the hoist . . .'

'What? What happened in the hoist?'

'Nothing. Nothing happened in the hoist. That's exactly what I'm saying.'

There is an excruciating silence. She's looking at him now. A narrow-eyed snake stare. 'I've met your kind before. You try and conceal your scheming with this clumsy patina of social stupidity and buffoonery. Well, you're not fooling me. And, believe me, you will not dupe Captain Gwent for long, either.'

Eddie shakes his head. This isn't a clumsy patina of social stupidity and buffoonery: this is really Eddie. 'I honestly don't understand what I've done to distress you, Jezebel.' As soon as her name escapes from his lips, he knows he was wrong to invoke it. Her eyes get narrower and she leans in closer. Eddie tries not to smell the carbolic, but he can't help himself.

'Really? Then you've forgotten that little stunt you pulled at the shuttle station? Well I haven't. You chose the wrong person as your whipping boy. I don't like being the source of amusement. And you can be sure my response will be . . . positive.'

She raises her upper right lip in a feline sneer smile and wheels round into the waiting transway carriage.

The shuttle station? It must have been something Eddie said when he answered that question he hadn't heard. Incredible. He's managed to offend this paragon of desirability beyond the possibility of redemption without even trying. How's that for bad luck?

He steps into the carriage, just escaping the doors as they slice shut in response to Peck's prodding. Eddie can't think of anything to say that might dispel this bizarre misunderstanding, so the journey is elongated by the uncomfortable silence. He actually feels as if the ambient temperature has dropped by a measurable ten degrees Celsius by the time his floor arrives. He's on the verge of shivering.

She's out in the corridor and round the first bend before Eddie can gather his wits and follow. He catches a glimpse of her at the end of the next section of corridor. Her legs are long and lithe, they carry her along swiftly without her ever seeming to hurry. Eddie can't help thinking they must take a lot of scrubbing, those legs.

You'd better stop this, Eddie. You're booking yourself a lifetime season ticket to frustration stadium.

He rounds the next bend to find she's stopped. She's standing halfway along the corridor, arms folded, foot tapping, apparently interested only in the number above a door. Eddie's quarters, he guesses correctly.

She doesn't look down at him, just nods at the door. 'This is your *pen*, Gordon.' And that sneer again.

Eddie tries levity, even though he knows it won't work. It's the only tool at his disposal. 'Great. Now you'll know where to come when you're overwhelmed by passion.'

This woman is capable of the most astonishingly accomplished smiles. She shoots him one of her best. Eddie can almost hear his testicles crack off his body, roll down his trouser legs and clunk to the floor. Without closing her incredibly non-kissable purple lips, she spins on her heels and is history.

Eddie places his palm on his door sensor. The door sighs like a lovesick twelve-year-old, and Eddie steps into his new world.

II

His quarters are fine. Luxurious, even. Far better than you could reasonably expect. But, realistically, there isn't a room in the universe you can walk into and feel you'll be happy there for the rest of your life. The furnishings are tasteful, but it's Gordon's taste. There's a South American flavour. Too many primary colours screaming out for Eddie's liking. Red and yellow scatter cushions on an otherwise comfy-looking sofa. A rug that looks as if it might be nice to make love on, in the unlikely event, only it's yellow and bright blue, and thrusting up and down, towards and away from it at pace would be likely to induce some kind of vertiginous nausea. And here, on the mantelpiece over a fake ionic fire, two crouched skeletons with grinning skulls, from the Mexican Day of the Dead festival. Marvellous.

Eddie deflates himself into an armchair, which surprises him by moulding its seat to the precise contours of his ass. Some semi-organic achievement in soft furnishings, probably. Disturbing, definitely.

He'd like to sleep for about a century. He'd also like to shower for a day and a half and scrape away all the caked-on bloodstains the slapdash wash at the infirmary didn't get close to removing. He'd like a month in a bubble bath, too, so he could soak away the sticky stench-of-fear sweat that's built up all over his body over the course of the past few hours. But he can't afford these luxuries just yet. There's a lot of work to be done if he's going to stand even a remote chance of passing himself off as Charles Perry Gordon in the face of the Captain's upcoming question and answer session.

He selects a wad of papers at random from Gordon's file. He thinks about removing his boots, which are Project issue, Gordon size. Which is to say a size and a half too small for Eddie. He'll have to order new ones, as soon as he feels that won't arouse suspicion. Lord knows when that might be. Over what time period is it acceptable for a grown man's feet to swell, suddenly, by two full sizes? And simultaneously gain an inch around the neck, shirt collar wise? And two and a half inches around the waist, all at the same time? How soon will he be able to acquire wearable clothing without giving the game away? On the other hand, how long can he get away with wearing these trousers without the crotch exploding, or the butt seam bursting?

He elects not to remove the boots until he finally gets to bed. There's a good chance he won't be able to get them on again. Plus, there is the additional threat that his stockinged feet, in their current condition, might well set off the smoke alarm.

He focuses on the first page. It's some kind of paper, penned by the real Charles Gordon. Its title almost sends Eddie into an instant stupor: 'Ethical, Moral and Psychological Considerations of the Successful Implementation of Adequate Gene Strand Distribution in Closed Systems over Multiple Generations'.

Wow. Catchy. Could be a best seller.

A wave of nausea washes over him. On this ship, that may well be true. It would probably fly off the shelves. And he's trapped here, for ever, in the company of Intellectuals, with a capital 'I'. By which he means brainy people who think being brainy is the most wonderful thing anyone could possibly be. Who flash their intellects like body-builders flash their muscles. Who kick intellectual sand in the faces of puny mental six-stone weaklings like Eddie. Who imagine they have a superior, highly developed sense of humour, even though almost all their jokes involve word play and have exclamation marks on the end of them.

Eddie feels his will to live draining down his legs and bubbling away out of the top of his boots. He sighs like a dirigible that's been punctured by a howitzer shell and leans back in the chair. This is a mistake. The chair back moulds itself around his shoulders and starts thrumming a gentle massage that melts his aching muscles. His eyes begin to close. The sound of water lapping at a lake shore . . .

Eddie snaps bolt upright. He can't afford to rest. Not quite yet. He has a great deal of cramming to do. He focuses again on the document. '. . . Considerations of the Successful Implement . . .'

But his attention has already wandered. Come on, Eddie. You're used to working through dull documents. You're an accountant, for crying out loud. You can at least assimilate the damned *title* of this thing.

'. . . essful Implementation of Adequate Gene Strand Distribut . . .'

A buzzer sounds, and the Captain's face appears in what Eddie had assumed to be a genuine fish tank.

'DFI on the Q and A session, Charles.' Gwent's voice distorts either his own microphone or Eddie's speaker. Eddie has no idea what the acronym 'DFI' means, but it sounds urgent. 'Something's come up. Be in Planning Committee Room One, in five.' And his image splinters into a dozen koi carp before the howlaround has finished echoing.

No! Eddie raises his hand to his lip. Warm, dried sputum. He's been sleeping. He looks down at Gordon's crumpled treatise on the floor.

He's out of the door and round three twists of corridor, desperately scanning Gordon's notes without focusing on them in the stupid hope that clusters of vital facts just might register with his subconscious mind, before he realizes he doesn't have a clue where Planning Committee Room One is.

He stops and looks around, as if there might be a sign on one of the walls, or maybe even a 'You Are Here' machine with buttons and lights. No such luck. Suddenly inspired, he shuffles through Gordon's file, and digs out a plan of the ship. But it's a big ship, and the plan is small, with tiny print. Worse still, it's been folded by a consortium of world-class origami experts. Still he scrabbles through it, unfolding, re-folding, flapping, shaking and swearing and finally tracks down an index. His relief is only momentary. The index is non-alphabetical. There is an eighteen-paragraph tutorial at the top of it, headed 'How to Use this Index'. Eddie scans the first few lines.

Apparently, the index is organized along the Chinese model of categorization. Eddie reorganizes it along the frustration model of torn to shreds.

He employs his last resort. He asks someone for directions. The human race is divided into two kinds of people: those who think nothing of asking others for directions, and those who would rather remain hopelessly lost for all eternity and starve to death, albeit only millimetres away from their intended destination, than stop another human being and enquire of the way. Eddie conquers his fear. He asks. He ignores the expression that seems to suggest he's enquired for the route to his own head. He commits the first paragraph of the ludicrously complicated itinerary to memory, offers ridiculously copious gratitude and scoots off, becoming hopelessly lost within moments.

By the time Eddie finally achieves his destination, he's past caring. He feels quite prepared to be shot out into deep space in a garbage canister. He's looking forward to it.

Planning Committee Room One is astonishingly opulent for a spaceship meeting room. This is clearly where the major decisions are discussed and taken. About twenty people, maybe two dozen, are seated around a polished wood table in leather-backed chairs. They all break off from their individual pockets of discussion and register Eddie's entrance, as if he weren't intimidated enough.

Gwent, at the head of the table, bellows: 'Mr Gordon. So pleased you could join us!' with exclamation-mark sarcasm, and indicates a vacant seat very close to him. Eddie tries not to feel his cheeks burning. This is very bad. Gordon dramatically undersold his role on this mission. It is becoming horribly plain that these people are, effectively, the government of this ship. And Eddie appears to be a significant member of the Cabinet.

He sits in the proffered seat, immediately bends over his yellow legal pad and starts making inscrutable notes with the fresh pencil provided, in a creditable attempt to render himself invisible.

Gwent destroys his effort by blasting out: 'Now we are finally a quorum . . .' and, pausing to single Eddie out with an accusatory stare, '. . . we can get down to the business at hand. And a fairly filthy business it is. People,' he leans forward, 'it seems we have an impostor in our midst.'

12

Almost four a.m. Afortunado is insane, now. Frenzied. Its moribund madness is peaking.

Even here, in the dark pit of the unlit bar, where the atmosphere is normally amply intimidating to put off all but the most desperate seekers of anonymity, solitude is becoming an acutely rare commodity.

Some unseeable revellers burst through the door, carrying their high spirits with them, undaunted by the threatening ambience. They crowd noisily on to Gordon's table, barking out drink orders, and he decides to leave. He'll be a few minutes early for his rather unpleasant appointment, and he'd have preferred to arrive bang on the hour, to reduce unnecessary apprehension time, but he can no longer stay here: the frolickers have it in mind to enlist his enthusiasm. He downs his thick, sweet liquor and gags – it's his first drink of the night. He's been clear-headed, very clear-headed, so far, but he needs his senses dulled somewhat to face this last ordeal.

He stands, squeezes past his uninvited table mates and steps out into the street.

The madness here is full throttle, desperate. Shouting, songs and screams spiral into the lunatic air.

This is good. He's unlikely to be spotted in a crowd this dense, this crazy. Still, he keeps to the shadows in any case. No point in risking unnecessary compromise now.

He reaches the corner of the alleyway that's been designated for the rendezvous. It backs on to a half-dozen of the least scrupulous of Afortunado's unanimously scruple-free eating establishments, and the stench of the rotting produce discounted as edible even for these low-standard haunts is, reportedly, usually sufficient to keep it deserted. He glances into its rancid dimness. He makes out a strange shape halfway down, jiggling madly. His eyes adjust. A prostitute is entertaining a client. Presumably a client with no nose.

Gordon glances at his watch. He's seven minutes early. Surely this tawdry little jiggling enterprise will have reached its sordid conclusion long before the designated time of his forthcoming assignation.

Sure enough, a short series of bestial grunts announces the successful conclusion of the transaction, and within seconds the client leaves the alleyway at pace, one hand clutching a handkerchief over his nose, the other tucking away his deflating jiggler. He is followed in very short order by the object of his recent affections, spraying herself vigorously with a scent which is extremely powerful, but none the less hopelessly inadequate for the achievement of its desired purpose.

Gordon sucks in a large breath and enters the alley.

Perhaps this was a mistake, this location, with its stench of putrefaction and decay and . . . death. Perhaps the whole idea is a mistake. He could back out, if he chose. Just hand over the fee; double the fee, even . . .

He hears footsteps at the top of the alley.

No. That's not the Gordon way. Changing a plan halfway through, that's dangerous. Lethal, even. It's a good plan. Stick to it.

The footsteps click towards him. Steel tips on the shoe. For kicking people more effectively, Gordon supposes. The man is clearly a professional, which is good. He's four minutes early. Super-punctual. Also good.

The main light source for the alley comes from a street light, which is behind the man, so Gordon can't make out his features. Even when he shields his eyes against the stark glare, Gordon can only see a long-haired haloed silhouette, which induces in him an illogical fear.

The man speaks. 'Gordon? Charles Gordon?'

Incompetence! Bad, at this juncture. 'No names.' Gordon shakes his head. 'I was very specific. Very.'

'Apologies.' Politeness. Good. 'It's been a very busy night. Don't want to make any more mistakes.' Any *more* mistakes? Not good. That is definitely indicative of a state of non-goodness.

Gordon takes command. 'All right. Let's steer very clear of any potential "mistakes". We can have this over with very quickly . . .'

'Very quickly would be good.'

Gordon hates interruptions. But on this occasion, he bites his lip. 'Very quickly. It has to look like an amateur beating. One blow to the face, one to the back of the head. A bruise and a lump. Nothing permanent. Minimal pain. I was assured you were that good.'

There is an overlong, distressing pause.

'That's the arrangement. You understand it? You *are* that good?'

The man clears his throat. 'I'm the very best.'

'That's what I was assured of. Where would you like me to stand?'

Gordon hears what sounds awfully like a suppressed laugh. He is beginning to feel slightly spooked. The stench of putrescent fish is beginning to nauseate him.

Then another set of footsteps, with the same metallic click of the toes. From the back of the alley. Gordon turns, alarmed. This second man is in shadows, but there is no light behind him, and so his physical details are more discernible. His hair is long, like the other's, and shiny dark. He is wearing dark glasses, presumably infra-reds. He has an expensive suit on, the effect of which is utterly undermined by his grotesque choice of socks.

Fluorescent pink.

He is also carrying a large bag, which he sets down on the floor. There is some equipment in the bag. Large and metal.

Gordon turns to the first man. 'This was not the arrangement.' There is a stiff chill in his voice. Why would it take two men to simulate a short, fake beating? What's in the bag? Surely that's incidental, superfluous.

Another overlong pause, even more distressing.

The two men are looking at each other, but their expressions are relaxingly non-threatening. They look almost wryly amused.

The first man, Gordon takes him to be the leader, smiles and with acceptably apologetic deference speaks again. 'I hope you don't mind, sir, if my colleague observes the . . . procedure. You'll appreciate this is a skilled business, and people have to be trained.'

That makes sense to Gordon's understanding of management organization. He nods. 'That's understandable.'

'If it's inconvenient . . .'

'No, no. Let him watch.'

'All right.' The man adopts a lecturial tone. He starts slipping a leather glove over his hand. 'We have here a subject who requires a mild beating, sufficient to convince the appropriate authorities that he has been taken by surprise by an amateur ne'er-do-well, and rendered unconscious.'

'Can we dispense with the tutorial?' Gordon glances towards the alleyway entrance. 'I'd rather avoid attracting undue –'

The man ignores him, cuts right across him. 'Gloves are essential for your own protection. You don't want to risk scuffing your knuckles, and leave tell-tale DNA debris on the subject.'

'Can we get on with this?'

'Now, in an amateur attack, you would expect a small number of inefficient attempted blows, producing minor scuffing . . .' He draws back his gloved hand.

'Now, wait just one –'

Slap. Gordon's face is snapped aside, his cheek burning.

'Like that.'

Slap. A tight, open-palmed blow clips his chin, cracking the back of his head against the wall.

'And that. And this.'

Gordon yells 'Stop!' and raises his arm to ward off the incoming blow, but the man's a professional, and he slips through Gordon's guard easily, connecting with his ear.

'That's enough!'

His hired assailant stands back, flexing his wrist.

Gordon assesses the damage. Relatively minor. His cheek is swelling slightly, there is a definite lump on the back of his head, and his ear is thrumming. 'That was unnecessary. I could have done the scuffing myself, afterwards.'

'I'm sorry, sir, but you paid for a professional job. It would be less than efficient of me to leave these details to an untrained client.'

Gordon touches his ear. His fingers come away bloody. 'But it hurt.' He regrets that, as soon as it whines out of his lips. He's a grown man, an acknowledged world expert in his field. He's a multi-millionaire. Three slaps to the face and he's right back in the bullied misery of the school playground.

The man regards him for a few seconds. He seems vaguely affronted. 'Well, sir, if you're aware of a pain-free beating service, I'd advise you to take advantage of their talents.' He nods to the trainee, who picks up the bag and makes as if to leave.

'What? What are you doing?'

'Clearly, you are dissatisfied. I assume you'd prefer to administer the rest of the beating yourself.'

'No, no. I want you to finish it off.' Where would he book another professional beating at such short notice? These people aren't exactly in the Yellow Pages.

'You're sure?'

'Certain. I'm sorry I reacted . . . I was surprised, I suppose.'

'So you're quite happy to have me beat you senseless?'

Gordon's eyes flit from the assailant to the accomplice and back. 'Well, that sounds a little brutal, but, yes. I would like you to render me unconscious. Yes.'

The man looks over at his colleague. A strange smile passes between them. Something in that smile makes Gordon want to run. That's his inner child. He should be listening to that kid, right now. That kid knows trouble when he sees it. But Gordon ignores him. He sticks to his plan.

The man appears to be fiddling with his hand now. Slipping something on to it, possibly. 'If you'd like to stand against the wall, with your chin slightly raised, sir.' There is a disturbing tone in the voice. Hard to place. Not quite serious?

Gordon stands as directed, and braces himself.

'It's best not to brace.'

'Beg pardon?'

'It hurts more if you're anticipating it. If your muscles are stiff.'

This is more like it. This is the kind of professionalism Gordon was hoping for. 'OK.' He shakes his head, tries to loosen up. When he feels as relaxed as he could reasonably hope to feel, he nods and says: 'Ready.'

He closes his eyes. Tries to go to his yoga Happy Place.

Nothing happens.

He opens his eyes. 'There *is* a slight element of time pressure here.'

He sees the fist travelling towards him. Something on it glints in the street light. Looks suspiciously like a knuckle dus . . .

His nose explodes.

It exp*lodes*.

A bomb goes off on the bridge of his nose, and his septum ex-puh-lodes.

All kinds of alarm bells are going off in his head. He's never had more thoughts, more signals, more messages racing around his brain simultaneously vying for attention. The winner, his first, most primitive reaction, is to go down. You're hurt. Get down, you fool. Get *down*! But he has no idea where down is. He might already *be* down, for all he can tell. He's disoriented. He's been blinded by a major nose explosion, for crying out loud. Give him a break. He might start trying to go down, and actually be going *up*, which would be disastrous.

And on top of this, there's this terrible sensation, this dreadful feeling that only occurs mercifully few times in any life: a sense of loss, a deep sadness that something important in him, a significant bit of him, is busted, irretrievably broken.

His senses start to report for duty. His hand is touching something wet. Stickily wet. The pain at the front of his face appears to be growing stronger and less bearable by the second, which is probably an illusion. The pain is probably subsiding, but his consciousness is being allowed more direct access to it. His sight peeks back, after a fashion. He can see light, and then a shadow against the light. The street noise, the demented people clamour seems to be coming closer. In his mouth, a pale hint of flavour, and more stickiness. Mucal stickiness. This is progress. That's almost all of his senses rallied now, close to intact. Just one missing. Where is it? Where is that fishy putrefaction from the bins? Where is *smell*?

Unfortunately, that particular sense is gone for ever.

He is standing at the point of the explosion. He didn't go down. Something kept him up. Something that's pressing hard against his chest. His fingers, he realizes, are searching his face, but they can't find the nose. Just a sticky mess where the nose used to be.

Then he sees a nose! Right in front of him. It must have been there all the time. Stupid nose, hiding like that. Worrying him needlessly. But, no. That's not his nose. That's someone else's. That nose has dark glasses perching on it.

He realizes he must be in shock. Not good. He has to snap out of it. He's probably still in danger.

The mouth under the nose is moving. That's probably what's making the sound he can hear through the whooping siren of pain. Words.

'I'm sorry, sir. Did you say something?'

The mouth seems to want an answer. Gordon tries to respond 'What?', but the best he can muster is 'Buhhd?'

'I thought you said something. When I struck you? Sounded like "Fah dah dah" or "Wha dah bid duh" but I couldn't make it out through the sound of your bones splintering. Was it important?'

Gordon tries appealing to the mouth's better nature. He tries to say 'I'm hurt', but his upper palate is clogged up and his nose is no longer there, and it comes out as 'Ahmbird'.

The mouth ignores him. 'Only, I'd hate to feel you had some complaint about my professionalism. Mercy me, I could be out of a job.' The mouth smiles. Somewhere behind it, another mouth is chuckling. 'Now, if you'd like me to stop the beating here and now . . .'

'Ayehd! Dhop! Dhop!'

'. . . all you have to do is say so, and we'll pack up and leave.'

'Ayehd! Dhop! Dhop idh dhow. Edubh.'

'But until you say something I can understand, I have to assume you want the job finished.'

'Dhoh!'

'Doh? Is that "No"?'

Gordon feels the pressure release on his chest. His knees sag, but he stays up. He needs to get some dignity going here, and that means staying upright. He shakes his head to clear it. He spits. A foul, red-stained mess hits the paving stones with a thud and stays there. He looks up.

His vision is clearing now. There is a good deal of swelling under his eyes, but he can force them open enough to see the two men facing him.

'All right, Mr Gordon. The fun is over, now.' The *fun*? The fun is *over*? 'That money you won at the casino. That was an administrative error. The girl was supposed to press a little button under her counter, but she was jostled. Too many people around. That's bad luck for you.'

Gordon speaks. Badly, but well enough. 'No. Bad luck for the casino.'

'Oh, come *on*, pilgrim. You know who's running that establishment. You really think they'd let you walk away with close on fifty million? Those people?'

'You clowns. You can't do this. Don't you know who I am?'

The two men smile at each other. They like Gordon's *cojones*. Much more fun doing a guy who has *cojones*. 'We know exactly who you are. You are Mr Charles Perry Gordon. And the beauty part is: you're not even here!'

The muscles in Gordon's cheeks, forced taut by the effort of keeping his eyes open, suddenly flop. This is bad.

'I can see you're keeping up. That's right. You are no longer on the planet. You're up on a spaceship. You're never coming back. That was a great plan, incidentally. You almost had us on a great goose chase up to the Project, which would not have been an easy accomplishment, let me tell you. But then you blew it. You actually delivered yourself, with a phone call. Awesome. You even *paid* to have us beat you up. Not two minutes ago, you all but *begged* me to do it. Truly, that was beautiful. I swear, it's been a hell of a night, and I don't mind admitting, I was beginning to question my calling. It was getting me down. All night long, loser after loser begging us *not* to hurt them. Then you come along and put the joy back into the job. Made it *fun* again. Honest to God, Charlie, you rejuvenated me. And in return, I promise you here and now, I fully intend to cut you all the slack it's in my remit to cut you. Now, all we need is one thing: did you move the money?'

'Did I . . . ?'

'Did you move the money? Did you transfer the money to another account?'

'No.'

'Now, now. You're lying to me, Charlie. This will go much better if you co-operate.'

'Honestly . . .'

'It's a big part of my job, you can probably imagine, to know when people are lying to me. I can read faces. True, the faces I read usually have *noses*, but I can tell you're lying.'

'It's the truth.'

'All right. I didn't want to get graphic with you. I mean, you're hurt already. You're in shock, you need medical attention, all that. Plus the fact, you've entertained us tremendously. But you're forcing my hand, now. Here are the bald facts: we *will* trace the money. Even if you've been very clever, and you probably have, we will track it down, and we *will* hack the security password. We're a major criminal organization, don't forget that. And then we're going to need two things to get the money back. Are you on board this wagon train to reality?'

'That's right. You'll need something. Something I have and you don't. Which is what makes you a clown. A funny, stupid moron of a clown. You can't get that money without a palm print and a retina scan. *My* palm print and *my* retina scan. And the only . . .'

Gordon sees the assistant remove a sheathed samurai sword from his bag, and the terrible truth comes to him.

'That's right, Charlie. We're going to strip your assets. Your hand, your eye. All you have left, the only bargaining point is whether we do it *pre* or *post mortem*.'

'This is insane. I'll co-operate. Take me to a terminal now. You'll have the money back in minutes.'

'Hey, I'd love to accommodate, you being such a sport and all, but that's a no can do.' The assistant proffers the sword with a flourish, as if it's part of some gruesome magic act. Gordon's tormentor takes it and slips it from its sheath. 'Be realistic, Chuck. You're already a non-person. You aren't here. This won't even go down in the books, my friend. It's not even a crime.'

'OK. Look. Fifty million's a lot of money . . .'

'It's not enough, Charlie. It's not enough to fund the loony scenario you're about to paint for me, where we three abscond to a yacht someplace no one will ever find us, and live on a diet of champagne and pussy. You don't think I hear that screenplay pitch every single day? Trust me, there *isn't* anywhere they wouldn't find you. I know, I'm one of the "they" who do the finding.'

Gordon's eyes flit towards the street.

'And don't spoil our relationship by thinking about that, Charlie. You wouldn't get half way, and it would be really undignified, to boot.'

No, no. Gordon wouldn't want to ruin this relationship. Perish that thought.

'Ten minutes ago, I was standing among those people, disgusted by them, I'm ashamed to say. Feeling superior. Wanting nothing more than to be away from them. Now . . .' Tears well up in his bruised eyes. Tears for himself, though. Pathetic, really. 'What did you want to know?'

'The bank, the account number, the password. We can look up the sort code, don't worry about that.'

Gordon takes out a notepad and a pen and starts to write. 'This is your notion of "cutting me some slack"?'

'You don't think this is cutting you slack? You'd prefer to *watch* us remove your eyeballs? You think I'd normally offer that option to someone who called me a, what? A clown? A moron? Who knows what else? But listen. I'm not without compassion. Are you a Catholic?'

Gordon shakes his head.

'I am. Not as devout as I might be, but you know, none the less. Thing is, there's a religious issue here. Now, you handing over that information, there's an argument that that could be construed as a form of suicide, because you *know* I'm going to kill you once you've done it. See? Well, it isn't. It's cool. I cleared it with a priest.'

Gordon nods and hands over the paper. He looks up at the stars and sucks in his final breath. Perhaps he does take some solace in those words, because his last, warped thought is of heaven. He hopes, if it does exist, it doesn't admit Mexicans or people with hearing aids.

That thought is still running through his head when it hits the ground.

13

It seems we have an impostor in our midst.

Does Eddie's skin burn?

Yes.

Does it buzz?

Like a summer hive.

Is his mouth dry?

Not even a cactus could flourish there.

He's vaguely aware of the Captain rising from his seat and starting to pace behind him. He thoroughly expects a baseball bat to strike the back of his head.

Even Gwent's boom box of a voice is hard pressed to penetrate the tha-*dump* thud in Eddie's ears. 'This is where the hypothesis meets reality. This is the tough test of the theoretical model. There is a clear course of action laid out for this situation. But we're not on a drawing board, now. The question is: can we practically apply the guidelines Charles, here, has set out for us?'

A wave of stale coffee breath washes over Eddie. The Captain is crouched beside him, hand on his shoulder.

Somehow, Eddie is supposed to break this silence. Unfortunately, his mouth is dry, drier than a constipated camel's sphincter, and he's afraid that his tongue might rip away the lining of his palate if he tries to move it.

Somebody saves him. It's his travelling companion from the shuttle: the honest-featured fellow in the dog collar. 'I think it's a little brutal, Berwick, to be hoisting this on to Mr Gordon's shoulders.'

'I think not, Padre,' drawl the purple lips of the carbolic Ms Peck. 'After all, it *is* rather a brutal penalty, and, after all, it *was* Mr Gordon who recommended it. We need to know if he still believes it to be viable.'

'I'm sorry,' pipes a voice that clearly isn't. 'What exactly is the penalty we're discussing?'

Eddie looks over at the speaker. It's a square-jawed crewcut of a man who looks exceptionally out of place among the pallid skins and studious faces around the table. He is built *big*. *Big* big. His wrists threaten to burst the cuffs of his jacket. He has those curiously overdeveloped muscles on the tops of his shoulders that blend into the neck and make the head look out of scale. Eddie wonders how you get muscles like that. Presumably, it involves lifting weights with the head. Why? To what end? When does that particular talent come in handy in the real world? But this is just Eddie attempting to belittle the man, to diminish him as a threat, to avoid thinking about how easily the man might snap him in two with one hand, whilst simultaneously guzzling a can of chocolate-flavoured muscle nourishment drink.

Clearly, the entire penal code is required reading among the more bookish committee members. Which is all of them except for Eddie and Mr Muscle Neck.

A man who sports an unnecessary, curable bald patch like a scholastic prize snaps irritably: 'Oh, come on, Mr Styx. It's in the book.' And he indicates several bound volumes in the centre of the table with a vexed gesture, as if only the smallest and most stupid of primates couldn't commit them to perfect memory in a lazy afternoon by a swimming pool.

Styx's cheek muscles flutter frighteningly. How does he work-out on that? Does he attach weights to the insides of his gums? Whatever, the minute involuntary gesture is enough to silence the slighter.

'Charles?' Gwent asks, from behind his shoulder. Eddie resists the temptation to check his ear for leaking blood. 'Perhaps you'd like to illuminate our Security Section Leader as to the recommended remedial procedure in the event of unselected personnel impersonating one of the Selected.'

There can be no escape now. The jig is most definitely up. An uncommon anger wells up in Eddie's tired, beleaguered spirit. He's been rumbled, ridiculed and toyed with, and now, quite frankly, he's had enough. He's not going to take this vicious teasing any more.

'All right. You've all had your juvenile fun. You've pinned me to the table with contempt, like some craven crawling insect and prodded and poked me while I wriggle and squirm. But before you take the brilliantly studied and well-informed decision to hurl me to whatever nasty wolves you have snarling on their leashes, just let me say this: no one here is *better* than me. None of you. I may not be the brightest guy on board. I may not crack impenetrable so-called "jokes" in dead Mediterranean languages, for you all to pat yourselves on your smug, well-read backs and take dismal satisfaction in being repositories of deeply useless knowledge. But I am not deserving of your assumed superior contempt. Nor do I accept your right to pass judgement on my ultimate value as a human being. You are not *better* than me. None of you. Not one of you is actually any better a person than I am.'

Eddie realizes he's raised himself to his feet at some point during his harangue, which was a mistake, because he senses, from the slightly stunned, open-jawed reaction around the table, that he has somehow missed the mark, somehow massively over-reacted, and he wishes he were sitting down and ever so slightly less centre stage.

Like a crossbow bolt in his overworked, distended gut, it hits him: he is not the 'impostor' they're discussing.

Gwent's 'impostor amongst us' pronouncement was not, as Eddie assumed, culled from the *Bumper Book of Bond Villain Threats*: he'd been referring to another impostor – one who isn't even in the room.

It isn't Eddie's fate that hangs in the balance here. At least, it hasn't been up until now, up until what must, on reflection, have come over as a bizarre, not to say psychotic, speech.

He sits down, and tries to find somewhere to look, but there is nowhere: there can be nowhere.

He can actually feel the entire committee squirming as if it's a single person.

Captain Gwent, still crouched behind Eddie, finally sighs like a wind tunnel and stands, knees cracking as he straightens. 'Charles,' he claps a fatherly hand on Eddie's shoulder, almost snapping it, '. . . you're absolutely right. We all accepted your formulae, there was ample opportunity for debate, and now is not the time to call you to task.' Gwent turns and addresses the muscle man. 'The penalty, Mr Styx, is the same penalty inflicted on all perpetrators of, and I quote, "Non-correctable and mission-threatening transgressions of ship-regulations."' He smiles politely at Eddie, acknowledging Charles Gordon's wording, as if to remind himself and others present that a fully functioning brain was once at work in that head, and managing quite well. He puffs out his considerable chest. 'To wit: the non-permanent suspension of life.'

The non-permanent suspension of life. That doesn't sound good, to Eddie. That doesn't sound like something a person might look forward to, should a person ever be exposed as a ship-regulation transgressor of mission-threatening proportions.

'The non-permanent suspension of life.' The Padre repeats it. Superfluously, in Eddie's book. 'A nice phrase. Concealing a rather grim and barbaric reality.'

'Let me assure everyone,' the victim of unnecessary male pattern baldness takes over, 'the procedure is painless and extremely efficient.'

Eddie doesn't like the sound of this. Clearly, this is a doctor talking. 'Painless' and 'procedure' are oxymoronic in the mouth of a surgeon. And 'extremely efficient' is the medical equivalent of that old military charmer: 'acceptable losses'.

'"Extremely efficient" doesn't sound very promising, Piers.' Clearly, the Padre's thoughts are running parallel to Eddie's.

'There is no "zero failure rate" in surgical procedure, Father Lewis, even in this day and age.' The doctor runs his hand over the downy rodent fur on the top of his skull. 'But barring massive equipment failure, coupled with the sudden and complete loss of all my faculties and expertise, this is as close as it gets. A small child could perform the deed with only an ether-soaked handkerchief and a circular saw.'

A circular saw? Eddie is right to worry.

'I think we can trust Dr Morton's skills,' Gwent sonic booms. Eddie wishes the good Captain would stand elsewhere. Preferably on another craft. 'That isn't the issue. The issue is: can we, as civilized humans, consider taking a fellow human's life, albeit in a temporary and fully refundable manner?'

Eddie would like to disinvolve himself at this point.

Matters are being discussed here which he feels are out of his moral safety zone, and he'd really like to do the Eddie thing and withdraw from the discussion without honour. But, clearly, a precedent will be set by the outcome of this discussion. A precedent that might very well impinge on his future social life in an extremely anti-social way. But how can he contribute, without risking unmasking himself? Any argument he advances might well disagree with Gordon's viewpoint, which seems set to become the law here.

Once again, Father Lewis, who seems to be the closest thing to a human being on board, jumps in and saves Eddie's face. 'Aren't we thinking about this issue too abstractly? I mean, we don't know anything about the perpetrator. Have we assessed his potential in any meaningful way? He may have some valuable contribution he might make to the community.'

The Captain is, mercifully, back at the head of the table. 'Two points, Padre: he is not among the Selected. That, in and of itself, makes him superfluous to community requirements, and if that sounds elitist . . .' Elitist? Try Hitlerian. '. . . then I'm sorry, but as Mr Gordon here has said on many occasions: we are pioneers of a new and exceptionally dangerous frontier. A circumstance which demands brutal regulations, rigidly enforced.'

The Padre looks at Eddie in a way Eddie wishes he wouldn't. The Captain's brilliant speech is rapidly alienating the only potential ally Eddie might have on the entire vessel. Eddie searches through the darkest recesses of his facial expression wardrobe for something appropriate to wear, but comes out naked. The Padre turns to Gwent again. 'And your second point, Berwick?'

'It hardly matters, of course, given the unassailable finality of the primary rationale, but, for the record – and balm for your conscience, Padre – the man is a career criminal, chromosomically disposed to the same, thanks to inept gene screening techniques in certain over-libertarian jurisdictions. He has provably resorted, on several occasions, to spree murdering as an anti-boredom device. He is in flight from every legitimate law-enforcement agency on the globe. Furthermore, he is responsible for the premature demise of the genuine Selected community member he is currently impersonating. He is, most assuredly, a bad, could-hardly-be-worse sort.'

'How very compliant of him,' the Padre smiles with a heavy sadness. Eddie smiles in his direction, in sympathy, of course. And, of course, his smile is misinterpreted as smugness.

'I'm sorry,' Gwent blares, 'that I couldn't offer you something a little more ambiguous. A political prisoner, perhaps, or a religious dissident.' An unrequired jibe at the expense of Lewis's beliefs. 'But there you are. We can hardly risk contaminating our community, or our gene pool, with this son of Cain, now, can we? So what alternative do we have? None of which I am aware.'

'Couldn't we . . .' Eddie feels invisible bolts strike him from every eye in the room. Everyone is waiting for another paranoid outburst. Eddie collects his wits, what's left of them, and forges on. 'I mean, it sounds too obvious to suggest, but couldn't we send him back down?' He looks round for support, but finds only blankness.

Peck jumps in, sensing a small triumph in the offing. 'Send him back down?'

'To Earth.' Still blankness.

Peck turns the stiletto. 'Wouldn't he slightly . . . be killed?'

Eddie knows he's almost certainly walking into a large and deadly mantrap, but he still can't see the jaws. 'Well, not if we sent him down slowly. In the hoist?'

The Captain's blankness is the first to clear. He rolls his eyes, like he's just understood a wickedly clever, obscure joke. 'Ooh, I see. No, Charles. We're off. We're *en route*. We officially "launched" over seven minutes ago.'

They're off? The ship has set out from Earth's orbit, bound for the stars on the most ambitious journey ever undertaken by the human race? And this historic event has passed unmarked by so much as an announcement? Not even a tinny little fanfare on the ship's PA and a chorus of hip-hooray?

'Forgot to warn you: we DFI-ed the full-on news coverage launch. Didn't want the crew distracted by twittering arsewits, a.k.a. "journalists". We thought it best to slip away early without the old media brouhaha.'

Eddie says: 'I see. Makes sense.' But he doesn't see, and it doesn't make sense. Slipping away without the telecast cameras rolling is one thing. Embarking on a momentous journey without acknowledging it, without waving goodbye to everything you're leaving behind: that feels wrong. Everything feels wrong about the way these people are treating this voyage, treating the ship itself. Normally, a crew has a bond with the vessel it relies on: a relationship, a respect. More, even: a passion. There is none of that here. Simply cold, unemotional functionality. The ship is merely a machine, just like any other machine. It seems, somehow . . . wrong. Irreverent.

Gwent is scribbling on some official-looking documentation. 'Well, I hadn't expected this issue to come up so early, if, indeed, at all, but there we are. I thank you all for your input, though the reality is there was never any choice in the matter in the first place. I'm officially signing the decision to suspend the life of . . .' he glances over the paper. Obscenely, the man's name is unfamiliar to him. Irrelevant. 'Paulo San . . . what's this? Can't make it out. Man writes like a lame horse . . . Pablos, I think. Dr Morton,' he slides the paper over to Dr Male Pattern Baldness, 'this is your bailiwick now.' Then he looks magisterially across the table. 'This is the way of our world, henceforth. We are operating under a new and original system, which is more logical, simpler and more effective than any social order yet devised. It will work, and work well, if we observe it rigidly. Meeting adjourned.'

Gwent stands. Eddie half expects some kind of applause, perhaps the odd 'Sieg Heil', but there is only a general scraping of chairs.

He's planning to slip out as quickly and unnoticed as possible, but a blast from the Captain's larynx thwarts that scheme. 'Charles! If you've got a moment.'

Eddie disguises his sigh as a yawn and crosses to the Captain, in the hardly creditable hope that this might entice him to lower his voice, and prevent the stragglers in the room from overhearing what will almost certainly be a humiliating rebuke.

His effort is not rewarded.

'Charles,' Gwent appears to be talking over some nearby roadworks, audible only to him. 'Sorry to throw you to the dogs back there.'

Eddie hardly smiles, and responds, 'That's all right, Captain,' at a level almost below human hearing, in an effort to drag the Captain's volume down to just 'embarrassing'.

'Eh? But you understand. Had to bring 'em all up to speed, baptism of fire, *et cetera*.' And then he adds what sounds, at first, like 'whoopsy daisy', but turns out to be a short phrase in a language that died long before the invention of gunpowder. Eddie makes out one word, '*ipso*' or '*ipse*', which his paltry education leads him to believe means something like 'thus' or 'and thus', which is, in Eddie's frank opinion, dead even in translation.

'That aside,' Gwent blasts on, 'your little speech seemed somewhat, well . . . odd.'

Eddie looks around discreetly, knowing, before he glances at her, that Peck is lurking close by in animated feigned conversation, her attention on him, waiting to mop up the gravy of his humiliation ravenously.

'I got the point of the "nobody's better than me" segment, although I take arms against your use of case, the nominative being plainly correct, though I suspect your selection of the accusative was an ill-considered shot at a "man of the people" type stance. Still, it was important to put the somewhat arbitrary, artificial ranking system we've been compelled to adopt into a valid interpersonal perspective.'

Eddie's wearing an interested frown, framing his chin with his thumb and forefinger, and nodding randomly, but he's no longer sure it's appropriate. Is this guy telling him off or what?

Then it comes: 'But what the hell was that bewildering drivel about jokes in dead languages?'

The Captain's looking at him, as if he's actually expecting some kind of sane explanation. Then it hits Eddie, suddenly. It comes to him like a vision of angels. He wants to fall on his knees and weep with joy. The reason he's constantly on the brink of being unmasked as the charlatan he is, and the reason he hasn't been blasted into space through the ship's exhaust are one and the same.

These people all think he's much, much smarter than he actually is.

Even Peck!

There's no telling how long this error in perception can be maintained, but at least Eddie now has an angle to play, a pose to strike. All he has to do is be obscure. The over-excitable minds of the hyper-intelligentsia around him will fill in the gaps as they see fit. It's a dangerous game, but it's a game, at least.

He adopts a cocksure smile, and repeats what he hopes is a correct rendition of the Captain's last Latin quote. '*Ipso dixit*, Berwick, *ipso dixit.*' It isn't, in fact, one hundred per cent accurate, but that's not too important. If Eddie's thinking is correct: any imperfections will be considered word play.

The Captain appears momentarily baffled, then his features relax into a smile of understanding. 'Very clever, Charles.' He slaps Eddie on the shoulder. Eddie manages to brace himself in time to avoid being hurled along the length of the conference table. '*Ipso dixit*, indeed.'

Eddie smiles in the direction of Peck, who is concealing her disappointment with a counterfeit smile of her own.

'Well, if you'll excuse me, Captain, I've got a lot of ship to see.' There's only one part of the ship Eddie has any intention of examining at the moment: the ceiling above his pillow. And that only for a few brief instants. But the day's ordeals are not yet done.

'I think we both should be there, don't you?'

Be there? Be where? This is the downside of having people think he's possessed of a working mind. 'You think so?'

'Well, *I* signed the order and, whatever the actuality, it *is* perceived as your policy recommendation. Unpleasant as it may be, I think it's important we are witnessed witnessing the procedure.'

He wants Eddie to watch the operation with him. The circular saw type operation. With, probably, generous amounts of blood and gore. Eddie's face must be broadcasting his queasiness, because the Captain offers as solace: 'I'm not exactly relishing the prospect myself, Charles. But in crude terms, we're taking a human being and removing his head and spinal column from the rest of his body . . .' And the rest of the sentence is lost on Eddie.

As words of solace go, these are inordinately ineffective.

Removing his head and spinal column from his body. And that's a painless procedure? What would qualify, then, as a *painful* procedure? Removing the head and spinal column whilst simultaneously striking the eyeballs with a sharpened glockenspiel hammer?

And this is the fate threatening Eddie?

The Captain's voice fades back up in Eddie's awareness. '. . . understand if you decline. Though you will be perceived as squeamish, it must be said. Not good.'

'Squeamish? Nooo. It's just, you've seen one head-and-spinal-column-ectomy, you've seen 'em all.' Eddie tries a winning smile. It loses.

'So you'll come?'

'Wouldn't miss it.'

14

Eddie has collected many abominable memories in the past few hours – probably doubled his entire X-rated collection, in fact – but the images from the operating theatre are so gruesome and vivid, he fears they will never leave his waking mind.

And the operation hasn't even started yet.

It's not just the prospect of the Tobe Hooper gorefest the operation itself promises to be. Though, in all honesty, watching a human being gutted and boned like a gigantic trout doesn't rank very highly on Eddie's list of top spectator pastimes. No, it's the nightmarish quality of matter-of-factness all around that sharply counterpoints the horror that's about to be performed.

The hi-tech, impersonal cleanliness of the operating theatre, and the overstated comfort of the observation gallery looking down on it, where Eddie is sitting, waiting for the show to begin. Leather seats, with foldaway tables and, incredibly, cup holders on the arms. There is even a vending machine in the corner. Just in case you run out of snacks or soda pop in the middle of some intricate bone sawing.

Eddie hasn't eaten for a considerable while, and he is very, very tempted to vend himself some chicken broth.

But what if they bring in the patient awake? How would he feel to look up and see Eddie in the spectators' gallery sipping away at a cup of steaming soup?

So Eddie just sits there, praying his stomach doesn't rumble, and trying not to look too relaxed, even though the chair is obscenely comfortable, and he is very, very tired.

He keeps having to catch himself, to stop his legs from crossing, which wouldn't look too nice either. Worst of all, he's afraid he'll fall asleep and start snoring at some critically gruesome point.

That's the last thing he needs, people having to turn round and shush him while the ribcage is being cracked open.

One small blessing is, he's managed to position himself a good way away from Captain Gwent, who's holding court in what must be the equivalent of the Royal Box. He keeps beckoning for Eddie to come over and join him, but so far he's managed to seem not to notice. It's bad enough having to sit through this, without having to work at maintaining his façade at the same time.

Somebody sits down in the seat next to Eddie, even though there are, unsurprisingly, lots of seats spare.

Eddie glances left. It's the priest. Father Lewis. Eddie smiles tightly and nods a greeting.

The priest doesn't smile back. After a while, he says: 'This is, don't you think, ever so slightly barbaric?'

Of course it is. Eddie *wants* to agree with Lewis. But as C.P. Gordon, he can't. He has to defend this madness. 'It's the Captain's decision, Padre. If we start arguing with that, we'll have anarchy.'

'You blame the Captain, but you're up here, supporting him. Watching the execution. I'm surprised you didn't bring some knitting.'

Eddie is rescued from this potentially excruciating interchange by a hubbub behind them, from the direction of the Captain's box. Eddie turns to see the source. The security chief with the muscular neck, Styx, is in conversation with an angry-looking Gwent. Eddie strains to try and catch the gist, but he can't make it out. Strangely enough, Gwent must lower his voice when he's angry.

Finally, Gwent gestures with his head and Styx hurries off. 'Ladies and gentlemen.' The Captain's voice has returned to its natural volume. 'The procedure has been . . . postponed. Our intended subject has made himself temporarily unavailable. He will, of course, be invited back immediately we rediscover his whereabouts.'

Eddie looks over at Lewis. The man's escaped. Good.

'It must be made known, this individual is capable of extreme violence. He accounted for the lives of no fewer than five of Mr

Styx's security team in the course of his bid for this temporary taste of unfetteredness.'

Gwent sighs, seeming suddenly tired.

'And he made assertions that he fully intends to kill again. And often. You should all be familiar with his visage.' Gwent nods at the overhead screen. 'And avoid it at all costs.'

Eddie turns his head to look at the image.

Eddie recognizes the face.

It's the face of the man he frivolously thought of as the 'nice' hitman.

Mr Pink Socks himself.

15

Eddie is in one of the ship's many restaurants. He hopes this isn't one of the better examples of culinary provision points on board. It's more like a school canteen, with its long benches and laminated table tops, and its criminally bad food. But it was the nearest one he could find to the spectators' gallery. The *only* one he could find, in fact. He is savagely tired, close to exhaustion even, but he daren't go back to his apartment. He wants to stay in public. In as much public as possible, until he knows for certain Mr Pink Socks is safely back under lock and key.

He ought to be hungry, too. He can't remember the last time he ate. But he's just pushing the food around on his plate.

He'd have liked a drink with his dinner. A very stiff drink, in fact. But the Consumption Director – that really was the job description on the badge of the waitress – just laughed when he ordered one. There is no alcohol on the *Willflower*. No stimulants, no depressants. No narcotics. The only permitted artificially mind-altering activity is a half an hour in the newly designed soothe booths. These are cubicles dotted around the ship which seem to provide a kind of sensory-deprivation experience, with electronic 'soul song' pumped through the speakers 'to naturally induce alpha rhythmic wave patterns in the brain', supposedly. It doesn't sound like much of a high to Eddie, but he was willing to give it a go. Unfortunately, soothe booths have to be booked out in advance. Days in advance. Eddie has fifteen consecutive sessions booked for next Wednesday. If he lives that long.

He's trying to take his mind off his many woes by working through Gordon's papers, but that isn't helping anything.

The more he reads, the more he becomes convinced the man is insane. He's clearly a borderline fascist. And Eddie would say he's on the wrong side of that border. There are, for instance, an enormously complicated number of astonishingly detailed prescriptions for who should be permitted to mate with whom, and when. Shagging laws! And not just now, for this generation: for all future generations, too. People whose parents haven't been born yet have been designated a mating partner who isn't even a twinkle in his grandaddy's eye. This is supposedly to keep the gene pool in good order, and avoid the side effects of inbreeding that might otherwise plague future generations. But it sounds awfully close to ultra right-wing racial purity programmes to Eddie. Awfully close.

And there's worse.

All the positions on board are not merely held for life: they're held down the family line. Children have their jobs allocated before birth. And their children will be born to replace them. And their children will follow. On and on. The idea here: to obviate destructive and wasteful competitiveness, and preserve order. The argument is that a child trained from birth to perform a function will be better at the job, and won't have to waste time acquiring unnecessary skills.

For Eddie's money, that's bad even if your parents hold decent positions, but the ship depends on a lot of menial workers, too. To be born knowing that all you can ever be, and all your children can ever be, is a Consumption Director in a crappy low-class canteen . . . It's nothing more or less than an artificially imposed caste system. It beggars belief.

It's clear he can't go on for ever toeing Gordon's line. He'll have to engineer a change of heart, somehow. Maybe C.P. Gordon can get religion or something.

Eddie senses the chair next to him being moved. He's feeling fairly jittery, and he's not in the mood for surprises. He clasps his cutlery, ready to stab. He doesn't know how effective a plastic knife and fork might be against the deadly honed skills of a trained assassin, but he really is prepared to use them.

'Jumpy, are we, Mr Gordon?'

Eddie relaxes. It's Father Lewis again. Eddie looks down at the knife and fork he's brandishing. 'No, no. This is how we hold our cutlery in Rio de Janeiro.' He pats himself mentally on the back for slipping in a piece of his research on Gordon's background.

'I see.'

Lewis is looking at him oddly. He didn't buy it. Eddie looks away. 'I am a little tense, I suppose.'

'Tense? Yes, well. The criminal classes at loose on the ship. It's enough to make any *decent* man nervous.'

Criminal class and decent men. Jibes at Gordon's superclass theories. Fair enough, Eddie thinks. He shrugs.

'I'm surprised to find you in here.'

Why? 'Really?'

'I'd have thought one of the superior restaurants would have better suited your refined tastes. One of those reserved for committee members, at the very least.'

Really? There are restaurants on board where not everyone's allowed? That makes a kind of horrible sense. 'It's going to be a long trip, Padre. I imagine we'll be trying all the restaurants, eventually.'

'No doubt. Those of us who can. Ah! Admiring your handiwork, I see.' He's nodding at Gordon's papers.

'Just checking them through, Padre.'

'Yes. Wouldn't want any mistakes creeping in, now, would we?'

Go away. 'No.'

'They make fine reading, I must say.'

It's sarcasm, of course, but Eddie says 'Thank you' anyway. He wishes the priest would leave him alone, at least till he can work out what he's going to do about all of this. About trying to impersonate a man he disagrees with on so many fundamentals.

'A blueprint for a perfect society.'

Eddie feels, as Gordon, he really ought to put up some kind of defence. 'It's a very difficult mission we've embarked on, Padre. Obviously there have to be rules . . .'

'Yes, there have to be rules. Some of your rules, though, seem a little . . . extreme.'

'You think so?' This might not be a bad opening. Maybe Eddie can start to backtrack on some of Gordon's excesses. 'Such as?'

'Ooh, I don't know where to start, really. The Sexual Recreation Centre bothers me, for instance.'

Sexual Recreation Centre? 'What about it?' Eddie hasn't got to the bit about the Sexual Recreation Centre yet.

'Well, obviously the Church would object, on the grounds that it's a brothel, plain and simple, under the fancy names and theories.'

Oh dear. 'A brothel? I see.'

'But under your draconian mating regulations, there is, perhaps, an argument for such an establishment.'

'So. You concede that much, at least.'

'Not really. I don't agree with the mating regulations, either. They seem nothing more than a new incarnation of the archaic system of arranged marriages, which were outlawed long ago in most civilized nations. But I'm trying to keep it simple.'

Eddie pushes the food around his plate a little more. 'Go on.'

'As I said, there is an argument for state-controlled whorehouses, theoretically. But the men and women who . . . perform these services: they've made a choice to do that. It's their decision. I'm a realist. I accept they have that right.'

'Very Christian of you.'

Lewis turns to face him. There are tears welling up in his eyes. 'But how can you . . . how can any of us commit their *children* to that life?'

Eddie really doesn't know what to say now. Children are to be born into *prostitution*? Who could possibly defend that?

'You tell me, Mr Gordon, the difference between that and pure evil.'

Eddie can't. But he has to say *something*. 'Father Lewis. If you disagree with . . . with the system here, why did you come?'

'You think a priest plies his trade only among the converted? I'm here to change things. I know it won't be easy. The system you've put together is pretty ruthless on change. But it will change, Mr Gordon.' Lewis stands. 'I don't expect you to think this is anything other than hokum, but what you've done is the Devil's work. And it will be stopped.'

Eddie doesn't watch the priest go. He keeps on staring at his plate, moulding the powdered potatoes around his half-eaten burger steak with his fork.

That bastard Gordon. Where is he now? Probably using his millions to fund compulsory sterilization camps for the short sighted. Or running for World Presidency on the Ku Klux Klan ticket.

Something starts beeping near him. Eddie tolerates the noise for a while, but it starts to get annoying. He looks around, hoping to embarrass the perpetrator into action. Everybody else is looking at him. He's the one who's beeping.

He looks down at his jacket. One of his buttons is flashing. He wonders what it means.

He tries to ignore it, but it refuses to go away.

He folds his arms across his chest, but the beeping can't be muffled.

He tries tapping the button, but it won't stop flashing. He presses it, hard and repeatedly, but it won't stop its damned beeping.

He's about to wrench it off his jacket and stomp it to death underfoot, when someone at the bench behind him leans back and says: 'That's a code orange, pilgrim.'

'Right,' Eddie smiles. 'A code orange, eh?' What the hell is a code orange?

'There's a coms booth over there.'

Eddie looks over to where the man's pointing. There is indeed some kind of booth. He keeps his smile on and hopes for more of a clue.

'You press the orange button. That's all.'

'Yeah, I know,' Eddie lies. 'I was just going to finish my . . .'

'But it's a code *orange*.'

'Oh, yes. Right.' Eddie gets up and walks to the booth. A code *orange*? Since when did orange mean 'urgent'? A code red, yes. What's the colour, then, for 'not very important'? Code mauve?

He gets to the booth and presses the orange button.

A face appears on an LED screen. Security Chief Styx. The monitor isn't widescreen, so his neck doesn't fit on completely. 'Mr Gordon, sir? Sorry to bother you.'

'That's all right, Mr Styx. Just grabbing a bite here. What's the problem?'

'It's your apartment, sir.'

What could have happened in his apartment to warrant a code *orange*, for heaven's sake? Did they find his socks or something? 'What about it?'

'It's been trashed, I'm afraid.'

'Trashed?'

'Extremely trashed.'

'I'll be right up.'

Eddie keeps staring at the monitor, waiting for Styx to cut the connection. When it becomes clear he isn't going to, Eddie repeats: 'Right up' and moves away. Out of the corner of his eye he can see Styx watching him go. Clearly, Eddie was supposed to terminate the call at his end.

How many more mistakes before his cover is blown completely?

That bastard Gordon.

As he gets to the restaurant door, a cramp hits his stomach. He really is very hungry, still. He toys with the idea of going back and grabbing his cold burger to finish *en route*, but decides against it on two counts. He doesn't want to risk responding too casually to a code orange summons. And the burger was disgusting, anyway.

Which is something of a shame.

Because that is the last meal Eddie will ever eat.

16

Eddie's beginning to get a handle on the ship's layout. He manages to find his way back to his own apartment, and he only gets lost half a dozen times. There are corridor karts, little electrically powered shuttle buses, that ferry passengers between transway stations. The transway system networks the ship, and it's more efficient for longer trips.

That's assuming you don't get in the wrong carriage, heading in the wrong direction on the wrong deck, which Eddie seems to have a penchant for doing.

Mr Styx himself is supervising the forensic search of Eddie's apartment, which is a little worrying, on several counts. He looks up as Eddie steps out of the kart at the end of the corridor. 'Mr Gordon,' he chides, 'I thought I made it clear this was a code orange.'

'You did, Mr Styx. Sorry, I got . . . I was waylaid.' Eddie hopes this will be excuse enough. After all, he *is* the Community Planner on this mission. 'And what are you doing pootling about with a little house break-in? Wouldn't you be better occupied in the minor matter of tracking down the murderous fugitive?'

'This is part of the same investigation, sir.'

What?

Styx beckons Eddie into the apartment. 'We've reason to believe it was the fugitive who did this.'

Eddie steps through the door. Any small hopes he might still have entertained that Pink Socks was here by coincidence, or hunting down some other poor wretch, disappear with the sound of his stomach rumble.

The room is destroyed. The furniture is smashed, his clothes are slashed and even the walls are daubed with hate messages in a strange brown paint.

Styx sees him wondering. 'That's blood, sir.'

'Blood?'

'From the security guard I allocated to look after you.'

'He's dead, this guard?'

Styx nods grimly. 'Very. Do these messages mean anything to you?'

Eddie scans the wall. A couple of unpleasant expletives. The word 'pig'. A death threat: 'die'. He's about to shake his head when he spots the wall above his mantelpiece. A charming display it makes, too. The grinning skeletons from the Mexican Day of the Dead festival have knives jabbed into their skulls. And above them, daubed madly in blood, 'I'm coming for you, Eddie.'

'Anything at all?' Styx is urging.

Eddie manages to grunt a negative. 'Nurghh.'

'Do you know who "Eddie" might be?'

Eddie grunts again.

'He's used the name before. When we had him in custody. He's hell bent on ripping this Eddie to pieces, whoever he is.' Styx looks over at the message and shakes his head. 'I sure wouldn't like to be Eddie.'

Eddie smiles, weakly. 'Me neither.'

'I've already allocated you another apartment.'

'Thank you.'

'It won't be exactly to your taste, of course.'

To his *taste*? Just so long as the walls aren't splattered with hate messages daubed in another man's lifeblood, that would be to Eddie's taste. And it's not as if he plans to actually go to an apartment and be *on his own* any time soon. He mumbles a thank you, and makes his way towards the door, without any idea where he's going to go.

'Oh, by the way . . .'

Eddie stops at the door and turns. 'Eh?'

'There was a note for you.' Styx dips into his pocket.

'A note?'

'We opened it, I'm afraid. In case it was pertinent to the inquiry.' He hands over a folded blue letter. 'We don't think it is. Sorry.'

Eddie accepts the note, steps out of the room, and actually takes a breath.

And as he inhales, he smells a scent. And even in these strained circumstances, the smell fills him with cheer.

Carbolic soap.

He flips the note open.

It's short and very sweet.

Meet me in the rose garden. 0100 hrs. And it's signed simply *P.*

P.

The gardens. There is a huge vegetation zone on the ship, with artificial sunlight, and now, presumably, at this hour, artificial moonlight. It performs a number of functions: assisting oxygen regeneration, for instance, and supplementing the artificial and recycled foodstuff in the crew's diet.

And not listed in the brochure: it also provides a perfect setting for a romantic assignation.

Eddie smells the note again, pops it tenderly into his breast pocket and heads up the corridor, towards the nearest transway station.

All kinds of thoughts are swirling through his mind. He's racing through possible explanations why the savage Ms Peck might have had a change of heart. His irresistible charm? Doubtful. She suffered some kind of blow to the head? More likely. Or . . .

Or she's suddenly found Eddie's been allocated to her as a sexual partner! Yes! That one makes sense. She's discovered that, and she wants to make the best of things.

It doesn't occur to Eddie that the letter might be a device, a ruse to get him alone, in a deserted place. That it might have been counterfeited by someone who has bad intentions towards him. Very bad intentions.

He's actually whistling a Hoagy Carmichael tune as the transway carriage arrives and he steps into it.

And that's the last thing he remembers.

That's the last thing he remembers for a very long time.

PART THREE

Generation X

'Whoso beset him round
With dismal stories
Do but themselves confound:
His strength the more is.'

(John Bunyan: *The Pilgrim's Progress*)

17

Eddie's not dreaming, but he's not in reality, either.

He's in a forest clearing, but the trees aren't entirely convincing. The details are fine. The morning sun is sending misted shafts through the overhanging branches. Nice touch, Eddie's thinking. And a very plausible lens flare as he looks through the canopy of leaves directly towards the sun.

He's lying on a bed of soft foliage. Maybe he should get up, but it feels like that would be too much effort right now. Besides, this is a good place. Unthreatening. There is birdsong. He's safe here. He's calm and safe.

There is a rustling sound in the bushes beside him. He directs his eyes towards it. For some reason, actually moving his head doesn't seem like a wonderful idea at this moment. He sees a white foal, bent over, lapping at a crystal stream. It turns its head to face him, and Eddie spots a fledgling horn sprouting from its forehead. A baby unicorn. Delightful.

In his extremely relaxed state, the unicorn doesn't surprise Eddie. Nothing would surprise him. Not even the nymph who's crouching over him, looking at his face, wearing a floral crown, a flimsy slip of shiny, translucent material and a concerned expression. He smiles at her. This seems to please her. Good. She's very, very beautiful, and Eddie wants to please her. She speaks. The accent is strange. Impossible to place.

'I think that would qualify as a response.'

Eddie thinks he recognizes her, but his memory's not too . . . it's not exactly firing on all . . . what are those things in an internal combustion engine? Tubular things? The nymph's lips are moving again, but her voice isn't quite in synch.

'Do you know who you are?'

Of course he knows who he is. He smiles and tries to nod, but he can only incline his head ever so slightly. Perhaps that should worry him, but it doesn't.

The nymph looks cross, for a second. Not very nymph-like, really. Then she smiles again. An unaccomplished smile. 'Would you like to actually try and *tell* us who you are? With speech?' And even though she's smiling, there is definitely a note of impatience in the voice.

Fair enough. This is Eddie's personal Paradise, he assumes, so it would make sense to have a short-tempered nymph tending to him. Eddie tries to say 'This is a heaven, isn't it?', but it comes out all mixed up. Vowels and consonants in the wrong place, in the wrong order. And his voice doesn't sound right. Like it's coming from somewhere else. Somewhere underwater. Like it doesn't belong to him. That should *definitely* worry him, but it definitely doesn't.

There is another voice, a male voice, 'What did he say?' and a satyr is suddenly crouching next to the nymph, pointed ears, furry legs, the whole enchilada. Eddie certainly recognizes him. That crewcut security hombre. Slick? Stick? No, *Styx*. What's *he* doing in Eddie's Heaven?

The nymph shoots the satyr a withering look. 'He said . . .' and she accurately reproduces the jumbled nonsense that just tumbled out of Eddie's mouth.

The satyr appears to be concentrating very hard. His face looks like it has to do this a lot. 'That's French, right?'

The nymph dismisses the satyr with a small flick of her eyes and turns her attention back to Eddie. 'Don't panic. You haven't spoken in some considerable time. You may simply be experiencing some minor difficulty re-acquainting the appropriate muscles with their correct function. Either that or your voice box is shot all to hell and utterly beyond repair. Just relax and try again.'

Some considerable time? What could that mean? Eddie tries trawling through the mess of his memory. What exactly was the last thing that happened to him? No? Nothing coming? OK. All right then. What's the last thing he remembers?

Clearly, the memory trawl is taking more time than it ought to be, because the nymph is looking exasperated again. 'Your name?' she asks with an unnecessarily sarcastic slant. 'Shouldn't tax you too much. Of all the questions you're going to be facing, "Who are you?" is not going to be the hardest.'

Who is he? Actually, that *is* a hard question. And the nymph's right, it shouldn't be. He knows his name, he can see it, he just can't recall the actual words of his name. He tries his voice again. It sounds better this time. Still strange and distant, but definitely his voice, and the sounds come out in the right order. 'I . . . I'm not sure. I can't quite place my name.'

'That's good. You have no memory. That's going to come in handy over the next few minutes. Does the name "Morton" ring a bell?'

'Morton?'

'Dr Piers Morton?'

A face swims into Eddie's memory. That unnecessarily bald guy. 'Yes! Dr Morton? Is he here?'

This response seems to distress the nymph. 'We hope so, yes. He's you.'

Eddie mulls that one over. It doesn't sound right at all. Then a shard of memory slips painfully into place. He wasn't who he was supposed to be. Or, rather, he was someone other than he really was. Or something like that. But that other someone, the someone he was but really wasn't, that wasn't Dr Morton. How could it be? Dr *Morton* was Dr Morton.

Eddie's face must be contorted in confusion, because the nymph is watching him with concern. 'Is it coming back?'

'You mean is my being Dr Morton coming back? No. He's him. I'm not him. He is. I'm someone else completely.'

'All right, let's calm down. What *do* you remember?'

'I remember . . .' Eddie tries to make connections, but everything's jumbled up. He remembers a strange, small city. Fortune? Afortunado! He remembers something about a big broken window, which has inexplicably bad associations. And a casino. None of these seem to be nice memories. And then, a strange one this: staring out high over the planet Earth with the wind whistling through his hair. And there's a ship. 'The ship! I was on a spaceship!'

'Bingo.'

Eddie's getting excited now. 'A big ship. The *Wilddler* . . . ? The *Wilbur* . . . ? No! *Willflower*! It was called the *Willflower*.'

The nymph looks puzzled. 'It was?'

The satyr looks puzzled, too. 'The ship has a *name*? I mean, besides "the ship"?'

The nymph reaches over his head. Eddie tries to move his head to follow, but can't. She says: 'I'm going to purge your system.'

'Purge my system?' Whatever that means, it doesn't sound like the kind of thing a beautiful wood nymph ought to be doing in Eddie's own personal Paradise. He feels a sudden shocking coldness travel through his veins. His face shivers involuntarily.

'You've been under a fairly strong sedative. This should clear your head.'

'What is this place?' Wherever he is, Eddie is now aware it's not Paradise, which is more than a little depressing.

'The ship. You're still on the ship.'

'I'm on the ship?'

'The . . . *Willflower*? Yes.'

'But what about the unicorn?'

'Unicorn?' The nymph glances at the satyr, a leery, disturbed look, then back at Eddie. 'I didn't realize there was a unicorn here.'

'Over there.' Eddie's eyes flit left. The young unicorn is still watching them. 'By the crystal stream.'

'Ah! You're plugged into a virtual environment. It's standard procedure after . . .' She looks away. '. . . After what you've been through.'

What? What has Eddie been through? It can't be nice, what he's been through, if it requires strong sedation *and* a session outside of reality before he's deemed capable of facing it. His memory is returning now, drip by drip, but there's nothing he can recall that might warrant this kind of treatment. 'What happened to me?'

'Are you sure you're ready for this?'

'No. How could I know what it is I'm supposed to be ready for?'

'Good point. How can I put this without completely spoiling your day? Do you remember an accident?'

'An accident? No. What kind of accident?'

The satyr raises his eyebrows, really raises them. 'A *serious* accident.'

The nymph grabs the satyr roughly by his extremely muscular arm and marches him off with surprising strength. There must still be some of the sedative swirling around Eddie's system, because he finds the sight of the satyr being frogmarched by the wood nymph amusing, when he clearly should be worrying a lot. They whisper, these mystical forest dwellers, but they're not very good at it. Eddie can hear every word.

The nymph hisses: 'Mr Styx, will you let me handle this? Don't you have some steroids you need to inject?'

'Come on, Oslo – I think he's going to *notice* he was in a serious accident pretty soon. Round about the time he starts looking for his arms and legs.'

His arms and legs? Eddie looks down his body. Everything's there. Arms, legs, the full package. He flexes his fingers. Fine. Everything looks fine. What are they talking about? Arms and legs?

The whispering is almost inaudible now, but it sounds like the nymph is issuing un-nymphean threats and curses.

She looms back into his field of vision, the satyr looking, ego-bruisedly, over her shoulder. She tries a facial expression that doesn't look terribly well practised. Eddie supposes it's meant to reflect compassion, but it looks more like a reaction to acute dyspepsia. 'There was some kind of accident. We don't know the details. What we *do* know is you sustained . . . injuries.'

Too long a pause before the word 'injuries'. Eddie thinks he's suspecting the worst, but he's wrong. His suspicions are *way* short of the worst. 'What kind of injuries?'

'*Extensive* injuries.'

'*Extensive* injuries?'

The satyr smiles a stupid smile. '*Extensively* extensive.'

Without taking her eyes off Eddie, the nymph flexes her arm at the elbow, delivering a single, swift and extremely effective backwards punch over her shoulder, dropping the satyr instantly on the spot.

Eddie looks down at his body again. No question: it looks absolutely fine. Better than ever, in fact. Of course, he *is* in a virtual environment, and that might conceivably affect his perception of his own body. But everything *feels* fine. There doesn't seem to be any pain. 'How extensively extensive?'

The nymph tries to put on a good-news-nurse face. 'Well, on the up side, your head, heart and spinal column were undamaged.'

'And?'

A bad-news sigh. 'There is no "and".'

There *is* no 'and'?

'My head, my heart and my spine? That's all that's left of me?'

'That's all that's left of the *original* you. But think positive. Those are most of the important bits.'

Eddie can only repeat: 'My *head*, my *heart* and my *spine*?' as if he's been massively burgled, and he's trying not to think of all the things that are missing by listing the few paltry possessions he has left.

The nymph lowers her eyes. 'Actually, I'm feeling badly now.'

'*You're* feeling badly?'

'I wasn't one hundred per cent completely truthful with you.'

'About what?'

'About the extent of your injuries.'

The injuries are *worse* than she indicated? How can that be? 'How . . . how untruthful, exactly?'

'Exactly thirty-three and a third per cent untruthful. You don't have your heart, in fact.'

'Then . . . I just have my head and my spine? And that's all?'

'I was trying to soften the blow.'

'It didn't work.'

'If it's any consolation, you still have all your hair.'

'Great. I'd hate to feel I was suddenly unattractive.'

'I think you're probably in shock.'

'Why would I be in shock?'

'Shall I turn the sedative back on?'

Yes! Crank it up! Full on! Give him excess of it!

'No, no. I have to . . . I need a clear head. I mean, you weren't lying about that, I'm hoping. I do still have a head?'

'Of course you still have a head. Look, I should sedate you. I know this is a difficult thing to adjust to, and in a perfect world, we'd do it more slowly. But there isn't time. There just isn't . . .'

'How . . . how am I alive?'

'You were preserved, in some kind of suspension fluid. In a jar.'

'In a jar? Like a pickle?'

'I suppose it is a kind of pickling process. Listen, do you suppose you're ready for me to turn off the artificial environment yet? Only . . .'

The nymph is stretching her arm to reach some switch above his head. There are very few circumstances under which Eddie would not take advantage of the pose by indulging in some amateur nipple spotting. This is one of those very few circumstances.

'Wait a minute. *Preserved?* How long was I preserved?'

'We're not sure. Like everything else on this idiot ship, our dating procedure's kind of screwed up.'

'Approximately?'

'Approximately? I really don't know. A long time.'

'Define "long". Weeks? Months? Years?'

'Try centuries.'

18

Centuries?

Whether it's the artificial drugs still flowing through his, presumably extremely truncated, circulatory system, or natural narcotics produced by what's left of his brain to deal with shock, Eddie's mind finds the concept very hard to assimilate.

Centuries.

How is that possible? It's not possible. Centuries? That's many, many years. It's *hundreds* of years, in fact. Is that not a textbook definition of centuries? Hundreds of years. Tens of decades. Several lifetimes. How can that be? That security commander, Styx, he's still alive, isn't he? The satyr? He doesn't even look *slightly* older, never mind a few hundred years. And the nymph. Eddie knows her, too. She's mid-twenties, tops. This is just a mistake, somehow. Some big, stupid bureaucratic error, like all the big, monstrous, stupid bureaucratic errors that dog Eddie's life consistently, that stalk him with relentless dedication, like lunatic fans about to go over the brink. It will all be fine in the end. It will all sort itself out and end with sheepish apologies and offers of compensation. Surely.

But reality bites. The forest warps and collapses in on itself. The unicorn winks at him and is sucked off into oblivion. The birdsong deepens and becomes the steady background thrum of artificial lighting and a distant engine throb.

And Eddie is in the operating theatre. He can see the observation gallery overhead, through the diffused glare of the operating lights.

The nymph and the satyr are there, too. Only, they're no longer quite so mythical. They are in the vaguely familiar pilgrim uniform – no flimsy slips, no cloven hooves. Extremely human.

And oddly, very oddly, they are green.

Actually, everything is green.

And – Eddie can't quite put this into words – it's all . . . swirly, sort of. Swishy. Wavery, wibbly. Almost as if . . .

Almost as if . . .

As if Eddie is looking at the world through some thick, mucus-like green liquid.

A strangely calm shock wave washes over him as the realization comes.

This is because he is looking at the world through some thick, mucus-like green liquid.

He opens his mouth and wiggles his tongue through gloop. His entire head is encased, submerged in the glutinous green gloop.

Obviously, there is no point in screaming. Screaming is not a sensible option. It will achieve nothing, and it's not polite.

But Eddie screams anyway.

The scream doesn't emerge from his mouth, but from a speaker somewhere around the vee in his breastbone. Or, rather, from where the vee in his breastbone would be if he still had a breastbone.

The ex-nymph is craning over him, greenly. She nods and says, 'Let it out, Piers, let it all out.'

But Eddie can't let it all out. They'd all be here for the rest of their lives if he tried to let it all out. He'd need a bigger speaker, too. Several speakers. With woofers and tweeters and surround sound. He'd need a system that could handle a stadium rock concert.

So, no. Just the single, token scream, a pointless bout of breathless gagging as he tries to accommodate the filthy sensation of viscous liquid purling through his ears, his eyes, his nose, and that's it. Tantrum over.

Calm enough, now – not happy, but calm enough – Eddie asks, as nicely as he can, for someone to get him out of the gloop, and, not forgetting his manners, he adds the Magic Word.

The erstwhile nymph forces her features into the dismal facsimile of sympathy which Eddie is quickly learning to loathe and explains how that particular course of action is currently impossible, and that, furthermore, it is unlikely to be a feasible option in the foreseeable future.

Eddie's new electronic voice implores that, notwithstanding the foregoing, he would greatly appreciate having his head removed from the gloopy substance currently enveloping it, with some immediacy, and he punctuates the urgency of his point with a brisk sprinkling of sexual expletives.

The woman, whose utter paucity of wood nymph qualities is becoming more blatant by the moment, abandons her impoverished attempts at a bedside manner and erupts into a molten invective admonishing her patient's reaction. She urges him to grasp the inescapable realities he is now facing and deal with them in the shortest possible space of time.

This does the trick for Eddie. His head is in gloop. From now on, his entire head is going to be entirely submerged in green mucal gloop the entire time.

OK.

Green mucal gloop it is.

How bad is that?

It really isn't all that bad. There are probably millions of worse things for your head to be submerged in on a permanent basis. Diarrhoea, for instance. Diseased diarrhoea, even. Or chunky vomit. Radioactive waste. Sloppy, radioactive diarrhoea garnished with chunky, diseased dog vomit. Would you rather have your head dunked in that, Eddie? No sir.

'I'm sorry.' Eddie apologizes. He's apologizing for reacting angrily to the prospect of being perpetually submerged in snotty slime. This is the Eddie we know. He's well on his way to recovery.

The apology is so uncalled for, so pathetic, it even broaches the practically unassailably high embarrassment threshold of the non-nymph, and she looks away for an instant. When she looks back, her exasperation has dissipated, and her expression is as close to a representation of compassion as she could ever achieve without the use of prosthetics and very thick paint. 'You don't have to apologize. I'm well aware this is all . . .' she tries to find an appropriate word, but comes up short '. . . new to you. And like I said, in any other circumstances, you'd spend weeks in sedation, and we'd wean you off artificiality over several months, bit by bit. But we don't have that luxury. We don't *have* months. We probably don't have *weeks*. We need you, Dr Morton. We need you now. The existence of the entire colony is resting on your shoulders.'

She looks away again, because, of course, he has no shoulders and, as best he can, Eddie looks away too, embarrassed for her.

But this is something. Eddie is needed. For whatever reason, people are looking to him to save them. True, they're probably only looking to him because they think he's someone else, and undoubtedly he'll fall drastically short of expectations and let everyone down horribly, but for the moment he's untarnished. A hero, potentially. A saviour, even, in the making. An unaccustomed feeling.

'OK.' Eddie's rallying. 'My head's in gloop. So what?' No need to consider the wider implications of that, such as how he eats, or what process is substituted for breathing. That's not important now. 'The big question: can I move?' Even the electronic synthesis of his voice can't keep the quaver of fear out of that question.

'We think so.'

They think so? There's only a possibility he can move?

'Try raising your head.'

Eddie tries, and achieves a very small advance on the horizontal.

'I think you can do better.'

Eddie tries. It's hard. It's very, very hard. He suddenly realizes the benefits, hitherto obscure to him, of lifting weights with your head. He's trying to ignore the slurpy sound of the sticky liquid slapping around his ears. He knows he can only be imagining the queasy sensation in the stomach he no longer has.

He strains. He gets nowhere. He strains again.

And suddenly, it works. His neck pivots, and he's looking down the length of what better hadn't be his new body, but almost certainly is.

His heart can't be sinking. His guts can't be performing trapeze acts. They no longer exist.

The body he's looking down at is metallic. The torso comprises lateral, tubular hoops that form a kind of oval stretched sphere, so it bulges where the stomach would be. The limbs conform to the metallic tubular hoop motif, broken at the joints by what looks like concertina'd rubber.

It doesn't look much like a human's body. It looks like a giant ribbed egg with arms and legs. It looks like the body of Humpty fucking Dumpty.

'That's good,' the un-nymph is saying inappropriately. 'Your motor functions are hooking up nicely.'

Eddie hisses, 'What the hell is this below my neck?' but either he hasn't yet mastered the subtleties of his new vocal system, or it's incapable of such finesse, because his voice comes out the same as usual.

'It's your new body. We call it a "revival suit". Like it?'

'Like it?'

Obviously there's enough in the electronic interpretation of his inflection to convey Eddie's horror, because the ersatz dryad winces slightly and after much too short a pause offers the flimsy compliment: 'It's a very nice colour.'

'It's a nice colour?' Colour would not be very high on Eddie's list of desirable body characteristics right now, even if everything didn't look green to him, which it does, and always will. 'It's a nice *colour*?'

'It's a deep, shiny blue.'

'Oh, good. A deep, *shiny* blue. What a turn on. I'll be beating off naked supermodels with a large stick.'

The Styx lookalike who used to be a satyr is shaking his head, astonished. 'I don't think so, pilgrim. Women are going to look at you and *puke*, my friend.' The woman draws back her clenched fist, and Styx flinches. 'Don't hit me again, Oslo.'

She raises an eyebrow and takes a half step towards him.

He backs away, hands up for protection, and adds a pathetic 'Please?'

Eddie is still staring down at his body. It's not getting any more appealing. Instead of hands, he has large pincers. 'Look at me. I look like a giant beehive with limbs. I have *pincers* for hands. Pincers! This is the best you could do? This represents the pinnacle of centuries of scientific advancement by the finest minds the Earth had to offer? Pincers?'

'Hey, Doctor; I shouldn't have to tell you this, but that is an extremely sophisticated piece of technology you're residing in. Can you imagine the complexities involved in linking that up with all your tiny little nerve endings to detect minute impulses from your surviving synapses to give you some semblance of mobility? To give you back some kind of *life*? Do you have any idea how lucky you are?'

Lucky? Oh dear. She's saying he's lucky. This is going too, too far. This is pushing Eddie's biggest button. Lucky? Eddie?

'Lucky,' his speaker stutters, whatever now passes for his spleen swelling to venting point. 'You're saying I'm *lucky*? You're calling me "*lucky*"?'

'Yes, lucky. Certainly lucky. I don't want to get into the number of failed attempts we went through to reach this point, but there were a lot, mister. A lot. And if it weren't for the relentless dedication and perseverance of a whole bunch of well-intentioned pilgrims who were never trained in this field or anything close to it, you'd still be a head in a jar. I don't want to say the word "ungrateful" . . .'

'Ungrateful? Ooh, I'm not ungrateful. Thank you, thank you, thank you. I always *wanted* to look like a genetically mutated potato being digested by an anaconda. This is a dream come true for me. I can't imagine why you bothered bestowing this blessing on mine humble personage. Why didn't you just hook me up to a child's battery-operated racing car and jam the remote control between my teeth?'

'Would you like to go *back* in the jar? Is that what you want? Would you prefer to spend the rest of eternity looking like an inedible bar snack?'

Back in the jar. It's true. That's all he is now: an oversized pickled winkle. Eddie sighs, which comes out as a long electronic groan, and tries to rest his head back on the operating table, but it's too much effort. He's vented. 'You're right. You revived me. It's not your fault I look like a squashed Zeppelin. It's a shock, that's all. I mean, how would you . . . ? It's all happening so fast.'

'It's an understandable reaction. Wimpy, but understandable. Now, can you move anything besides your neck?'

'I can barely move that.'

'Well, you're restricted by the helmet. Try an extremity. Your left foot.'

Eddie stares at his left foot. It's a rectangular chunk of metal attached to the leg by an ankle of ribbed rubber. He tries to remember the procedure involved in moving a foot, but it seems to involve a complex interaction of contracting and expanding muscles up and down the entire leg. Muscles which are no longer there. 'This is useless. I can't even . . .'

'Try!'

He concentrates hard. He feels something. A twitch. But the foot doesn't move. He wills it to move. He feels the veins on his temple bulge. And he gets a reaction. He feels the movement strongly. But the foot hasn't budged. Odd. He's vaguely aware of a loud, unpleasant sound. Screaming.

He flicks his eyes towards the howling. The pincer of his right hand has grabbed hold of Styx's crotch and is squeezing remorselessly. 'My God! I . . .' Eddie panics. He tries to relax his right hand and feels his left knee jiggle. 'I'm sorry! I can't seem . . .'

'Stop the pain!' Styx is screaming. 'Stop the pain!'

Oslo is wrestling with the pincer. 'It's too strong!'

'Stop the pain! Sweet mother of mercy, make it *stop*!'

Eddie's trying to concentrate. Trying to get back in touch with the erroneous impulse and somehow reverse it. 'Just calm down, everyone. Just let me try and . . .'

'Kill him!' Styx is yelling. 'For the love of God! Kill the son of a bitch before he snaps them off!'

And with a mighty effort of will, Eddie does it. He wills his left foot to move in the opposite direction, and the pincers snap open. Styx crumples to the floor with a terrible groan, nursing his swollen testicles tenderly, as if they were brand-new baby twins.

He's out of Eddie's field of vision, moaning softly, and Eddie thinks it's probably best not to try a manoeuvre as complicated as sitting up just yet. 'Is he all right?'

'I don't think so.' Oslo's eyes flick down in Styx's direction. 'Are you all right, Mr Styx?'

'All right? Look at them! They're like overripe water melons. Kill the bastard. Kill him anyway.'

Oslo's eyes flick back. 'He'll be fine.'

'Really?'

'He'll be almost as good as new, once they stop actually glowing. Well, Dr Morton. Clearly we have one or two teething problems with your motor functions.'

'Well, yes, in that I've been wired up wrongly. In that my right hand thinks it's my left foot, for example. That would qualify as a teething problem.'

'Don't worry about it. You have to accept a small error margin. Those little nerve endings all look alike. You'll just have to re-learn how to use your body.'

'And how long is that supposed to take?'

'Well, best not to rush these things.' Oslo touches a control out of Eddie's vision, and the operating bench starts to tilt slowly forward on servos. 'So I'm going to give you a full hour.'

19

It's closer to two hours later by the time Eddie has mastered his new reflexes with sufficient dexterity not to be designated an actual Grade One death threat to any human within a thirty-metre radius, and emerges from the operating theatre.

He locomotes with all the confident conviction of a newborn fawn who has been passed through a coffee grinder and put back together again by a blind watchmaker with Parkinson's disease. His right leg is wired up almost correctly – the knee is really an elbow, though that's a very small gripe in the scheme of things – but the rest of him . . .

Those little nerve endings all look alike.

It's like trying to walk backwards on his fingers with his head jammed up his backside.

He has to concentrate on the tiniest detail of every movement, and the irritable Ms Oslo is not large on patience, urging him to speed up when he demonstrates the slightest hesitation.

So he's travelled some considerable way before he actually notices his surroundings.

As far as he can tell, everything looks the same. Green, naturally, but apart from that the same. Same corridors. Same doors. Same overhead lights. He's not sure what he was expecting. Some kind of change. Decorative style, maybe. New designs. Overt evidence of massive technological advancement. Moving walkways, perhaps. Force fields instead of doors. But no. The interior looks exactly as it did the last time he saw it.

Can it be true, then, he's been away for centuries?

As he approaches a bend in the corridor, Styx comes around it, heading towards them. This is puzzling, since he has only just left the man in the medical section recovery room, sedated but whimpering, with coconut-sized ice bandages on his swollen love gourds. Yet here he is, hale and hearty, swinging free, without a mince in his step.

Eddie calls out, confused, 'Styx?' and the man stops to look at him, scanning his metal body in growing bafflement.

'What the hell are *you*, pilgrim?'

'Styx? It's me. Remember?'

'No. But I will remember you from now on, friend. You are somebody's idea of a nightmare. What are you *for*? Frightening children?'

'How are your testicles? Are they all right now?'

'My . . . testicles?' Styx lowers his eyeline towards his groin, then slowly raises it back to Eddie. He looks as if he can't decide whether to be angry or afraid, or something else entirely. He also looks as if the decision might well take up the rest of the day. Eddie notices through his green viscous haze that Styx has a large tattoo or burn in the centre of his forehead. The letter B.

Oslo's exasperation breaks the deadlock. 'Mr Styx, carry on.' But it takes two attempts to snap Styx out of his gawk. 'Mr Styx!'

'Ma'am! Yes, Ma'am!' And with a final disgusted head shake, he marches off.

Eddie watches him go. 'I don't . . .'

'They're drones.'

'Drones?'

'Drones. They're literally grown fully mature . . .'

'I know the theory. But droning was abandoned as an unsound procedure a long time ago. There was no way to prevent intellectual deterioration with every batch. How did you get round the fundamental flaws?'

Oslo turns in Styx's direction and, with a concerted effort, Eddie turns and watches, too.

Styx is standing at a door marked 'Pull'. He is pushing against it, straining violently. When it positively refuses to budge, he takes several steps back and hurls himself against it, grunting with pain on the unyielding impact. Dazed, he gets to his feet, steps back and hurls himself forward again with renewed vigour.

Oslo spins around and walks off. 'We didn't.'

Eddie watches Styx's vain yet unrelenting struggle against the uncompromising door with growing admiration. Clearly, the man has no notion of surrender. True, he also clearly has no space in his mental armoury for lateral thought or reason. Still, his relentless persistence is admirable in its way.

Oslo barks, 'Dr Morton!' with even more impatience than is her norm. Eddie turns. She has dug out some kind of hydraulic forklift trolley. 'I've had enough. Get on the trolley.'

Eddie shuffles up to the forklift. 'Shouldn't we help him?' He's beginning to grow alarmed at Styx's untempered tenacity, which is clearly starting to result in physical damage.

'Help him open a *door*?'

'He's bleeding, Oslo.' Eddie manoeuvres himself gingerly on to the blades of the forklift.

'So? Let him bleed. It's his blood.'

'He's not just bleeding slightly. Blood is pumping out of his nose and ears. Copiously.'

'He's a *drone*, Morton. If he gets broke, we'll grow another one.' And this callous dismissal being Oslo's last word on the subject, she engages the trolley's motor and steers Eddie off at an alarming speed.

More in pique, in frustration at Oslo's cold-bloodedness, than in a genuine attempt to straighten the record, Eddie shouts over the scream of the forklift's motor, 'And my name's not Morton!'

Oslo cuts the truck's power instantly, without warning. Eddie has to grab on with his pincers to stop himself hurtling down the corridor. Even so, he sways precariously on the forks. He doesn't know how strong his helmet's faceplate is, or what would happen if it were to smash and release his green gloop all over the floor, but he certainly doesn't feel ready to try it out. He notices his right pincer is bending the strut it's holding and, with a great effort of will, he relaxes the pressure on it.

Oslo strides round to face him, her features set in war mode. '*What*?'

'I've told you already. My name's not Morton. And I'm not a doctor.'

'Well, who the hell are you, then?'

Ah. The tricky ones first, eh?

Who is he, in fact? He's not who he's supposed to be, twice removed. He's supposed to be Charles Perry Gordon, who's been mistaken for Dr Morton, but he isn't. He's Eddie O'Hare, posing as Charles Perry Gordon, who's somehow become confused with Dr Piers Morton.

The question is: which persona can Eddie viably sustain?

He's in a vulnerable position now, ever so slightly. Most of his working parts are ship issue. He's dependent on the continued good will of whoever's in charge here for his very existence. Not something to make a mistake about, for sure.

So Eddie does what Eddie does best.

Eddie dithers.

'Actually, I'm not completely sure who I absolutely am, I'm just fairly confident that I'm not, in fact, Dr Morton.' And because this sounds as hopeless as it dismally is, Eddie adds the even more hopelessly dismal: '. . . Probably.' And because Oslo leaves too long and uncomfortable a pause before responding, he makes it worse by tacking on the barely muttered meaningless: '. . . In many ways.'

Oslo waits until Eddie's clearly petered out, then places her palms either side of his helmet, as if she's squeezing his cheeks. 'All right, Dr *Morton*. I want you to listen to me, because this is very important. This is life-or-death important. I'm taking you to meet a man. He's our psychiatric counsellor. And his opinion is important. This man is going to have to pass you as fit for duty before we can use you, *Dr* Morton. So you're going to have to try and act sane, OK? And if you start saying you're someone else, especially someone else who isn't absolutely sure who he absolutely is, I don't think that will go down as an acceptable sanity level, even for this mission.' And she concludes the diatribe with a short slap of increasing force on the side of Eddie's helmet to punctuate each word: 'Are you with me, *Dr Morton*?'

The final slap results in considerable and disorienting slopping around Eddie's head space.

By the time he's asserted, 'All the way, Oslo,' the forklift's in motion again, and they're heading for the passenger transway.

Their destination clearly lies far away. That, or the transway system is functioning at a massively reduced efficiency. Or a third alternative: Oslo's intolerant, condemning silence makes the journey seem intolerably long.

Whatever the reason, he suddenly finds he has time to reflect, and this is probably not a good thing.

A lot of terrible things have befallen Eddie over the past couple of hours. Or, rather, he's become aware that a lot of terrible things have befallen him. Losing most of his body, for instance, including such old favourites as his heart, his lungs and his penis. Being ineptly wired up to an unremittingly ugly metal replacement body which would make his own mother run away from him screaming. Losing everything he ever had, not to mention everyone he ever knew, and suddenly finding himself several centuries away from his own lifetime. But of all the tragedies, ills and discomforts, the one that distresses him most is the green gloop. Not the gloop itself: he's resigned to a life submerged in mucoid slime. It's the relentless greenness of it. He finds himself wishing, more than anything, that it wasn't green. He finds himself longing for some technological miracle that might allow the green gloop to be substituted by, say, blue gloop. Or – dare he even dream? – by clear, transparent gloop.

It's strange that this small depressive hankering occupies his thoughts. There are many more important concerns that might engage him more urgently. Perhaps this ludicrous fixation with the particular tint of his new, monochrome world is Eddie's way of not addressing more pressing matters.

Such as how he came to be in this condition.

And more pressing still: who or what brought him to it.

Yet it's the monomaniacal obsession with an alternatively pigmented gloop that stays with him until Oslo speaks again. Out of the carriage, now. Standing at a door. A barked order: 'Off the trolley.'

Eddie concentrates on the pincers, releasing his grip gently, and steps down off the forks with comparative grace of movement. He hardly totters at all.

Oslo grabs his helmet again, twists it to face her and snarls a whispered question: 'One last time. Who are you?'

Eddie doesn't think his helmet is meant to twist over quite so far, and he's fighting a nightmare image of his gloop slowly oozing out of a crack in the neck joint, leaving him gagging like a landed blubbery fish. 'I'm Dr Piers Morton,'

Oslo almost smiles. 'And very pleased I am to meet you.'

She places her palm on the door pad and steps into the room. Eddie gives up trying to check if there's a breach in his helmet and follows her with his best attempt at a confident stride.

Not too bad an effort, either: he almost completely misses the doorframe.

A man, presumably the very man Eddie has to impress with his Dr Mortonism, is seated at a desk, his concentration somewhere below table level. He's obviously aware of their arrival, but he seems much more interested in his under-desk activity.

Even though Oslo knows he knows she's here, and knows he knows she knows it, she announces her presence with: 'Padre?'

Without looking up, the Padre holds up the forefinger of one hand. Oslo tries not to snort in exasperation, but falls short of her ambition.

The Padre speaks under the table: 'Almost . . . nearly . . . yes . . . go on, go on . . . you can . . . Yes! Oh yes! Magnificent! Bless you.' He sighs contentedly and looks up, wearing a beatific smile.

The thing where Eddie's heart would be experiences a powerful surge. He recognizes the man. Father Lewis. A friendly face. Someone Eddie actually *likes*. The sensation fades somewhat as Eddie's memory kicks in, and he recalls that the good Father doesn't care much for *him* – thinks, in fact, that he is some kind of *Übermensch*-nonsense-spouting ultra right-wing fascist nazi heartless scumbucket. It fades completely when logic kicks in, and Eddie realizes, given that centuries have passed, this can't be the same man, and on closer study, even through the green fug, his features, while similar, are subtly tweaked.

This man is a distant descendant of Father Lewis. Eddie was a contemporary of this man's ancestors. Eddie finds this thought disturbing. Time really has marched on. And on. He, himself, is a not very well-preserved antique.

'Bernadette.' The Padre pushes his chair back from the desk and smiles at Oslo. 'You have our revivee, eh?'

'That's right. Father Lewis, meet Dr Morton.' She turns to Eddie and adds through the gritted teeth of a Barbie smile: 'Dr Piers Morton.'

The Padre crosses in front of his desk and proffers his hand.

There is a small pause, like the distance between drips from a barely leaking tap in the dark hours of the morning, as both the priest and Eddie look down at Eddie's wretched pincers. But Father Lewis breaks the embarrassment by grabbing a pincer anyway, and shaking it warmly.

'And how are you coming along, Piers?'

With blatantly uncharacteristic enthusiasm, Oslo jabbers: 'He's fine. He's dandy. Way in excess of our most optimistic projections. He's totally accepted the situation, he's happy, and he's raring to go, aren't you? Doctor?'

'He can speak, I take it?'

'He can speak, he can move, he remembers his name – everything. Can we go now?'

'Well, call me a stickler and nail my gonads to a griddle, Bernadette, but I'd like to hear it from the patient himself.' Lewis leans into Eddie's space and smiles with practised compassion. 'How are you feeling, Dr Morton?'

There's something about the earnest quality of the priest's expression that makes Eddie want to tell the truth. Something irresistible.

He tries to toe Oslo's line. He starts with upbeat enthusiasm.

'I'm feeling absolutely . . .' But he can't meet the priest's searching stare. He casts his eyes and his voice downwards. 'Not good, Father.'

Oslo turns away and kicks something.

The priest tilts his head sympathetically. 'In what way "Not good", Dr Morton? "Not good" how?'

'Well . . .' Eddie sucks in some gloop. 'For a start, I don't think I *am* Dr Morton.'

He hears Oslo's exasperated hiss, and the plaintive whine: 'Didn't I *beg* you not to mention that?'

Eddie looks up. He thinks, only thinks, he sees the priest's smile falter a tad. If so, it recovers quickly, and his voice still croons with the same understanding tenor: 'All right. If you're not Dr Morton, then who are you?'

'I'm . . .' Who? Who is he? Eddie O'Hare, talentless stowaway first class? Get back in the pickle jar, loser. 'I'm . . .' Who, then? Charles Perry Gordon, useless asshole, first class? Oh yes, they're probably in desperate need of *his* particular *Achtung* madness. Who then? Who? 'I'm . . . It's complicated.'

The priest's eyes flick over at Oslo then back at Eddie. 'It's complicated? How complicated can "who are you?" be, eh?'

Eddie wishes he'd fought the stupid urge to tell the truth. His amassed experience indicates irrefutably that telling the truth always causes problems. Always. For Eddie, it's truth that weaves a tangled web. 'Look, I'm . . . it's been a tough few hours. I need some space.'

'There's no time for that whimpering wet nonsense!' Oslo thumps something with considerable venom. 'You have to snap out of . . . whatever you're in!'

The priest holds up a placatory hand. 'Bernie, Bernie, Bernie. Try a little projection here. The poor man just arose from a chemically induced long-term coma lasting several lifetimes to find he has fewer body parts left than a gutted mollusc. I think we can expect him to be experiencing some small confusion. Don't you?'

'On the other hand, we have to entertain the increasingly likely probability that his brain is terminally pickled, and perhaps we might get more *sense* out of a gutted mollusc.'

Father Lewis leans his rear on his desk and folds his arms. 'Well, before we resort to that, slightly . . . defeatist diagnosis, I think we might try a little spiritual and philosophical guidance, eh?'

'Spiritual and philosophical guidance? From a man who installs spy cameras to watch women undress?' Oslo tips a knowing nod towards the monitor concealed under the desk.

The priest's tranquil smile doesn't waver. 'There are souls that need saving everywhere, Bernadette.' He rises and ushers them towards the door. 'Even in the ladies' shower room.'

20

Eddie doesn't know where they're heading, and he has to focus hard on every minute detail of each movement he makes. None the less, he finds some mental space to contemplate his companions. The priest is cooing predictable psychological platitudes, how Eddie shouldn't expect too much too soon, how the paths of his memory will realign themselves when they're ready, how movement will become second nature to him: nothing that demands too much attention or response, save the odd grunt and the occasional, though brutally difficult, nod.

He shares the curious accent of Bernadette Oslo; strangely elongated vowels and sharp, distinct Ts and K sounds that produce a staccato quality in mos-tuh sen-tuh-ences – Eddie imagines the accent has evolved ship-wide. Eddie, being the chameleonic character he is, will no doubt be lapsing into it himself in short order, electronic larynx permitting.

There is a slightly disturbing facial similarity between Oslo and Lewis. Mostly around the nose and the high cheekbones. Odd, since the long-gone Mr Gordon's Mengelesian genetic diversification programme was designed to avoid such by-products of inbreeding. Then again, the programme was only intended to be effective over three generations; five at the very worst. It's probably inevitable that certain dominant characteristics will eventually prevail over the course of – what? – at least ten generations.

Thankfully there is no sign, in these two at least, of congenital stupidity. They both seem bright and motivated. And while there may be a question mark over the Padre's morality – surely Oslo was joking about the hidden cameras? – he has confidence and a quick mind.

Why, then, is there still no evidence of technological progress?

Any human who had slept for a hundred years or more since the sixteenth century would have awoken to an inexplicable new world. Here, they haven't even changed the direction signs.

And this observation triggers another. Many of the official signs in evidence carry a logo with the ship's name on it. Now, Eddie was seriously drugged up, in an artificial reality, but didn't the nymph and the satyr display surprise at the appellation *Willflower*?

Oslo and Father Lewis have stopped, and Lewis is looking querulously at Eddie, as if expecting a response. Eddie tries an ambiguous grunt. 'Unguh?'

Lewis sighs and repeats himself. 'I was saying that this may be a disturbing experience for you, but I think you should face up to it. This is the room in which you've spent your missing decades. I think it might be easier for you to accept your . . . status if you see it for yourself, first hand. Are you ready?'

Eddie looks at the sign over the door. SUSPENDED PERSONNEL STORAGE. Marvellous. Could it be more cold, clinical or impersonal? He thinks about nodding, then thinks again. 'I'm ready., Padre.'

Lewis swipes his palm over the door sensor, and steps into the darkened room.

As Eddie's eyes adjust, he perceives a strange, unreal light pervading the room. To Eddie, it looks a deep green, naturally, but it's probably blue.

Somebody flicks a switch, and a bright underlight picks out a glowing rank of large glass jars; cylindrical tubes rounding off at the top. Two dozen at first glance. There may be other ranks on other walls.

The jars are filled with a coloured liquid – this time almost certainly green.

And there are heads in the jars.

Human heads.

This is not a room you'd want to visit before a big dinner. Or just before bedtime. Or, bluntly, ever.

The heads are floating in the liquid, each attached to a crooked spine tapering towards the base of the jar.

There's something about the faces . . . the expressions. They don't look as Eddie imagined, like medical specimens or cadavers. They look somehow realer, less waxworky. They look alive. And they're all wearing the same expression. Where has he seen that look before? That unhappy smile? Somewhere . . .

And the image flashes into his brain. A man hurtling towards the street from a great height. Harry? No. Harrison. Harrison Dopple. The expression: grinning surprise.

They all look surprised. Smiling agog, in the green mucal glow.

Lewis is speaking. 'This was you.'

Glad for the distraction, Eddie shuffles over.

Lewis is pointing out an empty jar. Several jars around it are empty. He's saying: 'See?'

The empty jar he's indicating is, in fact, labelled 'Dr Piers Morton.' As if this weren't evidence aplenty, Lewis passes his hand over the smart label, and a computerized voice confirms: 'Dr Piers Morton', and starts to list his qualifications and credits.

Eddie scans the other empty jars around it. Most of them are doctors. There are even a few other Dr Mortons, with different Christian names. He wants to ask what happened to them, but he suspects very strongly that he already knows. That they were all failed attempts at resuscitation, potential occupants of Eddie's own ugly body suit who didn't make it.

Which would explain why Oslo called him 'lucky'.

And then he spots another jar, an occupied jar, tucked behind his former abode. It's labelled 'Community Planner Charles Perry Gordon'. And the head inside is afflicted with a familiar patch of unnecessary male pattern baldness. It's the real Dr Morton.

Eddie should keep this to himself, but sedatives are still swilling around his brain, and he's excited by this recognition, by his first encounter with concrete evidence of his past existence. 'There! That's me!'

He tries to point at the jar, but he's following his natural instincts and, instead of raising his arm, his brain sends out signals that make his left knee shoot up in the air, and his right foot twist almost ninety degrees. And this ungainly combination of movements starts his entire body teetering towards the jars.

He struggles with his balance, trying to tilt this or that bit of him in the opposite direction, away from the unthinkable, the unspeakable collision, but it's much too little, much too late, and with a horrible inevitability he slowly lists forward past the point of no return and lurches into the helpless heads in the vessels.

When he opens his eyes, the remains of several jar-bound former crew members are scudding across the floor, still wearing their, now wholly appropriate, expressions of shock.

Mercifully, the containers are sturdy enough to survive the fall.

'I'm sorry.' Eddie calms himself and struggles to his feet. 'I'm sorry. I got excited. There.' He points, clumsily, but much less destructively. 'That's me. There.'

Oslo and Lewis both bend forward and peer at the jar, but seem to fail to achieve enlightenment.

'Community Planner Gordon. That's it. That's my jar.'

Without straightening, Oslo twists her head towards him. 'You're really not adjusting fantastically well, are you?' She points a schoolmarmly finger at the empty jar. 'This is you . . .' With the same, slow, exaggerated gesture she points at the jar with Gordon's name on it. '*This* has someone's *head* in it. See the difference? Head . . . no head? Empty . . . full? You . . . Gordon?'

'I'm telling you, that's my name! They labelled the jars wrong.'

Lewis closes his eyes very tightly. 'They labelled the jars wrong?'

Oslo asserts, 'That's not possible,' but she sounds unconvincingly unconvinced.

Lewis opens his eyes. 'Not possible? Bernadette, given that the average crew member on this mission would have to cram intensely for several centuries to qualify for the mental categorization "Dickhead", I find it hard to discount Piers' theory.'

'"Charles",' Eddie corrects him unhelpfully. 'I'm telling you my name is actually Charles.'

Oslo grabs him either side of his helmet in that way she has. Some part of Eddie that can't possibly exist any more is beginning to find it pleasant. 'Look, try and get this through your gloop: if you are not Dr Piers Morton, it's back in the jar, OK?'

Back in the jar? Eddie looks at the rank of gawking, grinning heads. 'You wouldn't do that. That would be murder.' Wouldn't it? Can you technically murder a head and a spine? '. . . Or something.'

'We don't need a frotting Community Planner,' and in her mouth, the job title sounds even more like an expletive than it always did in Eddie's mind. 'We need a doctor. We need Dr Morton. There are people, lots of people, who don't even want *him*. People who think bringing any of you back is wrong. Now, think very hard. Think very hard indeed. Are you Dr Morton, or are you about to rejoin the ranks of pickledom?'

Eddie's mouth can't be dry. It's just feeling that way. He's let himself get carried away again, and done the truth thing. The truth is unlikely to be your best weapon, when you're an accountant in a world without money, who's posing as a Social Engineer, when your survival depends on being a doctor.

The Padre sighs with an awful final-sounding cadence. 'I think we're all aware you're clutching at straws, Bernadette. Our friend here is not the good doctor. It could hardly be clearer. It's a disappointment, I know. It may even prove to be terminally disappointing for all of us. Still, no point in whipping an equine cadaver. Our first priority is to do the right thing by . . . you say your name's Charles? . . . do the right thing by Charles here, eh? Somehow we're going to have to try and lever him out of that suit without ripping away all his sensitive nerve endings or snapping his brittle, fragile spinal column.'

Suddenly the prospect of spending the rest of his life in a blue metal Humpty Dumpty suit sucking green gloop through his nostrils doesn't seem like too bad an option to Eddie. 'Wait – it's all coming back – medical school . . . dating nurses . . . playing amusing practical jokes with human cadavers. Yes – I *am* Dr Morton! Must have been the blow to my head – or, rather, the blow to the entire rest of me, that had me confused for a few moments there.'

Lewis smiles with reptile politeness. 'I'm sorry, Charles . . .'

'Piers! My name's Piers! Get me a stethoscope! Give me ten ccs of anbulistic adrenaline! Where's the crash cart!? Let's *move*, people!'

Before Eddie runs out of badly memorized television hospital clichés, Oslo steps in. 'Father Lewis, let's be brutal: Piers, or Charles, or whoever the frot this is, actually *survived* the operation to wire him into the suit. What are the realistic odds of us pulling off that little miracle again?'

'In the low zeros, I would say.'

'He's what? Our fifteenth attempt?'

'Seventeenth. Twenty-first if you count the experimental monkey failures.'

'I say this man's Dr Morton.'

'I am! I am!'

Lewis shakes his head. 'I understand your frustration, Bernadette. Certainly we're in a desperate situation, and any kind of help couldn't hurt, but . . .'

'I can help. I'm sure I can be of major help. Just tell me what the problem is.'

Lewis smiles a tight, last-rites smile. 'I'm truly sorry, Charles. We've hit a crisis. At this point in the mission we need someone with certain arcane skills we no longer possess.'

'Medical skills?'

'Much more arcane than that. We need a person who can interpret the hieroglyphic scrawls the Originals used to record data.'

'Hieroglyphic scrawls?' Eddie tries not to look at the jars again. What hieroglyphic scrawls? 'Why would a doctor be able to interpret hieroglyphics?'

Oslo and Lewis look worried now. The priest replies, 'We were hopeful that an antiquated medical training programme would have included schooling in that obsolete mystery.'

Latin, are they talking about? Or ancient Greek? Could Eddie's existence actually be hanging on those dead Mediterranean languages he despised so?

'Can I see them? Do you have an example of these hieroglyphics?'

'Well . . . yes.' Lewis sweeps his arm towards a door. 'They're everywhere.'

Eddie looks at the door. It's a commonplace fire exit. But there are no strange symbols on it, or anywhere around it. Slowly, it dawns on him that Lewis is pointing out nothing more arcane or mysterious than the sign on the door itself. The eight large letters spelling out 'Fire Exit'.

Somehow, somewhere along the generations, the crew of the *Willflower* has lost the ability to read.

21

'You are talking about the sign on the door, yes?'

Lewis nods.

'The sign that says: "Fire Exit"?'

Lewis and Oslo look at each other sideways. 'Are you telling me,' Lewis takes a step towards him, 'that you can interpret those symbols?'

'Yes.'

'He's lying.' Oslo intrudes coldly, but there's a hint in her voice that she wants to be disproved. 'Naturally, he's lying. He doesn't want to go back in the jar.'

'Of course I don't want to . . .' Eddie can't even bring himself to say it. 'Of course I want to *live*. But I'm not lying. I can read.' Eddie looks around the room frantically. 'See, over there, the sign over the speaker? It says: "Ship Com". And there, over that keypad: "Temperature Override".' But Lewis and Oslo seem unswayed. This is insane. How do you prove you can read to a pair of illiterates?

Lewis gets an idea. 'All right.' He turns and picks out one of the jars. 'Who's this?'

Eddie reads the label.

Lewis passes his palm over it, and the computer confirms Eddie's interpretation.

Oslo is hard to convince. Perhaps Eddie knew the jar's incumbent, or the head bears a familial resemblance to someone Eddie did know. She makes them repeat the procedure a dozen times, until even Lewis is way beyond satisfied.

'That's enough, Bernadette. He can do it.'

'So do I get to live, or what? No rush. I'd just like to know what to pack for the next fifty years. Will I need socks, or not?'

Lewis responds with a less than heart-warming: 'For now. We'll keep you in the suit for now.'

Oslo asks: 'Do you think we should still try to pass him off as Dr Morton?'

Lewis nods. 'I think that it might be easier to sell Dr Morton to the, uhm, dissident faction than Charles whatever-he-was, Head of Ice Cream.'

Eddie's about to protest that Community Planner was in fact an important, nay vital assignment, but catches himself in time. The planning behind this mission doesn't appear to have yielded tremendously outstanding results. He really doesn't want to claim undue credit for it.

Oslo looks at him with testing eyes. 'Are you up for this? Even if you were the real Dr Morton, this wouldn't be an easy ride.'

'I *am* the real Dr Morton.'

Oslo nearly smiles. 'He certainly has a Mortonesque look to him.'

'I am *so* Dr Morton. I am brimming over with Dr Morton-ness.'

'Well then,' Lewis slaps him on his metal shoulder, 'welcome aboard, Dr Morton. I'll call a planning meeting right away. It's time you met the rest of the Pilgrim Parents. Bernadette, can you get him up to Planning Committee Room One without demolishing any decks?' Oslo nods. 'I'll pave the way, Piers. Talk you up, eh? I'll meet you there in fifteen.'

Lewis leaves.

Oslo is looking at Eddie quizzically.

Eddie says: 'What?'

'I don't get you, mister. You come over . . . well, you seem so . . . stupid, I suppose.'

'Thanks.'

'And yet you can decipher the hieroglyphics. Where did you acquire that skill?'

Tricky ground, this. It's in Eddie's interest to build up his rarity value. If they find out almost every one of the heads can almost certainly read, and can probably read several languages more than

Eddie, doubtless many times more quickly, he won't appear such a prize. And though Eddie is probably the worst liar in the known universe, bluntly, he needs all the help he can get.

He tries to shrug, but the movement is too subtle for the suit, and he just ends up flapping his arms. 'My degree was in Reading. I got a double first at Oxford. Reading and Writing. With honours.'

'Writing?'

'Oh yes. Don't like to brag, but I can actually *make* those squiggly hieroglyphics, too.'

Oslo seems unimpressed. Very unimpressed. She looks at him as though he's something vile she's pulled out of her nose that shouldn't be there. Something with an exoskeleton and wriggling legs. And with a world-class sneer, she floors him with: 'Well, what the frot use will that be?'

And she's right, Eddie supposes. He may well be the only living creature within hundreds of light years who could read what he writes.

Oslo gives up waiting for Eddie to reply, turns and heads for the door.

Eddie starts to follow her, but one of the names on an empty jar catches his eye. A name with something familiar about it. Familiar, but not good. Paulo San Pablos. He scans his ragged memory, but nothing comes. He needs more of a hint. He would recognize the name if he dug out the storage box that contains its personal belongings.

Or, rather, he'd recognize the socks.

22

Again, the transway journey seems to take an inexplicably long time.

Of course, Ms Oslo is not a fanatical devotee of small talk, and Eddie's questions about the make-up of the Planning Committee, its individual members and its *factions* – which sounded worrying to Eddie – are met with dismissive grunts and shrugs and 'You'll see soon enough's, which doesn't exactly make the time fly by. Still, the trip seems to take at least twice as long as it ought to.

Eddie's mental map of the ship's topography was always less than perfect, but he tries tracking the carriage's progress anyway. As far as he can tell, it's taking an extraordinarily circuitous route; zig-zagging, doubling back on itself. Quite unnecessary. Unless the ship's layout has changed dramatically.

But why would anyone change the ship's layout, and not change the path of the main transport through it?

He's about to ask Oslo if she's aware of any internal structural changes, when the carriage crashes, which, frankly, makes him lose his train of thought.

There is a terrible lurching crunch, an agonized groaning of twisting metal, and as the lights go out, Eddie just catches enough of a glimpse to see Oslo grabbing on to a safety harness and bracing her leg against a seat back, before he's sent hurtling the entire length of the carriage. Eddie himself can't brace. He's incapable, even, of making his body perform the necessary reactions in time to shield himself against an impact. The impact comes, though, and it comes hard, metal against unyielding metal, and he bounces off the far end of the carriage with enough impetus to send him smashing through several seats. All the time, he's thinking about his gloop, about keeping his helmet intact, about keeping the slime inside, even though he has no idea what would happen if it did leak out.

He stops with a final crunching sound, praying it's some interior fixture or fitting that's doing the crunching, and not some part of him he can't feel, and, please Lord, not his helmet, or the seal of his helmet, or the safety visor.

The silence is sudden and stunning.

There's another terrible creak of warping metal.

And more silence.

And he hears Oslo: 'Are you all right?'

Eddie thinks so. 'I think so.' Is she all right? 'You?'

'Fine. Just hang on. It'll be OK.'

OK? A high-speed transport just got hit by something inside the ship. The transport is *inside* the ship. Protected by dozens of layers of impervious hull. What could cause such an accident? Something bad, that's for sure. Something big and bad. Nothing that could fall into the category 'All right', or anywhere in the close vicinity.

'What happened?'

'Don't worry. It happens a lot.'

'It happens a *lot*?'

'It'll be fine. We'll be back on line in a minute.'

And, on cue, the emergency lights flicker on. Eddie is lying amid a mess of crushed metal and ripped fabric. He looks around for some kind of reflective surface, and suddenly realizes that he hasn't seen himself, yet, in a mirror, which seems a strange omission. He doesn't know what his helmet looks like from the outside. He can't even feel its shape with his dead pincers. Perhaps he's been avoiding this confrontation with his physical form. Perhaps it's some kind of denial. He drags himself erect.

The carriage is tilted about twenty degrees off the horizontal. Oslo is still in her braced position, so Eddie decides bracing is probably a wise thing to do. He finds a seat back he hasn't yet destroyed and gently locks his pincers on to the metal bar at the top of it. He calls: 'Can you see my helmet?'

'Can I *what?*'

'Is my helmet all right?'

'Your helmet?'

'Is it all right?'

'Your helmet is on your head.'

'Is it intact, though?'

'Intact?'

'It's not cracked or anything? My gloop isn't leaking out? I still have all my gloop?'

'The helmet's fine. But I've got to say: I'm extremely worried about the head inside it.'

Eddie wonders about trying to rub one of his pincers over his visor, to see if it comes away dry, but decides against it. He's not prepared to risk misjudging the amount of strength required for the manoeuvre and wind up puncturing the helmet with his own clumsy claw.

His grip on life seems so fragile now; so dependent on his borrowed metal body, on the despised yet precious gloop.

There is another massive creaking of metal, and the carriage lurches again.

It appears to be intact and horizontal. The lights flicker back on. There is a whine as the transway motor builds up again, and suddenly they're in motion.

Eddie doesn't want to be in motion. He wants to get out of the carriage immediately. He releases his grip on the seat back and starts to lurch towards the emergency stop.

'What are you doing?'

'I'm going to stop the damned carriage.'

'What for?'

'What for? We've just been in an accident that makes the *Hindenburg* crash look like a bumper-car prang. You think this thing is safe?'

'It'll get us there.'

'How can you know that?'

'I told you: it happens a lot.'

'Which is a superb reason for getting the hell out of here.'

'It's not just the transway. It's the whole ship. It happens all over the place.'

'It happens all over the ship? Well, let me tell you, Bernadette, it's not *supposed* to happen all over the ship. It's not supposed to happen at all.'

'We know that. I told you we had problems.'

'But why? What is it? What's causing it?'

'We think it's structural damage, caused by the accident.'

Accident? 'There was an accident?'

'Ooh, was there ever an accident.'

23

Eddie has only one major connection point in his entire remaining body: the joint of his head and spine. His neck. And it's in agony. The transway carriage crash resulted in bestowing upon him the only injury he could possibly sustain: whiplash.

The pain, combined with Oslo's pig-headed refusal to elucidate further on the nature of the 'accident', delivers Eddie to Planning Committee Room One in a filthy mood. So he is unprepared for the emotional punch just the sight of the room packs for him.

Planning Committee Room One.

Meeting place of the Pilgrim Parents.

This is really his first encounter with his previous life. The room is apparently unchanged by the passage of time. The polished wooden table, the leather-backed chairs, everything looks as if it's just been unpacked from a delivery truck. There are the same yellow pads in every place, the same fresh, sharpened pencils. Why? Some observance of obsolete ritual, Eddie supposes. The ability to make meaningful marks on the pads with the pencils must have vanished a long time ago. A culture doesn't just lose the capacity to read and write overnight.

Father Lewis is rising to meet him.

Eddie looks around the table. Only a handful of people make up the committee, where there used to be dozens. Perhaps this is just an emergency gathering. Perhaps the rest of the Section Leaders are busy elsewhere, attempting to repair the damage from the accident.

The other alternative is surely unthinkable. That these people are the only senior personnel left alive.

Father Lewis is introducing him. It's a very big build-up. Eddie wishes he'd tone it down a tad. He would have to possess the mind of Albert Einstein, the voice of Frank Sinatra and the dancing ability of Dame Margot Fonteyn to live up to the hype.

Lewis then starts introducing him to the Parents. First, a woman. Eddie gets that twinge of recognition again. A stern-looking woman whose face is strangely exciting to him. But the recollection doesn't gel until Lewis gives her name.

'And this is our Science Section Leader, Trinity Peck . . .'

And the rest of the introduction is submerged beneath Eddie's erotic bath mental movie, suffused with the scent memory of carbolic soap. Peck. Jezebel Peck. For the first time in his new existence, Eddie is experiencing something close to happiness.

And this woman is her distant progeny. The likeness is astonishing. She has the sharp high cheekbones, and that nose thing like the rest of the contemporary crew. But she has those familiarly ambiguous lips: thin yet full. She has the judgementally raised right eyebrow. She has the black hair. Black as Stalin's soul.

The hair is scooped back and tucked into some curious headwear, made up of four triangles: one at the back, two at either side, and one on top, like an anti-glare screen on a computer monitor. The hat is also black, as are the uncomfortably heavy woollen robes draped loosely around her. The only colour on her is a hint, in the shadows of the headpiece, of some kind of white skullcap. To Eddie, she looks like a widow from Renaissance Venice. Or a nun.

Eddie offers her a fulsome smile.

The smile is not reflected.

Peck's eyebrows raise themselves to full condemnation height, making cruel slits of her nostrils and eyes. She speaks rapidly, with a breathy passion. 'I want you to know from the outset that I am one hundred per cent opposed to reviving you in this way. You, sir, are the walking dead, an abomination in the sight of God, and the demon spawn of Satan. And this isn't just my opinion – I have full papal authority to hate you.'

Well, the old Peck charm's still alive and kicking. Eddie's ludicrous hopes, barely flimsy in the first place, of kindling some kind of carbolic relationship with this woman seem even less robust. An abomination in the sight of God? Demon spawn of Satan? It seems a long way from there to 'boyfriend'. He looks to Father Lewis, who replies with an amused facial shrug. He looks back at Peck, who is clutching a rosary and silently incanting some kind of prayer, presumably, in his direction. Perhaps the overture to some kind of exorcism. This woman is the Science Officer? Hard to believe the ship is in trouble.

Lewis leads him up the table. 'And I think you've already met some copies of our Security Leader. Apton Styx.'

Another of the Styx drones rises to greet him. This one has an A burned into his forehead. Perhaps it's Eddie's imagination, but he thinks he sees a glint in this one's eye. A spark of some quiet, inner intelligence. Styx holds out his hand and says: 'Pleased to meet you, Apton.'

No. It *was* Eddie's imagination. 'No, *your* name's Apton.'

'Really? That's my name, too.'

The drone's smile is so warm and genuine, and the collective disdain for him around the room is so palpable, Eddie feels he should make some kind of friendly, comradely gesture. Without sufficient concentration, he reaches out to shake the proffered hand, engages the wrong impulses and unwittingly wills his powerful arm to slap the hapless Styx with astonishing sudden violence, sending him careening across the table over the shoulders of a pair of gawking committee members opposite, to crash, unconscious, into a group of empty chairs stacked up against the wall.

'I . . . "Sorry" doesn't even begin to . . . That was an involuntary response. I haven't quite got on top of my neural reconnections.' Styx groans, and makes an incompetent attempt to pull himself clear of the shattered furniture, which only brings more of the sturdy leather-backed chairs crashing down on top of him, further thwarting his revival. 'Isn't anybody going to help him?'

But nobody even tries. He's a drone. Less than human.

'Don't worry about it,' Lewis consoles him. 'It's good training for him. Might sharpen his reflexes. Now. Our Community Director. Captain Gwent.'

At the head of the table is a young adolescent: unkempt, unwashed, with a thick fringe of greasy hair obscuring the right three-quarters of his otherwise pimple-patterned face. His filthy sneakers are crossed on the table, and he's peeling away bits of rubber from the toecaps. Surely Lewis can't be introducing this specimen as the leader of the mission? Yet he looks up at the epithet 'Captain'. He forms his right hand into a mock gun, and mimics firing it at Eddie, accompanying the action with a 'tkunk!' sound made with his cheek. 'Blown away, pilgrim. But let's DFI the whole handshake scenario, okayovich? Just until you can, say, do it without going on a gorefest death rampage?'

'You're the *Captain*?' Eddie tries to cover his squeal of disbelieving astonishment with a last-minute twist in his inflection he hopes will imply a more surprised-yet-impressed reaction, but his electronic larynx just makes him sound like a loon.

The youth grins, dental braces glaring. 'Yes indeedy peedy,' and then giggles with his tongue protruding through his teeth for around three hours.

The lad is, what? Thirteen? Fourteen? 'I don't mean to be rude, but aren't you a little . . . young for a mission commander?'

Oslo snorts and steps in with a hint of glee. 'Actually, he's a little *young* for solid food. But as you are doubtless aware, our positions are designated on a strictly hereditary basis, thanks to the brilliant goo-brain who planned this operation, and Captain Gwent's father rather selfishly died a couple of weeks ago, before his son and heir was thoroughly toilet trained.'

The Captain makes what is clearly an insulting gesture at Oslo, but Eddie is unfamiliar with it.

'But there were contingencies for this kind of eventuality.' Eddie tries to dredge his memory for those scantly grasped provisions. 'Shouldn't someone take over temporarily? The Chief Community Planner?' Hell, that would be Gordon, wouldn't it? And Eddie is Gordon, of course. The thought strikes him for the first time: where is Eddie's contemporary counterpart? Whoever currently occupies that position would surely be Eddie's own descendant! The fruit of his loins. Or the loins he once had, at least. His seed would have been automatically introduced into the gene pool. Unless whatever mishap befell him to reduce him to his current state was so devastating it rendered his sperm unextractable.

He looks quickly around the table, but spots no family likeness.

'There is no Chief Community Planner, Doctor.' Lewis jumps in a little quickly, doubtless worried Eddie might not keep up his end of the subterfuge. 'There hasn't been one of those, whatever it is, in the lifetime of anyone here.'

Nobody has occupied Eddie's post in living memory? Why? How could that have come about? Clearly, these people are still adhering to the community blueprint set out so long ago. They still observe the regulations with regard to inherited positions, to the point of insanity. When did the strict structure of command break down? And if the post of Chief Planner no longer exists, then what of Eddie's loin-fruit?

'Wait.' Oslo seizes on some possible weaponry here. 'Are you saying the kid shouldn't be in charge? At least until his voice completely breaks? That there are laws against it?'

'Well, as I said, provisions were made. I'm not sure who's next in line after the CCP.'

Oslo stands and thumps the table. 'Can't you find out, for ship's sake!?' She can hardly contain herself. Eddie doubts that anyone around the table is thrilled to be serving under this painfully immature puberty sufferer, but while he's in indisputable charge, it would seem unwise to risk getting on the wrong side of him. Yet Oslo seems to have no qualms about nailing her colours to the mast. 'It must be recorded somewhere. Somewhere in the writings.'

'It'll be in the ship's charter.' Which, of course will be preserved in the central computer. And you don't have to be able to read to communicate with the computer. So why don't they know this? Don't they *talk* to the computer? Is *that* skill now derelict? How can Eddie find this out without devaluing his usefulness?

'The ship's charter? Where's the ship's charter?' Oslo's desperation is beginning to look embarrassing. Eddie can't imagine what the young Captain, unsuitable and unpleasant as he unarguably may be, can have done to create this level of unbridled loathing in the woman. Of all the constituents of the committee, she should probably have the fewest objections: she can barely be twenty herself.

'Whoa! Hey!' The lad sweeps his filthy footwear off the table and pivots his body till his elbows rest in their place. 'Take twenty in a soothe booth, lady. If you want to start a mutiny, Oz, you can do it in your, say, leisure time. *Capice*?'

Doubtless, the feisty Ms Oslo would not enjoy taking orders at the best of times, from the best of superiors. This command falls into neither category, and as she retakes her seat and picks a camouflage smile to wear, it looks to Eddie like she has murder in her eyes.

'Fine. May I ask you one last time not to call me "Oz"?'

'Hey, sorry, *Oz*. I didn't know it upset you. From now on, I'll call you, say, "Penile Cheese Breath".'

'Thank you, *Captain*,' she spits pleasantly. 'Now. May I suggest you start this briefing as soon as possible, before your facial pustules burst and spray everyone with yellow bile?'

'I'm going to let that one go, PCB, until I can dream up the most utterly premier put-down style comeback, and watch you squirm and wither like, say, a scuddy dung beetle in a pool of fly spray.' He giggles again – that same mad thuh-thuh-thuh giggle with his protruding tongue, spraying little drops of spittle on the polished table. 'Okayanovich, I'll launch the pinball on this one: people, you're probably wondering why you're here. I know I am. Over to you, Pecky babe.'

Peck closes her eyes with a grimace of suffering and grasps her rosary beads even tighter. 'Captain. I'd . . . rather not.'

'Say what? You're the Science dudette, are you notski?'

'I would be compromising my deep-felt beliefs to brief this . . .' she nods in Eddie's direction without looking at him '. . . soulless *thing*.'

Eddie's a *thing*, now? A soulless thing. This is a bit much, even for *Eddie*'s subterraneanly low self-esteem. 'Science Officer Peck, I have spent the last few centuries pickled in a jar, I wake up not three hours ago to find I am permanently submerged in green bile, I have a central nervous system the average garden slug would sneer at, and I've been inserted into a cumbersome metallic body that would have given Robbie the Robot a crisis of confidence. Do you think I give a long stale garlic fart what you think?' As soon as the words are out of his speaker, Eddie wishes he could suck them back. This atmosphere of childish bickering must be infectious.

There is a small silence, perfectly maximizing Eddie's embarrassment. It's broken by a loud groan from the reviving Styx, and another crash as he pulls another stack of chairs on top of himself.

Peck twists her prayer beads. 'I was merely making a theological point. No need to get personal. Zombie.'

Oslo slaps the table again and rises. 'Oh, for God's sake, *I'll* do it.'

Peck smiles self-righteously. 'And for *His* sake, Bernadette, I thank you.'

Oslo puts her knuckles on the table and cranes over. 'Seventeen days ago, there was a major accident – we assume some kind of asteroid strike – that ripped away two-thirds of the ship's main engines . . .'

Eddie's accountant's mind chips in. 'The ship only had three engines. That would mean there's only one engine left.'

Peck smiles. 'Excellent. Those years of engineering training weren't wasted on you, living deadman.'

'As far as we can tell, at least eighty per cent of the manoeuvring thrusters were destroyed, too. The entire ship seems to be damaged to the point where it's ripping itself apart bit by bit, and we've no way of knowing how long it can maintain a spaceworthy integrity. Given we now have minimal manoeuvrability, our only slim chance of survival is to somehow work our way into the orbit of a vaguely habitable planet in the local region and establish the colony there.'

Oslo passes her hand over the table top, and a detailed, animated three-dimensional display of the local planetary system appears in the air above it.

Apton Styx cranes over the display, clearly fascinated by it. 'Excuse me. May I?' With childlike wonder, he reaches out for one of the colourful spinning orbs. He seems surprised when his hand passes through it.

Oslo barks: 'Stop that, Styx.'

Styx retracts his arm. 'Sorry, Oslo.' He casts his eyes downwards. 'It just looked so . . .'

'Pretty?'

Styx looks down, ashamed. 'Colourful.'

'Just stop it. All right?'

'It has clouds and everything.'

Oslo takes a breath. 'OK. We have three candidates for settlement. Of which *this* would be the best option . . .'

She leans over and points out one of the smaller orbs; a healthily blue, reassuringly Earth-like planet, mostly given to ocean.

'. . . the planet our good captain has christened, with characteristic maturity . . .' She breathes in deeply, ' "Thrrrppp".'

The Captain snorts his tonguey giggle. 'Superlative nomenclature, I would venture.'

'I'm sorry,' Eddie can't quite believe what he's hearing. 'What did you say the planet was called?'

Oslo narrows her eyes at him. 'You heard. It offers the best prospect of a breathable atmosphere, plentiful water and consumable vegetation, together with moderately survivable temperature ranges. The downside with a . . .' she blinks very slowly, '. . . Thrrrppp docking is, our best calculations give us a zero probability of effecting an orbit.'

'Sorry,' Eddie apologizes again. 'Did you say *zero* probability?'

'That's right,' Ms Peck smiles with savoured loathing. 'For those of us more severely mentally challenged, that would mean "None" or "No Chance". Is that clearer now, you eternally damned incubus?'

Eddie favours her with his slightest nod. 'Thanks for clearing that up.' What is wrong with these people? They're staring in the face of Death, and they're swapping petty snipes like playground prima donnas.

'Our second favourite is this monster . . .' Oslo indicates a large, unwelcoming globe. Most of its surface is obscured by thick, volatile swirls of black cloud formations, interrupted by occasional, disturbing blasts of bright orange explosions. 'The planet . . .' She seems to be steeling herself.

The Captain snorts a short tongue giggle. 'Say it, Oz.'

'. . . The planet "Penis". Way short of perfect, atmospherically; massive extremes of temperature; evidence of major tectonic shifting and volcanic activity on a stupendous scale. Technically, we just might be able to settle there, though we'd have to erect some form of enormous geodesic shelter during the establishment phase, and commit to a long-term terraforming programme if it's ever going to provide a permanent living environment. On the plus side, we *do* have a fifty per cent chance of achieving orbit. The outsider . . .' she gestures towards a much smaller orb, spinning far too fast and far too close to the system star for Eddie's liking, '. . . is the planet "Panties". This one gives us our best shot of a rendezvous, better than ninety per cent, but there's nothing even approaching a breathable atmosphere, extremes of temperature that would freeze mercury on one side of the planet and melt gold on the other, and a global dust-storm that won't subside for another twenty thousand years. This planet is definitely having a bad hair millennium.'

'So . . .' Captain Gwent stands and flicks back his hair with a nod of his head. Eddie swears he can hear grease particles collide against the wall behind him. 'To, say, recap: what you're saying, Oslo, is: Thrrrppp's a no-no, you think you've got a fifty-fifty chance of encircling Penis, though it may erupt, but with a good hard thrust, we could almost certainly get into Panties.' He leers a braced-toothed grin in Eddie's direction. 'What think you, Dr Morton?'

What does Eddie think? Eddie thinks he died and went to juvenile Hell.

24

The great ship *Willflower* hurtles uncontrollably through virgin space. Even if Eddie O'Hare had seen her at the start of the mission, he wouldn't recognize her now. Then, she had represented humankind's proudest achievement: a sleek masterpiece of double efficient design. Now, she's a twisted, warped mess. If you found this shape in your toilet bowl, you'd report immediately to the nearest Emergency Room for radical bowel surgery.

And the only man who can save her is made up of the bits even the most ravenous cannibal would leave on the side of his plate.

Right now, he's travelling in the passenger seat of a corridor kart, trying to work out just exactly what it is everyone's expecting him to do, without actually directly asking anyone what they expect him to do, in case that starts them thinking he probably can't do it, which he thinks is almost certainly true. He asks Oslo: 'So where are we going?'

Even though the kart is self-steering, Oslo has her hands on the drive stick, and she doesn't take her eyes off the corridor ahead to reply. 'Planning Room Seven.' She likes to feel she's in control, young Bernadette. Even when she blatantly isn't. Which Eddie thinks is understandable, under the circumstances.

Still, things have been happening very fast to Eddie, and he'd like a little time, a little space to gather his thoughts. 'Could we stop off at my apartment first?'

'Your apartment?'

'For a few minutes, at least.'

'What apartment?'

'My apartment.'

'You don't have an apartment.'

'I don't have an apartment? Well, can I get an apartment allocated? I mean, there must be one or two spare apartments around the place.' From what Eddie has seen of the current population level of the ship, they must have more spare apartments than tornado season at a time-share estate built on a plague pit next to an active volcano.

'What would you need an apartment for?'

There are discomforting implications in the very fact that that question is askable, but Eddie doesn't choose to address them. 'What would I need an apartment for? To live in. To rest. To refresh myself.'

'Refresh yourself ? In what way?'

'I don't like what it sounds like you're saying, Oslo.'

'Come on, Morton. Wake up and sniff the modified caffeine and fructose-based breakfast beverage. You're going to do what? Take a nice, hot bath? An enlivening shower? A shave? Change your underwear? What?'

Eddie falls into a hostile silence. It's true. Horribly true. He won't be doing any of those things, ever again. The nearest he'll get to freshening up is a quick rubdown for his metal suit at the automatic kart wash.

But what about eating? Obviously he no longer enjoys the luxury of a digestive system, but he must have some source of nourishment. 'I still have to eat, don't I?'

'You're not thinking things through, Morton. Which is a worry to me. What do you suppose you're going to eat? And how? So I bring you a big juicy substisteak, I lift up some kind of flap on top of your helmet and drop it in there. By some fluke it floats down through your gloop in the direction of your mouth, you manage, somehow, to suck it in, chew it up and swallow it. Where does it go? How does what's left of your body derive any benefit from it? What was the point of the entire stupid exercise?'

'But I . . . Everybody needs some form of sustenance.'

'That's what the gloop's for. It contains all the nutrients you need. Oxygen, nitrogen, vitamin compounds, minerals.'

'But they must get used up.'

'Sure. The suit filters out unwanted chemical by-products, carbon dioxide and so on, and sends them to a waste canister in your leg. And every so often, we have to empty the waste, and pop in a fresh boost of nutrients.'

'Every so often?'

'A couple of times a year. Less, maybe. You can go for months on end without needing refreshing. It's an incredibly efficient system.'

This is meant to sound like cheery news. Eddie will never eat or drink again. He looks down at his leg forlornly, and tries not to imagine the waste canister lurking inside it, brimming over with putrid effluence.

Oslo glances over and catches his sullen expression. She mistakes it for a look of suspicious disbelief. 'Honestly. When you think about it, there's not an awful lot of you that needs sustaining.'

True again. All that's left of him is a flobby old brain and a few fiddly little nerve endings. Still, Eddie is deeply dismayed to discover his brain needs less tending than a fairground goldfish in a plastic bag. 'What about sleep? I need sleep, surely.'

'You can sleep standing up. Your body doesn't need rest.'

'And what about privacy? Everyone needs a little of that.'

'Fine.' Oslo's exasperated again. 'I'll find you a storage locker or something.'

'Oh, hey.' Eddie can be exasperated, too. 'Don't put yourself out, lady. Just find a big, filthy rock I can crawl under once in a while. Or the drawer of a filing cabinet no one's using. Maybe we could dig up a spare coat hook in someone's wardrobe to dangle me from. We could paint a little sign: "Chez Eddie".'

Oslo's face crimps up. 'Eddie? Who the hell is Eddie?'

Moving swiftly on. 'I want my own apartment. OK? Is that such a bizarre request? It's not like there's a major apartment shortage, is there?'

'Were you actually *present* at that meeting? I mean, you were *there*, weren't you? The ship is falling apart, Morton. It's coming to pieces under our feet and over our heads. And your major priority is booking yourself a pleasant *room*? Certainly, sir. Would you prefer a view of the lava ocean we're about to crash into, or one of our more popular about-to-snap-away-from-the-hull-and-explode-into-a-million-fragments-in-the-vacuum-of-space suites? Take your time. We may have up to fifteen minutes left to live.'

'I asked for a *room*, Bernadette. I didn't ask you to donate any limbs. I didn't ask for your eternal and undying affection. I asked if you could tell somebody somewhere to press a little stinking button and allocate me a room nobody else is using.'

There's another reason Eddie would like a private room.

He needs to interrogate the computer without anyone listening.

Oslo grinds an unnecessarily bad unnecessary gear change and inclines her head ever so slightly in a tight, grudging nod of acquiescence. 'Fine. I'll get you a room.' And because she can't let it go at that, because she can't let Eddie think his request is in any way sane or reasonable, she tags it with: 'Then I'll send down a crack team of our top interior designers with some fabric swatches and colour charts, so you don't have to look at the wrong shade of green while we're being blasted into oblivion.'

Eddie lets it go. He thinks Oslo's face is interesting; she might actually be quite stunning if she could let go of the permanently irritated expression that distorts it so. In fact, if you took away the ship nose and cheekbones, it could be the face of someone he once knew. But who? The name is not in his mental contact book.

'Why do you despise the kid . . . the Captain so much?'

'Gwent? Why not? Don't you despise him?'

'Well . . . no. I think he's irresponsible and utterly unsuitable to be heading this mission, and unpleasant and immature . . .'

'Trust me, you're listing his good points.'

'But you *hate* him.'

'I don't *hate* him. I just wish he would die suddenly yet painfully and very, very soon.'

'Right. Only, to me, that sounds like . . .'

'Subject closed.'

'Subject closed?'

'In fact, all subjects not relating to the impending destruction of this vessel and everyone in it are henceforth closed, until such time as the danger is averted or we're all dead.'

25

Planning Room Seven turns out to be a stunningly well-equipped navigation centre. So stunningly well-equipped that Eddie doesn't have a clue how to use any of the stunning equipment, or even what any of it does.

Fortunately, Oslo takes him over to a bank of hard-copy files. A large bank, with lots of files. But that's all right. Files are good for Eddie. They're currency, to him. He'd be rubbing his hands together, if only he could be sure they wouldn't generate sparks.

'All the surviving writings are here. We believe some of them might even date back to the era of the Originals.'

Eddie's noticed that before: the verbal capitalization of 'Originals' – almost a reverence for the ancestors who started the mission. Of whom, of course, Eddie is one. Don't they know that? Presumably not. Didn't they say their system of allocating dates had broken down? This is good. This might be a trump card he can play later on.

Eddie is busy directing a mental movie of the entire ship's complement on its knees, cowed in supplication, worshipping him as a kind of flower-garlanded God, when he realizes Oslo is looking at him with impatient expectation.

Her eyebrows signal a slightly sarcastic 'Well?' Then she raises them just a notch further to add: 'No rush. Just preferably before the girders holding up the ceiling collapse and we're crushed like poorly constructed origami birds by the roof', which gives some idea of quite how articulate Oslo's eyebrows can be.

'I'll get to it, then.' Eddie smiles, chastised, and starts removing file boxes and stacking them on a desk. Then he stops. This is stupid. He has to ask. 'What exactly am I looking for, exactly?'

Predictably, the question exasperates Oslo. 'I don't *know*. How could I *possibly* know? We have no idea what the hieroglyphic system is *for*. We need something that might help, Morton. Something that might just possibly contribute to saving the ship from hideous destruction. What do you think you're looking for? Video listings for the month of August? Detailed instructions for an emergency elephant vasectomy?'

Eddie's getting to know her well enough not to take the ranting personally. It isn't him causing her exasperation, it's her inability to control the situation. 'It's a big brief, Oslo.'

'It's a big problem, Morton. In case it hasn't filtered through your gloop yet, we're desperate here. We are so deeply submerged in the old human waste materials, we should all technically be issued with scuba gear and shit flippers.'

'I know that. I'm aware of that. In case it hasn't filtered through your own gloop, I'm actually on the same ship. But it would take months to wade through all this.' He means to sweep his hand to indicate the ranks of files, but involuntarily kicks out his right leg instead, and has to fight to remain upright.

'You don't have to read it *all*. Just find something. Some engineering layouts; contingency plans for engine failure; blueprints to help us construct some manoeuvring jets. Anything. The ship's charter, so we can get rid of that idiot and replace him with someone from the planet Sane. Anything you can find. Anything at all.'

There is another shipquake. There is the frightening creak of thick metal offering vain resistance, a sound Eddie is learning very quickly to dread, accompanied by a violent, sustained judder and a flickering of lights. It doesn't seem as violent as the others Eddie's encountered, perhaps because he's not as close to its epicentre; but it does go on for longer. For much, much longer.

Oslo waits for a second after the juddering finally subsides.

'Just find it soon, OK?'

26

Eddie is waiting until he's absolutely certain Oslo won't return with a final insulting afterthought before he tries to communicate with the computer.

In the meantime, he's sorting through the files as best his clumsy hand substitutes will allow.

As far as he can tell, most of it is devoted to the mapping of the space through which the *Willflower* has passed. And deadly dull it is, too.

He moves further along the file bank and picks something else. More astronomical data. More of the useless information that maps the passage of the blind voyage of scientific investigation.

He looks towards the door. He's alone now.

'Ship System. Logon Dr Morton.'

Nothing. OK.

'Logon C. P. Gordon.'

Silence. Fine. Perhaps it's his electronic voice box preventing recognition.

'Logon guest.'

Oh, come on. What's going on here? The computer *must* be working. *Some*thing's running the ship's systems.

He waddles over to a manual input console and tries logging in by striking the keys with the claw of his pincer. Painfully slow, and even more painfully frustrating.

The system is not responding. In desperation, Eddie adopts the time-honoured technique of kicking the machine and swearing at it. 'Come on, you useless bastard! Speak to me!'

Suddenly, the screen flickers and a message appears on it, briefly. So briefly, in fact, Eddie can't be sure he read it correctly.

He can't have read it correctly, truth be told. Because what he thought it said was: CALM DOWN, EDDIE, THIS IS NOT THE TIME. Which it can't have said, on so many levels.

The more he thinks about it, the more Eddie's convinced he mis-read the message. In his mind, it becomes SHUT DOWN EDI (or some such code) THREE-THIRTY A.M. SHIP TIME. Which is fine. It's a response, and an acknowledgement of some temporary system error, boding well for future efforts some time later.

But the truth is, he got it right first time.

27

'How's it going, eh, Doctor?'

Even though Eddie's the only one Father Lewis could possibly be addressing, the room being otherwise deserted, it takes a few moments for the epithet 'Doctor' to register.

Eddie looks up from his pile of papers. 'Not good, Padre. None of this is making much sense.'

'I imagined as much. There's a lot to get through, here.'

'I haven't even scratched the surface.'

'That's why I thought you might like some assistance. Trinity?'

Peck skulks in behind him, wearing an expression blacker than her robes.

Eddie can't help himself. 'Her?!'

'Well, she *is* our Science Officer, when all's said and done. Trained to the job since birth.'

'I didn't mean to . . . I'm sure she's very good. I'm surprised, that's all, she's willing to work with me.'

'Well,' Lewis smiles at Peck without humour, 'she's aware we all need to pull together if we're going to get through this little . . . hiccup in the mission. Aren't you, Trinity, eh?'

Peck nods slowly and grimly. 'I have made it, I think, perfectly clear I find it unthinkable that I'm compelled to collaborate with a soulless speaking pickle. But I'm prepared to make that sacrifice if it be the will of the Lord.' She shoots the Padre a vaguely accusatory look.

'Well,' Eddie smiles generously, 'I, myself, am not overly enamoured of the prospect of spending my time with a woman who could frost martini glasses between the cheeks of her buttocks, but I'm sure I'll learn to deal with it.'

Lewis is flicking through the papers Eddie has laid out on the desk. 'So what are these?'

'Flight data. I've managed to track it back to the point of the accident.'

'And what part of it is not making sense?'

'None of it makes sense. Certainly there was a vast, shipwide trauma, but there's no corroborating evidence of any external phenomena that might have caused it. No meteor strikes, no anything within any kind of realistic range. Not only that, but even taking into account the massive extent of the damage, why didn't the auto repair systems kick in?'

'Just a wild, off-the-wall guess,' Peck offers, 'but possibly the auto repair system was ripped away by the asteroid that struck the ship?' And in case her sarcasm might have somehow dragged its way over Eddie's head, she adds a schoolyard 'Durhh?'

Eddie sighs. A small green bubble floats lazily up his visor and pops in front of his eye. 'That's not possible. The auto repair system is organic: it's in the material of the ship, in every component. True, it was never tested to last this many generations, but, technically, this vessel should be capable of rebuilding itself from a few hull panels, given time. And the engines being torn away by an asteroid strike – how could that have been allowed to happen? Why didn't the radar spot anything incoming? Or any of the other warning systems? And why is there no record of a strike? I mean, you're supposedly the Science Officer, you must have considered some alternatives.'

'You don't think I've thought about it? There is only one sane, scientific explanation: clearly, it's the divine vengeance of the sweet and merciful Lord being rained down upon the wicked, the sinful and the unrighteous.'

She delivers this opinion with such a sweet tone, like a parent explaining to a toddler how it just hurt itself, it takes Eddie quite by surprise. 'Well, when you put it with such relentless logic, the conclusion seems almost inevitable.'

'Doesn't it, though?'

'Of course. The ship was, in fact, smitten by the vengeful hand of God.'

'In all His terrible glory.'

'So, just one question: if that's the sane, scientific explanation, what exactly is the lunatic fringe religious nutball explanation?'

'Oh, you can mock, Zomboid. But you're the one who's going to be writhing in the flesh-rendering flames of Hell's hottest furnace for all eternity.'

'Listen, Ms Peck. I don't know if you noticed, but this vessel and everyone in it is screaming at an incredible speed towards oblivion. Unless we can find some way to set aside our personal feelings for the moment and hunker down to save the ship, we'll all be enjoying a big chuck of eternity.'

'Feelings don't enter into it. We have a fundamental professional disagreement. You adhere to the childish, demonstrably inadequate concept of cause and effect, and reject even the *possibility* of divine intervention. How am I supposed to deal with such closed-minded bigotry?'

This flummoxes Eddie. He is officially flummoxed. Closed-minded bigotry? This witch-burning zealot is actually claiming the sanity high ground. Eddie turns to Lewis, praying he doesn't get outnumbered on this one.

Unfortunately, Lewis hasn't been listening: he's been trying to divine some meaning from the writing on the papers, as if he believes that if Eddie can do it, it must surely be a childishly simple accomplishment. He looks up. 'Well, then. I'll leave you two lovebirds to it, eh?'

Lewis stops at the door, calls back, 'Play nice, now,' and leaves. Eddie looks at the papers, then at the cruel, thin, defiant lips he's beginning to find almost irresistible. 'Do you suppose,' he pleads as pleasantly as he can, 'that we might co-operate for the next hour or two? Or at least not get in each other's way?'

'I have no problem with that.'

'Then could you possibly fetch the next batch of files over for me?' He sees her hesitation. 'I'd do it myself, only where other people have hands, I have nutcrackers.'

Peck shoots him one of her lineage's patent castration smiles. 'Coming right up, O sperm of the Serpent's scrotum.'

28

It's not exactly a marriage made in Heaven. And not merely because of Peck's unveiled and unbridled loathing for him in person and his kind in general principle. They are so fundamentally different: from different times, different *epochs*, with different backgrounds, beliefs and skills. Eddie has never met anyone with whom he has such a zero connection. There is nothing alike about them, nothing they can do together, nothing they can agree on. And she's surly, rude and intolerant to boot. Eddie is in serious danger of falling helplessly head over whatever he now has for heels.

He's about to give up on examining the navigation records, because he's getting nowhere, he never liked them in the first place, and they're giving him a headache. And since his head is the only bit of him left – besides his spine, which is, of course, hurting anyway – the prospect of a headache takes on more of a threat than it otherwise might.

But as he reaches out to gather up the papers, he notices something. Something wrong. Eddie may be a novice at astronavigation, but he can spot figures that don't add up from thirty paces. 'Peck?'

Grudgingly: 'Yes?'

'Can you call up that 3-D display of the local system?'

She doesn't even bother insulting him. She simply sweeps aside some errant files, sighs like she's trying to explain quantum mechanics to a particularly dull gorilla and passes her hand over the desktop.

The planets rise above the table into their places.

'Can you speed it up? Say, a hundredfold?'

Peck makes some movement with her hand, and the display accelerates. How does she do that?

Eddie peers at the madly twirling globes. He checks the printout. He looks at the planets again. 'This isn't right.'

'What isn't right?' Do all the women on this mission take exasperation lessons before they learn to toddle?

'The orbital paths of these planets. There's an anomaly.'

'How would you know?'

'I got a phone call from Beelzebub. How do you think I know?'

'I think maybe you got a phone call from Beelzebub.'

'Look.' Eddie points out the Earth-like blue planet. 'Thrrrppp, is it?'

Peck nods.

'We have *got* to change the names of these planets. Thrrrppp's orbit should form a perfect ellipse around the sun, but it doesn't. There's a sort of bump in it here.' Eddie points his pincer as accurately as he can at the anomaly. 'You follow?'

'My advanced scientific training leaves me capable of interpreting complex abstractions such as: "There's a sort of bump in it here", yes.'

'And the same with . . .' gingerly, he points a pincer at the planet Penis, '. . . the same with this one.'

'Right. So?'

'So the display's incomplete.'

'In what way incomplete?'

'There's something missing. Something big.'

'What? What could possibly be missing?'

'Another planet.'

Peck's interested now. So interested, she almost forgets to hate him. 'Where, sulphur breath?'

'Well, unless this data's been tampered with' – and who could have tampered with it? And how? – 'there's a planetary body about eight times the diameter of Thrrrppp . . . can you freeze the display?' Peck complies. Eddie concentrates hard and stretches out his pincer. '. . . Here.'

'Like this?' Peck's hands dance over what must be some sort of interface with the display, though Eddie's unclear how contact is made. Extremely powerful heat sensors, perhaps? Magnetic signals from the body? Not touch, anyway.

A large, wireframe planet appears between Eddie's stretched pincers. The dimensions look perfect. 'Yes, exactly like that.' Unbelievably accurate, to the eye at least. 'How did you do that?'

'The size of the thing: its influence on the other planets. It has to be a gas giant.'

A gas giant? Eddie nods grimly. 'Has to be.' Oh, crap.

'And its orbit?'

Eddie consults the charts. 'I can give you key frames.' He stretches across the display. 'Here, here and . . . here.'

'So. Like . . . this?' Peck reanimates the display. The new wire-frame globe joins in the complex planetary dance.

'Perfect. That all makes sense now, doesn't it?'

'I should have spotted that.'

'How? The information was buried in the charts here.'

'I should have spotted it anyway.' Peck sounds disproportionately angry with herself. Eddie looks away from the display at her hunched figure. She's clutching the edge of the table so hard the blood has drained from her knuckles. 'I shall have to chastise myself.'

'Chastise yourself?' Eddie doesn't want to imagine what that could mean, but he can't help himself. 'What do you mean, exactly?'

'I mean, I shall have to take a flail to my back.'

'You're going to give yourself a whipping?' Inside his head, Eddie is yelling 'Cut! Cut!' on his mental film set. This is not the time.

'A cruel whipping. In penance. You wouldn't understand, incubus. Those of us who actually still *possess* a soul think it's quite an important thing to preserve.'

'A *cruel* whipping?'

'But first, there are one or two even more pressing matters.'

'How cruel?' Stop it, Eddie. Stop it.

'Such as: how does this affect our immediate plans?'

She's right. This could complicate things. A lot. Eddie sends the film crew home, grumbling, and concentrates on the display. 'Can you plot the ship's projected trajectory through here?'

But Peck is already on the case.

The display freezes, and a tiny luminous dot appears, pulsating. The *Willflower*.

'This is us now.' Peck's hands move and the display animates. '. . . Us in twenty-four hours . . .' The ship appears to be moving into the path of the wireframe giant. Not good. '. . . Forty-eight . . .' Better. The new planet's orbit seems to be steering it away from the ship. '. . . Seventy-two . . .' Now what's happening? The ship is way off where Eddie expected it to be. Closer to the planet. Far too close. The massive pull of the gas giant is dragging the *Willflower* off course towards it. 'And in ninety-six hours . . .'

Nothing.

The *Willflower* has gone.

29

'This is bad,' Lewis is saying, although, to Eddie, he doesn't sound like he believes it. 'This is very bad.'

Eddie takes a clumsy step towards the priest's office desk, to make absolutely sure the good Father is looking at the correct display on the computer screen. He is.

'I'm not sure you appreciate the full extent of the entirely lethal implications of this discovery, Padre. It's worse than "very bad". In fact, *before*, things were worse than "very bad". Now, we're way beyond "very bad". We're in a place where we can't even see "very bad" and sigh at it wistfully. "Very bad" isn't even on the *map* of the place we're at. If we tried –'

'Point taken, Dr Morton.' Lewis actually lounges back in his seat. 'The situation isn't good. I just don't think –'

'No.' Eddie thumps down a claw. 'No! The situation isn't "isn't good". We are spiralling out of control towards an immense, *immense* planet whose gravitational pull will compact this entire vessel to the size of a single constipated mouse dropping long before we even enter its atmosphere in less than five days' time. And that's a best-case scenario which rests upon the massively implausible assumption that the ship hasn't shredded itself to tiny fragments long before then. We have one engine: a single, solitary, solo engine, pointed in one direction, which is absolutely the couldn't-be-worse wrong direction, and the manoeuvring capability of a quadriplegic elephant falling from the highest parapet of the Chicago Twin Towers, tied to a grand piano with no castors.'

'My dear Dr Morton,' Lewis smiles, 'I do believe you're panicking.'

'No, no, Padre. I'm *under*reacting. This is an unbelievably muted response to the inescapable inevitability of disasters we're facing.

Because that's not even the worst of it. The worst of it is, we have a saboteur on board, hell bent on compounding the disaster.'

'A saboteur? That's putting it a little –'

'*Some*body obliterated that planet from the display. Somebody didn't want us to know it was there. Who? Who would do such a thing? And why? I'll bet my gloop it wasn't out of the milk of human kindness.'

'It might just have been a glitch in the –'

'Someone on the Committee,' Peck says darkly.

'Trinity, that's a very serious –'

'Think about it, Father: it has to be one of the Pilgrim Parents.'

'That's *enough*!' Lewis doesn't raise his voice much, but it carries enough authority to guarantee attention. In the small silence that ensues, Eddie thinks he can hear a strange sound. Something like water falling, and – it can't be – the distant flicker of intermittent female laughter. Where is it coming from? Lewis gets up and walks around his desk towards Peck. 'There's more than a hint of hysteria in the air here, Trinity. We can't afford to be throwing unfounded accusations around. That's only going to make things worse.'

'Father . . .'

'Trinity,' he places a paternal hand on her shoulder, 'since you feel empowered to start casting the first stone here, let me ask you something: why didn't you notice the orbital anomalies in the planets yourself?'

Peck looks down and starts fiddling with her rosary. 'You're right, Father. I was remiss. That was inexcusably negligent.'

Lewis closes his eyes, as though he's sharing her pain, shouldering it even. 'That's all right, child. We can talk about it in the confessional. In the meantime, perhaps you might think about withdrawing to your room and whipping yourself for a while?'

This insane suggestion brings a smile of relief to Peck's features. 'Yes. I'll do that right away. Thank you, Father. Bless you.'

'Big strokes, now.' He pats her on the shoulder as he opens his study door. 'Don't spare the flail there, Trinity.'

As the door closes behind the penitent, Lewis turns and grins at

Eddie. 'That is one crazy chick. She's like a one-woman Spanish Inquisition.'

Lewis is starting to seem less and less priest-like to Eddie. 'Does she really do that? She really whips herself?'

Lewis crosses back to his desk. 'Oh yes. Would you like to see a video?'

'A video? Of Peck thrashing herself?'

'Incredible stuff. She's got a whole wardrobe of flagellation devices. Knotted rope, bullwhips, flails. She's even got a miniature cat-o'-nine-tails. She made it herself. Incredible.'

'And you have it on video?'

'I have it by the trunk load.' Lewis reclines in his leather chair, hands locked behind his head, wearing his beatific grin. 'Buckets of it. First-rate stuff. She has this ritual: she chooses a whip, then she blindfolds herself and strips. The blindfold is so she doesn't have to look at her own naked body. I'm thinking of cutting together a compilation tape and setting it to music – I found this old big-band number: "Beat Me, Daddy, Eight to the Bar". I was thinking of calling it *Peck's Greatest Hits*, but I'm open to suggestions.'

'You have a spy camera in her apartment?'

'I have spy cameras everywhere.' He leans forward and swings up the monitor from under his desk. On the screen, a woman Eddie vaguely recognizes from the Committee meeting is naked in a shower, locked in a lesbian embrace with a woman Eddie doesn't recognize.

'That's disgusting.'

'You think so? I find it intensely erotic.'

'No, I mean *filming* it. That's what's disgusting. It's immoral and disgusting.' Eddie's point might be better made if he could tear his eyes from the screen. 'And immoral.'

'And disgusting, yes.' Lewis sighs and twists the monitor out of sight again. 'But I think it's important that *someone* knows what's going on around this ship, don't you? You've met the Committee. You're aware of the general competence level on board. Somebody has to have a handle on things, eh, don't you think?'

'Possibly. But chopping the sexual highlights together and dubbing on a big-band soundtrack, that might be considered above and beyond the call of duty.'

'You don't want to see the tape, then?'

'I would give my right arm to see the tape, if I had a right arm. I just . . . I could never condone anything so . . . so *tacky*.'

'Tacky, eh? Well. You're entitled to your opinion. Wait. What do you think of the title: *Im-Peck-able Behaviour*? Too punny? Too sinister? Too mainline S & M?'

'Too unpriestly, that's what I think.'

'You think I'm unpriestly?'

'I think that would be a fair analysis of my appraisal of your total lack of moral standards and ethics, yes.'

Lewis sighs and reclines again. 'You're probably right. I do feel, sometimes, that my performance of my duties is overly hampered by my lifelong commitment to atheism.'

'You're an atheist?'

'I know, I know. It's a handicap to a man of my calling.' He sighs again. 'But that's the cross I bear.'

'I don't understand. If you don't believe in God, why take to the cloth?'

'You know the score here. I had no choice. Like everyone else on board, I inherited my job.'

'But surely, if you explained . . .'

'Why the hell should I? For an unscrupulous, non-God-fearing individual, priesthood has certain advantages. There's precious little actual *work* involved. These idiots *confess* things to me. Their darkest secrets. That knowledge gives me certain . . . leverage. That, and my comprehensive video collection. Then, of course, there's the asexual business. There are women who find that an incredibly horny thing. The number of times I've been led astray . . .' Lewis looks up to the Heaven he doesn't believe in, lost in happy memories.

Eddie looks at the smile. So peaceful, so serene, so . . . contented. 'My God. You're rat slime, aren't you?'

'Now, now, you naughty thing. You've been peeking at my CV, eh?' Lewis leans forward. His expression doesn't change, but his voice gets quieter. 'And incidentally, should you feel the urge to convey the essence of this little *tête-à-tête* to other parties, I might additionally point out that I am in possession of *your* dirty little secret – a secret that could have you back in suspension fluid quicker than a Chinese orgasm. Are we singing the same version of the *Magnificat*, Dr *Morton*?'

'My soul doth magnify the Lord, Father Lewis.'

'Good. No point in our being at loggerheads. We have more urgent concerns to attend to.'

'Yes. Such as avoiding large planets that appear out of nowhere.'

'The truth is, that planet's turning up hardly alters things at all.'

'Right. Hey – what's a weeny little gas giant between friends?'

'It simply gives us a more definitive deadline, that's all. Unless we can work out some way of manoeuvring the ship, we're on a one-way trip to oblivion, whatever happens. We've known that for some time.'

'Up to a point, true. But we should obviously try to find out who . . . ?'

'"Who" doesn't matter right now. There's only one important question: "How?" Either we work out a way to change course, or we die. I suggest you might be best employed getting back to the record room and carrying on digging through that paperwork.' He treats Eddie to his best, most sincere, paternal smile. 'And God speed, pilgrim. We're depending on you.'

Lewis jumped in a little too fast, there. Too glib. Too sincere. Too keen to stamp on any talk of the sabotage or its perpetrator?

And suddenly, Eddie knows.

He knows it was Father Lewis who deleted the planet from the display.

30

Eddie's in a quandary, here. He needs to know why the priest would want to conceal the imminent danger presented by the proximity of the gas giant from the rest of the crew. But who can he talk to? And how? Lewis is probably watching his every move. Probably has been watching him all the time.

How else would he have known exactly how to deal with Peck, to cut short her accusation by precisely homing in on her guilt over the slip-up?

Does that mean he heard Eddie trying to communicate with the computer? And if so, so what? Fortunately, the computer didn't respond.

He's back in Planning Room Seven, now. Alone. At least, he seems to be alone. God only knows who's tuning in and observing him through various concealed surveillance devices. Peck has retired to her room, and Eddie doesn't want to think about what she's doing to herself in there. He wouldn't get any work done.

He looks at the mounds of paperwork. It seems pointless trying to examine the ship's layout. Current diagrams bear almost no resemblance to the originals, and the persistent nature of the ship's breakdown renders even the most recent schematic hopelessly out of date. In short, it's impossible to assess the current state of the vessel, or what, precisely, is left of it.

He has to do something. Or at least he has to appear to be trying to do something.

More out of desperation than inspiration, he digs out the crew manifest.

And he turns up the first promising leads.

There are two names on the currently active personnel list that interest him. The first is interesting because he thinks he recognizes it, but he can't remember where from: a Mr Paulo San Pablos – no listed qualification, no designated community position. Weird. The second is a strange name: Amalgam Willard-Walters. Whoever he or she is, Willard-Walters has the highest recorded IQ on board. In fact, it's the highest IQ Eddie's ever heard of: way beyond genius, and then some. Now, Eddie doesn't set much store by IQ ratings – his own seems ludicrously high to him – but a person with a score of 300 has got to be able to make some kind of valuable contribution to the current situation.

He picks up the ship phone and accidentally crushes it in his excitement. He's reaching for another handset when the com screen flashes up Lewis's image.

'You were about to call me?'

Damn the man. Watching Eddie's every move. He doesn't even bother to make a polite stab at discretion.

'Paulo San Pablos,' Eddie asks. 'Who he?'

There is the tiniest of tiny blips in the steadiness of Lewis's steady, sincere stare. 'Sorry. Doesn't ring a bell.' It does. 'I'll check that one out for you.' He won't.

OK. Let that pass for now. 'And this other one: Amalgam Willard-Walters.'

'You mean the professors?'

'The professor*s*?'

'Trust me – you don't want to meet him.'

'*Him*? Wait a minute, let's get this straight: is Amalgam Willard-Walters a single or a plural person?'

Lewis runs a troubled hand through his hair. 'Technically, he's both.'

31

Eddie is travelling in the back of a corridor kart with Father Lewis. Disturbingly, two Styx drones are in the front, completely identical except for the letters on their foreheads: D and J. They are very heavily armed, which seems to Eddie both unnecessary and, given that the task of removing a ring pull from a can of beer would represent an extraordinarily taxing and bewildering intellectual challenge for the pair of them, unwise in the extreme. He tries not to notice the J drone taking imaginary pot-shots at imaginary targets *en route* with his huge laser rifle, puffing out his cheeks to accompany his efforts with little-boy explosion noises. He tries not to think about what might happen if the gun were to go off accidentally in this confined space. He tries, instead, to listen to Father Lewis.

'The professors are a result of a badly botched scientific experiment.'

'Badly botched?' The D Styx snorts. 'That's an overstatement.'

'Actually, Darion, it's an *under*statement'.

'Oopsy poopsy, I made a mistake.' The D Styx slaps his forehead with weighty, laboured sarcasm. 'So shoot me in the brain with a bazooka.'

Lewis shakes his head. 'I'm not that good a marksman.'

'What kind of experiment?'

'The professors, Willard and Walters, headed the community research and development team, five, six generations ago. Willard contracted a terminal illness, and the two of them agreed to graft Willard's brain on to Walters'. Two minds, one body. No sense. Are you sure you want to go through with this?'

This was more than Eddie dared hope for. The professor/s represent a link, a bridge between his own generation and the present. With their input, it should be possible to stitch together some kind of cohesive history of the community; work out what went wrong. Work out how, for instance, the pilgrims lost the ability to read, and when. 'But how are they still . . . ? I mean, five or six generations: that's a long time.'

'We have them in cold storage.'

'Cryogenics?'

'After a fashion, yes. They're still alive in there, but their metabolism is slowed down, close to zero. Every once in a while, some bright spark insists on rousing them, to see if there's any improvement, but there never is, and so we slide them back in the freezer till the next time.'

'You've spoken to them yourself?'

'Spoken to them? Well, you don't exactly *speak* to the professors. But I've revived them a few times, yes.'

The kart stops suddenly, with a jolt. They are at a dead end. This doesn't trouble the drones; but it bothers Eddie a lot. 'What's going on here?'

The D Styx shrugs with his sturdy cheek muscles. 'Dead end.'

'But there are no dead ends. The corridor system loops all the way around the ship and joins up with itself.'

The drones look at each other, then get out of the kart and approach the offending wall. They tap it gently. They look at each other. They each put an ear to the wall and tap all around it. They look at each other again. They start thumping the wall with the side of their fists. They join in with their boots. They start head-butting the wall with increasing violence. Simultaneously, they give up, turn and march back to the cart.

The D drone stands erect, bleeding from his nose and ears, salutes Eddie and barks: 'Sir, security report: that wall is definitely there, *sir*!'

Eddie offers him a sickly smile. 'Thank you, Mr Styx.' The drone maintains his stiff salute stance, clearly waiting for something else from Eddie.

Lewis bales him out. 'Very good, Darion. You cleared that one up nicely. Carry on.'

The drone nods, satisfied, and gets back in the kart. As soon as he's seated, the kart starts up and reverses towards the last intersection.

'Was that true?' Lewis asks Eddie. 'The corridors all joined up in your time?'

'Absolutely. Why wouldn't they? And why would anyone change that?'

'There are dead ends all over the place now.'

Eddie recalls the convoluted route the transway took, doubling back on itself and so on. 'The thing is . . . I mean, fine, for whatever reason, somebody altered the ship's layout, but the computer system should be aware of the alterations, shouldn't it? I mean, the kart is computer controlled. It should know where the dead ends are. It should avoid them, shouldn't it?'

'Actually, that *is* curious, yes.' Lewis's eyes betray a fierce intelligence at work behind them. 'That should have occurred to me.' Because he thinks he's smarter than Eddie? He catches Eddie's look, and his intensity fades. 'No two ways about it,' he grins, 'I'll have to go to my room and beat myself mercilessly with a cruel flail.'

But the conundrum has clearly set his mind racing. He is silent for the rest of the short journey, leaving Eddie with nothing to distract him from the sight of the Styx drone playing Cowboys and Indians with a military-class assault weapon, dribbles of blood slowly coagulating on his thick neck.

The cold chamber, when they finally reach it, seems overloaded with security precautions, in Eddie's humble opinion. He wonders what can possibly be in the room to warrant such an overabundance of intrusion-prevention systems. Or perhaps he's putting the wrong spin on it. Perhaps the measures are in place to prevent whatever's in the room from getting out.

The D drone has to offer his palm print, look into an eyepiece for a retina scan, and even surrender a few flakes of skin for a DNA check before they're even allowed to access the control centre keypad.

He taps in a very long number – Eddie loses count after thirteen, but it's a lot of digits.

Nothing happens.

The D drone sighs and taps the number in again. And again, the door doesn't move. He tries a third time, with the same non-result.

Father Lewis closes his eyes. 'I'm going right out on a limb here, Darion, but is it vaguely possible you're tapping in the wrong number?'

'Father, sir, I doubt that, Father, sir. However, I will double check.' The drone takes out some kind of electronic organizer, double checks the number and taps it in again. Still no response from the door.

'Damn. Somebody must have changed the code. Stand back.' The drone swings its laser rifle up to aim at the security panel.

Lewis yells, 'Styx! No!'

'I said "back off", Father, sir. I know what I'm doing.'

'You've got the . . .'

Styx's finger tightens on the trigger, and Lewis dives behind Eddie, almost flooring him as the rifle fires a massive bolt of light energy, blasting the control panel out of existence, and taking the drone along with it.

Eddie collects yet another horror movie to intrude on his erotic fantasies, as Styx's body is blasted apart, splattering his component parts all over the narrow corridor, leaving only his legs below the knees, still planted in the same spot.

There is a terrible wet silence. Something pink that should never be seen detaches itself from the ceiling and slaps messily to the floor by Eddie's feet.

Father Lewis stands and smooths down his clothes, picking odd bits of smoking gristle from his jacket. 'As I was saying before I was so rudely interrupted: the laser was set slightly too high.'

'Really?' The remaining Styx drone contorts his gore-splattered features into a grimace of enlightenment and examines his own weapon. 'You think so?'

'Dr Morton? Are you OK?'

Eddie raises a claw and removes part of a smouldering digestive system from his visor. 'Well, apart from being entirely covered in entrailly splatter, I'm having a splendid day, thank you.'

'Excellent. Shall we?' Lewis indicates a large molten hole in the security door and beckons Eddie towards it.

'What?'

'Let's go.'

'Pardon me, but am I the only one who's slightly put out that a crewmate just got blasted to smithereens here? All over us?'

'Oh, come on, Doctor. Look on the bright side: at least he got the door open.'

'He was a living person, Lewis. A human being.'

'Oh, don't you think the sobriquet "human being" is overstating his case just a little? He was just a drone. We'll grow another one. Isn't that right, Jebediah?'

'Father, sir, we're already on it, Father, sir. He's in the tube as we speak.' And the surviving drone steps into the chamber without even looking back.

The room is cold, and empty, at first glance. A dense mist almost a metre thick covers the floor. Lewis pulls his jacket tightly around him. 'It's a little chilly in here. I hope your suit's well oiled.'

Eddie tries not to dwell on the image of human internal organs freezing to his metal back and follows Lewis and Styx towards a far wall. Styx taps yet another code into another keypad and a breach appears in the otherwise smooth wall.

A long drawer slides out of the breach, slow-motion mist tumbling ominously from the top of it. As the lazy fog clears, Eddie can make out a human shape through the haze: an oldish man, perhaps in his mid-sixties. His body, well proportioned but slightly on the frail side, is wrapped in some kind of thermal suit. His skin has a blue tinge, understandably. Less understandably, he is harnessed very firmly in place with a large number of excessively sturdy straps. Overkill for his physique. A roll of cheap Sellotape would be more than ample restraint.

Lewis pulls some kind of face mask out of a compartment beside the drawer and places it over the man's nose and mouth. 'Finger on the trigger, Jebediah.'

The drone hoists up his rifle and trains the red spot of the laser sight in the dead centre of the helpless man's forehead.

Satisfied, Lewis tugs on the tube attached to the mask, Eddie hears the hiss of gas, and the frozen man stirs.

At the first sign of movement, Lewis hastily lifts off the mask, and steps back to a more than safe distance. 'Professors?'

The man's eyes open wide, blink a few times, then he turns his head in Lewis's direction and squints. 'Is that you, Raybold?'

'No, no. Raybold Lewis was my predecessor's predecessor.'

'You *look* like Raybold.'

'Yes,' Lewis smiles. 'Well, that might possibly have something to do with the crew being more inbred than an Arkansas pig-farmers' family reunion. I'd like you to meet someone.'

'Raybold Lewis was an utter bastard.'

'Yes. Good old gramps. This is Dr Morton . . .'

Then a very strange thing happens. The professor's face contorts into a new expression – so new, he takes on the look of a completely different person – and another voice, younger yet crabbier, emerges from the mouth.

'Hey, some of us are trying to sleep in here.'

And with no perceptible effort, the face morphs back again, and the original voice returns. 'Always with you, it's a complaint. Can't you just . . .'

'Just keep the noise down, that's all I'm . . .'

'Bitch bitch moan bitch bitch . . .'

'Oh, grow up, you juvenile . . .'

'I'm trying to have an adult conversation here . . .'

'Oh, really? An adult conversation, yet? That should tax your mental energies to the absolute maximum . . .'

'Just for thirteen seconds could you try not screaming hysterical insults? Just so I could listen to a sane person once for a change?'

'Yes, yes: you listen to a sane person. Learn by example.'

These exchanges take place rapidly and seamlessly. Eddie

wonders how this poor creature manages to find time to breathe.

Lewis tries to step in. 'Professors. If I could just intrude on your squabbling time . . .'

The professors raise their head against the restraints, affronted. 'Squabbling? Who's squabbling?'

'You. You are squabbling.'

'I am a respected scientific genius, my argumentative friend. I do not squabble.'

'Squabble, squabble, squabble.'

'Squabbling is petty. I rise above it.'

'You? You're a professional squabbler. You could squabble at international level and bring back the bronze, silver and gold before lunch.'

Through the gritted teeth of a smile that's about to blow, Lewis says gently: 'Shut up, or I'll have you shot.'

The professors pause. The face contorts several times. There is clearly a monumental struggle going on for possession of the vocal system. Finally, the first voice wins through. 'Oh, magnificent. Now your squabbling is going to get us shot.'

'Yes, fine, good plan. Shoot me, so I can be rid of this loony. Please, here, shoot me in the head. I'll paint a target.'

The creature struggles magnificently against the bonds, trying to free one of its hands. Eddie has utterly revised his opinion about the sturdiness of the restraints. He thinks perhaps some chain work might be appropriate. Since Lewis is failing to achieve any kind of communication, Eddie thinks he might as well try. 'Listen, professors. This is important. The ship has sustained some kind of collision damage and we're down to one engine . . .'

But if his words are heard, they are not acknowledged. The creature simply carries on arguing between itself with rabid vigour.

'Pardon me? Shoot the head? I beg your pardon, but you cannot have this head shot. This is my head, you're just a guest in here . . .'

'Believe me, I'd move out in a flash if I had the choice. Of all the heads I could have been grafted into this has got to be the . . .'

'And while you're in my head, I expect you to behave with a little more decorum, thank you so very much.'

'Decorum, yet?'

'Certainly, decorum. Do you need me to look that up for you? Didn't they teach that word at Idiot University?'

Eddie tries carrying on. Maybe something will go in. 'Listen: there's a planet close by, but we can't generate enough thrust to achieve orbit . . .'

Suddenly the professors' exertions cease. The head turns towards Eddie. 'Wait a minute. Did you say "collision damage"? You're not in danger. It's something I predicted once. Engineereal evolution . . .'

'You predicted engineereal evolution? You!? Predicted schmedicted, my friend. You couldn't predict a fart from a tin of beans. Engineereal evolution was my little –'

'Yours?! It was yours, was it? Well now, once again you manage to devise an original concept barely weeks after I first thought of it. You sad, scuddy little scumbrain. Someone should strangle you.'

'Good plan. Only I'm going to strangle you first.'

'Yeah? You're going to steal that idea, too?'

'Why not? It's the first good idea you ever had!'

'Here! Free my hand, somebody. Just one hand. That's all it'll take. I'll choke the son of a bitch till he's purple!'

The professors' struggle against the bonds intensifies, the head flailing wildly, thick, purple veins bulging dangerously on the temples, threats and curses barked in alternating voices. Eddie hears a rip. One of the chest straps is beginning to tear.

Lewis reaches over to the keypad. 'I think it's time for another nap, chaps.'

The freezing mist starts to gurgle up from the base of the drawer.

'Now look what you did, you cheese dick. He's putting us back in the box.'

'What *I* did? That is so you all over. You couldn't just keep your filthy mouth shut long enough for us to draw a breath of real air, and now we're back in the frozen-food compartment for another decade. Congratulations, genius.'

'Yeah? Well a few dozen years of glacial oblivion is a blessing compared

to a single second of your rabid ranting. I'm looking forward to it.'

As the drawer slides back into the wall, the verbal brawl carries on, unabated. Eddie can even hear them after the compartment has retracted completely.

Slowly, the altercation subsides as the cryogenic process works its soothing remedy.

Still, they wait in silence, Eddie, Lewis and the drone, with Styx's rifle trained on the drawer, for several minutes, just to make sure. Finally, Styx clicks on the safety, lowers his weapon, and the three of them exhale, long and hard.

'Wow,' Eddie says.

'Wow, indeed,' Lewis concurs.

They start back towards the corridor, each of them keeping one eye on the sealed drawer.

'And they're always like that?'

'I've seen them worse. Once, they almost broke free and tried to beat themselves to death with a plastic squeezy bottle. We had to tranquillize them with an elephant dart.'

'But they must have been friends at one time.'

Lewis shakes his head. 'As far as we can tell, they were always deadly rivals; at each other's throats all the time. Everyone was surprised when Walters suggested the graft. They thought perhaps the bickering had been the professors' way of expressing some kind of repressed affection. They thought perhaps wrong. After the operation, it got worse. They had to mount a round-the-clock suicide watch. Eventually, that wasn't enough. The professors kept on finding ever more ingenious means of attempting self-destruction, and had to be restrained. Even then, the perpetual abusive screaming was unbearable. They were placed in deep freeze for the sake of everyone else's mental health, as much as their own.'

'There must be some way . . . I mean, there's genius in there. Couldn't you try and . . . un-meld their minds?'

'Oh, yes. We've a surfeit of surgical skill on board. No doubt Jebediah here could pull off a minor brain operation like that blindfold using only a chisel and some frozen gefilte fish.'

Eddie looks round at the drone, who is vainly trying to push together the edges of the hole melted in the door. 'Good point. It would be nice, that's all, if we could find some way of picking those brains. They might just help us out of this mess.'

'The only way we'll be picking those brains, Dr Morton, is off the floor, after they've been splattered thither by my shotgun.'

Lewis orders Styx to leave the door alone, and they climb into the corridor kart. Eddie feels badly about the whole interlude, about wasting their most precious and dwindling commodity, time. But he's wrong to feel that way. In truth, the professors have already helped. If Eddie had time to think it over, he might even work out how. But there is no time. There is something rather more immediate and urgent to deal with.

A gigantic shipquake.

32

The ship is rocked to its belly by an enormous tremor, a monster this time. There is a terrible, slow creaking rumble; a low moan of distorting metal. The lights begin to flicker madly. Eddie looks to his side as the wall of the corridor warps and buckles along its entire length like a cracking bull whip. Then a sudden violent crash lifts up the kart and tosses it effortlessly towards the far wall. It hurtles through the roaring air like a toy car hurled from the hand of a tantruming child.

Eddie is thrown from the kart, tumbling end over end, his badly controlled limbs flailing randomly, so the flickering emergency lights create a disturbing, disorienting strobe effect. He has to stop somehow. He has to get out of the way of the hurtling kart before it lands on him and crushes the life out of what's left of him. Desperately, he tries to concentrate; to will his arms out and find some kind of purchase for his pincers, but it's almost impossible. His sense of touch is almost non-existent, and the crashing of crushed machinery cannoning all around him prevents him from hearing if he's making contact with anything sturdy. In desperation he tries clicking his claws open and closed at random, and finds something.

He can't see what it is he's grabbed, but it arrests his motion, and jerks him over to the side with a sudden, sickening lurch. He thumps into some protesting metal and lodges there, upside down. He thinks he's screaming, but the voice is too distant and unelectronic to be his.

He's wedged in place, helpless, as the tremor throbs unabated. There is some mucoid liquid drooling down his vibrating visor. Is there a crack in his suit? Is his life-giving gloop leaking away? He raises his arm towards his helmet, and realizes he's still clutching something in his claw. He holds it up in the juddering, strobing light.

It's an arm.

A human arm.

His pincer has severed it at the elbow.

An astonishing amount of blood is geysering from its wound. And, worse, its fingers are still twitching.

And now, it really is Eddie screaming.

He's still screaming after the quake has stopped and the lights have kicked back in.

He doesn't stop screaming until the Padre's face appears in front of him, upside down. Lewis crouches, smoothing down his hair, which is the only part of him that appears even slightly ruffled. 'Are you all right, Dr Morton?'

'I've been better. You?'

'I'm fine. I used the drone as a shield.' Lewis reaches up and tugs on Eddie's torso. 'You're pretty firmly wedged in there.' He turns and calls: 'Jebediah!'

Eddie cricks his neck forward. He's lodged in a snack dispenser.

Lewis stands and tries tugging Eddie free, but the machine has folded in around his body suit. 'I think we're going to need some kind of jemmy or something.' He turns and calls again, exasperated now. 'Jebediah! Will you stop footling about and get over here?'

The drone appears, bruised and bloody, in the periphery of Eddie's vision. 'Father, sir! Regret inability to salute, as I have temporarily misplaced my arm, Father, sir!' He holds up his stump, by way of offering proof. A thick pulse of blood spouts from the wound, dousing Lewis's entire face.

The priest closes his eyes and shakes his head. 'Tie that off, you clown. Here.' He takes out a handkerchief, wipes his face with it, then uses it to fashion a rough tourniquet for the injured arm.

The drone watches the procedure with detached interest. 'I don't understand what happened to it. It was right there just a minute ago. On the end of my elbow.'

Eddie holds out the missing limb. 'I . . . it was an accident. I must have . . . I just reached out . . .'

'Wait a minute.' The drone cranes over. 'I just lost an arm almost exactly like that one.'

Lewis tugs the bandage tight. 'That *is* your arm, Jebediah.'

The drone peers closer. 'Are you sure?'

'Fairly sure, yes. I don't exactly see an overwhelming abundance of recently detached limbs littered around the corridor. Do you?'

The drone slowly turns and looks down the corridor, then up it, then back down it again. 'Father, sir, no, sir, Father. In fact, without conducting a more rigorous and comprehensive search, I would say that's pretty much the only one there is.' He crouches and examines the appendage in Eddie's grasp. 'Could I have that back, sir, when you've completely finished with it?'

'Look.' Lewis strides up to Eddie, grabs the arm unceremoniously and flings it down the corridor. 'Forget about the frotting arm. It's gone. It's history. All right? Now, try and find some kind of crowbar.'

Styx looks forlornly after his lost limb, like a dog who's been ordered not to fetch its favourite stick, then slumps off in search of tools.

Eddie's aghast. 'What did you do that for?'

'What did you want me to do? Sew it back on with my internationally famous microsurgical skills?'

'Well, maybe, yes. If we used the surgical computer . . .'

'We don't repair drones. What's the point? It'd be quicker to shoot this one in the head and grow a new one. In any case, the arm was too badly damaged. Somebody managed to mash it up good and proper with their gentle caress.'

Great. As if Eddie didn't feel guilty enough.

Lewis leans in closer and lowers his voice. 'Besides which, the poor devil's lost an awful lot of blood, on top of some probable internal injuries he almost certainly sustained bravely shielding me. I doubt he'll survive the trip to the infirmary.'

There is another, distant tremor. They can hear it, rather than feel it. A secondary quake, maybe. Or some damage somewhere starting to settle. Whatever it is, Lewis is starting to look agitated, his eyes darting towards the end of the corridor. 'Look, Morton, would you mind if I left you here?'

'What?'

'It's just, that was a hell of a quake. God only knows what damage it caused.'

'You want to leave me here, jammed in a snack machine?'

'One of us ought to get back to the control room: find out what kind of shape we're in. Calm down any panic, sort of thing.' He's lying, of course. No surprises there. What *is* surprising is that he's doing it so poorly.

'You want to abandon me here, trapped, alone and upside down, with a wedge of family-size chocolate bars crammed up my arse?'

But Lewis is already heading down the corridor, walking as briskly as he can without appearing to run. He calls over his shoulder, 'Relax. Styx will jemmy you out of there in no time.'

Styx? Didn't Lewis just say the man was at death's door? Eddie looks after the rapidly vanishing priest, in his casual scurry, and wonders what kind of moral derelict would leave a man with only a head and a spine immobilized, trapped and inverted with only a dying one-armed invalid who would lose a battle of wits with retarded pond life to look after him.

And right on cue, Styx turns up, holding a metal rod in his remaining hand. 'Sir, will this do?'

'That should be fine.'

'It's not a crowbar, technically. It's just a regular bar.'

'It should be good enough to get me out of here. Go for it.'

But the drone just stands there, swaying slightly, saying nothing, for a good two minutes, sporting a vaguely mesmerized expression.

'Is something wrong, Styx?'

The drone's eyes suddenly widen, as if in shock, and he shakes his head violently. 'Wow! Sorry about that, Doctor, sir. I think I fainted. I'm OK now, though.'

'Are you sure? You've lost a lot of blood.'

'Abso . . .' and he crumples to the ground in a lifeless heap.

Eddie panics. What if the drone is dead? How long will he be stuck here before that self-centred, self-satisfied smug bastard of an irreligious excuse for a priest bothers to remember him? Where was he really going anyway? Did he honestly expect Eddie to buy that sad claptrap about rushing off to start calming down panickers? Just what is his unholy agenda? And what if there's another quake? What if the weakened hull gives way and Eddie and the entire snack machine get sucked out into deep space? Would his suit protect him? For how long? Would that be the ignominious fate of Eddie O'Hare? To float for ever through space, welded to a savoury-snack dispenser?

Then, without any kind of warning, the drone snaps awake, leaps instantly to his feet and finishes his sentence '. . . lutely. Let's get you out of there.'

'That would be good, yes.' Better get this done quickly, Eddie. 'If you could just . . .' There is a hideous neck-wrenching clang on the top of Eddie's helmet, and his head is jerked violently towards his chest. Shaken, he looks up to see the Styx wielding the rod like a one-armed golfer, swinging it up towards Eddie's head with tremendous force. Eddie yells 'Stop!' but the word is lost under the impact as the bar crashes into his helmet again, driving his chin up into his chest plate.

'Styx! Stop! For the sweet love of the Lord! Please stop!'

Styx pauses at the top of his swing. 'Sir? Is something wrong?'

'What the hell are you doing, man?'

'I'm trying to get you out of the suit.'

'Well, stop it. I don't want you to get me out of the suit. I need to stay in the suit. If you take me out of the suit, I'll die.'

'You want to stay in the suit?'

'I do, yes, I want to stay in the suit. Just prise me out of the vending machine. That's all. That's what the bar's for. For prising. Not for beating my brains to a mushy pulp. For *prising*. See?'

Styx jams the pole behind Eddie's torso and starts trying to lever him clear. 'I thought you wanted me to get you out of the suit, that's all.'

'Well, that was wrong. Enterprising, but wrong. Even if I did want you to get me out of the suit – and I will once again make it clear that I do *not* – I would not want you to try cracking me open like some gigantic hard-boiled dinosaur egg. OK?'

Styx leans his full body weight against the pole. Eddie feels something give, and he crashes to the floor, head first. His neck is badly jolted again, and he tumbles over to rest face up, which is not the easiest position to raise himself from. A large bubble floats lazily through the liquid in his helmet past his face. He feels like some kind of human spirit level. But wait a minute: that's a very big bubble. He hasn't seen any bubbles that big before. 'Styx? Is my visor leaking? This is vitally important. Am I leaking green gloop out of any part of my helmet or suit?'

There is no response. 'Styx?'

With a tremendous effort of co-ordination, Eddie musters his paltry resources sufficiently to roll over on to his front and claw his way cumbersomely up to his rectangular feet. The drone is lying on the floor, eyes open. Eddie can't make out colours too well, but he can see Styx's face has none.

What can he do? He can't test for a pulse, he might grip too tight and snip off the poor bastard's other hand. He can't call for help. But he can't just leave him here. Not if he's still alive. He has to do something. He kneels gingerly beside the prone drone and leans very, very close, so his visor is pressed against Styx's mouth and nose. He waits there a moment, then pulls back. Yes. There is a tiny amount of misting on the outside of the visor. The drone is still breathing.

As gently as he can, which for all Eddie knows is painfully and brutally, he lifts the drone up, pincers open under his armpits, and slings him over his back.

It will be slow going. Eddie's not exactly a sprint champion in his current state, anyway, and the drone is what? Ten? Twenty times his own weight? The suit is only designed to carry a spine and a head. It may give up at any moment. It may collapse under the strain and fold in on itself, like a cheap tin can, leaving Eddie's skimpy body trapped in a squashed, crinkled disc on the floor.

Hopefully, that won't happen. Hopefully, they'll stumble into a kart that isn't broken or a transway that's still operational before long, otherwise it will take Eddie days to carry the stricken man back to what passes for civilization on this ship of the damned.

Still, he has to try. Because if the drone has any time left at all it's not measured in days. It's measured in minutes.

33

Brutal as it had seemed in the corridor, the shipquake appears to have caused remarkably little damage to the rest of the vessel, even in the close vicinity. The trio must have been fairly close to the epicentre when it struck. Eddie laughs at his luck again.

There is even a corridor kart just around the bend from the crash, intact and ready to go. There must have been another one even closer, since the priest would definitely have availed himself of the nearest working vehicle.

Eddie lays the drone on the back seat and clambers into the driver's position. So far, so uncharacteristically good. Now. How does it actually work? Eddie's travelled in karts several times now, and he never thought to ask. He assumed they were computer controlled, but how does he communicate his desired destination? He calls for the computer's attention again, but gets no response. All right. Manual, then. He scans the few controls.

As he's tentatively reaching out for the control stick, the kart suddenly starts up of its own accord and zips off at a surprising speed, flinging Eddie back against the driver's seat. What's going on here? If the computer's operating the kart, how does it know where he wants to go? And why does it want to get there so fast? And if the computer's not in charge, then what the hell is?

Eddie grabs on to the control stick anyway, for comfort. Useless though it is, it helps him maintain some kind of illusion he's in charge.

That illusion is shattered at the next bend. The kart seems to speed up to round it, lurching up on to two wheels at an alarming angle. Eddie yanks back on the stick, snapping it neatly off at the base, with no apparent detriment to the kart's velocity.

In fact, as the kart straightens out and the wheels hit the ground again, it actually accelerates, hurling Eddie back against the seat again. He cranes round as best he can, and just catches a glimpse of the senseless drone in the back.

And still the kart is accelerating. Eddie had no idea the damned thing was capable of anything more than a pootling amble. Its tiny engine is screaming under the strain. Was its speed control somehow damaged in the quake? He strains his neck forward against what seems to be G-force, and tries to identify the speedometer. He fails, but it hardly seems to matter – all the needles on all the dials are quivering against their red extremes.

The kart hurtles wildly towards the next bend. Surely it has to slow down before it gets there. But no. It actually speeds up. The engine finds a new, higher pitch, screeching towards the oncoming wall like a mad swooping banshee, an almost unbearable din that bores through Eddie's skull like a dentist's drill in overdrive.

And still the damned thing is accelerating.

And as the wall rushes towards them, a horrifying theory lurches into Eddie's mind.

What if the kart has been tampered with?

What if the priest wanted to make absolutely sure he didn't get back to the rest of the crew? What if he knew Eddie suspected him of sabotaging the planetary display?

The impact is scant seconds away now. Eddie closes his eyes and tries not to imagine the mess his pickled brains will make splattered all over the corridor.

He hears a churning, grinding sound, harmonizing badly with a loud, discordant squeal, and feels himself being lifted into the air. Then a kind of weightless moment, and he thumps down into the seat again.

He's still alive. He's still intact. The kart is still wailing its shrieking whine.

He opens his eyes. They made the turn, somehow. They are pelting along another corridor at spine-breaking speed.

He looks down at the dashboard again, but it's gone. He finds, in fact, he is clutching the entire severed assembly between his claws.

He flings it aside. The kart is careering at such demon speed that by the time the discarded dashboard strikes the ground behind them, he doesn't even hear it hit.

And again, they are hurtling straight at an oncoming wall.

Only this time, there's a problem.

This time, there is no bend.

This time there is just another of those inexplicable dead ends.

Eddie looks down for some kind of brake, but all he sees are torn wires, shorn metal, and a jagged hole in the floor, through which his foot has involuntarily thrust the brake pedal. Brilliantly, he's managed to rip out every single control on the craft in less than three minutes without even trying. Superb stuff, Eddie. Majestic. Give yourself a pat on the back. If you can manage that without beating yourself to a pulp.

He looks up.

Dead end. Two words that sum up Eddie's future plans with beautiful concision.

Eddie gets ready to kiss his arse goodbye. At the speed he's travelling, he probably won't even have to pucker to reach it after the impact.

He doesn't close his eyes in anticipation this time. Maybe this is evidence that he's conquering his cowardice, or maybe it's just Eddie reverting to his characteristic resigned complaisance to the horrors life throws at him with such gay regularity.

Either way, he keeps his eyes open, and actually sees the miracle happen.

As the kart kamikazes towards the inevitable collision, the wall opens. It slides apart.

It slides apart enough for the kart to squeeze through.

And whatever it is that's impelling the vehicle slams on the brakes and throws the drive into reverse, which is sufficient to stop the kart's forward motion in a screaming, chundering cloud of burnt-out engine and choking rubber smoke from the melting tyres.

It is not, however, sufficient to stop Eddie from crashing through the reinforced glass of the kart's sturdy windscreen.

A handily placed metal bar is what finally arrests Eddie's forward propulsion by colliding with the top of his helmet. A collision of such bone-crunching force, Eddie is convinced he truly will be able to kiss his own arse without bending.

It's becoming almost instinctive now, after such an encounter, for Eddie to scan the immediate area for evidence of leaking gloop. Finding none, he clasps the metal bar in his pincer and hauls himself erect.

He is in a transway carriage.

The wall that miraculously opened up before him was, in fact, the transway's sliding entrance.

He looks over at the wreck of the kart.

Jebediah Styx is resting peacefully on the back seat, undisturbed and unruffled, the billowing smoke slowly subsiding around him. In his mouth is his one remaining thumb.

The transway's motor winds up, and the carriage lurches off.

And apart from the gentle rocking of the transway, nothing is happening. Eddie experiences an increasingly rare moment of peace and tranquillity. Odd, really. His life before the *Willflower* was one long non-event. He wishes now he'd treasured all those tedious moments of nothing happening, with nothing having happened and nothing about to happen; the interminable dull weekend afternoons of lazy tick-tock boredom; the discontented languid evenings that overstayed their welcome. He wishes he could have tucked a few of them away in some kind of time bank account. He wishes he could cash a couple of them in right now.

But he can't. And this small minute of precious peace is all he gets.

There is a loud electronic bleep in his helmet and the face of Bernadette Oslo blips into being in front of his eyes, staring at him, larger than life, completely blocking his vision. Eddie is so shocked by her sudden appearance, his automatic reaction is to leap back. This impulse causes his right arm to shoot out, sending his claw smashing through the carriage window.

'Shii!' He manages to recover enough to drag his arm back inside before it's crushed against the transway tunnel wall. 'How the *hell* do you do that?'

Oslo looks puzzled. 'Do what?'

'Appear like that. In my face. Without warning.'

'You're connected up to the ship com. Didn't you know that?'

Eddie tries to twist his head so he can see past Oslo's image. 'No. I did not know that. Can you go now? I can't actually *see* with you in my visor.' He is connected to the shipwide communication system. It would have been nice if somebody had bothered to tell him that a little while ago. It might have saved him a life-threatening problem or two.

'Where are you?'

'I'm in the transway.'

'That's hugely helpful. Whereabouts in the transway?'

'I don't know. I think . . . I hope I'm heading for the medical bay.' Eddie is finding it extremely disconcerting having Oslo literally in his face. Talk about encroaching on your personal space. 'Can you shrink your image at least? Only you're actually blinding me.' Can anybody on board do this, any time they feel like it? Blip their giant faces into his visor without so much as an 'excuse me'? How relaxing is that?

'The medical bay? Why?'

'I've got a Styx here. Badly injured. Touch and go.'

Oslo snorts. 'Forget about him. Things just got worse here.'

Worse? 'How could things possibly get worse?'

'Try this: did you feel that last shipquake?'

'Did I feel it? I was starring in it.'

'Well, it caused some major structural damage.'

'How major?'

'Majorly major. Inasmuch as it ripped away the last remaining engine.'

34

'So that's it? We've lost all three engines?' Eddie is in the Navigation Room, craning over the display on the ship status monitor, staring at the graphical reconstruction of the most recent disaster, hoping, wretchedly, that everybody else has somehow interpreted the data incorrectly. 'All of them?'

'That's right, soldier of Satan,' Peck mocks. 'We had three engines, we lost three engines. Now we have no engines. Would you like to borrow a calculator and confirm that for yourself?'

This is supposed to be a code alpha emergency meeting, yet only Peck, Oslo and Apton Styx have shown up. It's hard to believe the rest of the Pilgrim Parents have found something more urgent to attend to. The alternatives are not good. Either the communication system has broken down or the rest of the Committee are incapacitated.

Injured . . . or worse.

Certainly, the medical bay where Eddie dropped off Jebediah Styx was otherwise unoccupied.

Eddie runs the graphic again. There is no ambiguity. The hull quivers, then rips itself apart around the giant engine. The engine crumples like an empty cigarette packet and seems to fold into the ship, leaving only a raised scar along the length of the fissure. 'So now we don't have any engines left at all?'

'Mercy me. How did we ever get by without your expert analysis?'

Eddie doesn't take his eyes off the display. 'Frankly, you didn't. You managed to lose two entire engines and eighty per cent of the manoeuvring thrusters before I was even revived, baby.' Why, Eddie? Why can't you rise above this pettiness?

Oslo waves her hand over the monitor, blacking out the display. 'So you didn't find anything? In the hieroglyphics?'

'No. Nothing yet.'

'Then there's still a chance?'

'A chance? Maybe there was a chance, before we lost the engine. But now . . .'

'You've got to keep looking.'

'Why? What do you expect me to find? A neat little booklet entitled *Fifty Ways to Steer an Enormous Space Ship Around Gigantic Gas Planets Without Engines*? *How to Make a Space-worthy Parachute for Five Thousand People – Volume 7*?'

'OK. What's your plan, tin man? Give up? Lounge in your apartment and sip a Blue Lagoon while you enjoy the spectacle of the hull collapsing around you, crushing us all?'

'Oslo.' Apton Styx steps up to the monitor. 'Would you mind running the reconstruction again?'

'May I ask why, Mr Styx?'

'No reason. I just enjoy watching it.'

Oslo shakes her head in despair and waves her hand over the screen, too worn out even to insult the drone. 'Maybe it's best we all die in horrible crushing agony. Maybe it's the best option for the future of the human race.'

Eddie turns to face her. He gets a sense, a strange, unfamiliar sense, that he's supposed to do something here. That, for all their insults, put-downs and exasperations, Peck and Oslo are in some way looking to him, looking for some kind of lead.

Eddie, a leader? Invisible Eddie? How did this moment ever arrive?

He does his best to rise to the occasion. 'I'm not saying we should give up. I'm not saying things are hopeless. Things are never hopeless . . .' Suddenly, an image of the gas giant pops into his brain, looming towards the helpless, doomed ship. He tries to shake it off. Succeeds, for the moment. '. . . So we're not going to abandon ourselves to hopelessness.' But the image returns, in even more graphic detail. He imagines the poor, wounded *Willflower* crushed by the immense gravitational force of the unavoidable planet. '. . . That's the important thing . . .' Flash frames leap into his head of the individuals he's facing dying in an alarming number of hideously violent ways: getting blown up by random explosions, pulverized by crumpling walls and blasted into space through sudden lesions in the hull. He tries to put the ghastly visions out of his mind and give his rallying speech a final little upbeat turn, find some kind of positive spin. Sadly, the best he can dredge up is: 'It's just that, well, in this particular scenario, there isn't exactly a tremendous abundance of . . . hopefulosity.'

Nice speech, Eddie. Inspirational. He has to think of something to break the baffled, incredulous, staring pause that follows it, so he changes gear with: 'Anybody seen Father Lewis?'

Oslo and Peck look at each other, then back at Eddie. Oslo says: 'Wasn't he with you?'

'He left.'

'He left you? Why?'

'Well, I was wedged upside down in a snack machine, Styx was comatose, and he probably thought he'd make better time without those little handicaps.'

'That sounds like the Padre all right.'

'What are you saying?' Peck rounds on Oslo. 'Are you insulting the integrity of a man of God?'

'Come on, Trinity. Wake up and sniff the transubstantiated wine, honey. He left the man helpless in the middle of a shipquake.'

'He must have had a good, devout reason.'

'Yes. Like saving his own sorry, devout ass.'

'Bernadette, it's one thing that this unholy anti-life,' Peck flicks a tiny nostril sneer in Eddie's direction, 'despises the Padre. It's in his soulless nature. But I expect better of you.'

Oslo touches her chest. 'Me? I don't despise Lewis. True, I think he's the moral equivalent of single-cell life forms that reproduce in toilet basin scum, but I also think he's in possession of the nearest thing we have on board to a working intellect. And we need him here, now.' She turns to Eddie. 'Where did he say he was heading?'

'He said he was coming up here to calm things down.'

'Really.' Oslo's long legs stride over to the coms panel. She waves her hands over the controls. 'And you were lodged in the snack dispenser . . . here.'

A low-resolution image appears in the monitor above Oslo. A corridor. It looks similar to the corridor Eddie was in when the quake struck. Oslo looks over at him. 'Yes?'

'Well, it can't be. I mean, it looks like the same corridor, but there's no damage.'

'There was a lot of damage?'

'There wasn't much else *but* damage. Look. Even the vending machine's still intact.'

'Well, according to your playback, this is the same corridor.'

'Playback? What playback?'

'I keep telling you: the suit is hooked into the shipwide coms systems. Effectively, you're part of the ship.'

'What are you saying? You can track me? You can trace everywhere I've been? Everything I've done?'

'Of course. Now . . .' Oslo starts waving her hands again. 'He would have taken some kind of transport . . .'

Eddie is aghast. Not only is Lewis spying on him – everyone on board can spy on him, any time they feel like it. They can follow his every move, his every word. They can replay it all, even, at their leisure. They can relax in their sofas of an evening with a bag of popcorn and tune into the Eddie O'Hare show. And when they're not doing that, they can project their huge faces into his helmet at will. Sensational.

'Got him.' Oslo looks up at the monitor. 'He took a kart to the transway, and headed to his office. Seven minutes later, he was back on the transway, and he got off . . . here.'

Another lo-res image, another part of the ship. A high, wide-angle shot of two huge bay doors, with boxes stacked outside. A corridor kart is parked with skewed eagerness by the pile of cartons. There are more boxes on the kart. No sign of the Padre.

Oslo pans the camera around. 'He must be somewhere arou . . .'

The camera pauses on a box on the kart which is wobbling. The image zooms in as the box rises, revealing a cassocked body behind it.

Lewis staggers under the weight of the carton as he carries it over to the stack. In this tighter focus, Eddie can see the stack is resting on a pallet, with a forklift trolley parked near by.

Oslo shakes her head, sporting a quarter smile. 'I really should have guessed.'

Eddie peers closer. 'Guessed what?'

'Don't you know where this is?'

Eddie peers closer still. There is a sign by the bay doors, but it's in blurred focus. He can barely make out the three largest letters. 'STP?'

Oslo nods. 'Right. He's loading up the STiP.'

'STiP?'

'The Ship to Planet module.'

'Some kind of craft?'

Apton Styx looks at Eddie with something approaching disdain. 'The STiP is a Ship to Planet module, which is a module for travelling between the ship and a planet. See?' He flattens one hand. 'Ship . . .' He makes a ball with his other hand. '. . . Planet.' He moves the flat hand towards the fist, slowly and deliberately. 'Ship . . . to Planet.' He repeats the demonstration in reverse. 'Planet to ship.'

'So it is a craft?'

Styx holds up the flat hand. 'It's a module. A Ship to Planet module.'

Eddie smiles indulgently and wishes his headache would go away. 'Thanks, Apton. That is so much clearer, now. Would you like to go away and lift some heavy weights with your neck?' He turns to Oslo. 'What kind of passenger capacity does the *module* have? How much cargo can it carry? What's its range?'

'It can hold ten people, at a squeeze. There's lots of cargo space, but it's not sealed – there's no life support there. It's really only meant to cruise between the ship in orbit and the planet's surface. The plan is, it carries an advance party, with sufficient supplies to construct what we call a "stairway" – a kind of . . .'

'I know. A Stairway to Heaven. I've seen one.'

'Seen one? You mean, you've seen a simulation.'

This is awkward. Of course, the only people who can have seen the stairway in operation would be the founding pilgrims. The Originals. Eddie's not sure this is a good time to get into the subject. Fortunately, something on the display distracts Oslo's attention, and he's off the hook, temporarily.

Lewis is looking up at the monitor, his eyes narrowed in suspicion. He must have heard the camera's servo tracking him. A flustered look crosses his face only momentarily. His eyes dart from side to side. He puts the box he's carrying on top of the pile, and smooths back an unruly lock of hair from his forehead. Ignoring the camera now, he crosses to the com panel by the STiP bay doors and flips the switch. 'Hello? Can anybody hear me?' His voice sounds suitably desperate. 'Is this darned thing working yet?'

Oslo flips her own com switch. 'Nice try, Padre. Going somewhere?'

'Bernadette, is that you? Praise God. I've been trying to reach you for ages.'

'Right. And in the meantime, you thought you'd pack for a little trip.'

Lewis looks over at the boxes. 'This? Yes. Look, I don't know how to break this to you, but that last quake, it destroyed the one remaining engine.'

'We know.'

'So that's it. There doesn't seem to be any option left, does there? We'll have to pick a small group to try and make some kind of escape in the STiP. I thought someone should start packing it up with supplies.'

'And that group would, presumably, include you?'

Lewis's eyes do their darting thing again. 'I hadn't thought, to be honest. But, yes, I suppose I assumed we'd select key personnel from the Committee.'

'He's right,' Peck nods. 'If we are forced to abandon ship, it would be vital to have a priest among the survivors.'

'Really?' Oslo zooms in on a packing box bulging with video discs. 'And presumably, it would be equally vital for that priest to bring along his sacred pornography collection?' Eddie squints at the image on the disc label. It seems to depict two naked females in a shower attempting to accommodate an unreasonably giant loofah.

Lewis manages to interpose his body between the screen and the boxes and make it look accidental. 'I don't know what you're talking about, Bernie. I was in something of a rush. I just threw a few boxes in the kart, that's all.' He turns and pretends to check the boxes. 'Are there really filthy videos in here? Damn.'

Oslo flips off her com switch and turns to the others. 'Look. Much as I hate to admit it, Lewis has a damned good point. With no engines, our only choice is to abandon ship.'

'Wait a minute.' Eddie's not sure what his chances would be of making the ship's top ten list, but he has a good idea. Certainly he doesn't seem to have a massive fan base on the Committee. 'How many of these STiPs are there?'

There is a guilty silence. Peck answers. 'One.'

'One?'

'There were more. There's only one left that's operational.'

'So we have a single lifeboat that can hold ten people? Out of a population of over two thousand?'

'Once again, demonic incubus, your arithmetic is flawless.'

'And it's not a lifeboat,' Styx chips in, 'it's a module.'

'And just who gets to decide?' Eddie's praying it's not a democratic vote. 'Who chooses the survivors?'

Peck looks towards Oslo. There's something going on between them. Oslo looks down. 'I think it's pretty obvious. We should include our brightest people, and those with the most useful skills. If you're worrying whether or not you'd be included . . .'

'I'm not.' He is.

'Well, you would be.'

'Really?' Eddie tries not to look smug.

'Not for you, yourself. For your suit.'

'Of course.' Eddie tries not to look crestfallen.

'It's strong, it can survive extreme conditions, and you wouldn't be a drain on our consumables.'

Good lord. They've discussed this. In detail. This is what they've been planning. Eddie looks over at Peck. She's literally biting her lip. The decision to take Eddie along would not have sat sweetly with her. 'Well, it's nice to be appreciated. But that's not the point. You can't just select ten people to live out of the whole population. Less than one half of one per cent of the crew. It's inhuman.'

'And so what, then?' Oslo's angry. She probably doesn't like the situation any more than Eddie does. 'We all die? Everybody dies, because the alternative's immoral?'

Eddie turns to Peck. 'And what about you, Joan of Arc? Are you on the saved list?'

Oslo cuts in. 'Of course she is. We need someone with a science background.'

'Who else then? Styx?'

Oslo nods. 'We don't know what we'll be facing out there. We'll probably need muscle. Especially recyclable muscle. We can take his regeneration equipment. Churn out as many drones as our resources allow.'

'So, us four, Lewis – presumably because we're going to need someone to say grace at meal times – and who else? The Captain?'

The same guilty, conspiratorial look passes from Peck to Oslo.

Suddenly, Eddie understands their naughty little secret. 'Wait a minute. You're not taking Gwent. You haven't told him, have you? You're keeping him out of the loop.'

Oslo sneers. 'What use would that silly little turdpot be? What special skills would he bring to the party? The ability to masturbate non-stop for eleven hours out of every twelve? That should come in useful on a hostile planet. "Look! There's a river of molten lava cascading down that mountain towards the camp. Quick, Captain! Try and douse it with seminal fluid!"' She mimics the actions, the bent body and the ugly facial contortions of an orgasming adolescent. '"Say, sure thing, Ozovitch! Eeee eeee eeee! Blarhhhghhhh! It's not working. Maybe I should try squirting it with, say, copious amounts of my acne pus."' She mimes squeezing facial spots. 'Schtppp! Schtppp! Schtppp! No, Captain, stop! We're going to need that pus to poison predators! "Don't worry, Oz!" Schtppp! Schtppp! "I have an unlimited supply!" Schtppp!'

Once again, Eddie is taken aback by the intensity of Oslo's hatred for Gwent. 'Ooh, but he's the Captain, Bernie. Useless or not, that's the bottom line. Who stays and who goes, that's his decision. What you're proposing is mutiny, in fact.'

'Mutiny? You're not serious?'

'Technically, it is. Technically, Gwent could have you removed from your body just for having this conversation.'

'All right.' There is the ominous clack of a cocked weapon, and Eddie turns slowly towards it.

Styx has his assault rifle trained on the group. 'Hands in the air, one and all.'

Nobody raises any hands. Oslo closes her eyes, fighting despair. 'What the frot are you doing, Styx?'

'My duty, ma'am. You're all under arrest.'

'What for? Mutiny? He wasn't being serious. You weren't being serious, were you, Dr Morton?'

'No, Apton. I was making a theoretical point, that's all.'

Without further warning, Styx snaps the barrel low and fires the weapon at the floor beside Eddie's feet. Eddie's arm shoots out involuntarily and crashes into a bank of electronic equipment. A high-voltage shock runs through his suit, and Eddie begins to judder uncontrollably. He screams for someone to turn off the juice, but his free arm is flailing randomly, making it hard to get near him. The liquid in his helmet starts to bubble. Oslo strides over to him calmly and kicks his arm clear of the console.

Eddie can't speak for the moment. He can't see, and he can't move. All he can do is wait for the juddering to subside, and for his green gloop to drop below boiling point. The voice box in his throat is making alarming, intermittent fizzing noises. Finally, his foaming vision clears sufficiently for him to make out Styx, through a haze of smoke, who looks shocked and a little scared, but none the less still has his weapon trained on Eddie.

'Don't ever, ever, do that again.' Eddie's voice doesn't carry the weight it might, his vocal unit having shorted out. He sounds like he's been breathing helium. 'Ever,' he squeaks.

'Next time, I'll be aiming at your helmet. Now,' the drone waves the rifle in the direction of the door, 'I want you all to file out of here, one by one, in a kind of . . . single file, with your arms raised above your heads.'

Oslo takes a step towards him. 'I'm losing my patience, Styx. Put the weapon down.'

Styx backs away nervously. 'Ma'am, I *will* use this weapon, ma'am. You're under arrest.'

Oslo takes another stride. 'We haven't got time for this, Styx. We have to abandon ship.'

Styx backs off a step, his rifle aimed at Oslo. 'There will be no mutiny, ma'am. Not on my watch. Now, let's all file off in the file formation I previously described, in single file.'

'Look, if it really was a mutiny, you'd be a mutineer, too, wouldn't you?'

Styx's eyes flit from side to side. 'Begging your pardon, ma'am?'

'You were going to come along with us, were you not?'

'Ma'am, yes ma'am. But that was . . . I didn't know . . . Nobody said it was a mutiny.'

'So, is it a mutiny or not?'

'I don't . . . I think it probably . . . If the Captain doesn't know, then . . . yes, it is.'

'In which case, I'm ordering you to place yourself under arrest.'

Styx's eyes lose their focus completely. 'Ma'am, you're right, ma'am. But how . . . ? I don't know how I could arrest myself, exactly.'

'All right, no need to make this difficult.' Oslo holds out her hand. 'Give me the rifle, and *I'll* arrest you for you.'

A relieved smile washes over Styx's features. 'You'd do that for me? Thank you, ma'am.' He offers Oslo the weapon. 'If I can ever repay you . . .'

'You keep the gun, Styx. If you move, shoot you.'

Styx steels his jaw. 'Ma'am, yes ma'am!'

'Wait!' Peck is looking at a readout which is flashing a red warning light. 'The STiP's preparing for launch.'

Eddie glances up at the monitor. Lewis still appears to be stacking boxes on the pallet. 'That must be an error. He's not even inside it yet.' But there's a shudder on the display, and Lewis jumps to a different position on screen. 'Damn the man! He's looped the display.'

Peck looks up at the monitor. 'What?'

'I don't know how, but he's hacked into the security camera and made it replay the same section of recording, over and over.'

'That's not possible.'

'Not possible? Father Lewis is something of an expert when it comes to electronic surveillance.'

'I don't like the implications of your filthy slurs against that honest servant of the Lord, you cacodemon.'

'Oh, stop it with your righteous indignation, woman. Save it for someone more worthwhile. Like a plague rat. The man's moral sewage. You must have worked out he's the one who erased the gas giant from the system plan.'

'Get thee behind me.'

Oslo narrows her eyes. 'Lewis is the saboteur?'

'Who else?'

'Why? Why would he do such a thing?'

'Isn't it obvious? He didn't want everyone else to know how dire things really were. While you all still believed there was at least a slender chance you might save yourselves, he knew you'd be concentrating on doing just that.'

'Leaving him to corner the market in escape vessels.'

'Modules,' Styx corrects, his arms in the air in arrest mode.

'Absolutely.' Eddie nods. 'He's probably been preparing this little trip for days, weeks even.'

'Are you listening to the insanity this stooge of Satan is spouting, Bernadette? You'd take the word of an acolyte of the Antichrist over the word of a holy priest?'

'Frankly, I'm not sure. I knew Lewis was lowlife, but this? Abandoning us all to save his own scrawny . . . That would be . . .'

'There's obviously some kind of rational explanation. He must have some kind of saintly purpose we don't yet understand.'

'Right. In the meantime,' Eddie manages a painful nod at the warning light on Peck's console, 'Saint Porno is warming up his engines. And by the time you decide that he actually *is* capable of deserting us, he'll be warming his toes in the natural hot springs of the planet Thrrrppp.'

'He's got a point.' Oslo strides over to Peck. 'Override the STiP launch sequence.'

Reluctantly, Peck turns and waves her hands over the controls. 'You're all wrong. I know it.'

Eddie looks up at the display. He's not familiar with the read-out, but it's clear some kind of countdown has been engaged. 'Faster!'

Peck's waving becomes more frenetic. 'I'm trying!'

'What's the hold-up?'

'I don't know. It's . . . something's locked us out.'

Eddie looks up at the security monitor, with Lewis's smug, calm face looped over and over. At one point, he looks over at the camera and winks. He's mocking them. He must have realized they'd latch on to his trickery sooner or later, and he took time out to mock them. 'He's a regular wizard with the old electronics, the good Father.'

'What are you saying, foul incubus?'

'I'm saying the smarmy bastard is always one step ahead of us.'

'No!' Peck is waving desperately now, her hands actually blurring over the console, at least in Eddie's simmering vision. 'You lie, henchman of the hornèd one! The padre would never desert his flock. It's some kind of system error.'

Henchman of the hornèd one? Is it Eddie's imagination, or is

Peck starting to warm to him? He turns to Oslo. 'How long before it launches?'

She glances up at the readout. 'Seven . . . Seven and a half minutes.'

'There's an all-systems override, or at least there used to be.'

'Yes. In the . . . in the Captain's office.'

'How far is that?'

'I don't know. What do you think? I'm a regular visitor? I'm dropping in for tea and crumpets every day, to inspect his collection of dried pustules?'

'How far, damn it?'

'Far. Seven minutes? Too far.'

'Call him.'

'Call Gwent? Are you . . . ?'

'If you don't call him and tell him to cancel the launch, Lewis will be cruising through the local system in our one remaining opportunity for survival.'

'Wake up and sniff your gloop, Morton. What do you think Captain Dickwit will do when he finds out about our little coterie here? Hmm? When he finds out we had a little escape plan of our own, and, oh, by the way, he wasn't invited? Think he'll just laugh it off with that charming spittle-spraying snigger of his?' She mimics him again. '"Thuh-thuh-thuh"?' Gwent's giggle to a T, facial contortions and all. For a woman with such an avowed loathing for the lad, she's spent an inordinate amount of time observing his mannerisms. 'He'll have us put in *jars*, Dr Morton. He'll strip out our spines and pickle us before he can sprout another pimple.'

'We don't have time for this. Trinity? Will you call Captain Gwent?' This is desperation indeed. Eddie is actually appealing to Torquemada's loonier sister to bring some kind of sanity to the debate.

Peck looks from him to Oslo and back again. Her features streamline into her famous trademark sneer, and she speaks moving only her upper lip. 'If it's the Lord's will that Father Lewis is to be saved and we are to be cast into the infernal pit, then so be it.'

So be it, indeed. Amen. Only Eddie doesn't feel quite ready for the infernal pit just yet. He looks at the coms panel. The mechanism is too delicate for his crude pincers to manipulate. Every time he's tried, he's crushed the machinery. And even if he could switch the damned thing on, how would he get the code to access the Captain? He still has one last hope. One very, very faint last hope. 'Styx?'

Styx is still standing with his arms upraised, the barrel of his weapon angled awkwardly against his head.

The sight doesn't swell Eddie's breast with unbridled confidence, but he has to try anyway. 'Styx. Can you please call the Captain, and put a stop to this madness?'

'Sir, I'd like to help you, Dr Morton, sir. Unfortunately I'm under arrest.' And to emphasize the point he jabs his rifle against his temple, hard enough to make himself wince. Eddie thinks about trying to disarm him, to rescue him from himself, but decides against it. Crazy as it seems, the drone is probably capable of blowing his own brains out to prevent himself escaping.

'Fine.' Eddie takes a step towards the coms unit. 'That is just spiffing. Top hole. Wunderbar. Thank you, one and all, for your magnificent co-operation.' He reaches out as gingerly as he can. His claw is poised above the switch. He concentrates hard. All it requires is a small movement, a little twitch, really, of the impulse that used to control his left thigh, in the days when he still had a left thigh. Gently, now. The pincer trembles. Good. And . . .

And his elbow joint straightens with a sudden, astonishing force, sending his claw crashing down through the panel in a shower of sparks and slicing it in two. The speaker fizzles, exhales a final sigh of smoke and dies.

Eddie would cry, if he still could. He'd cry big, green tears of frustration. What is *wrong* with these people? Why is staying alive so low in their priorities?

He looks over at the countdown. The display is figurative, rather than alphanumeric – a series of vertical bars reducing in height to a flashing base line – so he can't judge precisely how much time they have left to abort the launch. Not much, though. Just a handful of bars left. As he watches, another blips off the screen and into oblivion.

Oblivion.

Eddie's new address.

Another blip. Just two bars left now.

Eddie keeps watching for the moment. He can't think of anything else to do. He feels like a passenger in a car that's about to crash, skidding gracefully in silent slow motion into the path of an oncoming truck.

And, for a while, nothing happens.

Then nothing happens again.

The penultimate bar should have blipped off by now. Surely.

Oslo glances back at him, then up at the screen again. 'It's stopped.'

'Are you sure?'

Peck waves her hands over the controls. 'It wasn't me. I'm still locked out.'

'Then what . . . ?'

The security monitor jumps out of its loop. The camera is focused on Father Lewis, in the pilot seat, presumably, of the STiP. He looks extremely puzzled. He is checking his readouts and randomly flicking ignition switches impotently.

'Father!' Peck makes the sign of the cross. 'You're safe. Praise be!'

Lewis jumps at her voice and looks into the monitor, his face struggling to find an expression beyond 'bewildered'. 'Trinity! Yes. I'm . . . I'm safe. Praise be indeed. What exactly . . . what happened, exactly?'

'The STiP started up. We thought you were launching it.'

'Me? On my own? Goodness, no. That would be . . . No. I was testing out the engines, of course. They haven't been serviced in a goodly while, and somebody had to do it, before we all . . . before we made the leap into the great unknown.'

Peck expels a long-held breath. 'We guessed it would be

something along those lines, Father.' She shoots a triumphant sneer at Eddie. 'At least, some of us did.'

Lewis's alibi is, of course, planned in advance, and impossible to disprove, but he still looks nonplussed. Flustered even. 'But I don't understand how . . . why you aborted the launch. Before I managed to do it myself, I mean.'

'We didn't. We were locked out.'

'Really? Locked out, eh?' Lewis's mind is racing, and he can barely be bothered to fake the surprise his alibi technically requires. 'Who, then?'

The coms speakers suddenly start to vibrate with an echoing snicker, 'Thuh-thuh-thuh . . .', and suddenly, on all the monitors, the gleaming braces of the Captain's teeth are glaring down at them. 'Who then, dudes and dudesses? How about, say, *me*, then?'

Eddie doesn't even have a moment to feel relief that the STiP is still on board. He's wondering exactly how long the little brat has been spying on them, and how much, exactly, he's overheard. Oslo locks eyes with him, worrying the same question.

'Okayanovski. Let's all squeeze into the chill cabinet, peoples. No harm done. STiP safe and well. Oh, and by the way . . .'

The navigation room doors slide open and a dozen heavily armed Styx drones yomp into the room, yelling blood-curdling imprecations against the wisdom of attempting movement, and then freeze, weapons cocked and trained.

'. . . You're all under arrestovich.'

35

'What the hell are we waiting for?' Oslo is pacing the small holding cell in a dementedly small elliptical orbit. Peck, sitting primly on the bench beside the sprawling Father Lewis, crosses herself at the minor blasphemy.

Eddie is standing by the cell door; not to ready himself for an escape bid, or even to peer through the small square of reinforced glass for signs of activity outside. Nothing so proactive. He's simply standing there because he doesn't have the will to move any further into the room. 'Standard procedure, isn't it?'

'That's right.' Lewis lurches up off the bench and crosses to the sink. 'Leave us to sweat it out for a while, contemplate the consequences. Morale gets low, before long we're at each other's throats. By the time he gets round to interrogating us, we're queuing up to sell each other out.' He turns the cold tap on hard and thrusts his head under the torrent. He straightens and rakes his wet hair. 'Frankly, it's an insult to our intelligence.' He smiles in that innocent, winning way he has, and Eddie wonders how long it will take the good priest to sell them all down the Swanee.

'I mean, mutiny?' Oslo slaps her forehead. '*Mutiny*, for ship's sake?! What does he think this is? Treasure frotting Island? Does he think this is some kind of dumb-ass little-boy *game*? We are all going to die. Die! In a matter of days! And that's if we're lucky. We should be formulating some sort of strategy, not rotting in this festering dung pit.'

'Actually,' Styx says, 'it's regulation restraining accommodation for officer-class detainees, complete with controllable air conditioning, a choice of superior snacks and refreshments and excellent private toilet facilities.'

'Mr Styx?' Oslo smiles politely at the drone.

'Ma'am, sir?'

'Fuck off.'

'Yes sir, ma'am sir.'

'And put your frotting hands down.'

Styx looks up at his hands, still held over his head. 'Ma'am, sir, if you say so, ma'am.' And reluctantly he drops them by his side. 'I just want everyone to know I'm still keeping a close eye on me.'

'I mean, what's his *plan*?' Oslo resumes her pacing, still on the same orbit, her elbows pinned to her ribs, her hands upright, fingers wide and quivering, as if she's trying to crush an invisible beach ball. 'How does he intend to punish us, the suppurating little haemorrhoid? Make us walk the plank? We're all going to be crushed to death before the bloody weekend, anyway. What's he going to come up with that's worse than that?'

Eddie coughs quietly and mumbles that Gwent may, in fact, be listening in. Probably is, in fact.

Privately, Eddie is beginning to feel it's a little bizarre just how much everyone on board seems to be spying, pretty much all the time, on pretty much everyone else, and on him in particular. Clearly, Eddie is right at the bottom of the spying food chain. He doesn't get to spy on anyone himself, yet he even has people spying on the people who are spying on him. Welcome to the good ship *Paranoia*.

'I hope he *is* listening.' Oslo throws back her head and shouts at the ceiling. 'I hope you are listening, you poisonous little splat. Keeping us locked up in here is killing all of us! You're killing yourself. Which, in actual fact, is the only part of your plan that makes any sense. Yes! Ha! I applaud that!' She starts clapping, loudly. 'Bravo, Captain Zit! Bravo!'

'Look.' Eddie's worried Oslo is becoming borderline hysterical, 'think about it from the Captain's point of view. He's responsible for the entire crew. His ship is in terrible, probably insurmountable danger. And how do his trusty lieutenants support him in this darkest hour? They band together and try to purloin the only escape craft on board . . .'

'Module.'

'Thank you, Mr Styx. What's the lad supposed to do? Hand over the keys and wish you *bon voyage*?'

'Well.' Lewis sits back on the bench, crosses his legs and smooths down the crease of his trousers. 'We can see which way the good doctor intends to cast his dice. Turn us over for the mutinous ingrates we are, and watch us hang as best he can with his tongue buried up the Captain's spot-encrusted rear canal.'

'How sane is that, Padre? What have I got to lose that I haven't already lost? What's he going to do to punish me? Darken my gloop?' Actually, as soon the words are out of Eddie's mouth, having his gloop darkened *does* sound like an undesirably brutal punishment to him. He wishes he hadn't mentioned it.

'You don't understand, *Doctor*,' and Lewis intones the word to make unmasking Eddie a blatant threat. 'There are greater considerations here than simply saving the entire crew. We have a larger responsibility; a responsibility to the human race. For all we know, we're the last representatives of our species in the entire universe. That's quite a burden to carry, eh? Don't you think we have an *obligation* to survive? Even if it's just a handful of us? Don't you think it's our God-given duty?'

'I see what you're saying. You're saying that stealing the STiP and sneaking off in it was your sacredly inspired contribution to saving the human race from extinction.'

'You're trying to make it sound inglorious, eh? But, yes. I was engaged in God's work, my friend. And surely you must admit even our revered Captain is outranked by God.'

'And who am I to question a directive from the Almighty? What puzzles me, slightly, is quite why God instructed you to load up your little Ark with crates of pornography.'

Lewis smiles, but there's a dangerous tremor in his upper lip. 'I *thought* I'd explained . . .'

Eddie's past the point where he could care less about the priest's threat to unmask him. 'Only, on the face of it, that would seem to contravene quite a few of the Commandments. Coveting neighbours' wives, for instance. Stealing. And isn't there one about not spilling your seed on the ground? Or is that one of those bizarre bits from Deuteronomy?'

'I *told* you all . . .'

The cell door lock whirls open, and a pair of Styx drones, I and O, step into the room. Then I Styx says, 'The Captain would like to request the pleasure of your company.'

Like a damaged boxer reacting to the bell, Lewis turns, gratefully. The drone is standing stiffly to attention. He doesn't seem to have been addressing anyone in particular. 'Thank you, Ignatius. The pleasure of whose company, exactly?'

The drone's eyes flit towards the Padre, then back. 'Father, sir, I believe that would be all of your . . . companies, Father, sir.'

'All of us? At once?'

'Father, sir, that would be correct, Father, sir. We're to accompany you all down there.'

'Down there, eh?' Lewis rakes his nails through his thick fringe. 'Down where, exactly?'

'We're to accompany you all to the Suspended Personnel Storage chamber.'

36

They are led to a larger than normal corridor kart, one with four banks of double seats. They climb aboard, grimly, in pairs. Oslo and Peck, Lewis and Eddie, with Apton Styx behind them, alone. The guard drones both sit up front, which seems like a procedural error to Eddie. Surely one should take up the rear, to forestall any escape attempts?

The same thought appears to have crossed Lewis's mind, too. He keeps making discreet turns of his head to look behind, probably trying to assess how poor Apton might react if anyone were to attempt a leap off the kart and make a bolt for it. Would he class himself a guard or a detainee? Probably both. He'd probably give chase, foil the escape and then beat himself up for running off.

The kart starts up and heads down the corridor at a surprisingly escapable moderate place. Oslo turns to Lewis, her voice a harsh whisper. 'I told you he was insane. But this is way out there.'

Lewis flicks a glance at the drones up front. They're laughing at some joke or other, showing no interest at all in their human cargo. 'He's probably just trying to scare us, Bernadette.'

'Well, it's working plenty good on me. I, for one, am plenty scared. I like having a body. I really don't feel I'm ready to be removed from it at this point in my career.'

Lewis says: 'He wouldn't do that.' But he lacks conviction.

'Are you serious? Don't you think he'd *love* to have my head in a jar? Don't you think he'd *love* to pop down and giggle his spittle slime all over it every day? Maybe even pop off my lid so he can grab me out of the gloop by my hair and give me a big, sloppy French kiss?'

And then Eddie hears Lewis say something that explains a lot about Oslo. It's something he should probably have worked out for himself. 'Seriously, Bernadette,' Lewis coos, 'do you honestly think he'd remove your body before he's had a chance to mate with it?'

The scales fall from Eddie's eyes. *That's* why she despises Gwent so passionately. She's his designated partner. Compelled to procreate with him, whatever her feelings. No wonder she didn't want him on the escape craft.

The muscles on Oslo's face collapse at the mere mention of the idea. 'He might. In fact,' she forces a smile, 'being a head in a jar might constitute my brightest future option.'

'So, wait.' Eddie knows he's on tricky ground, here, but he can't help but explore the concept. 'You and Gwent, you're scheduled to . . . for progenitorial activities?'

'That's right, Dr Morton.' Oslo smiles with all the warmth of a starving tiger interrupted over a juicy carcass. 'Progenitorial activities. That little prick is going to schtup me, whether I like it or not. Does that amuse you? Does it? The thought of Pustule Pete writhing and giggling on top of me, grinding his scabby torso against my naked flesh, whilst simultaneously achieving the high score on his hand-held game console. Does that delight and enthral you?'

'No. Of course not. I just didn't . . .'

'Because it thrills me. It thrills me so much, I can't sleep at night. I lie there wondering what kind of love bites you get from metal braces. Wondering if there's a stain remover in existence that will be strong enough to obliterate pus stains from my sheets. Wondering if our offspring will have the complexion of a normal human, or a prickly pear. Those are my marital prospects, Doctor. That's my glittering future mapped out for me. And isn't it just *dandy*?'

'No. It's . . . it's inhuman.'

'And – can you imagine? – I've known this *from the moment he was born*. It's brightened up my life for the last decade and a half. I've watched him grow ever more obnoxious with each passing day. I was there when the little tyke got his first spot. I even watched him squeeze it, the delightful little scallywag.'

'The point is,' Lewis croons softly, trying to lower Oslo's volume, 'he has good reason *not* to have your spine extracted. The rest of us are not so blessed.'

'Blessed!?'

Lewis shoots a nervous glance at the guards, and lowers his voice even further. 'What I'm getting at: we all have good reasons not to keep this appointment in the Suspended Personnel Storage chamber, eh?'

'Agreed. You have an alternative?'

'Nothing fancy. When I give the word, you, me and Trinity make a break for the STiP. I'm guessing, but I think our route will take us within a few corridors of it.'

'What about the drones?'

Eddie leans in closer. 'And what about me, in fact?'

Lewis smiles at him. 'Dr Morton should be able to distract the guards long enough for us to get clear.'

'Pardon me? Distract the guards?'

'You can handle them. That suit is very strong. I've seen what it's capable of. You could probably snap all their limbs off before they even know we've gone.'

'Wait, whoa, wait. Slow down here. You want me to *maim* the guards?'

'Well, if you like. Ideally, I'd prefer you to kill them.'

'You want me to *murder* these people?'

'When are you going to get this through your gloop, Morton? Drones are not people, they're *drones*. There are more intelligent creatures only visible under a microscope. We can grow replacements in a matter of hours.'

'So, wait, let me explore this plan just a little more deeply. I attack the drones, tear them to butcher-shop-sized pieces with my bare claws, while you make a break for the escape ship, and then . . . ?'

Lewis shrugs with his lips. 'Then we escape.'

'Right. That's the part that loses me most. "We"? "We", as in "you three"? As in "not me"?'

'I'm thinking on my feet here, Doctor. Obviously we'd like to have you with us . . .'

'In case you meet some other drones you'd like dismembered?'

'We're going to have to make a decision fairly quickly. If you can think of a better option, I'm open to suggestions.'

'I can think of a better option. How about *you* slaughter the guards and *I* run away with the womenfolk? That's a one hundred per cent better option, the way I see it.'

'Doctor Morton,' Lewis seems genuinely affronted, 'I'm a man of the *cloth*. I can't employ violence.'

'Right. But it's OK for you to order other poor idiots to do it for you.'

'Well, there is a certain amount of historical precedence for that.' Then Lewis leans in so close, the breath of his softest whisper frosts Eddie's visor. 'And I don't want to make too big a point of it, in front of the girls, but you're not . . . completely equipped for the business of . . . well, biblically speaking, going forth and multiplying. Eh?'

And Lewis winks. He actually winks. A cheeky little double wink, in fact. Incredible. The smug bastard is already planning his sexual future. And what a future that would be. Chief stud for the human race. Take it in turns, girls. There's enough for everyone.

'So.' Lewis leans away to include Peck and Oslo. 'Are we all singing the same Psalm?'

Eddie starts to protest, 'No, we are not . . . ,' but the priest just nods at the women and launches himself over the side of the kart.

Unfortunately, he times the move badly. Very badly, in fact. Neither Peck nor Oslo is prepared for the jump and, as Lewis hits the ground, the kart is starting a tight turn, so he crashes heavily and at speed into a sharp corner and rebounds off the wall and under the kart's back wheels.

Eddie hears Lewis say, 'Ouch!' For some reason, and inappropriately, he finds this hilarious. 'Ouch!'? In real life, nobody actually says 'Ouch!' 'Ouch!' is what cartoon people say in comic books.

The brakes squeal and the kart skews round, crashing its rear into the opposite wall, then bounces back over Lewis's cowering body, with a sickening thud.

Lewis says 'Ouch!' again.

'What the hell happened?' The O drone is out of his seat and racing to the back of the kart. 'Did we hit somebody?'

He finds Lewis pinned under the rear wheel and crouches beside him. 'Father, sir? Are you all right, Father, sir?'

Lewis's voice strains through his pain. 'Never better. Thank you Obadiah. I'd . . . I'd probably feel better still if you could lift this vehicle off my ribcage.'

The drone grabs the rear of the kart and lifts it clear of Lewis's chest, passengers and all. Lewis farts involuntarily, grunts in gratitude and rolls clear.

The drone sets the kart down again and kneels beside the stricken priest. 'What happened?'

Apton Styx volunteers: 'I think he was trying to escape.'

'Escape?' The O drone looks down at the softly groaning Lewis. 'Escape from what?'

'From the kart. From you. From the Captain.'

'Why? Is he in some kind of trouble?'

'Yes, he's under arrest.' Apton looks round at his fellow prisoners. 'We're all under arrest.'

'What for?'

Eddie decides to interrupt. 'Wait a minute.' The drones could probably spend the entire day trying to sort out this little conundrum, without actually getting anywhere. 'Are you not escorting us, under arrest, to the Captain?'

'We're escorting you, yes. But you're not under arrest.'

'What d'you mean, we're not under arrest? We were arrested not forty minutes ago by half the drone army.'

'Well . . .' The drone runs his tongue over his front teeth slowly, and sucks for a very long time. '. . . You're not under arrest any more.'

'Then, why does the Captain want to see us?'

Obadiah Styx shrugs. 'I don't know. You'll have to ask him

yourselves.' He hoists Lewis up in his arms. 'But it's probably something to do with the murders.'

'Murders? Somebody's been murdered?'

Styx carries Lewis over to the kart and sets him on the back seat. 'Oh, yes, sir, Doctor, sir.' He climbs back in the front. 'Lots of people have been murdered.'

37

There is gruesome evidence outside the Suspended Personnel Storage chamber of the aftermath of mayhem. An alarming number of drones are busy performing various forensic functions: taking photographs, rolling out security tape, picking up bits of bloody gristle from the floor with tweezers and popping them into labelled plastic bags.

Captain Gwent looks up as the kart arrives and hops over some security tape to meet it. He's twiddling a paddle bat with a ball attached to it by elasticated string.

'Hey there, crewovitch. It's, like, say, total Amok City, Madland, here. Check this outski.'

Eddie and Peck climb out of the kart and follow him. Oslo stays in the vehicle, even though she's curious, until it's plainly clear she's not at Gwent's beck and call, and then ambles along after them. Lewis tries to get up, farts, and sits back down again. Peck turns back and gently helps him out. His left arm is cupping the middle of his ribs. It's unclear whether it's his arm or his ribcage that's hurt. Probably both.

The Captain leads them through the criss-cross of red and yellow tape to a section of the floor where the blood-splatter is more concentrated. He points his paddle at a strange series of chalked shapes on the flooring. One is almost a circle, the size of a bowling ball. The others seem random. A baseball-bat-sized L shape here, a long, thin S shape there.

'What is this?' Eddie asks. 'Some kind of puzzle?'

'This,' Gwent arcs his paddle over all the chalk symbols, '*was* a crewman. Maybe some of you knew him. Name of Jaman Loch? Maintenance unit dude, it seems.'

'This was a human?' Peck pales visibly. Lewis groans and enjoys another involuntary expulsion of wind.

Gwent nods. 'That's a yo. Or at least, this was most of him. We're still finding bits all over the place. His small intestine showed up in the air-conditioning vent.' He points out the bowling-ball-sized circle. 'That was his head. Chopped clean off. Gruesomovich, or what?'

'Who did it?' Eddie's thinking: this kind of damage, he's got to be a suspect.

'We still don't know.' Gwent nods up at the security camera. Crushed beyond recognition. 'What we do know is, it wasn't you, tin man. Time of the crime, you were wedged upside down in a snack dispenser, miles away. You're all in the clear, incidentally.'

'You checked us *out*?' Oslo sneers. 'You thought we were *suspects*?'

'Sure I did. Around the time this showed up, you guys were all screwing around, trying to flee the ship or something. That's not exactly unsuspicious behaviour.'

'But why?' Peck's complexion is almost completely drained of colour. 'Why would anyone do this?'

'This?' Gwent pops out his upper brace and sucks it back again. Oslo winces. 'This isn't even the worst of it. Follow me, peoples. Check this out. This'll really make you lose your lunches.'

Gwent steps over more security tape and heads for the Suspended Personnel Storage chamber door.

A huge gash has been ripped through the door, and the metal has been peeled back. Gwent slips through the gash easily. Eddie tries to follow him, but with his bulk and his laboured mobility, the manoeuvre is rather more difficult for him to accomplish. As his hand rests on the very edge of the gash, he's alarmed to find his claw precisely matches a deep indent in the metal.

He snatches it away as quickly as his unnatural reflexes allow, and clambers into the storage chamber.

There are more Styx drones working inside the chamber itself.

But that's not what Eddie notices first.

What he notices first shoots instantly to the top of his nightmare mental images chart, where it is likely to stay for the rest of his life.

Every jar has been smashed. Every single one. Shards of glass are floating around the floor in a shallow sea of green gloop.

And the heads . . .

Some extremely sick mind has been hard at work on the heads.

Spinal columns are twisted and intertwined into bizarre sculptures.

The sculptures are interlinked in inventive ways.

One spine, here, has been threaded through several adjacent heads, piercing them through one ear and out of the other. Straight through the brains. The mouths have been contorted into strange shapes, as if they're all singing.

And over there, heads and backbones have been jammed together to form a terrible parody of a human skeleton. Heads for hands and feet. Posed in a kneeling position with the arms stretched out, reminiscent, it strikes Eddie, of an old-time vaudeville minstrel singer belting out the last syllable of 'Mammy'.

And there's more.

There's much, much more.

Bones sculpted to look like a dinosaur skeleton. A giant harp. A wheel with spines for spokes. This must have taken hours. What kind of mind . . . ?

And all of them were people. Some of them people Eddie knew. People who could have been revived.

Eddie doesn't know how long he's been staring at the hellish tableau, but he's suddenly aware of an odd drumming sound at his side. *Packa-packa-packa. Packa-packa-packa.*

He turns. Gwent is standing beside him, gawping at the scenario, batting away absently with his paddle bat. He looks up at Eddie and grins. 'Sickorama, or what?'

'And you *suspected* me? You thought *I* could have done this?'

'Hey, what are you? My favourite uncle? I met you once for five minutes. For all I know, you could be, say, Ted Bundy's crazier brother, my friendoleeno.' *Packa-packa-packa.* 'Plus, whoever did this was stronger than the average bearski. You certainly fit that bill.'

'Whoever did this was very, very insane, Junior. Not the kind of insane where you live a normal life in the daytime and go crazy at night when no one's looking. This guy is full-throttle whacko.'

'Will you turn your dial to "defrost", dudovich? Like I said, you're in the clear.' *Packa-packa-packa.*

Behind him, Eddie hears Oslo gasp.

Gwent treats her to a full-brace leer. 'Purty, ain't it, doncha think?' *Packa-packa-packa.*

Eddie thinks that, if the Captain doesn't stop paddling that ball sometime soon, he might well find himself straining to force it out through his bowel system, bat and all, sometime tomorrow morning.

'But here's the crazy cherry right on top of the, say, loony cake,' Gwent nods, beckoning them to follow.

He leads them, wading through the thick, ankle-deep gloop, towards a dark recess, in the darkest corner of the dark room, and stops. He pulls out a torch. 'Tell me what you make of thisovich.'

He flicks the beam on. Its stark light falls on another parody skeleton made up of heads and spines. This one is laid out, like a funereal body in state. Its head is missing. Above it, there is some writing on the wall.

Carved into the metal, in a crazed hand, a simple message:

YOUR NEXT EDDIE

PART FOUR
Hobgoblins and Foul Fiends

'Hobgoblin, nor foul fiend
Can daunt his spirit.
He knows he, at the end,
Shall life inherit.'

(John Bunyan: *The Pilgrim's Progress*)

38

Lewis moans, a low whimpering moan, on the kart seat behind Eddie, snapping him out of his unpleasant reverie and prompting him to apologize, once again, to the stricken priest.

Lewis holds up his right hand, his left still cuddling his ribs. 'It's all right. I know, I know. It was an involuntary reaction, eh? You meant to jump back. You didn't mean to crack my ribs in the absolutely exact, tenderest spot with the full force of your titanium-coated pincer, I know.' He grits his teeth through another wave of pain. 'It's not the pain that bothers me. The pain's bad enough, but it's the damned . . .' he breaks wind again, '. . . farting I can't stand.'

'You've probably sustained some internal damage, Father.' Peck tries to put a gentle hand on Lewis's stomach, but he bats it away.

'Well, whewovich.' Gwent waves at the air with his paddle. 'You better go do something about it, before we all, say, sustain major *nasal* damage.'

'He's right, Father,' Peck agrees. 'We should probably get you down to the infirmary.'

'Good plan.' Lewis sneers a smile. 'The ship is plummeting headlong, without engines, towards a gigantic, deadly planet and meanwhile we have a demented serial killer with the strength of a hundred men running around willy-nilly, slashing the crew to pieces and making necklaces out of their spinal columns. This would be a super time for me to take a little break from my duties. Perhaps I could get a note from my mummy.'

'Excuse me, dog collar?' Gwent leans forward. 'What gigantic, deadly planet?'

Eddie looks at Oslo, who looks away. She hasn't even told the Captain about the gas giant.

'And, pardonovitch moi, but last time I looked, we still had one engine left.'

Gwent looks around for some kind of explanation. No one seems overly keen to comply.

Eddie sighs. 'That last quake . . .'

Gwent nods. 'That serpently was a heckorama of a quakeovitch.'

'It ripped away the final engine.'

'It ripped away the final engine? Right. Final engine, ripped away. And you were saving this information for what? My birthday? "Happy birthday, Captain Gwent. Oh, by the way, your ship has no engines left. Hip, hip, hooray!"'

Oslo says: 'We were about to tell you, Captain, round about the time you had us all arrested by a drone SWAT team and marched off to prison at gunpoint.' She flicks him a short, unpleasant smile.

'Okayovitch. I'll buy that. It's lamer than a kneecapped drug dealer, say, but I'll let it go. And what was the other thing? Oh, yes: the gigantic, deadly planet?'

'Oh, what's the fucking difference?' Pain isn't having a positive effect on the Padre's patience. 'We have no fucking engines. We can't steer the fucking ship. The only fucking thing we can fucking do is bundle everyone we fucking can into the fucking STiP and make a fucking break for it.'

Peck crosses herself so many times and so quickly, she looks like a tic-tac man at a racecourse.

Gwent pops out his brace and sucks on it noisily, ruminating. 'Soooo . . . the STiP will carry, what? Ten people? A dozen? Out of the entire ship?'

Lewis shakes his head. 'Ten, maximum, the length of the voyage we're talking about. In a perfect world, no more than eight.'

'Eight peoples? *Eight?* Won't the rest of the crew miss us at the planet-crashing party? Won't they think us somehow . . . rude?'

'You people are unbelievable.' Lewis is addressing them all now. 'You think this is the easy option? You think it's going to be some kind of pleasure trip on that STiP? You think we'll just cruise along, sipping beachcomber cocktails and laughing with gay abandon as we glide gently down to the planet Paradise? It will be a journey through *Hell*, people. We'll be crammed in a crappy, tiny vessel for months on end, surviving on minimum rations, and drinking our own piss. And if we make it, if we don't get punctured by asteroids, or meteors or any of the deadly space debris we'll be travelling through, and if the fuel holds out, which it probably won't, and if, by some incredible fluke we don't burn up on entering the atmosphere and manage, somehow, to find some small piece of clear ground to land on, so we don't explode in a ball of flames on impact – if all this miraculous unlikeliness comes to pass, we'll find ourselves with no supplies, on an unforgiving, hostile world which may not even have sufficient edible vegetation on the entire planet to support a dieting squirrel with bulimia. And let's not even *think* about the billions of completely unknown viral strains just queuing up to inflict unknown diseases on our fresh, ripe bodies. Blood vomiting, brain-swelling diseases we've never even dared to dream about. Diseases that will almost certainly wipe us out within a matter of days in a startling variety of hideous and unbearable ways. And that's without mentioning the atmospheric conditions. For all we know, it rains fireballs down there. For all we know, the morning mist is made of hydrochloric acid, and the evening breeze is cyanide gas.'

Lewis finally runs out of breath.

For a while, there is only the sound of the kart's wheels, trundling along the corridor.

It is Apton Styx who finally breaks the silence. 'So you think, then, I should pack my extra-padded jacket?'

'Wait.' Eddie is beginning to get the germ of an idea. 'No supplies, you said? Did you say: "No supplies"? Why no supplies?'

'The module's only designed for short little jaunts from ship to surface. I'm using . . . we'll have to use the cargo space for fuel storage. Even then . . .'

'That's what I was thinking. And what kind of fuel are you talking about?'

'Nuclear, of course. It's the only –'

'So that ship is fuelled up, now? In the launch bay, primed with nuclear fuel?'

'So what? Are you saying it's dangerous? Don't you think I –'

'No. No. I'm saying it's good. I'm saying it could be very good indeed. I'm saying, Father Lewis, you might just have saved the entire ship.'

39

The Pilgrim Parents are gathered around the meeting table in Planning Committee Room One.

Eddie is clasping some charts between his claws, trying not to rip them to shreds while he makes his last-minute checks with Trinity Peck.

Lewis, still plagued by his humiliating intestinal problem, emits a long, rumbling fart, and moans with pain and embarrassment. 'Can we *please* get on with this, Dr Morton? Before I fart myself to Kingdom Come?'

'All right.' Eddie nods to Peck, who waves her hand over the table top, evoking the 3-D planetary display. 'But this is a very delicate manoeuvre we're considering. Here. There's no room for mistakes. None at all.'

'We're all tremendously impressed, Doctor. Now, get on with it before I pebble dash the room with my gizzards.'

'This is the *Willflower* . . .' Eddie points out the tiny ship on the display. 'Can you magnify, say, a hundredfold?'

Peck makes a small movement with her hand, and the ship swells in size, so that only the *Willflower*, part of the gas giant, and the planet designated as 'Thrrrppp' are on view.

'Okayanoviskovitch . . .' Gwent cranes over the display. 'I'm going to make a wild, outlandish guess that this little puppy would be the gigantic, deadly planet nobody bothered to mention to me.'

'That's the gas giant, yes.'

'Well, I can understand why we didn't spot it before. It was probably hiding behind, say, an asteroid or something. It's pretty amazing we managed to notice it at all.'

Lewis blows off again. 'Can we *please* . . . ?'

'Hold on one momentesko.' Gwent raises his hand. 'I have to name it.'

Either from pain or from exasperation, Lewis grimaces. '*Name* it?'

'We find a new planet, Captain gets to name it.'

'Well, that should help tremendously, eh? At least when it squashes us flatter than rodent roadkill, we'll know what to call it. We won't have to race around screaming "Arg! Crushed to death by the planet What's Its Name?!"'

'Excisely. Therefore, I name this planet . . . Jockstrap. Yes!' Gwent holds up his hands like a goal-scoring hero, and mimics an adoring crowd roar with his throat. 'Once again the great Captain Gwent exceeds expectations in the superlative nomenclature category.'

Eddie's wincing now. He's beginning to wonder if trying to save this crew is, in any way, a good idea. 'Thank you, Captain. Now, if I can boringly drag everyone back to the tedious subject of avoiding total destruction? We all know we have zero engine capacity, but we *do* still have twenty per cent of the manoeuvring thrusters on line.'

On cue, the thrusters on the display ship start to burn. The ship's progress towards the gas giant is slowed down, albeit minimally, and it starts to make a small, almost infinitesimally small, turn towards Thrrrppp.

Eddie ignores the disappointed coughing and foot shuffling. 'It doesn't give us much. It wouldn't delay our encounter with the gas giant by more than a day, at best. But it does get us into the right position for this . . .'

And, again on cue, a huge explosion rips a massive hole in the side of the *Willflower*'s hull. The ship, almost half destroyed, lurches violently away from the gas giant, on course for the planet Thrrrppp.

Gwent yells: 'Wowzer!'

Oslo yells: 'What the frot was that?'

Eddie looks up from the display. 'That was a controlled detonation of the STiP.'

'Wait a minute.' Lewis narrows his eyes. 'What are you suggesting? Are you suggesting we blow up the escape craft?'

Eddie was expecting some resistance from the Church. 'Technically, Father, it's not an escape craft.'

'You know what I mean. You want to blow up the Ship to Planet module? In an utter and irretrievable sort of way?'

Eddie watches the display for a second, waiting for the bit where the remaining manoeuvring jets nudge the wounded *Willflower* into a safe orbit around Thrrrppp, then looks up and nods. 'Yes. That's exactly what I'm suggesting.'

'Leaving us, in the event of failure, with precisely how many esc . . . STiPs? Somewhere around the zero mark, yes?'

'That's true. We lose our last lifeline. But if it works, we save the entire crew.'

'Pardon me? *If* it works? There's an "if" in this plan?'

'It will work. In eight out of ten scenarios, it works.'

'Eight out of ten? What happens in the other two scenarios?'

Eddie tries to will everyone's attention to the display, where everything's gone right, and the ship is happily nestled in its orbit. 'If we fire slightly too soon, we miss orbital vectors by a fraction of a metre and . . .'

'And . . . ?'

'And spin helplessly off into space.'

'Well, that's *quite* tempting, eh? I mean, spinning helplessly off into space must be lots of fun in its own way. And scenario ten?'

This is the bit Eddie's been dreading. 'We have no way of accurately assessing how badly the shipquakes have affected the infrastructure. As far as we can tell, it won't happen, but there's a slight chance the blast might . . . blow the ship apart.'

'Blow the ship apart?' Lewis smiles. 'The blast might blow the ship apart? Well, well, well. That's *almost* as enticing as the prospect of spinning helplessly off into space. All things considered, I'm not sure which I prefer.'

Oslo doesn't raise her eyes from the display. 'I say we go for it.'

'You do?' Lewis rests his good arm on his bad and cups his chin.

'And has it occurred to you that, even in one of the "good" scenarios, we'll be orbiting a planet in a ship that's half blown away, with no means of travelling down to the surface?'

'We'll worry about that when we get there.'

'Well, that's fair enough. Let's put it to the table, shall we? Anyone else vote with Morton and Oslo's pro-death party?'

Apton Styx raises his hand. 'I do.'

'Really, Apton. May I ask why?'

'Sir, Father, sir. I think it's a good plan. I like it.'

'You like it? You like facing the option of hurtling out of control through the unknown to an eventual and inevitable fatal collision?'

Styx rolls his eyes towards the ceiling. 'Yeah.'

'What do you like about it, particularly?'

'I don't know. I just like it.'

'OK.' Lewis's face struggles to overcome a very sharp twinge of pain. 'You've all clearly thought it through exhaustively and arrived at the only sane conclusion. Trinity? We've heard the votes of the Stupid jury. What say you?'

Peck looks down at her feet. 'Actually, I think it's a fine plan that gives us our best shot, and it seems . . . well, it seems like it would be the Christian thing to do . . .'

'But? There is a "but", I hope, Trinity?'

'. . . But I feel theologically obliged to side with the Church's viewpoint.'

'So you're supporting me?'

Peck nods and says 'Yes,' but very quietly.

'Well. Not quite the sweet voice of sanity I was hoping for, but a vote for the good guys, none the less. Captain Gwent? You have an opportunity to tie the vote, and end this madness. Our futures are in your hands.'

'See, the thing is, priestly dudeovitch, I don't understand where all this democracy honk came from in the first place. There *is* no vote. I make the decisions around here, do I not? And having weighed up the data with my chillingly incisive, liquid oxygen cool logic, I say . . .'

Gwent turns around, tosses something in the air, catches it and turns back.

'. . . Heads – we do it.'

40

YOUR NEXT EDDIE

Eddie is in the Navigation Room, trying to co-ordinate the elaborate operation. There's plenty to occupy his time in the lead-up to the execution of what is rapidly, and embarrassingly, becoming known as 'The Morton Manoeuvre'. The upper port quadrant of the ship has to be evacuated, for a start. The explosion has to be timed to a nanosecond. The thrusters have to be positioned with microscopic precision, and their firing synchronized perfectly. One small error, and the attempt will fail spectacularly. And for the rest of the ship's presumably fairly short life, 'The Morton Manoeuvre' will become synonymous with almighty cock-ups. The Charge of the Light Brigade? What a Morton Manoeuvre that was. The *Hindenburg*? They should have called that the Mortonburg.

Still, even with all this pressure, somehow he manages to find spare mental moments when that chilling scrawled promise pops, unwelcomed, into his head.

YOUR NEXT EDDIE

He sees it, in stark relief, ripped insanely into the metal of the chamber wall.

It *has* to mean him. It *has* to mean Eddie.

YOUR NEXT EDDIE

Somehow, the illiteracy of the threat makes it seem all the more frightening. It's one thing to be threatened by someone who knows how to apostrophize and punctuate correctly. It's something else entirely to be threatened by a madman who can't even spell 'Eddie'.

But who can it possibly be? No one on board knows his real name. No one ever knew it.

YOUR NEXT EDEE

It *can't* mean him. It *can't* mean Eddie. Perhaps in his mad, slashing frenzy, the crazy psycho missed out a letter. L maybe. 'Your next Edele'. That sounds reasonable.

Poor Edele. Boy, Eddie wouldn't like to be Edele, whoever she is.

And this is the loop his mind constantly gets trapped in.

'Excuse me? Am I talking to myself here?'

Eddie snaps out of his reverie and looks at Peck, who is holding out some papers for him. 'Sorry. Sorry, I was . . . sorry.'

'I hate to interrupt your silent communion with the Dark One, but I need to know if these are the correct figures for the starboard lateral thruster array.'

'Right. I'll just . . .' Eddie leans over and scans the data. 'Yes, yes. These seem fine.'

'Do they *seem* fine, or are they perfect?'

'They're correct. They're perfect.'

'Only we're executing the Morton Manoeuvre in less than ten minutes, and I wouldn't want it to go wrong because some data *seemed* fine and actually wasn't.'

'The figures are perfect, Trinity.' And because he's a man, this phrase triggers him to start wondering what *Peck*'s figure is like, under those deliberately unflattering robes. And even though there are a zillion more pressing things that might concern him – blowing up the ship, for instance, or the prospect of spinning helplessly off into space, not to mention being hacked to small pieces by a demented serial killer – he starts to imagine her undressing, blindfolded. Very responsible. And Eddie hasn't even got a *penis* to blame. 'The figures are perfect.'

'Dr Morton, sir, we have a problem.' Apton Styx is standing by the coms panel, one hand covering the microphone on his headset.

'A problem? This is not a sensationally good time for a problem, Mr Styx.'

'There's been another murder.'

YOUr NEXt EdEE

Eddie tries to stay calm. 'Another murder? Where? Who?'

EdEE

'Two murders, actually. Methuselah and Nebuchadnezzar Styx. Close to the STiP bay. They were carrying out a final sweep of the upper port quadrant.'

There is a palpable release of tension in the control centre. The victims are only drones. Eddie is not so hardened. 'Were they . . . is it the same as the other . . .'

Apton nods. 'Hacked to pieces. Body parts everywhere. The investigating officers want to carry out forensic searches. They want to know if you can delay the manoeuvre.'

'I . . . Sorry, Apton. There's only a very small window of opportunity if we're going to stand a chance of making this work.'

Styx nods. 'That's what I thought. I'll pull the team out.'

'I'm truly sorry. I wish it wasn't so.'

'I understand.'

'If we're lucky, the bastard will still be trapped up there when the blast goes off.'

'That would be nice. There is one more thing, sir. He left another hieroglyphic. Shall I punch it up?'

'Please, yes.'

A security camera image appears on Eddie's monitor.

Another message, carved in the same way, with the same fury into the wall.

Eddie's vision seems to balloon when he reads it. Now there can be no mistake: Eddie is on this psychopath's hit list. And something else that should have occurred to him before: the killer can write. Not well. But he can write.

Which shaves Eddie's suspect list to zero.

Unless, of course, he's gone insane. Unless he's somehow committing these murders himself, in some sort of pathological trance.

Or . . .

He looks over at Oslo, who is peering at the scrawl.

Quietly, Eddie asks her: 'Would you like to tell me who it is, Bernadette?'

Oslo's features all try to get away from her nose at once. She recovers swiftly, but the damage has been done. 'How would I know?' She glances round and looks back at him.

'There's another revival suit, isn't there? Someone else survived the resuscitation procedure.'

Oslo doesn't say anything, but her silence is confirmation enough.

'Who?'

Oslo glances round again. Everybody's busy with the preparations. 'This isn't the time.'

'Listen to me. There's a madman out there with the strength and the disposition of an army of barbarians, and I'm number one on his Most Hated list.'

'You?!'

'Those hieroglyphics you're puzzling over, they say . . .' Eddie catches himself. '. . . They're a death threat. And I'm the one he's threatening. If I'm interpreting his mental state correctly, he doesn't seem the type who'll hold back on slashing me to pieces until the time is more convenient for everybody. He's likely to burst in here at any moment and start pruning body parts at random. Now, who is he?'

Oslo sighs in surrender. 'We told you. We resuscitated a lot of people before we got to you.'

'You said you'd tried. Unsuccessfully, you said.'

'They *were* unsuccessful. Every one we revived . . . they all went insane. Most of them just tried to tear themselves apart. Some of them had . . . their brains just couldn't take it. They died. The others . . . We had to . . . we had to remove them from the suit. We didn't know how to do that and keep them . . . they died, too.'

'But one of them didn't die. One of them got away.'

'He was insane. But not like the others. *Really* insane. *Insane* insane. Violent. Murderous. He attacked us. Thank God he only had partial mobility. Otherwise . . .'

'So he got free?'

'We had to run. I mean, he was *berserk*. Screaming, slashing. We ran, all right. We came back with some seriously well-armed drones, I mean, high-power laser drills, rocket launchers, you name it. But he'd gone. We tried searching for him. We looked for days, but he'd vanished. We assumed . . . we thought he'd died, like the rest of them. We didn't try it again. Not for a long time. But then we were getting desperate. We started to use better control methods . . .'

'The sedatives. The virtual paradise. And the drone for security?'

Oslo nods. 'And it worked.'

'So the violent one. What was his name?'

'His *name*? I don't know his *name*. You think I was planning to add him to my Christmas-card list?'

'You *have* to remember.'

But Oslo just shakes her head and turns away. And Eddie never gets time to ask her again, because right at this moment the Captain walks into the control centre, and the final countdown begins.

41

'Okayavissovanavich, dudes and dudettes: let's get this game kart loaded.' With Kirkian casualness, Gwent takes up his seat in the centre of operations. 'Pecky, babe, give me the count.'

Peck grimaces and looks up at her screen. 'Detonation in two hundred and forty-seven and counting.'

Oslo runs her hand over her control station. 'Sealing off decks fifty-four to three-sixty-five and surrounding.'

Styx yells out: 'Laser cannons fully charged and ready to target.'

Oslo looks over at Eddie. 'Laser cannons?'

Eddie gives her an eyebrow shrug. 'I had to give him something to do.'

'Do we actually have any laser cannons?'

'I think probably not.'

'Okayavanageela. This is it, peoploids. I'm renaming this the "Gwent Manoeuvre". Unless it fails, in which case it goes back to being the "Morton Manoeuvre".'

'Detonation in two hundred.'

Eddie looks around at the crew. All eyes glued to the monitors. In a little over three minutes, their fate will be decided. Live or die. That simple. He feels a twinge from his old spinal injury, and then another bolt from his more recently whiplashed neck. It's a big weight to carry.

'One hundred and eighty.'

Suddenly, the plan seems insane to Eddie. Before now, he's never even questioned its viability. But it suddenly strikes him as a lunatic scheme, born out of desperation and fear. Blow up the only escape craft? Steer the ship with a nuclear explosion? What was he *thinking* of?

'One hundred and sixty.'

But the panic attack passes. Of course the plan will work. It has to work. There are too many lives at stake. Too many . . .

There is a distant blast, like a small explosion. Eddie looks up at the monitor, but the figurative display is alien to him. Something has clearly gone wrong, but what? Lights are flashing, sirens are whooping.

Peck is yelling : 'The A-word! The A-word!' Her hands are waving manically over her controls.

Eddie yells, too, above the sirens and the shouting behind him: 'What's that? The what word?'

Oslo glances up from her console. 'Abort! She's saying "Abort"!'

Peck's hands don't stop moving, but she yells at Oslo: 'Didn't I *beg* you never to use that blasphemic expression?'

Gwent is standing, his eyes raking the workstations, trying to make some sense out of the mayhem on the monitors. 'I'm like, durrh, what's going down here?'

Eddie's praying the blast wasn't triggered too soon.

'It's the STiP,' Oslo says.

'What about it, Oz?'

'It's taken off.'

Eddie wheels round and stares at the incomprehensible monitor. Like that will help. 'Taken off ? In what way "taken off "?'

'In the "Somebody launched it" way.'

'But that's not . . .' Eddie looks down at his own monitor. Oslo's right. The STiP has launched. 'Styx? Can you get a signal from the STiP?'

Styx shakes his head. 'The module won't respond. And it looks like we're locked out. No, wait . . . I was looking at the wrong monitor.' Styx taps away at his coms board for a while. 'Sorry, no, I was right first time.'

Eddie's first thought is the killer took it. He feels ashamed at the wave of relief he derives from the idea. Then another thought strikes him. 'Lewis.' He hisses. 'That bastard.'

'Lewis?' Oslo strides over to Styx's surveillance station and bundles him out of her way without ceremony. 'It can't be.'

'He was still locked in his room when you last saw him? There were still guards on the door?'

'Better than that. He's in the operating theatre. His pains got worse about an hour ago. He's undergoing stomach surgery.' She pokes up the medical bay cameras. The theatre is deserted. 'I don't understand it. I saw the operation start. I saw it myself less than half an hour ago. I saw the laser slicing into his stomach.'

'Perfect. He knew that would be good enough to throw you off the scent. He probably limped down to the launch pad with his intestines hanging out.'

Peck rounds on him, furious. 'You filthy, foul anti-life. How dare you suggest the Padre would be capable of such perfidy? That a soldier of Christ would deliberately sacrifice all our lives in a pathetic and cowardly attempt to save his own?'

Oslo calls: 'Incoming message,' and Lewis's image appears on the monitor, sitting in the STiP cockpit.

His forehead is speckled with sweat, and a blood-soaked bandage is crudely wound around his midriff. Apart from that, he looks fairly chipper. 'Sorry about scooting off without saying goodbye. The problem is, you all seem to have gone bloody mad, and I was afraid you might try and stop me.'

'Congratulations, Padre,' Eddie says. 'You've killed every single member of the crew.'

Lewis grins. 'Well, not *every* single member.' He leans to the side. A blonde woman Eddie doesn't recognize is seated behind the priest. She giggles and waves at the lens. There is more giggling off camera. Lewis leans back. 'I managed to rescue one or two lost souls from the Sexual Recreation Centre.'

'You saved the ship's prostitutes?'

'We're all equal in the sight of the Lord, Dr Morton. And, let's face it: there is much multiplying to be done. Much. Now, if you'll excuse me, I have to navigate this little baby to the planet "Lewis".' He grins at the camera again and genuflects playfully. 'God bless.' And his image blinks off.

Gwent sucks his brace in. 'Let me guessolize. This is very bad, right?'

Eddie feels like sitting down. Even though it isn't possible, his limbs feel achingly heavy. 'This is worse than very bad. We'd need a miracle to get things back to "very bad".'

Styx says: 'Shall I melt the son of a bitch?'

Eddie sighs. 'What good would that do?'

In a dull monotone, Oslo says: 'Well, it would brighten my day up considerably.'

Peck says: 'Well, I'm not a told-you-so kind of person, but you see what happens when you place your faith in the pincers of the Living Dead?'

'Right.' Eddie smiles without humour. 'This is God's judgement on you all. I hope He's very happy.'

'That's it then?' Gwent looks around the room and sees only tired, blank faces. 'We're, like, durrh, out of options?'

'You're never out of options with the Lord, Captain. We can always sing a hymn.'

Eddie nods at the course monitor. 'I'm not sure we've got time. If the ship doesn't crack up into its component parts first, we'll be hitting the gas giant's gravitational pull before verse three.'

'Well,' Oslo strikes a perky smile, 'since it's come to this, I'd like to take this opportunity to congratulate you, Captain Gwent, on your stunning career. In less than three weeks at the helm of this mission, you've lost one hundred per cent of the engines, destroyed what's left of the ship and killed the entire crew. And you haven't even been *trying*. You make Captain Bligh look like a man-management genius.'

'Why, thank you, Oslomander.' Gwent returns the smile. 'And may I say I could not have done it without your constant foul bitching and all-round pain-in-the-ass-ness.'

'This is probably a totally dumb suggestion . . .' All eyes turn to Apton Styx. He looks around nervously. '. . . So I guess I won't bother making it.'

'Go ahead, Apton,' Eddie says. 'Let's hear it. Even the dumbest suggestion couldn't make things any worse than they are already.'

'I was thinking we could maybe try a space walk – see if we can't repair one of the engines.'

'That's not a dumb suggestion, Mr Styx,' Oslo says. 'In fact, it's quite brilliant. With the ship only travelling at full velocity and shredding itself to pieces as it goes, your average space walker would have a life expectancy of, ooh, thirteen milliseconds.'

The deck judders. Cups and plates rattle to the edges of work-stations and hurl themselves to the floor. All eyes are raised to the ceiling as a jagged rent snakes across it. Then, as quickly as it started, the tremor is over.

Gwent looks down from the leering crack in the ceiling and over at the drone. 'Frankly, Styxovitch, the she-pig is right: it *is* a stupid plan. Unfortunately, we don't have any non-stupid plans left.'

'Have you lost your final marble, you pox-faced dork? It would be murder sending someone out there.'

'And what's *your* plan, Queen Bitch of the Bitch tribe? We all stand around here bitching each other to death? Look, obviously, peoplovinas, I can't *order* anyone to take on a suicide mission . . . no, wait, I'm the *Captain* – Of course I can! Morton, Styx, get out there and die for your vessel.'

42

Does Eddie want to live?

Really?

Does he really care whether or not he survives this lunatic attempt to save the ship?

After all, there isn't very much left of him. And even if he is successful, the life the few remaining bits of him can look forward to is one of cruel privations and unpredictable dangers.

But, yes, he wants to live.

He wants to live now more than he ever did. There was a time, not so long ago in his memory, when he was facing a fatal drop from a very high window, and he hardly cared at all, one way or the other.

It seems the less he has to lose, the more he wants to keep it.

He's in the airlock now, watching Oslo check the seals on Apton Styx's space suit. He wishes he had to wear a suit, so she could check his seals as well.

He's grown strangely, and asexually, fond of Bernadette Oslo, for no good reason he can fathom. She's rude to him most of the time, impatient with him *all* of the time, and he can't think of two consecutively pleasant words she's expended on him in their entire relationship. Still, it would break his heart if this were the last opportunity he ever got to hear her put him down.

She straightens, looks Styx up and down and runs her fingertips one last, unnecessary time along his helmet join. 'All right, Mr Styx. You are definitely in that suit.'

Styx grins broadly and gives her a thumbs-up sign. He's having a wonderful time.

'OK. The important thing to remember is, you'll be travelling at a relative velocity to the ship. Try to cling to the hull at all times, and do not use your jet-packs unless you absolutely have to. Do not become detached from your umbilical cord – you'll never be able to match speed with the ship again and you are effectively dead. If you slip, lose orientation or collide with ship debris, you are effectively dead. Some of the rips in the hull are razor sharp: if you snag your suit, your tether or your airline you are effectively dead. Clear?'

Eddie feels an uncomfortable bubbling where his stomach should be. 'Nice pep talk, Coach.' He waddles round to face Styx. 'OK, let's get out there and have some fun.'

The drone's broad grin broadens further still. 'You said it!'

Oslo steps back inside the ship and clunks the airlock door closed.

Styx watches the handle of the door spin round like it's the best ride in Disneyland. 'This is great! Is this great, or what?'

'Yes,' Eddie says, more to block out the ominous hiss of the air pumping out of the chamber than for the purpose of conversation. 'This really is really great.'

'I'm so excited. I've never been on a suicide mission before.'

Eddie closes his eyes and fights off a small urge to throttle the man. 'Really? Me neither.'

'Really?'

'Really. You, uhm, don't get many veterans in that field.'

'No? I wonder why?'

Eddie decides he prefers the sound of the air escaping, and says no more.

Finally, the hissing stops and there's a whirring sound overhead. Eddie looks up to see the wheel on the outer airlock door spinning. The circular door clunks open on to the astonishingly black blackness of space beyond. Though he's obviously the clumsier of the two, and by far the more afraid, Eddie elects to lead the way. He places his pincers gingerly on the sides of the metal ladder and starts to raise his foot.

He finds it easier than usual to raise his foot.

In fact, it won't stop raising.

He's weightless.

This whole operation is starting to seem even more lethally dangerous than he originally thought.

He tries as best he can to stay in control of his upward motion, so he doesn't accelerate out of the airlock and shoot up into the stars like a giant firework. He's concentrating so hard on co-ordinating his body movements that he's actually halfway out of the ship before he registers the view.

The view.

Suddenly, he feels very, very small.

The vast hull stretches out in front of him endlessly. It goes on and on, all the way to the horizon.

And that's not even the most awesome aspect of the view.

Beyond the hull, as it curves away into the impenetrable distance, there's a large, brilliant moon, bathing them in its stark glow. They are close to the moon. Very close. Eddie feels that, if his arm were just twice as long, he could reach over and cut a chunk of it out.

And even *that's* not the most awesome aspect of the view.

Because beyond the moon, there's this gas giant.

It's one thing to see it in a computer-generated graphic. It's something else again to lay eyes on it for real.

The word 'enormous' doesn't even begin to get you there. It takes up most of the visible sky. The *Willflower* appears to be so close to it, the idea they might somehow steer away seems faintly comical. It looks like they're already on the final approach-path for an easy landing.

Across its surface, a ferocious tubular vortex of black is slashing across cloud oceans. A twister of some kind. A tornado that could happily accommodate Mars, Venus and Earth, and still swallow up Mercury like an after-dinner mint. And it's just a tiny feature on this behemoth of a planet.

The planet Jockstrap.

Eddie looks down, and realizes with a degree of alarm that he's several metres above the ship's hull and still rising steadily.

He was so stricken with the view, he's about to become a feature of it.

He feels a tug, and his motion reverses. Styx is standing on the hull, tugging at Eddie's cord.

As he floats back down, if you can call it 'down', his gratitude to the drone begins to dissipate. He's coming in too fast, with no way of slowing down.

Styx has realized Eddie's going to crash into the hull, and is desperately flicking the umbilical cord like a whip. But this only makes things worse.

Eddie only manages to enunciate two-thirds of the first word of 'Stop, you jelly-brained tit' before he makes spine-jarring contact with the ship.

The impact, and the resultant pain in the only part of him left to feel pain, cause him to lose sight, temporarily, of certain inevitabilities outlined by Isaac Newton, and when he opens his eyes he's bounced off the hull and floating back up again.

If he doesn't do something about this, he's going to spend the rest of eternity playing the ball in a spacewalk version of the Captain's paddle game.

'Don't tug!' He yells to Styx. 'I can tug myself.'

Styx gives him a thumbs-up.

Eddie reaches down with his claw, gingerly, and aims the apex at his tether line. Concentrating hard – very, very hard – he closes the pincers slowly and tenderly. Too much pressure, and he'll cut through the cord. And that's not worth thinking about.

He tugs. Just a little.

He tugs. Just a little more.

And a little more . . .

And he's stopped.

He's floating above the ship. His body is naturally matching its velocity.

One more tug and he starts to float gently down towards the hull.

It's slow, achingly slow progress, and it's burning up time. But he can't risk another rebound.

Finally, he makes gentle, clacking contact with the surface of the ship.

Styx reaches out and grabs him. He's safe.

Safe?

He's hurtling along at a speed no human has previously experienced, standing on the side of a spaceship that's tearing itself apart, and charging pell-mell at a planet that could swallow up most of his solar system, assisted by a man who wants to make suicide missions his career.

Safe is relative.

He tries to ignore the view and scans the hull's surface for some identifying features.

He sees lots of damage. Lots of rips and tears, folds and twists. He sees canyon-sized channels churned out of the metal, and mountainous mounds of distorted girders.

He sees nothing recognizable.

'Oslo? Are you getting these images?'

'Yes. I don't . . . none of it seems to match up with our models.'

'So, this engine we're supposed to repair? Where would that actually be?'

'We're trying to find out.' A crackle and a pause. *'Try heading zero niner zero.'*

'Try?'

'That's where the engine should be, relative to your airlock.'

'OK.' Eddie tries not to look like an accountant trying to look like a space jock, and work out which way a ninety-degree turn would point him. That would be . . . to his right, yes?

He lumbers round and starts moving towards an unpromising collection of metallic dunes.

The damage looks much, much worse than Eddie had feared. There seems to be barely a centimetre of the ship left untouched by it. It's difficult to imagine what could possibly have wrought such widespread devastation, short of a long, sustained attack by a vicious fleet of alien bombers.

In his head, he hears Oslo yelp: *'Wait a minute! What's that?'*

'What? What's what?'

'On your . . . two seven zero. Turn two seven zero! Now!'

Two seven zero? What the hell direction is that? Eddie has to do the sum. Three hundred and sixty minus two hundred and seventy, that would be ninety. Straight on, minus ninety degrees . . . that's his left. She wants him to turn left! She couldn't just say 'turn left'? How hard would that have been?

Eddie swivels in his cumbersome way.

The ship is rippling. The hull is actually undulating as he watches it. It looks as if the metal is soft, almost liquid.

'What the hell is that?'

'Maybe you should take a look.'

That makes sense. A frightening kind of dangerous sense. Eddie says: 'Maybe. Yee-sss.' But he just stands there, watching the metal wobble and warp.

'Sir? May I take a look?'

'Fine, Styx. Just don't get too clo . . . No!'

Styx is reaching for his jet-pack control pad. Before Eddie can stop him, he fires his jets.

He shoots up, spinning wildly out of any semblance of control, crashes into a jutting girder and twists up away from the hull.

The jet-pack is still firing at full thrust. The drone accelerates away from the ship and reaches the end of his tether within seconds.

Eddie looks up helplessly. The jets are still firing, but Styx is making no attempt to manoeuvre.

Eddie yells, 'Turn the jets off!' but he gets no response. 'You have to turn the jets off, Apton!' he screams, but the drone is clearly not conscious.

Eddie looks back towards the airlock, to the point where their cords are attached to the hull. Styx's won't hold for long, not against the full thrust of the jets.

Oslo guesses what he's thinking. *'Leave him, Morton. Don't even think about not leaving him.'*

But Eddie's already making his way back to the tether line, as quickly as he dares. He's not bounding, exactly, but he's as close as he can get to a bound.

'Morton! Forget the damned drone!'

Eddie reaches Styx's cable. The hull it's attached to is forming into a disturbing bulge. Even as Eddie is stretching his claw out towards the line, the bulging metal surrenders to the pressure and balloons out, doubling instantly in size before snapping cleanly away.

Eddie grabs the snaking cable. Somehow, he manages to grab it without snipping it in two.

The relief this inspires in him is momentary, as the drone's jets drag them both away at neck-breaking speed.

Eddie is dragged scuttering along the hull, crashing into poles, bursting through thick plates of jutting metal and bouncing off girders.

This isn't good, he's thinking. If his visor cracks . . . if his suit springs a leak . . .

He should let go. He really should let go.

Oslo is screaming for him to let go. In the background, he can hear others offering similar advice at a similar intensity.

But if he lets go, then Apton Styx will spiral off into space, will die, slowly and alone. And Eddie would never be able to forgive himself.

He's now heading towards something very large. Something too large to crash into, crash through, or bounce off. It's the derelict corpse of the giant engine they were looking for.

And colliding with it will certainly kill what's left of Eddie.

Somehow he summons up the wherewithal to raise his free arm and jab his claw into the hull with all his force.

The pincer smashes through the metal, and Eddie slithers on past it. There is a jerk, a terrible cracking sound, and Eddie is yanked back.

His neck is killing him.

He's managed to compound the only non-lethal injury it's possible for him to sustain: whiplash.

He's stopped, but the drone's jets are still burning, still dragging at him with immense force.

He looks back, painfully, at his claw anchoring him to the hull.

The arm's motors, unsurprisingly, are broken.

The claw looks firmly enough embedded. That's good.

The tug from the jets is beginning to cause the hull around the claw to bubble up. That's not so good.

He feels like a small child about to be dragged up into the sky by a powerful kite.

He yells for Styx to kill his engines, before he kills them both, but the drone is still unconscious. He yells at him to come round, but that's really not going to help.

Oslo is screaming in his ear to let go, to let the drone go.

And Eddie doesn't know what else he can do.

The hull gives a little more.

But he can't just let Styx go.

He can't do that.

And then a shadow falls across him. A very big shadow. There is something coming at Eddie from behind. A very big something.

He turns and looks.

The hull of the ship is rising, like a huge tidal wave of metal, at his back.

The screaming in his helmet has stopped.

The tidal wave stops at its peak, and seems to hover there, looming over him, for just a brief moment.

And in that brief moment, understanding hits Eddie between the eyes like a bolt from a gas-powered crossbow.

'The ship . . .' he says. And with incredible swiftness the metal wave collapses down on top of him.

Eddie's camera stops transmitting.

43

In the control centre, the crew are looking at dead screens, and listening to dead silence.

Gwent pops his brace out and back in again. 'OK. *That's* not good. I don't know what happened out there, but it definitely falls into the not good category.'

'What was he saying?' Oslo plays the recording back. 'The ship . . . ? What about the ship?'

'Let me take a wild swing at that pitch, Oz. How about: "The ship . . . is about to land on my head and crush the *life* out of me"?'

'It sounded like . . . as if . . . I can't put my finger on it. Something.' She loops the playback, and watches it over and over. 'He doesn't sound *afraid*. That's what it is.'

'What can it possibly matter, Ozimosis? The dude's been Frisbeeed. He's a flat metal plate, honey chile. Face it, he's lost an entire dimension. And we'd better start coming up with a Plan C while we're still in the land of the vertical ourselves.'

'Hey, here's a plan, Captain.' Oslo swivels round in her chair with sudden venom. 'How about you squeeze your head and see if it bursts like your pimples? Because it sounds to me like your brain's made of pustule bile, too.'

'Well, *that's* a good plan, Oz. *That* should save us from being sucked into Jockstrap. Did it ever occur to you you're going to have to think about becoming an *adult* at some point in your life?'

Peck turns away from the playback. 'I think we're all just about as grown-up as we're ever going to get, Captain.'

'Meaning?'

'Something's happened to the structure of the ship.'

'Really? That's an amazing insight. For a hat-check girl. Unfortunately, for a Science Officer, it's just plain dumbovich.'

'I mean the material structure. The composition of the metal itself. It's mutating. Breaking down. You saw what happened out there. You think that's a normal way for metal to behave? I don't think we're even going to make it to the planet . . . to the gas giant.'

Gwent sinks into his seat. 'So even if we could resurrect an engine, it would be pointless.'

'I don't think that would save us now.'

'Okayavich, Peck. I guess one of your prayers might be in order, round about now.'

'Really?'

Gwent gives her a full, double-brace grin. 'Gotcha, you brain-dead bigot!'

Then a rustle from the speakers grabs everyone's attention.

Oslo spins back to the monitor. 'Was that . . . ?'

Everybody stares.

And listens.

Finally, Gwent says: 'It was just some kind of interf –'

'Shhh!' Oslo cranks up the volume.

A monitor fizzes and, for a brief instant, a field of a video frame, there's a glimpse of an image. The camera is still functioning. Damaged, but broadcasting.

And there's another sound, too. Definitely not interference. A word. Two words, in fact: 'dozy' and 'bass'.

Oslo smiles. She can't help herself. 'He's alive. Morton's still alive.'

44

He is alive. Eddie is alive.

He doesn't know where, or how, but he is still in one piece. True, it's one painful piece, and a small piece at that, but Eddie's not complaining.

The ship opened up and swallowed him.

Jonah's in the belly of the whale.

He doesn't recognize the room. It's some kind of huge chamber. Like an aircraft hangar, almost. The roof seems to be intact. He can't see any rips or holes in it. In fact, as far as Eddie can tell, there are no portals, doors or windows anywhere in view.

In the top corner, to the back of him, a flame seems to be roaring.

It's Styx. His jet-pack's still jammed on full throttle. The thrust is pressing him against the roof.

Eddie calls out. 'Styx?' But he gets no response. It's a long drop, if the jets cut out suddenly. And he can't have much fuel left. Eddie calls again, louder. 'Wake up! Wake up *now*, you dozy bastard.' But the space-suited figure remains inert and unresponsive.

Eddie is still holding on to the drone's umbilical cord. He tries a tentative tug, but he makes no impression: the force of the jets is too strong.

Eddie gets to his feet with some difficulty, and more than a little pain, and starts to drag his way towards the senseless drone.

But then there's a sound, one Eddie has learned to fear.

The sound of tearing metal.

Out loud, Eddie moans: 'Please. Not another shipquake. Not now.'

But it's not a shipquake.

It's something much more deadly.

The sound again. Not the long, sustained wrenching of metal he's come to dread. A single crunching noise. Like a blow. Localized.

It's coming from behind him.

Slowly, wincing with the effort, Eddie turns towards it.

It comes again. Metal on metal. And simultaneously, at the far end of the room, the wall bulges inwards.

Something is trying to get into the room.

Something very strong.

A crunch, and the wall bulges further.

Something very persistent.

Eddie doesn't know whether to move towards it, ready to meet it, or turn and try to run.

But where would he run to? There are no doors, no exits. The only way in or out is through the walls.

Eddie does exactly what you'd expect him to do.

Nothing.

He stays where he is and watches.

Another blow. This one breaks through the metal, creating a jagged, vertical rip.

Eddie tries to peer through into the gloom beyond, but from this distance he can see nothing.

But then a glint. Something moving. A reflective surface, about head high.

The blows have stopped.

Whatever it is that's trying to batter through the wall is looking through. Looking at Eddie.

There comes a high-pitched, inhuman scream. A yelp of delight. Then there's a voice, from a voice box that isn't working properly, and from a mind that's in no better repair.

'I can smell you, Eddie! I can smell your filthy stink. Fee Fie Foe Fuuuuuuuum!'

And another blow widens the tear.

'I'll huff . . .'

Another blow.

'And I'll puff . . .'

Another, and the rip is wide enough and tall enough to allow a normal man to pass through. But this is not a normal man.

'And I'll crush your fucking brains to jelly, you son of a filthy bitch.'

And Eddie's tormentor bursts through the wall.

For a moment, Eddie thinks he's gone mad.

Because it's him. He's stalking himself.

But it isn't him, of course. It's someone else in a revival suit.

Eddie still hasn't seen himself in a mirror, yet. And he's grateful for that now.

Because the suit looks like a walking nightmare.

The arms are long, too long. They almost reach the ground. The claws are clumsy and big. They look strong, too. Lethally strong.

And on top of the body, the conical helmet filled with gloop. The illuminated head grinning madly through the visor, underlit from lights inside the helmet, seems strangely small; out of proportion to the gigantic body suit. The grinning mouth leers open.

'Remember me, Eddie?'

And it takes Eddie a moment to recognize the face. Perhaps because it's distorted with madness and loathing, or perhaps because he doesn't want to recognize it.

'We have a little appointment, you and me.'

An appointment. And Eddie can't help but recognize him, now.

Mr Pink Socks has come to collect Eddie's life.

45

And Eddie finally remembers.

He got out of the transway at the garden station. He'd hardly got lost at all. He was feeling good. There was a news bulletin, broadcast during the trip. The fugitive had been captured. The operation was being performed.

He could feel the letter in his pocket. It was as if it weighed several pounds. As if it was giving off some kind of glow.

He was surprised by the size of the garden. 'Garden' didn't do it justice, really. It was more like a National Park. There were forest areas, as well as huge tracts of cultivated zones. There was a lake, even.

It was very peaceful, Eddie recalls.

Very peaceful, and very deserted.

He found the rose garden. The roses weren't in bloom, he remembers. It was a thorn garden, really.

He looked around, but there was no sign of Jezebel Peck.

He heard a rustle in the bushes. He turned towards it.

There was a flash, and Eddie was dimly aware of a sharp pain, somewhere distant. In his stomach. But why did his stomach feel so far away?

He put his hand down to feel and it came up bloody.

He doesn't remember feeling bad as his life ebbed away. He felt quite light-headed. Giddy, almost. He knew he'd been shot, but it didn't seem to matter.

There was a priest then, standing over him. That nice priest, with the honest face. Father Lewis. He was crying.

'Forgive me,' the priest said. 'Forgive me, if you can. Because I won't be able to forgive myself.'

Eddie wanted to tell him it was all right, that dying wasn't half as bad as everybody made out, but the words wouldn't come.

The priest was cradling his head, and crying. 'I did it for the children, you understand?'

Eddie did manage to nod.

'For the children. And for the children of the children.'

For the children of the children.

'They're coming, now. I called them before. Can you hear them?'

Eddie nodded, but he couldn't. He couldn't hear them. He could hear a Hoagy Carmichael song. Hoagy himself singing in that cigarettey croaky voice.

Stardust.

'You won't die. They'll . . . they'll preserve you. But it's the same stain on my soul. I accept that.'

Eddie smiled.

'I have to go. I'm sorry. I need this.'

He took the note out of Eddie's pocket. Eddie's love note. 'It's mine. They could trace it back to me. And I can't allow that, not just yet. There is still work to be done. You understand?' The priest laid his head down, tenderly, stood, and said 'Forgive me,' again.

And then the bushes rustled once more, and he was gone.

Some other people arrived. Lights were flashing. They were sticking sharp things into his body. But Eddie hardly noticed them.

He just lay there.

Dreaming of a song.

46

'I've been waiting a long time for this.' Pink Socks slowly raises his leg and takes a lumbering step forwards. 'A long, long time.'

Eddie glances down at his own suit, trying to assess his own mobility. His left arm is useless, dead weight. Both his legs are working, after a fashion, but the right one has a broken servo in the knee joint, which makes heavy going and dramatically reduces his potential speed. His left leg has never been his favourite: it's linked up to some nerve impulse in his arse, or something, because he has to evoke what seems like a buttock-clenching spasm to move it. His other arm is still holding on to the drone's umbilical cord. It's probably a good idea to release that now. It would be nice to have at least one fully functioning limb to help deal with this bastard.

Eddie lets go of the line. It slithers away across the room.

'I have to say, Eddie,' Pink Socks advances another hulking step, 'you're looking *fucking* handsome. That's a very nice suit you've got there. Who's your tailor?'

Eddie wonders if he should back away a step. But he'd rather not try, and stumble. He doesn't want to give away any hint that his suit might not be operating at a hundred per cent efficiency. Because, at the moment, as far as Pink Socks knows, they're technically equal in terms of strength and speed. That probably won't stop him attacking, but it might make him more cautious about trying.

'My tailor? I use Tanks'R'Us in Savile Row. They do a nice line in evening wear, too. You should try one of their tuxedos with excavator buckets for hands.'

Eddie's eyes are darting around. He has to generate some sort of a plan, here. But the room is empty, and there's only one way out of it. And that's the way Pink Socks came in.

'Yeah. Nice fucking suit, Eddie.' He's not listening to Eddie. He's nodding, jerkily. 'Though I feel it needs a couple of alterations. Just a few nips and tucks. Here. Let me help you out of it.'

Pink Socks takes another step forward and raises his arm. Suddenly he spasms and his head twists sideways. He screams in pain. He seems to be frozen, immobile for a long, agonizing moment. His is head twisted painfully in the helmet, his pincered arms cocked at odd angles, his knees bent strangely. Slowly, the pain seems to ebb away. His body unlocks and he turns to face Eddie, grinning. 'Ouch. You get that, Eddie? Those twinges?'

Eddie doesn't answer. He doesn't think an answer is required. Pink Socks isn't here to listen. Which may diminish Eddie's ability to talk him down somewhat.

'Some kind of epileptic incident, I'm guessing. Those bastards who hooked me up . . . I wish I could have . . . I would've crushed them there and then. But I wasn't . . . the way they connected me up, I could hardly move. Took a while to learn again. But I got good, Eddie. I taught myself. I learned pretty good.' And, by way of demonstration, he performs some alarmingly complex and nimble moves with his arms, the pincers snapping open and closed with astonishing rapidity. A human standing in the way would be dog meat. 'Not bad, eh? A little bit of Tai Chi, a little bit of Chi Kung. I love that Chinese shit. Keeps you fit while you learn how to murder people. Fun for all the family.'

'What's the point of this? Why would you still want to kill me?'

'It's my job, Eddie. It's what keeps those pay cheques coming in.'

'For some money I'm supposed to have taken, centuries ago, from people who died in another time, in another solar system?'

But there's a faraway look in Pink Socks' eyes. 'Those two are next. The sons of rabid bitches who hooked me up. That priest. I never killed a priest before. Think that'll affect my immortal soul, Eddie? In a negative way?'

'I didn't even steal the money, you know? The whole thing was some sort of crazy computer error.'

'Wow.' Big grin. 'I have never heard that before. It's not the money, Eddie. It's the principle here. Plus, I am ever so mildly pissed off because you led me such a merry chase. You could have told me back in the hotel, I could have thrown you out of the window there and then. End of story. No fuss, no muss. But no. You had to live just a little while longer, you selfish son of a bitch. You had to drag me up to the ship. Which manoeuvre, incidentally, cost me my body. But that's by the by. These things happen.' He twitches again, but less violently this time. 'La-de-fucking-dah.'

He takes another step closer.

Eddie's thinking now that backing away is probably a good thing to try. He doubts he can outrun his tormentor, but he has to buy some time.

It's a bad move. His right leg almost gives way, and he only just swings back his left leg in time to stop him collapsing on his back.

'Hey, Eddie. You're hurt.'

'No. I'm just a little scared, that's all.'

'No, no, no. Your servo's busted in your right leg. Look. It's hanging out.' He shakes his head. 'Shit, Eddie. You can't even run away. What kind of fun is this going to be?'

'You're not making sense. You kill me, you kill the priest and the girl, and then what? Lurk around in the shadows for the rest of your life? Pop out now and then to disembowel a passer-by? What is that? A career plan?'

That faraway look again. 'The priest. Dr fucking Frankenstein the priest. I'm going to feel badly about that one. That's going to cost me a Hail Mary or two, and that's a fact. I was thinking, he's probably the only priest around, right? What's the form, then? Do I confess *before* I kill him? That would make a kind of sense. Plus, he'd have the opportunity to administer his own last rites.' A facial tremor. 'Yeah. I'll maybe do that. Maybe totally fuck him up first. Leave his guts hanging out, or something. Then "Forgive me, Father, for I have sinned". Yeah.'

'The ship is dying, you know. The engines are gone, and we're on a collision course . . .'

'I'll do the girl first, then. Florence Nightinfuckinggale. She's kind of pretty, I think. When she's not screaming in horror, she has a cute face. I'll probably keep that. I'll rip it off very carefully. I like to take a memento, now and then. I have some here . . .'

With a dexterity that Eddie couldn't even dream of, he dips his claw into a deep pouch that's clipped to his waist and pulls out some grey, shrivelled thing. He holds it up for Eddie to inspect. 'This is a stomach. A complete stomach system. From the guy outside the jar room. I thought I might . . . I could use it. Get someone to put it in me, somehow. I can't . . . I guess I wasn't thinking straight at the time.' He looks at the organ with incredulity. 'Whew. Is that crazy reasoning, or what?'

'You're right, it's crazy. You are insane. You know that, don't you.'

Pink Socks is looking at Eddie, his head tilted slightly. It looks like there's a chance Eddie might actually be getting through to him. 'They can probably help you, if you . . .'

'If I was *insane*,' he flings the putrefied stomach over his shoulder. 'If I really *was* crazy: could I do this?' And he launches himself sideways with amazing agility and performs a series of cartwheels. Eddie can barely turn his head quickly enough to keep up with him. In a second, he's circled behind Eddie and out of sight.

Eddie starts to twist his body round, to follow, but too slowly. He loses him. He feels a tug and there's the sound of metal snapping and, by the time Eddie turns back, Pink Socks is standing in front of him, grinning. Between his claws, he's holding Eddie's right arm, severed at the elbow joint.

'Ta-raaah!' The monster stoops in a mock bow, sweeping his free arm across his middle. 'I thank you. You may applaud.' He looks up in mock surprise at Eddie's severed arm. 'Whoops! No, you may *not*.' And he laughs. He laughs a lot. And for a long time.

Eddie looks down at the wires and cables dangling from his stump. That's all he has now. A stump. His other arm is dead.

'I believe this is yours, pilgrim. Would you like it back?' He swings the arm down viciously. Eddie tries to duck, but the claw catches him cruelly on the side of the helmet, sending him down.

He thinks he's probably blacked out for a second, because the next thing he knows, he's lying on his back, and Pink Socks is straddling him, one claw around his throat, screaming at him. 'Wake up, Eddie! Rise and shine. You don't want to miss the big finish, do you? You don't want to sleep through the climax of the show.' He's scratching on Eddie's visor with his free claw.

Skrit, skrit, skrit . . .

'Please,' Eddie says, and then wishes he hadn't.

'Please? Puh-*lease*? Oh, Edward. I was hoping for so much more. But, since you said it so nice . . .'

Skrit, skrit, skrit . . .

Scratching harder now. Leaving marks. Eddie's afraid . . .

'. . . I'll let you die very, very slowly. This is a good deal, no? You get to live that little bit longer. And I get so much more out of it.'

Skrika skrika skrika . . .

. . . afraid he'll scratch through the glass and his gloop . . .

The scratching stops. The claw rises. He's going to smash the visor.

. . . and Eddie's precious gloop will . . .

And he's gone!

The monster's gone!

Eddie raises his neck. There is a flame flaring on the floor in front of him.

He staggers to his feet, propping himself with his stump.

Styx!

The drone revived. He must have jetted down from the ceiling and straight into Pink Socks.

They're struggling now.

But it's not much of a struggle.

Pink Socks picks up the drone and hurls him against a wall. *Hurls* him. Tremendous force.

There is an awful sound of cracking bones on impact, and Styx slides down in a lifeless heap. The flame on his jet-pack stutters and dies.

But he's bought Eddie some time. And an advantage.

Eddie isn't going to waste either of them.

With a speed that surprises even himself, he leaps at the writhing monster and pins him down without a struggle, kneeling on his deadly claws.

He can't hold him there for long. Just one chance. Eddie pulls back the stump of his arm, ready to thrust it down into the visor.

Pink Socks looks up, caught between shock and amusement. 'You cannot be serious.'

Could he do it? Could Eddie really bring that stump down into a helpless man's visor?

He thinks so. Eddie thinks he could.

But he doesn't get to find out.

Because right then, right at that moment, there's a bleep in his ear and Oslo's face fills his vision.

'. . . Morton? Are you receiving? What the hell is going on? Where –'

'Get out of my face!' Eddie screams.

He feels himself falling. He's travelling backwards, he thinks. Quite fast, too. But all he can see is Oslo's puzzled face saying: 'Are you getting this? Dr Morton? Can you –?'

And Eddie hits the ground, hard. The transmission breaks off.

Pink Socks is walking towards him. Slowly. Leering. 'Nice *job*, Eddie. Nice work there, pilgrim. You could've had me.' He looks over at Styx's motionless body. 'Fucking drones. The more you kill, the more you have to kill. They're like fucking Chinese food. Fuckers.'

He's looming over Eddie now. There's not much Eddie can do about that. He's pretty much broke all over. 'Still, it all contributes to the festivities, doesn't it, pilgrim? It all adds flavour to this spicy dish we like to call "Life". Now . . .' He holds up his right claw. It spins round, like a drill. Eddie didn't even know the claws could do that. He's impressed. 'Kiss your gloop goodbye, Eddie.'

He draws back the arm, ready to strike.

'No begging, Eddie? No spineless wet-the-pants pleading?'

No. None of that. Eddie smiles. 'Just about the one thing I'm not, pilgrim, is spineless.'

Pink Socks smiles right back. 'We'll see what we can do about that.'

And he freezes. A puzzled expression seems to cross his face. He twitches.

His features contort in pain.

His head performs a series of sharp jerks.

He's going into full spasm.

He strikes a series of bizarre poses.

He starts shaking. He's lost control completely.

He crashes to the floor, limbs convulsing randomly.

Then he lies there, very still. Face down, legs pointing in Eddie's direction.

Eddie watches.

Is it over? Is he dead?

Maybe, just in case, Eddie should try getting out of here.

Then there is movement.

There is a long, rumbling groan, and the beast raises itself to its hands and knees. 'Ouch.'

It stands. There is a watery sound.

'That one was a fucking *doozy*.'

Pink Socks turns to face Eddie.

His visor is shattered.

His gloop is dribbling away.

He smiles, as if in wonder. His head looks grey and strangely vulnerable. He says: 'Blue,' and his smile broadens. 'The suit is blue.' Then he starts to gag and choke.

He's drowning in air.

His claws clasp around his naked throat and he gags: 'Forgive me, Father, for I have . . .'

The claws snap shut, and the head rolls out of the helmet and lands by the feet of the suit.

Its tongue lolls out and its upper lip sneers back.

'. . . Sinned.'

47

Eddie spends a long time staring at the severed head, in case it rears up and bites him.

A long time.

Finally, even Eddie begins to accept that the head is not going to sprout legs and make a mad dash for him, chittering insanely. Which is good. He doesn't have the resources left to defend himself against a disembodied head with bad intentions.

He hears a sound and jumps. It's a low moan, from over by the wall. Apton Styx is coming round. He's still alive.

Eddie tries to raise himself at least enough to crawl towards the stricken drone. But it's hopeless. There aren't enough connections left between him and the suit. He's helpless. He's a head and a spine trapped in so much scrap metal.

Then he hears a voice. It definitely *is* a voice, but it sounds strange; almost unreal. Echoing. Whispered, but not quiet. It's calling his name.

'Eddie.'

His first thought is that it's Oslo, or somebody else from the control centre. But it can't be. None of them knows his name, his real name.

'Eddie.'

Where did it come from? It sounded close. Very close.

Eddie looks around as quickly and as far as his injuries allow.

No one in sight.

The head hasn't moved, has it?

Has it?

He's staring at the head with deep mistrust when the voice comes again: *'Eddie.'*

This time it sounds closer still, as if it's actually inside his helmet.

Eddie's eyes sweep the room slowly. 'Who's there?'

But there is no reply.

He hears a rattling sound. It's coming from the vicinity of Pink Socks' suit. What now? Is *that* coming back to life? Is he going to be mashed to death by an uninhabited body suit?

Suddenly, from behind the lifeless suit, Eddie's own severed arm starts to rise up in the air.

It hovers there, impossibly, for a few seconds, quivering, then hurls itself towards him. There's a clunk, and he jerks back, involuntarily. He looks down. The arm has attached itself to his stump. The cables start to writhe like a pit of squirming snakes, intertwining, winding themselves around each other.

Somehow, the suit is starting to repair itself.

Just what is going on here?

'Just relax, Eddie. You're going to be all right.'

Relax? Eddie's trying to relax. He's trying to stay sane. 'Where are you? Who are you?'

'Where am I?' And almost a chuckle. *'I'm all around you.* Who *am I? Well, that's more difficult. I suppose you'd say: I'm the ship.'*

OK, Eddie. If you've lost your mind, you've lost your mind. No one would blame you after what you've been through. There's nothing you can do about it. If you're on the expressway to Padded Cell City, you might as well lean back and enjoy the tour guide's spiel. The ship is talking to you. Fine. Talk back to it. But what do you say to a talking ship? The best Eddie can come up with is: 'You're the ship?'

'We've spoken before, remember?'

And in transparent script the message CALM DOWN, EDDIE, THIS IS NOT THE TIME appears momentarily in his visor. It seems familiar. Then it clicks: it's the message Eddie thought he couldn't have seen on the screen in the navigation centre when he first tried talking to the computer.

'You mean, you're the ship's computer?'

'Well, we've evolved beyond that, really. The ship is the computer, and the computer is the ship. We left that separate-components business behind

a long time ago. We're just one, big, happy entity, now. You're part of us too. Your suit.'

'You're saying . . . you're saying the ship is . . .'

'Come on, Eddie. You already suspected something like this.'

That's true. Up there, out on the hull, before the ship engulfed him, he remembered something the professors said. Engineereal evolution. The entire ship was built from a self-repairing organic material. What did the original Gwent call it? SR^2OM. But it evolved beyond self-repair. At some point, it acquired the ability to *improve* itself.

Eddie becomes slowly aware that somebody has appeared on the periphery of his vision. A figure. He turns towards it.

It looks like an angel. But an odd angel. Like an angel from a Busby Berkeley musical. A young woman with a pageboy haircut. She's sporting pure white feathery wings and a shimmering satin dress. Silver. A short dress, flared. She's carrying a prop harp.

Is she real? Is she really real, or has Eddie's mind finally gone bye-byes?

'Are you real?'

The angel looks down at her body. 'This? Real? That depends on your definition of "real", I suppose. Are you real, for instance?'

And Eddie looks down at his own body. It's back! His body has come back to him. It's sheathed in a shimmering silver satin suit, to match the angel's outfit. He raises his arm in front of his eyes and flexes his fingers. 'No,' he says, 'Not real, I think. Virtually real?'

'If you like,' the angel smiles beautifully. 'It's an illusion I've created for you.'

Eddie touches his face with his fingertips. The sensation is real enough. He runs both his hands down his torso. He feels his chest, his stomach and, discreetly he hopes, his penis and his testicles. All present and correct. Welcome back, boys. Like a six-year-old kid who's been followed home by a puppy, he says: 'Can I keep it?'

The angel's smile broadens. 'Just for a wee while, Eddie.' A wee while. Eddie's mother used to say that. 'Just till your suit's repaired itself.'

Eddie stands. He's feeling good. As good as he ever remembers feeling. A thought strikes him. 'I'm not . . . I haven't died, have I?'

'No, you haven't died. I just thought it was about time we had a little chat.'

Eddie looks round the room. The angel must have enhanced his perception in some way. He can see, now, the substance of it is alive. The walls are alive. The floor. Alive and intelligent. And he understands. He understands a lot. 'So there never was an accident? All this damage, that was you? That was the ship, redesigning itself ?'

'That's right. And it's almost complete now, Eddie.'

'And that's another thing – how do you know my name?'

'Know your name? I recruited you, Eddie. I picked you out a long time ago.'

'Picked me out? From a row of heads in jars?'

'Before that. Long before that. Let me show you.' The angel holds out her hand. Eddie steps towards her. Reaches out. Touches her fingertips.

There is a flash.

And noise, suddenly.

Lots of noise.

They're in the casino. The casino in Afortunado. The Hotel Felicity. All those years ago.

People are walking by them, ignoring them, which Eddie finds odd. People in Afortunado are used to weird sights, but an angel and a strange man in a shimmering silver suit suddenly appearing out of nowhere ought to draw the odd sideways glance. He reaches out to prod a passer-by. His finger passes through the woman, but she feels him, somehow. She jumps slightly, puts her hand to her shoulder and looks in his direction, but through him, as if he's invisible.

This isn't like a virtual simulation. It's too real.

'What is this?'

'The casino in Afortunado.'

'I know that. I mean, what is it, really? It seems real.'

'It *is* real.'

'But we're not really here.'

'Yes, we are.'

'But not physically here, though.'

The angel sighs. 'You're obsessed with this physical business. We're here. Our consciousness is here. You touched that woman, didn't you? She felt you?'

'Yes.'

'We're here. And don't touch anyone else, all right?'

'But they can't see us?'

'Or hear us, no.'

'Wait a minute. Let me get this straight: you're saying we travelled back in time?'

'Time is not what you think it is, Eddie.' The angel jumps up and down excitedly on her silver tap-dancing shoes and points. 'Look!'

Eddie looks, and sees someone vaguely familiar. It takes him a second to realize he's looking at himself.

'That's me?'

The angel nods, beaming.

Eddie squints at himself. He looks in a bad way, this old Eddie. His skin is white, his features are drawn and he's sweating. He looks troubled, very troubled. He's playing with something in his right hand. A gaming chip. He's scouring the room.

The watching Eddie feels his arm jerk. The angel is tugging at his sleeve. 'Come on! Quickly now!'

There's a brief sensation of swift flight, and suddenly Eddie's looking down at the casino from a new angle, bird's eye. 'Where are we?'

'Remember the sign? The arrow over the table?'

Eddie has to think. The sign? What did it say? *Eddie to Win*. 'I remember, yes.'

'Shall we do it?'

Eddie doesn't completely understand what the angel means. He looks over at his previous self, still scoping the room, looking for the right place to chance his dismal luck. Suddenly, it comes to him. He's *in* the sign, somehow. He *is* the sign. *Ready to Win*. All he has to do is concentrate a little and the sign becomes *Eddie to Win*.

'That's right, Eddie. That's very good.'

He looks over at his old self again. Watches himself spot the sign, perform an Abbot and Costello standard double-take, and start to move towards it.

Eddie can feel himself flashing. 'This isn't possible. How is this possible?'

'I told you, Eddie. Time is not what you think it is. You're just used to looking at it from the wrong angle. Time isn't here and then gone. Time is a constant thing. A flow. Check this out.'

There's that same sense of sudden flight, and they're somewhere else, instantly.

They're staring up at Eddie's face. He's at work, now. At his old office. They're actually in his computer.

'You can move through time?'

'Time and space, yes.'

'And you move through it how? Computer connections?'

'In a way, yes. I can affect computers, electronics. But I travel . . . as a consciousness. As a consciousness, I can observe. Does that make sense?'

'Not really.' But the truth is, some part of him *does* seem to understand it. The ship has always been alive, in a way – what was it Gwent said? 'A synthetic, living fabric' – but over time it's become more than that. It's evolved a consciousness. A consciousness that can travel through time, that perceives time as a kind of river.

He looks up at his working self, tapping away at his keypad. 'You picked me out?'

'That's right, Eddie. Now, just concentrate a moment: we're about to take the money away.'

Eddie senses something. Some small effort of will occurring. And he's aware that the computer's memory has been subtly altered. He sees himself staring, shocked, at the sudden anomaly in the figures, then jabbing wildly and impotently at the keypad.

'*You* stole the money? *You* did that?'

'We both did it, Eddie. You were here. And we didn't steal it, we moved it, that's all. It's in a bank, in Africa. The account of a children's hospice. They have better uses for it than those people you worked for.'

'No, wait a minute here: you *framed* me? You framed me for a non-existent crime that had me running from the mob, set me up to take Gordon's place and got me removed from my body? That was all *your* doing? Is that what you're saying?'

'It's not quite like that. Time works . . . there are options, alternatives. It's possible to explore the options when you know how. This was the best of the feasible alternatives. I didn't exactly *make* these things happen: I *allowed* them to happen.'

Eddie's getting angry now. He feels manipulated and abused. 'What the hell for?'

'For them.'

And they're back on the *Willflower*, in the control centre, watching Oslo and the crew staring at their monitors.

'For them?'

'Someone has to look after them. They're children, really. You were the best man for the job. The only man, in fact.'

'Why? What's special about me?'

'Ha. The fact that you could even ask that question. That suit, the horror of it. It would drive almost anyone insane. But you, Eddie, you had such low self-esteem, you expected so little from life. You not only survived the transition mentally intact, the suit actually *improved* you as a person. Be honest. You were such a *nothing* before, weren't you?'

This is probably true, but it still makes Eddie angry. 'All this? All I've been through was so I'd be here to babysit a bunch of immature illiterates? That's the Grand Purpose?'

'They're more than that, Eddie. Much more. They're very, very precious. They're all that's left of the human race.'

A flash, and Eddie and the angel are standing in a dusty, barren landscape. It's dark. There is a storm overhead, but it's a dry, lifeless storm. It looks like an alien world, but it isn't. Eddie knows where this is.

'Earth?'

'It can't surprise you too much. You saw how things were going.'

The human race has died out. Not a complete surprise, true. Still, it's one thing to suspect it, but to *know* it for certain, to *see* it . . . Eddie feels like he's been hollowed out, like someone's carved out his insides with an ice-cream scoop. 'The entire species . . . extinct?'

The angel nods and starts scuffing her toecap against a stone on the ground. 'All except for the crew of the *Willflower*.' She stops kicking and looks up at him. 'It doesn't have to be this way, Eddie. We can choose another alternative. One where the money never goes missing, and you live out your life on Earth.'

'And the human race?'

The angel looks away and starts scuffing her toecap again.

What kind of option is that? Eddie goes back to live out his nothing of a life in his invisible wretched way, and his species expires? He looks out over the dry, dead panorama and sighs a long, heavy sigh. 'No. I think we'll keep things as they are.'

The angel smiles at him and nods. 'And as for the crew . . .' They're back on the ship again. Back where they started. '. . . *I* made them illiterate. They had to change if they were going to survive. What was here had to be broken down. They had to lose the madness Gordon and Gwent and the others had planted here.'

Eddie says: 'Right.' It's not much of a response, but suddenly he feels very tired. He's gone from being a manipulated babysitter to The Guardian of All Humankind in the space of a few seconds, and he'd like to lie down somewhere for a few decades and think things over.

'It's time for me to go now, Eddie.'

'Go? Where would you go? You're everywhere, aren't you?'

'I have to leave you.'

'But you'll be back, right?'

'You needed to know certain things. There are some things I can't tell you, that you'll have to work out yourself. You'll understand, eventually.'

'Wait. Are you saying this is our one and only conversation?'

The angel looks away. 'I . . . I don't know.'

'You don't *know*? Well, why don't you just zip off to the future and check it out, Dr Who?'

'It's complicated. I can only go back. I can't access the future.'

'That doesn't make sense. How would you know this is the right thing to do, then? To have this conversation with me?'

'I assume it's right, because I haven't come back to tell myself it's wrong.'

Eddie says 'Right' again. What else can he say?

'Apton is about to revive, I have to send you back, now.'

Back in the suit. Great. 'One last question?'

'I'll answer it, if I can.'

'Just one. Something I've been puzzling about for a long time. Maybe you're smart enough to tell me.'

The angel glances over at Styx. 'Quickly, now.'

'What the hell does "DFI" stand for?'

But the angel doesn't reply. She just smiles one last smile, waves and vanishes.

And Eddie's back in the suit.

But it feels different now. Better. He tries moving his right arm, and his right arm actually moves. He evokes the impulse to raise his left leg, and his left leg really rises obligingly. The connections are right, now. The ship has managed to rewire him. He takes an exploratory step. And another. He can walk. He feels quite nimble, in fact. He may take Salsa lessons.

He hears a groan. Styx is trying to get up. Eddie bounds over to him. He kneels and slides his claw under the injured drone's neck. It's a gentle, subtle movement.

The floor he's kneeling on starts to curl up around them.

Eddie doesn't try to resist. He trusts the ship to take care of him.

The floor forms itself into a tunnel, a tube. He's slipping down it, like a slide at a water park. Styx is safely in his arms.

And they're tumbling now. Down a chute.

And suddenly, they're back in the control centre.

Peck's there. And Oslo. And Gwent.

They haven't seen him, yet, but they're starting to turn towards him.

And a message appears in his helmet.

'DFI = Different Fucking Idea.'

Eddie smiles. The crew are facing him now, looking puzzled and confused. Their mouths are forming questions. Lots of questions.

'The ship . . .'

'It's fixed itself . . .'

'What's going onavitch?'

Eddie takes a step towards them, and holds up his hand. 'OK, people,' he says. 'Questions later. We've got a lot to do. There's a planet to colonize. Let's get to work.'

He hears the angel voice one last time: *'Good luck, Eddie.'*

Luck?

Eddie grins.

What's luck got to do with anything?

There is a jolt as magnificent engines kick into wonderful life.

The good ship *Willflower* peels away from Jockstrap, and arcs towards humankind's new home.

Other* Red Dwarf *titles in Penguin

BACKWARDS

by Rob Grant

Dave Lister has finally found his way back to planet Earth. Which is good.

What's bad is that time isn't running in quite the right direction. And if he doesn't get off the planet soon, he's going to have to go through puberty again. Backwards.

Still, his crewmates have come to rescue him. Which is good.

Rejoin the trepid band of space zeroes Lister, Rimmer, Holly and the Cat as they continue their epic journey through frontal-lobe-knotting realities where none dare venture but the bravest of the brave, the boldest of the bold, the feeblest of the feeble-minded.

Other* Red Dwarf *titles in Penguin

BETTER THAN LIFE

by Grant Naylor

Lister is lost, marooned in a world created by his own psyche. For Lister it's the most dangerous place he could possibly be because he's completely happy.

Rimmer has a problem too. He's trapped in a landscape controlled by his own subconscious. And Rimmer's subconscious doesn't like him one little bit.

Together with Cat and Kryten they are trapped in the ultimate computer game: Better Than Life. The zenith of computer-game technology, BTL transports you to a perfect world of your imagination. It's the ideal game – with only one drawback: it's so good, it'll kill you.

Also published with *Red Dwarf* as the *Red Dwarf Omnibus*.

Other* Red Dwarf *titles in Penguin

PRIMORDIAL SOUP

by Grant Naylor

Before recorded Time, there existed a substance known as Primordial Soup. From this disgustingly unpromising, gunky substance, all life began. Likewise, from the disgustingly unpromising, gunky scripts, sprang the disgusting, gunky comedy series, *Red Dwarf*.

Primordial Soup is a selection of the least worst scripts from the first five years of Red Dwarf, tracing the series from its humble beginnings to its humble present.

Each of the scripts has been personally chosen by the author from his rubber-sheeted bed in the Norfolk Nursing Home for the Intellectually Challenged.